Beauty

AND THE

CLOCKWORK

BEAST

OTHER PROPER ROMANCE NOVELS

A STEAMPUNK
PROPER ROMANCE

Beauty
AND THE
CLOCKWORK
BEAST

NANCY CAMPBELL ALLEN

SHADOW
MOUNTAIN

Library of Congress Cataloging-in-Publication Data

Names: Allen, Nancy Campbell, 1969–   author.
Title: Beauty and the clockwork beast / Nancy Campbell Allen.
Description: Salt Lake City, Utah : Shadow Mountain, [2016] | 2016
Identifiers: LCCN 2015041339 (print) | LCCN 2015042601 (ebook) | ISBN 9781629721750 (paperbound) | ISBN 9781629734071 (ebook)
Classification: LCC PS3551.L39644 B43 2016 (print) | LCC PS3551.L39644 (ebook) | DDC 813/.54—dc23
LC record available at http://lccn.loc.gov/2015041339

Printed in the United States of America
RR Donnelley, Harrisonburg, VA

10 9 8 7 6 5 4 3 2 1

To Kirk Shaw,
for planting the idea,
and to Pam Howell,
for finding it a home.

"You are very obliging," answered Beauty. "I own I am pleased with your kindness, and when I consider that, your deformity scarce appears."

"Yes, yes," said the Beast, "my heart is good, but still I am a monster."

"Among mankind," said Beauty, "there are many that deserve that name more than you, and I prefer you, just as you are, to those, who, under a human form, hide a treacherous, corrupt, and ungrateful heart."

—*Jeanne-Marie LePrince de Beaumont, 1750*

Chapter 1

It had never been proven that Lord Blackwell had killed his wife, but then the man in question hadn't actually denied it, either. The death of his sister the very next day hadn't helped matters at all, and rumors circulated and swirled, as rumors were wont to do. According to London gossip, the police had questioned him as a formality and then left him alone.

Lucy Pickett pondered the rumors as the airship gained altitude. She stood at the railing and looked out at the dark London sky, wondering if it was wise to be going straight into the beast's lair. Cousin Kate insisted Blackwell Manor was haunted, and anything was possible, but Kate had always had a flair for the theatrical. And dramatic girl that she was, she'd gone and married into the Blackwell family.

The night was awash in an ethereal glow that had little to do with charm and everything to do with fog and gas lamps. The air below Lucy was ribboned with even, controlled streams from the Tesla coil sub-stations, providing convenient electricity for those who could afford it.

The airship continued to climb, and Lucy left the cold night air of the outer deck and opened the glass-paneled door to the interior. The airship was nice enough, but when she compared it with those from her brother's fleet, she found it lacking. Daniel Pickett had impeccable taste, and his ships were not only stylishly turned out, they were comfortable as well.

She had become spoiled in her travel, and the fact that none of Daniel's ships had had a flight scheduled that night for Coleshire was vexing, but only mildly so.

Lucy sat in her assigned seat, pleased that the flight wasn't full and that she had the entire row to herself. Feeling a slight draft, she scooted to the open window and looked down again at the city. London became a toy village as the airship reached cruising altitude, and she tugged on the heavy fabric window coverings, blocking the breeze and the sight of the city below.

She returned to the aisle and, taking advantage of the absence of seatmates, lifted the partial black lace veil from her eyes and removed her stylish top hat to which the veil was attached, placing it gently on the seat beside her. The headpiece's adorning feathers, lace, satin roses, and small goggles had withstood the rigors of her busy schedule in the few months since her purchase of it through London's premier haberdashery. Madame Dubois was the shop's most recent acquisition. Supposedly she was from Paris, but Lucy had it on good authority that Madame Dubois was from a little town on the Welsh coast and had adopted her former tutor's French accent. Either way, the woman worked wonders with hats, and Lucy wasn't inclined to care much about her fabricated nationality.

Lucy leaned her head against the cushion and closed her eyes. Her recent research trip to the Continent had been wonderful, but she was tired. With any luck, she'd be able to catch an hour of sleep before the airship touched down in Coleshire, seat of the Blackwell earldom and her cousin Kate's new home.

Kate—beautiful and vibrant, and earnest in her relationships. She'd fallen in love within a matter of days with the younger brother of an earl, then married and moved before the dust had settled from their whirlwind courtship. Daniel had been responsible for introducing the two, and Lucy was beginning to wonder if it had been a wise course of action. Kate seemed happy, but a letter awaiting Lucy upon her return from the Continent had concerned her enough that she'd booked passage on the first available flight.

With a frown, she pulled Kate's letter from her reticule, along with a still-sealed missive from the Botanical Aid Society of London.

> *Lucy, I am afraid. Jonathan is delightful and a very gentle husband, but this house . . . It has eyes, a presence. A ghost. I feel someone watching me night and day, and Jonathan's brother—Lord Blackwell—can hardly be bothered with our concerns. He refuses to hire a Medium to investigate the manor and insists there is nothing unusual. The man has no heart, I am convinced. What's worse, I fear I may be ill. My energy is lagging, and I have been enduring excruciating headaches . . .*

Lucy smoothed the creased paper. She'd read the letter at least fifty times, and she had to admit that, despite Kate's proclivities for story-telling, there was a note of uneasiness in the letter that had given Lucy pause the first time she'd read it—and every time since.

For all of Kate's dramatics, she was as healthy as an ox and not given to bouts of hypochondria. She had always prided herself, in fact, on her robust health. For her to be ill—it might be nothing at all. Or it might be something, and that was what had upset Lucy's sense of well-being.

Lucy was content when those in her realm were happy, and very rarely had she ever come upon a circumstance she couldn't somehow manipulate for the better. She could host a ball and work a room to her advantage, barter and cajole, charm and finesse. And when she came upon stumbling blocks, she removed them one by one with relative ease.

But Lucy wasn't a Medium. It wasn't as though she would arrive at Blackwell Manor and be able to exorcise Kate's supposedly ghostly visitor. She wasn't even certain she believed in ghosts. Vampires, shape-shifters, zombies—they were all anomalies verified by science. And science, she trusted. As an accomplished research botanist and public spokesperson for the Botanical Aid Society of London, she was comfortable with things she could prove with fact.

Lucy considered what she knew about Kate's new brother-in-law, the Earl of Blackwell. Her brother, Daniel, had fought with Lord Blackwell in the war and spoke very highly of him. She had never met the earl, however, and all accounts of the man were less than complimentary. It was readily acknowledged that he had a good head for business and had saved the family estate from ruin by marrying an American heiress, but he had few friends, and most people found him intimidating, if not downright frightening. The fact that Blackwell's young bride had died under mysterious circumstances one month after marrying him did nothing to aid his reputation.

Lucy sighed and opened the envelope from the Botanical Aid Society. It was quick and to the point.

While our search for the Anti-Vampiric Assimilation Aid must continue full steam ahead, Director Lark feels that you must enjoy a few weeks' holiday to rest and recuperate. While your time abroad was likely pleasant, she is well aware how little time you take for yourself. She insists that you do not darken the door of these offices until well into next month.

In response to your recent request, the following is a summary of what we've accumulated from the research team to date:

It appears that the Vampiric Assimilation Aid allows the vamp to walk among the living undetected for a period of only one year, not two, as we previously suspected. After approximately twelve months, the Aid wears off and is no longer effective. The vamp then cannot eat regular food, walk in sunlight, or disguise the fangs.

The vamp appears to lose a significant amount of speed and agility while under the influence of the Aid. The ability to transform into black mist also seems to be affected and can only be held for a limited time. Vamps in mist form may still inflict damage on victims, however, requiring the immediate application of anti-venom.

We have just learned from officials in Glasgow that a

vamp who ingests a significant amount of human blood can temporarily reverse the Aid's limitations—but only for roughly three hours.

Be on your guard, as always, Miss Pickett. While cloak-and-dagger stealth is not necessary, use discretion with whom you share sensitive aspects of your work. And be aware that while Bow Street tells us the threat to the public is significantly lessened because of the mandatory vamp banishment to Scotland, the recent advent of the Vampiric Assimilation Aid has made it all the more easy for the undead to hide among us.

The letter was signed by the director's assistant, Gregory. Lucy folded the paper and returned it to the envelope. She closed her eyes and suppressed a shudder at the unbidden memory of a young woman's body that had lain in a London alley, eyes open wide, skin unnaturally pale, blood drained. Evidence of green vampire venom had pooled around the signature bite marks at the victim's jugular vein, the skin gray and showing signs of decay. Though Lucy had already begun working at the Botanical Aid Society, it was that macabre sight that had propelled her to petition for a coveted spot on the Anti-Vampiric Assimilation Aid team.

She enjoyed her work; it allowed her to travel and to study botanicals, and she was very content. Her recent trip, in fact, had yielded promising results, and she was anxious to pursue her observations in the London lab. Yet now she was on an official holiday—one she didn't necessarily feel the need for. However, it would allow her the luxury of spending time with Kate without feeling rushed.

Lucy sensed someone standing in the aisle next to her. She cracked one eye open and glanced at the automaton flight attendant who had appeared noiselessly at her side. The attendant appeared as a human woman, but Lucy knew her metal-and-clockwork interior was cloaked with biologically-engineered facial features and limbs.

"Would you care for some tea?" the automaton asked. Her black eyes blinked mechanically.

"No, but thank you," Lucy murmured.

The attendant inclined her head in acknowledgment and stepped to the next row, her movements nearly as smooth as those of an actual person. Perhaps it was for the best that automatons—or "'tons"—could still be distinguished from the human population. Science was evolving at a rapid rate, however, and advancement in 'ton programming had progressed to a point where personality traits were available for the choosing. The differences between human and 'ton might not eventually be so easily discernible.

Sleep was frustratingly elusive for Lucy, but it wasn't long before the airship began its descent and then settled onto a landing field where docking workers secured it to the ground. The noise from the propellers eventually quieted, and Lucy donned her hat and gathered her portmanteau. She held her luggage claim ticket in one gloved hand.

After disembarking and handing her ticket to a 'ton airfield attendant, she waited while he retrieved her trunk from the cargo hold and then, with an android strength impossible for a human, carried it to a waiting, open-topped horseless carriage.

"Blackwell Manor, please," Lucy said to the carriage driver. She attempted to give him the address, but he nodded and rolled his eyes.

"I know where it be, missy." He gestured with his shoulder while preparing to release the brake. "Get in, then."

The airfield attendant closed the rear boot and then offered his hand. She took it, noting the coldness of the metal through her glove. The 'ton sketched a brief, stiff bow and then returned to the airfield. Lucy lifted her hem and climbed into the carriage, which jerked forward with a grinding of large, clockwork gears that were in sore need of lubrication.

Perhaps the journey would have been a little less disconcerting by day. As it was, the world was dark. Tree limbs stretched across the narrow lanes like thin, black arms, forming an eerie tunnel punctuated with pockets of dense fog so thick that the dampness invaded Lucy's clothing, chilling her to the bone. If she ever decided to visit her cousin at night again, she would see about finding a covered carriage with heated bricks for her feet.

The path twisted and turned, and she lost her bearings as they wound their way farther into the countryside. Every now and again she saw a small inn, pub, or humble cottage, but a sense of isolation crept upon Lucy as the conveyance traveled deeper into the forest.

Thirty minutes passed before the vehicle finally came to a stop in a circular drive. The full moon hung above an enormous house of black stone with sharp angles and turrets that stretched into the sky. One saving grace, she supposed, was that there were lights on in some of the windows. Had the house been entirely in the dark, she might well have instructed the driver to return her to the airfield.

She heard a loud *thud* as the driver dropped her trunk on the ground next to the carriage and then opened the door for her. Looping the strings of her reticule over her wrist and grabbing her portmanteau, she took the driver's hand as he helped her disembark. She raised a brow at him when he made no attempt to pick up her trunk.

"Do you suppose you might at least carry it up the front steps for me?" she asked.

He smiled, the skin around his black eyes crinkling. "For another coin, I might be able to do that."

She glanced at him askance and set down her portmanteau. Opening the reticule, she withdrew a coin while still watching the amused face of the driver, a 'ton who had clearly been programmed to be savvy. The conveyance company likely brought in a fair amount of coinage from this one.

"Carry it to the stairs, and then I will give you this." She waved the coin at him between two fingers but closed her fist around it when he leaned toward her.

Eventually, trunk and portmanteau at her side, she found herself at the top of a wide stone staircase leading to a vast front porch that spanned the entire width of the house. The driver quickly made his way back to the carriage with her gold coin in his coat pocket.

He looked back at her once, his smug smile faltering as his eyes rose to examine the house behind her. "God be with ye, then." He wasted no time firing up the vehicle, leaving with a loud grinding of gears and puffs of steam.

Lucy turned toward the enormous pair of front doors that brooded over the porch and yard. She lifted the cold, wrought-iron door knocker and banged it resolutely against the door, wincing at the resounding crack that split the night. It took another thirty seconds and two more eardrum-splitting assaults with the knocker before the door finally began to creak inward.

Between rumors about the "Beast of Blackwell Manor" delivered by gossipy young girls at tea in London and the odd reaction of the carriage driver, Lucy found her heart beating rapidly as she waited in the cold night air. A sliver of light shot across the porch and into Lucy's eyes, and she leaned back slightly as she looked with equal parts curiosity and dread at the person on the other side.

An elderly gentleman, a human, apparently, opened the door wider and gave her a perfunctory bow. "Miss Pickett? Welcome to Blackwell Manor."

Miles Phillip Charles Blake, Lord Blackwell, sprawled in a stately chair before a hearth in the earl's chambers at his ancestral hunting lodge, some two hours' journey on horseback from Blackwell Manor. He twirled a tumbler of amber liquid, wondering if he would actually drink it this time. He knew it was folly—when he drank, he talked. By his own edict, however, he was the only person in attendance at the hunting lodge aside from a skeleton staff. There was no harm in losing himself for a moment in the dulling oblivion the drink would provide. It wasn't wise for other reasons, however, not the least of which was that he would need his faculties about him for the next several hours.

In his other hand, he held a cryptic note written with the use of a typewriting machine.

I know your secret.

It was the ninth such note he had received in as many months. He felt his chest tighten as the words stared back at him. He was no closer to discovering the note's author than when he received the first one, and that did not sit well with him in the least.

He had enemies, of that there was absolutely no doubt, but a good majority of those could be crushed with his influence and status, if nothing else. He couldn't control the world, however, and some felt they had nothing to lose.

Leaning forward, Miles tossed the note into the fire. Oliver would be livid. His friend and former army captain was a consulting detective for Bow Street, as intelligent as he was ruthless. He had been collecting the notes, testing them in laboratories in an attempt to learn more about the person or entity who had sent them. As the flames licked around the parchment, first charring the edges black and then devouring the whole of it, Miles wondered how he would explain the foolish act of rebellion to Oliver. It was as though his world was spiraling out of control, and burning the paper had been one thing he could do to reclaim his life. It had been a stupid impulse, and Miles was not one who made a habit of doing stupid things.

Briefly closing his eyes, he reached into his pocket and withdrew an elegant copper watch suspended on a long chain.

Four hours. He had four hours.

He tightened his fingers around the tumbler until the logical voice in the back of his brain told him he'd crush the thing if he continued. So he threw it into the fire also, noting with satisfaction how the thick glass shattered and the flash of the flame as the liquid hit it.

It was the third night. From midnight until dawn, he had to hope nobody was anywhere near the hunting lodge.

Chapter 2

The butler, who introduced himself as Mr. Arnold, arranged for two 'ton servant boys to carry Lucy's trunk and portmanteau to her room on the second floor. While he was giving the boys instructions, Lucy looked around the cavernous front hall. Only two of the many wall sconces were illuminated, giving the space a gloomy feel that made Lucy shudder in spite of herself.

Mr. Arnold led Lucy into the parlor on the right, which, she noted with relief, was cheerily warm with a fire in the hearth. Several lamps chased away the gloom. The walls were covered with floral-patterned paper, and a thick rug adorned the floor. Intoning that he would fetch Mrs. Blake, the butler quietly closed the double doors behind him.

Lucy took a deep breath and sat near the hearth, holding out her hands to the warmth before settling back in the chair. She listened to the crackling fire and the ticking of a clock on the wall until Mr. Arnold opened the doors again.

"My apologies, miss, but Mrs. Blake is already asleep for the evening, and her husband has asked that she not be disturbed. I would be happy to show you to your room."

Lucy glanced at the clock. It was late, but not ridiculously so. Kate was a night owl, and Lucy had telescribed her with the time of her pending arrival. Something was definitely wrong.

"Very well," she said, rising from her chair. "Are there Tesla connections in the bedchambers, by chance?" Lucy followed Mr. Arnold from the parlor and up a wide flight of stairs to a hallway on the second floor.

"Yes, miss. We have a fully-functioning Tesla Room on the main level with connectors in each room."

She nodded, and they continued to the end of the hallway, where he opened the last door on the right.

"Mrs. Blake has put you in one of the turret rooms. There is quite a lovely view of the front yard during the day."

Lucy nodded. "Thank you, this is very nice." A fire blazed in the hearth, casting a cozy glow over the rich wood paneling and cream-colored wallpaper.

With a bow, the butler left, closing the heavy door behind him.

What in the world had she stepped into? There was no sign of Kate, and she'd just been shut most effectively into a large, rambling manor house that resembled a small castle. One that Kate feared was haunted, no less.

Lucy noted a large brass key in the door lock and turned it, hearing a loud *click* as the bolt slid home. Withdrawing a handheld telescriber from her reticule, she located the Tesla connector behind the right bedside table. She plugged into it and scribed a quick message to her mother that she had arrived safely and would communicate again soon.

After she unpacked her trunk, hung her clothing in the wardrobe, and changed into her long, white nightgown, she washed her face with water from the basin on the dry sink and then climbed into the big bed. Her worries about not being able to rest faded as her eyes drifted closed mere moments after her head hit the pillow.

An insistent banging on the door jarred Lucy awake, and she squinted at the early morning light filtering through the turret window. The sun was hidden behind gray clouds, but at least it wasn't raining yet.

"Lucy!"

She climbed out of bed and made her way to the door, rubbing her eyes and trying to get her bearings. When she unlocked the door, it flew open to reveal Kate, whose face was a myriad of expressions ranging from joy to relief. "You're here!" She clasped Lucy in a tight embrace.

"I am." Lucy smiled and pulled back to examine her cousin. "Have I overslept, then?"

"No, no." Kate closed the door. "Breakfast isn't for another hour yet, and we all dine together in the breakfast room. But when I received the message this *morning* that you'd arrived last *night*, I nearly throttled Jonathan for not waking me!"

"He wanted you to rest, I'm sure." Lucy climbed back into bed, patting the spot next to her. "Suppose we just dispense with social chatter and get right to the heart of the matter. What is wrong?"

Kate joined Lucy, a frown marring her pretty brow. "I hardly know where to start." She clasped Lucy's fingers with her own.

Lucy stifled a yawn and settled back into the warm spot she'd only just vacated. The fire needed to be lit, but it could wait. "Begin by describing your illness."

Kate shrugged. "I am not my usual self. You know how often I walk—why, I normally cover several miles each week with daily jaunts around the countryside. Now, when I venture outside, I am weak before I've even made it beyond the back gardens. Which are horrid, incidentally," she added with smile. "Your botanist's heart will cry buckets when you see them."

"You are feeling fatigued, then?"

Kate nodded. "And my appetite is sparse."

"That is odd. You eat like a horse."

Kate stuck her tongue out at Lucy.

"Could you possibly be expecting a little miracle?"

Kate flushed. "No. I am not expecting."

Lucy pursed her lips and gave her cousin her thorough regard. Kate seemed her normal self, if perhaps a bit tired. "And why is it you think the house is haunted?"

Kate's eyes widened. "I see someone," she whispered. "I hear things late at night, feel the presence of someone in my room when I know I'm alone."

"What of Jonathan? Has he also experienced such things?"

Kate shook her head. "He believes me, though. As opposed to his wretched brother."

"Daniel speaks quite highly of the earl." Lucy watched Kate's reaction.

Kate waved a hand dismissively. "Heaven knows I adore your dear brother, and were it not for him, Jonathan and I would never have met, but I am forced to wonder about his judgment where it concerns Lord Blackwell."

"He cannot be all bad. He allowed his brother to wed a few scant months after two family deaths. And it was very bad of you, you know, to marry while I was abroad."

"It was sudden." Kate's eyes lit up as she smiled. "But oh, Lucy, Jonathan is so wonderful. He writes poetry—he is the world's most gentle soul." She paused. "And you are correct about the earl's generosity in letting us wed so soon. I do believe the only soft spot in the man's heart is for Jonathan. Because they are still in mourning, however, we were unable to have any sort of celebration. We've talked of hosting a gathering for family and close friends—we shall see."

Lucy nodded, scrutinizing Kate's features. "You are awfully pale, cousin. I shall see about mixing a special drink for you. I would assume there is an herb garden, or at least a good supply in the pantry?"

"Yes. There's a greenhouse just off the kitchen, in fact. Mr. Grafton keeps it in tip-top condition."

"And this room is lovely. You selected it for me?"

Kate nodded and looked around. "There are four turret rooms on the second floor that are kept in good condition for guests. The other guest rooms are never used and are closed up. The servants' quarters and the widow's walk are on the third floor, along with the observatory, though we do not go there. That is Lord Blackwell's lair, as is the entire south wing."

Kate paused and then grasped her in an embrace that caught Lucy by surprise. "How long will you stay?" she whispered in Lucy's ear.

Lucy drew her hands up to pat Kate's back in reassurance . . . but from what? A crack of thunder outside heralded an approaching storm—typical for the season, but which still evoked a sense of unease.

"As long as it takes to be sure you are well." Lucy pulled back from her cousin so she could look at her face. "I'm not a Medium, Kate. I'm not sure I can be of any help if you do truly have spirits roaming these halls."

"Not spirits. Just one."

"How do you know?"

"I feel the distinct personality—one distinct personality."

"Do you have any idea who it might be?"

Kate paused. "I wondered at first if it was Lord Blackwell's wife, Clara. She died suddenly, you know."

Lucy frowned. "But you decided the ghost isn't hers?"

"No. I'm afraid it's Marie."

"The sister?"

Kate nodded. "She was brutally murdered the day after Clara died."

Lucy exhaled a long breath. "I knew she had died, but rumor said she'd been ill."

Kate's voice dropped to a low whisper though the two were alone in the room. "Rumor also says that Blackwell married Clara for her fortune and then killed her after they'd been married but a month. And then, with what happened to his sister . . ."

"What do you think?"

Kate lifted a shoulder. "He is so fearsome. And he never smiles."

Lucy fought a smile of her own. "That doesn't make him a murderer."

"There have been other issues, problems . . ."

"What sort of problems, Kate?"

Kate closed her eyes. "Dead animals on the property—drained of blood. And I heard Mrs. Farrell talking about a possible vampire attack in town."

"An attack on an animal?

Kate shook her head. "A woman." She paused. "You're working on something that might address such a thing, yes?"

Lucy nodded fractionally. "Something."

Kate was quiet for a moment and then smiled brightly. "Enough of this maudlin madness. You're here! Let me help you dress for breakfast."

"Very well. I shall let you play the lady's maid." Lucy leaned forward and kissed Kate's cheek before hopping off the bed and making her way to the wardrobe.

"It's a shame to put your hair up. Look at those long, dark curls."

Lucy shook her head as she chose a day dress. "There's entirely too much of it."

"Oh, Lucy! I've missed you so very much. Everything will be absolutely perfect now that the two of us are together again."

Breakfast was an uneventful affair. Lucy and Kate dined with Jonathan, who was every bit as charming and gentle as Kate had proclaimed. He said he was grateful that Lucy had come for a visit; she wondered if Kate had told him that she'd invited Lucy because she was frightened and not just because she'd been missing her.

Afterward, Kate introduced Lucy to the upper echelons of the human staff. Mrs. Farrell, the head housekeeper, was a tiny, thin woman who brooked no argument and expected perfection from her underlings. Mr. Grafton, the head chef, was large and loud, effusive and energetic in meeting "Mrs. Kate's dear cousin." Martha Watts, the weathered-looking stable mistress, tolerated no foolishness from her stable boys, and her domain was neat as a pin, a notable fact considering it was an abode for large, smelly animals, both natural and animatronic.

She had met Mr. Arnold the evening before, and there were a few additional human servants who helped the upper staff manage what Kate referred to as "the minions," non-sentient automatons that ran on programmable tin punch cards.

The 'tons personalities were nearly nonexistent, in accordance with Mrs. Farrell's wishes. According to Kate, she preferred a "tightly run ship" rather than an army of helpers with human foibles, but Kate told Lucy that their blank expressions and lack of discernible traits made an already gloomy house even gloomier.

If nothing else, however, the servants were well-dressed. The stable boys wore green uniforms with gold buttons that bore the Blackwell crest, the kitchen help donned maroon uniforms with silver buttons, and the grounds help wore blue uniforms with white buttons. The maids were outfitted in light gray dresses and white, stiffly starched aprons. There was little variety to the physical appearance of the 'ton help. Lucy imagined the family made good use of the name tags firmly affixed to the shirtfronts and aprons.

She had a brief tour of the manor's main rooms—those that were unlocked—and Lucy noted that the house was indeed well kept. Mrs. Farrell's emotionless army cleaned and polished, maintaining a beautiful home that still managed to feel somewhat cold. What should have been inviting was instead oddly off-putting, from the many locked doors to the heavy drapes closed over the floor-to-ceiling library windows. Places where the human staff gathered—the kitchen, various workrooms—were the only places that felt comfortably inhabited. A pall hung over the rest of the house, heavy and foreboding.

The portrait gallery was a showpiece. According to Kate, the original earl had delighted in boasting of his ancestry to his visitors, and, despite the fact that Blackwell no longer hosted grand parties, the gallery was still kept in pristine condition.

Kate pointed out portraits of the family. It was indeed a handsome, if somewhat somber, gene pool, but the painting of the late Lady Marie Blake, Jonathan's deceased sister, was particularly striking. She had posed in a resplendent red gown, her black hair curling in glorious waves, and the expression on her face was all but majestic. She had been an incredible beauty, and if the portrait accurately captured the spirit of its subject, intimidating. It was situated on an easel between two other paintings: a smaller one of a delicate-looking young woman Kate identified as the late Countess of Blackwell, Clara Appleton Blake, and a portrait of a rather large mother with two beautiful adult children who were Kate's new cousins-in-law.

It was when Lucy saw the gardens at the rear of the house that she realized how well Kate knew her—it did break her heart to see them in such disarray. Trees and vegetation were thick, tangled and unruly, stretching from the house to far across the expanse of the rolling, wooded Blackwell property. Lucy imagined one might be able to make sense of it from above, but at ground level, it was an overgrown mass that resembled a jungle.

The only spot of organization was the herb garden greenhouse just outside the kitchen door. Mr. Grafton clearly made good use of it—the rows of herbs were neat as pins, marching orderly, side by side. Lucy readily identified a good majority of the plants and made a mental note to examine the rest later and compare them with her reference book.

Next to the greenhouse was a wide stone staircase that rose upward as high as Lucy's line of sight onto a landing that served as a courtyard with access to the library's double doors. In the spring and summer months, with large potted plants, umbrellas and comfortable chaise longues, tables and chairs, the area would serve as a beautiful gathering place if the house's inhabitants were so inclined. Lucy pictured the whole of it, down to the last detail, and felt a wistful sense of loss that it would likely never be used and loved—even with Kate and Jonathan in residence.

"It *is* cold now," Kate said as they moved past the greenhouse and surveyed the flowerbeds and smaller trees that had once likely been beautiful. "Plants do die in extreme temperatures."

Lucy glanced at her. "These gardens were neglected long before the temperatures changed. The weeds are as tall as many of the plants, and these here should have been pruned and tied in preparation for winter." Lucy looked down the path that led to the darkened interior of the landscape. "And *that* hasn't seen attention for decades."

Kate nodded, seemingly resigned. "I understand Lord Blackwell's mother had directed the care of the grounds on the larger scale. She'd had an army of servants who kept the entirety of it in mint condition—well groomed, easily navigated. She hosted parties in the summer months that involved treasure hunts and mazes that stretched acres across the property for both children and adults alike."

"Her sons must miss her very much."

"She died while giving birth to Jonathan. Only Lord Blackwell remembers her. She adored dancing, I hear, and when she died, the old earl had the ballroom completely shut up. It's not been used in ages. And as for this immediate area surrounding the house—well, nobody cared much for it after Clara and Marie died. This was Marie's domain. She and the head gardener, Mr. Clancy, managed the whole of it together, and I'm afraid her death nearly sent him to his own."

"He's a human, then?"

"Partially. He had an accident as a youth that required limb replacement and a heartclock implant. His brain is still intact, but I hear he was never a chatty one to begin with. He came on as a young man when Jonathan's mother was in her prime, and when Marie grew older, they became close friends. Once Marie died . . . well, I doubt he's spoken two words to anyone since."

"And Clara and Marie died six months ago?"

Kate nodded.

Lucy frowned. "And you're sure Marie was murdered?"

Kate winced. She took a deep breath and began walking down the garden path that wound through the thick undergrowth. Lucy followed, tugging the collar of her fitted jacket snugly to her scarf against a cold blast of wind.

"She was torn to shreds," Kate murmured, and Lucy had to lean in closer to hear her. "It looked as though she'd been attacked by a wild animal or possibly a vamp, although there were no traces of venom, no puncture marks, and she'd definitely not been drained." Kate grimaced. "From what I understand, there was blood everywhere. Ghastly. Her death was ruled an accident, but Lord Blackwell and Jonathan both believe otherwise."

"And you don't believe it was an animal attack?"

Kate shook her head. "Marie had a gift with animals. She had always been able to communicate with them in a way nobody had ever seen. As a child, she could coax the lions and tigers at the London Zoo to eat right out of her hand, and they submitted to her when she reached through the bars to pat their heads or scratch their ears. Stray dogs in the village marketplace, feral cats, even circus animals—they all loved her."

They continued in silence for a few minutes, their steps soft on the damp ground littered with leaves and twigs. Lucy looked back as they walked around a bend; the house was completely hidden from view.

"Do you often walk out here alone, Kate?"

"Not alone. I come here almost daily with Jonathan. I hate to be shut up in that house." Kate was winded, and Lucy slowed her stride, linking her arm through her cousin's.

Lucy frowned in thought. "As Jonathan is heir presumptive, does he not have a separate estate? Perhaps from his mother's family holdings? One of the lesser titles?"

Kate nodded. "He does, but the property has been vacant for several years and needs some work done before we move into it. If we decide to, that is."

"Why would you not?"

Kate sighed. "Jonathan adores his brother. He worries about him, says there's something not quite right with him."

"Many soldiers often return from conflict with problems ranging from fits of temper to extreme melancholy. Daniel is . . . Well, he's not himself either. The Society has even asked me to consider researching possible solutions in the form of botanical aids."

Kate shook her head with a slight frown. "Jonathan doesn't know quite what it is, and I certainly don't know the earl well enough to offer an educated opinion."

They fell silent again and followed the path, which continued to twist and turn. Lucy was about to suggest they turn back when they came upon a gray stone wall that rose above their heads.

"What's this?"

"Marie's sanctuary. Full of roses and other plants I know nothing about but which you could probably identify easily."

Lucy slowed and examined the wall. Long tendrils of ivy spilled over the top of it from the inside. "It's enclosed?"

Kate stepped off the path, motioning to Lucy. "The door is over here." They walked around the corner of the stone structure to the third side, where Kate stopped.

The gate was a substantial oak affair, darkened from the rain. With a glance at Kate, Lucy tried the door handle. It held fast.

"Mr. Clancy—the gardener—and Lord Blackwell are the only two people with keys."

"And they want it preserved in her memory with nobody going in or out? I understand grief, but I would think they would want to keep it beautiful for her."

Kate bit her lip. "I don't believe anyone can bear to enter. It's where her body was found."

Chapter 3

Lord Blackwell, if I have your support with this piece of legislation, it could mean improvements in workhouses and orphanages all over the country. The others will follow your lead if they believe you are in favor of the changes—just think of the good you would be doing for the betterment of all mankind!"

Miles brushed past the eager young lord without sparing him a glance. "I haven't the time, Brunsworth. Try someone else."

"But Blackwell!"

Miles maintained his pace through the parliamentary building until he was finally out the front door. Of all the things that came with the earldom, the House of Lords was his least favorite. He had enough on his hands with the estate. His father had adored the attention and status that came with Parliament. Craved it. Miles wished for a way around it.

"Blackwell!"

Miles turned with irritation and a quick retort at the ready for young Brunsworth but paused when he saw who had called to him. Against his will, his heartclock stuttered as the man neared, followed immediately by a sense of rage Miles found himself working to contain.

"Randolph."

Bryce Randolph smiled, but it was little more than a thinly veiled sneer. "I haven't seen you much since our time abroad."

"I admit that rather surprises me." Blackwell calmly tucked his paperwork under his arm and donned his gloves. "You are one who favors the art of spying, after all. Not very discreetly, of course."

Randolph eyed him, a slight flare of his thin nostrils. Everything about the man was thin, from his physical stature to his personality. The only thing he had in excess was a sense of obsequious ambition and a transparent desire to be more important than he was.

Randolph smiled. "I thought it might interest you to know that I now hold a seat on the Predatory Shifter Regulations Committee."

"And why would that be of interest to me?"

"One would think a peer of the realm would actively concern himself in efforts to keep Her Majesty's subjects safe. I told the Committee that you and I served in the same company during the war, and that you would certainly keep me apprised of anything that would involve the interest of the PSRC."

Miles, still and silent, watched Randolph until the other man moved slightly, showing an inkling of discomfort. "I have an appointment to keep," Miles murmured and turned to leave.

"You should expect an invitation to appear before the Committee in the future. To share any knowledge you may have, of course," Randolph called after him.

Miles tamped down an urge to whirl around and shove the man through the building behind them. Running, avoiding, hiding . . . It was not in his nature to do so, and yet it had become necessary to his survival.

The Blackwell carriage stood at the ready and carried him quickly through the bustling streets of London. Traditional, horse-drawn conveyances battled for space with automated horseless carriages that spewed steam and ground gears. Market vendors vied for the attention of the masses that walked up and down the streets, shopping and conducting business. It was cold out, and the wide assortment of colored corsets, blouses, vests, trousers, and other accoutrements that were usually on display were covered by long cloaks and woolen overcoats.

The hats were easily visible, though, and rarely were there any two exactly alike. The haberdasheries in London's clothier district were very particular about that. Top hats with mesh veils, large flowers, and stylish goggles along the brims graced the heads of women whose elaborately braided and curled hairstyles had likely taken the better part of the morning to create. Men also donned top hats of varying styles and heights but typically avoided the fripperies the ladies seemed to enjoy.

A variety of automatons walked the streets alongside humans. Some were more humanlike than others, depending on the level of skill possessed by the programmer who outfitted them with the stiff tin punch cards that allowed them to function. Most households that used 'tons paid professional programmers to create the sort of servant they required. Many of the younger generation, however, were taught programming in school; as a result, a growing number of families across the country enjoyed the convenience of programming their own 'tons and were no longer at the mercy of a programmer's busy schedule.

Miles preferred to travel in one of the estate's enclosed horseless vehicles with a driver up top. His 'ton chauffeur maneuvered the vehicle with practiced ease, and not having to navigate freed Miles to review the thick stack of paperwork that invariably accompanied him whenever he ventured into London.

"Dr. MacInnes, then, my lord?" the chauffeur asked through a speaking device that broadcast directly into the body of the vehicle.

Miles pressed the talk-back switch. "Yes, Collins. And I will not be long—you will wait outside."

"Very good, sir."

Collins's accent was stuffy and cultured. Miles's father, the late Donovan Miles Percival Blake, had insisted all of his 'tons be programmed to emulate the class and sophistication of loyal, educated servants. Since his return from battle, Miles had found it rather grating and was considering having them all redesigned. He missed the comfortable cadence and diversity in language and class that had flowed around him during his time in India.

Miles looked out the windows at the gray London day. The sky was dark and a good match for his mood. He had long ago abandoned the hope of a normal life, one filled with the joys of hearth and home. He had experienced it for a short time as a child until the death of his mother, and once he realized that the family legacy—or curse—was fully upon him, he had squelched any latent, lingering desire for conventional happiness. All there was for him was to preserve the estate and leave it in good condition for Jonathan and his future family. It might well happen sooner rather than later. Miles felt his own days were numbered.

He gathered the heavy thoughts around him like a cloak as he exited the vehicle and climbed the steps to a well-appointed town house in the middle of Chillington Square. A swift knock summoned a pleasant looking 'ton, who, when he saw Miles's face, took a step back before standing his ground and pasting a smile firmly in place.

"Right this way, Lord Blackwell," the servant said, and Miles followed him, keeping his expression neutral with a fair amount of effort. Even automatons, *nonhumans*, recoiled from his appearance. He'd had the scar for years, but in those years, he could count on one hand the number of people who hadn't looked at him with a measure of fear, disgust, or morbid curiosity.

He entered Dr. Samuel MacInnes's office, and the servant closed the double doors quietly behind him. Sam glanced up from his desk, then rose, a broad smile crossing his handsome face. He approached Miles with long strides and enveloped him in a quick embrace and a slap on the back.

"How goes it, then?" Sam gestured to a pair of chairs in a seating area near a window that looked out over a small garden.

"Well enough." Miles sat and regarded his friend for a moment. Broad through the shoulders and athletic to the core, Sam had been one of Miles's closest friends and confidants during the war. He was the light to Miles's dark; he doubted Sam had an unpleasant bone in his body. More annoyingly, he was too perceptive by half.

"You're fatigued." Sam braced one booted foot atop the other knee and studied Miles with narrowed eyes and an expression Miles had come to know all too well.

"I am fine." Miles raised a hand. "Do not begin prodding me like one of your laboratory specimens."

"You should know that the new device is only weeks away from completion. We could conceivably conduct the transfer in a month. Perhaps less."

Miles frowned and looked out at the garden that had been pruned and clipped for the pending winter. "I do not know if it is even worth the effort. The risk to you is incalculable, and for what?"

"For your life. I should think that would be all the reason we need. And I am not worried about the risk. I can always claim ignorance."

Miles looked at his friend with eyelids at half-mast. "Nobody would believe it."

"I've performed the procedure for you once before. All we are doing now is updating the device. Perfectly reasonable, no cause for suspicion."

"Bryce Randolph has secured himself a position on the PSRC. If I wasn't certain before, I am now; he knows I'm a predatory shifter."

That gave Sam pause. He finally inhaled and let it out on a quiet sigh. "Has he threatened you?"

"Not in so many words."

"Does Oliver know?"

Miles shrugged.

"We continue as planned. I have some leisure time coming. I'll return to Blackwell with you this evening. I need to measure your vital signs after charging."

For all that he was grateful for Sam's unflagging help and support, he had to wonder if it was worth the bother. Prolong his life, and for what? To endure several more decades of society's fear? The constant worry he might accidentally kill a loved one? It wasn't in his nature to quit, however, and he wouldn't put Jonathan through the pain of another loss. He finally nodded at Sam. "Thank you for your help."

Sam grinned. "I shall think of a favor in return," he said and stood. "In the meantime, you will join me for lunch. I have no house guests this month and am finding it a trifle dull."

Sam was an expert at keeping a mood light. His eyes, however, had betrayed a glimmer of concern, and Miles almost wished he hadn't seen it. Sam was a good physician, and he had never coddled Miles or insinuated in any way that Miles couldn't care for himself. If his friend was actually worried, it didn't bode well. But whether he was concerned about Miles's appearance or the fact that Randolph had insinuated himself onto the Committee, Miles was unsure.

By the afternoon of the second day, after a short jaunt into Coleshire that had Kate drooping from exhaustion, Lucy knew there was definitely something ailing her cousin, but she was at a loss to explain it. With Mr. Grafton's permission, she mixed a few select herbs in a teacup and had Kate drink it. She tucked Kate into bed to rest and promised her cousin she would be able to entertain herself.

Lucy made her way toward her room at the far end of the hallway in the north wing. Kate had been clear that Lord Blackwell's suite of rooms was in the south wing, and he didn't appreciate visitors. When Lucy had asked if there was anything of interest in the south wing, Kate had told her the ballroom and billiard room were both located there.

Lucy frowned as she approached her room. Suppose Kate and Jonathan wanted to host a ball? Kate had use of the front parlor—should anyone brave the manor's fearsome reputation—but perhaps Jonathan would like to treat his friends to a rousing game of billiards. Such things weren't allowed because they were near the beast's lair? She sighed and pushed her door open. It wasn't fair, really, to call him a beast. Kate did, but only when there was nobody around to overhear.

He has that horrible scar . . .

Kate's words echoed in Lucy's mind, and she shook them off with some effort. Supposedly the man remained in residence, although he did travel frequently to London, and Lucy had to assume she'd meet him at some point. As much as she considered herself a fair judge of character and a kind person, she dreaded the moment she'd come face-to-face with the earl. He now loomed so large in her mind as the beast everyone claimed him to be that she almost hoped she might finish her visit at the manor without ever having to come in contact with the man.

With determined resolve, she made herself comfortable at the writing desk where she'd placed her notebooks and research materials under lock and key. Flipping through the pages, she considered the work she'd done on her recent research expedition. She'd proven herself to the Botanical Aid Society on more than one occasion with remedies she'd created for various ailments, and her current assignment was more significant than anything she'd done to date.

One of the sketches in her notebook depicted a vampire with mouth open, fangs exposed. Next to it she'd written various combinations of herbs and medicines she'd collected abroad that might counteract the illegal botanical aid known as Vampiric Assimilation Aid, which allowed vampires to exist among the living in broad daylight. Though many vampires had been eradicated from London, most had been exiled to Scotland during the past decade, and the new illegal aid had produced an upsurge in the population. When vampires couldn't be detected, they were free to either bite and kill or create more of themselves at will; undead who managed to control themselves were few and far between. Very rarely did a person turn and manage to maintain any significantly lasting semblance of his or her former soul.

She reflected on the letter she'd read during the flight to Coleshire regarding the most recent developments into vamp investigation. Noting the things Gregory had listed, she updated her own records and nibbled on the end of her fountain pen, heavy in thought. It was laughable that Director Lark believed Lucy could simply switch off work-related matters as easily as she would a Tesla lamp.

Wondering about the herbs she had been unable to identify in the greenhouse, and with thoughts of Kate's illness and bloodsuckers swirling in her head, she gathered her cloak, notebook, pen, and a waterproofed pink parasol that matched her day dress to stylistic perfection. Marching through the house, she made her way down the main floor hallway to the kitchen where she opened the back door.

"Tea, Miss Pickett?" Mr. Grafton's booming voice carried through the room as she reached her arm outside to flip open the parasol in anticipation of stepping out into the rain.

"Thank you, no, Mr. Grafton. I've a mind to sketch some of your lovely plants."

The portly cook made his way to her, wiping his hands on a cloth that hung from the apron tied at his waist. "Are you an artist, then?"

"No. A botanist."

"Ah! A female botanist. Most refreshing!"

Lucy's lips quirked into a smile. "I'd dearly love to believe you're sincere."

"But I am!" The cook placed a hand on his chest, his bushy brows drawn. "My mother was knowledgeable about plants. She was a natural healer." He paused. "Of course, the villagers thought she was a witch and put her to death."

Lucy blinked. "Put her to death? That's positively primeval. Even if she were practicing Black Magick, she should have been given the option of banishment."

Which was *still* a primeval option, in Lucy's opinion, but then some of the smaller towns and villages throughout the kingdom had yet to allow the practice of even Light Magick. People's fears usually ruled the day when it came to Magick users, vamps, or shape-shifters.

Shape-shifting predators were on an extermination list. Anyone, at anytime, was allowed to take down a dangerous shape-shifter with the Queen's blessing, and even those not usually considered "predatory" were often hunted for sport while the law looked discreetly the other way. Lucy's great-uncle was a fox shifter. He kept a very low profile.

Mr. Grafton nodded with a deep sigh. "Those were different times. Saved my life, my mother did, by sending me away with her friend hours before the mob reached our home."

"I'm very sorry."

"It was long ago," Mr. Grafton said, his voice gravelly. He shuffled his feet under Lucy's regard. "So you're a botanist?"

She smiled at the abrupt subject change. "I am a researcher for the Botanical Aid Society."

"Are you, now? Well, that's very fine. And what have you discovered?"

"A few botanical aids, treatments for certain common ailments."

"You don't say! We have an expert in our midst. I hope your earlier concoction helped your cousin? Mr. Jonathan tells me she is not feeling well these days."

"So I understand. Have you noticed a difference in her appearance or behavior since she took up residence here?"

"Well, I'm certainly not one to spend much time in direct contact with the family, but I do find myself wondering if she might be falling victim to the curse."

"Curse?"

Mr. Grafton flushed and cleared his throat. "Nonsense, of course. Nothing I should be wasting your time over. In fact, I must continue my preparations for tea."

Lucy watched the man as he retreated to the far side of the kitchen. Belatedly, she realized her arm, parasol open, was still hanging out of the open door. With a shake of her head, she stepped outside and took a deep, cleansing breath.

What curse?

The question lingered, and she determined to press for details after she made sketches of the herbs in the greenhouse. The bulk of them were readily recognizable, and she labeled them accordingly. There were a few she still was curious about, so she sniffed and even tasted some before drawing them carefully for later identification.

Curiosity got the better of her when she exited the greenhouse and saw the path that led to the rock-walled garden hidden deep in the undergrowth. Of their own volition, her feet moved down the muddy path as she readjusted the parasol and held her closed journal close to her chest.

Without the necessity of maintaining a slow pace for Kate, she reached the garden in a matter of minutes.

Making her way to the far side of the enclosure, she contemplated the heavy gate. She nudged it with her foot, then, shifting the parasol, shoved at it hard with her hand. She pulled the handle toward herself repeatedly before admitting what she'd already known to be true. The gate was still locked fast.

A low growl from behind startled her, and she whirled around to see an older man dressed in a raincoat with a cap on his head, under which shot tufts of white hair. "What do ye think ye're doin'? This is private property!"

Lucy stepped back from the gate at the look on the man's face before she regained a modicum of courage and stood her ground.

"My apologies, sir," she said. "I am visiting my cousin, Mr. Jonathan Blake's wife, and she is unwell. I thought to explore the grounds while she rests."

"Mrs. Blake ought to have told ye that certain places are ta be left alone." The man's eyes flashed at her, and she found herself once again fighting to keep from running away.

"Might you be Mr. Clancy?"

He flared his nostrils. "I might."

"As a fellow lover of horticulture, I ask your patience with my lack of manners. I only sought to observe the treasures on the other side of the wall."

He scowled heavily, his eyebrows lowering over brilliant blue eyes. "The garden belonged to Lady Marie. She . . . is no longer here to tend it."

Feeling as though she were trying to coax a small animal to her without frightening it, she weighed her next words carefully. Smiling as though feeling sheepish, she said, "I know better than to be poking my nose where I've not been invited. I suppose I was drawn to the garden out of curiosity—it seems quite grand. I've a fondness for plants that exceeds what most people might define as 'normal.'"

The old man studied her for a long moment, and she fought to keep herself from fidgeting under his tight regard. He finally withdrew a large iron key from his inner pocket. "Not much ta see in this weather," he grumbled as he fitted the key into the lock. "Can't imagine why someone would be out explorin' in all this rain anyway." He was forced to twist and wiggle the key several times before the audible *click* of the bolt sounded in the chill air.

The gate swung inward on hinges that squeaked a loud protest at the invasion, and Mr. Clancy motioned for her to precede him, his expression inscrutable. She entered the walled enclosure with a sense of awe as the garden itself seemed to steal the air from her lungs.

Lush, green grass and foliage carpeted the ground. There was a small, wrought-iron gazebo in the far corner, encased in thick green vines that dripped with rain, and an intimate seating area near it that consisted of iron chairs, a round table, and a bench big enough for two adults to sit comfortably side by side.

The interior of the garden was lined with large planter boxes that contained multitudinous varieties of flora, among which she spied roses, foxglove, meadowsweet, and lady slippers, which had long since bloomed. Large lilac trees graced each of the four corners and, as evidenced from outside, ivy covered the walls and escaped over the top. The lawn was overgrown, and there wasn't a plant in sight that wasn't in need of trimming or deadheading or just plain removal, but the beauty that the garden surely possessed when cared for was readily apparent.

"It is absolutely stunning," Lucy breathed and glanced at Mr. Clancy, who looked at the gazebo with his jaw clenched.

"She did love it," he finally muttered.

"When the weather clears, would you allow me to clean it up a bit?" Lucy asked. Her fingers itched to fix the mess, and she began mentally organizing the whole of it, deciding where she would start and how she would go about restoring order. With concerted effort, she refrained from flipping open her sketchbook and making notes. "I didn't know her, of course, but I would think this garden should be cherished and cared for as a tribute to Lady Marie, wouldn't you agree?"

Mr. Clancy finally looked at her. "No. It was hers and she's gone." His worn face was weary as though he'd seen the grief of a thousand lifetimes. His eyes looked strangely wet, and Lucy felt her heart soften by several degrees.

She nodded. "I understand. And I do thank you so much for allowing me to see it. It's splendid." She picked her way back to the threshold, watching her step to avoid patches of mud.

"Wait," Mr. Clancy called, and when she turned, he joined her at the gate. "Clean it if you must, then, but don't be pesterin' me for help. I've other duties ta attend."

Lucy smiled. "I promise not to pester you. Other than to ask you for the key."

He nodded, and although he didn't smile, she caught a gentle shift in his features. "But not after six o'clock in the evening. My arthritic knee acts up after dark."

"Noted." She gave him a nod and, after a brief moment of hesitation, shifted her parasol to offer him her hand. He looked at her and took it in a perfunctory shake.

"Ye're Mrs. Blake's relation, then?"

"Yes. First cousin."

He opened his mouth and then closed it again. "Well, a good day to you."

"And to you." They left the quiet sanctuary, and Mr. Clancy locked the gate behind them, pocketing the key. He gruffly told her that his quarters were in the cottage down by the stream and then left her in the falling rain.

Chapter 4

After checking on Kate, Lucy spent the rest of the afternoon in her room reviewing her sketches and comparing them to her plant reference guide. She also searched her notebook dedicated to medicinal herbs, wondering if there might be something that would restore Kate's energy permanently rather than just a temporary mend.

She heard the approach of a horseless carriage in the drive—a rather large one, from the sound of it—and she went to her window. Amidst some fuss and ceremony, she saw an older woman who began firing orders at the servants with a volume Lucy heard through the closed window. A young man and young woman emerged from the carriage as well.

Lucy's observations were interrupted as Kate knocked quickly and then entered, wearing a beautiful dinner gown. She looked better after having had a good, long rest. "Please come downstairs with me. The Charlesworths are here."

"I saw the carriage. Who are the Charlesworths?"

Kate sighed as she took Lucy's notebook and pen from her hands and placed them on the writing desk. "Mrs. Charlesworth is Jonathan's paternal aunt. She has two children, Arthur, who is slightly older than we are, and Candice, who is our age; you might remember seeing their family portrait in the gallery. Mrs. Charlesworth's husband passed on some five years ago. I shouldn't wonder if he took his own life as a means of escape."

"Mercy, Kate." Lucy moved her research materials into the desk drawer and locked it.

"I know, but if you refuse to be my confidant, then where shall I turn? At any rate, I don't care for Mrs. Charlesworth. She has a calculating look about her hideous face that sets my teeth on edge."

Lucy quickly exchanged her day dress for a dinner ensemble that was deep wine in color and trim in its fit.

Kate made a spinning motion with her finger, and when Lucy turned around, Kate tied the outer corset strings snugly against her back. She grabbed a handful of hairpins, pulled Lucy down into a chair before the vanity's large, ornate mirror, and began working on some of the more unruly curls of Lucy's coiffure.

"What does Jonathan think of the Charlesworths?"

"He doesn't much care for them either, but they are family. They don't go away." Kate finally settled for pinning the curls atop Lucy's head and allowed a few delicately twisting tendrils to fall gracefully to her shoulders.

"And Lord Blackwell?"

Kate made an inelegant sound. "Who in the world knows what he thinks? He just broods and sucks the life right out of a room."

"Where is the man? I've yet to even see his face." *That's the ticket, Lucy. Tackle the matter head-on.* She squelched the nervous fluttering in her stomach with a command to stop fretting like a ninny.

"Once a month, he goes to the family hunting lodge for four or five days."

"Does he hunt?" Lucy retrieved her matching shoes from the wardrobe and slipped them on. She selected a pair of gloves as well.

Kate rolled her eyes. "I would assume so. He is at the hunting lodge, after all." She shoved the gloves onto Lucy's hands and pushed her out of the room.

"You certainly seem to have regained your strength," Lucy muttered as Kate swiftly closed the door behind them.

"Words cannot express the depth of my distaste for that woman," Kate huffed as they made their way down the hall.

"Then why are we in such a hurry to meet with them?"

Kate stopped midstride and looked at Lucy with eyes that widened slightly as she bit her lower lip. "I am now mistress of the house. Blackwell doesn't have a wife or children, and Jonathan is heir to the earldom. There are expectations, you know."

Lucy nodded. "I do. I also know that I do not like the thought of someone making a nuisance of herself at your expense. Does Mrs. Charlesworth visit often?"

"Yes. I've met her once before, and Jonathan tells me they are often regular fixtures around the place." Kate resumed her pace down the hallway, and Lucy had to trot to stay at her side. "And she telescribed earlier today, insisting on hosting a ball in my and Jonathan's honor at their home in Stammershire. I've told them repeatedly it isn't necessary, that at some point we will just do it here, but Aunt Eustace insists."

"Oh dear, that is an unfortunate name."

"Yes. And I know she only wants to host this grand ball to keep up appearances for her lofty circle of friends."

"How lofty can they be? I had assumed she must have married a commoner."

"She did. But she was the daughter of an earl, and her husband made a significant amount of money"—she lowered her voice—"from the village rectory, or so the rumor goes. But nobody dares approach Eustace about the issue."

Lucy's mouth twitched, and she tried to fight a smile as they reached the top of the staircase leading to the front hall where she heard a cacophony of voices that lifted on the air. "He was a vicar, I presume?"

"He was," Kate whispered as they paused on the second step down. "But he also had inherited money, which is why it is so baffling that he would steal from his own parishioners."

"This place is a circus," Lucy murmured as they continued their descent.

"That's what I've been telling you." Kate smiled and linked her arm through Lucy's.

Once all the formal introductions were made, the family gathered in the dining room for supper. Through some quick maneuvering on his part, Arthur Charlesworth claimed the seat next to Lucy. Opposite them sat Mrs. Charlesworth and Candice, with Jonathan at the head. Kate rounded out the party in the hostess's seat at the foot of the table. She looked extremely ill at ease, and Lucy felt her protective instincts surging to the surface.

"And where is my errant nephew this time?" Mrs. Charlesworth asked Jonathan as the first course was served.

One of Mr. Grafton's automaton kitchen helpers placed Kate's food in front of her. Lucy noticed a subtle grimace cross her cousin's features before she looked up at the 'ton and said, "Thank you, Robert." The boy nodded and returned to the sideboard for more food. Kate had the right of it, Lucy decided. The lack of animation in the staff was disconcerting, to say the least.

"Miles is at the hunting lodge," Jonathan replied to his aunt. "He likes to visit every now and again for a few days. If he's not there, his time spent away is usually in London on parliamentary business. The majority of the time, he's here. It's your misfortune to keep missing him," he finished with a wink.

Lucy admired his smooth delivery. Had she not known from Kate that Jonathan wasn't overly fond of his relatives, she might have thought him at pleasant ease with the woman who—Kate was right—had a hideous face. It wasn't so much the features; it was the way she set them. Lucy wondered if the woman had ever smiled a day in her life.

Mrs. Charlesworth opened her mouth to reply, but just then, Arthur leaned close to Lucy and asked her how long she would be gracing Blackwell Manor with her beauty.

Lucy glanced at him as she ate a piece of asparagus. "As long as Kate wishes me to," she told the man after swallowing. "It's been ever so long since we have spent time together."

He smiled at her, and Lucy wondered how many hearts he had melted with that gift. That Arthur was handsome was an understatement. He had a thick head of sandy-colored hair styled to perfection, and his clothing hung well on his healthy frame. He wore his wealth and confidence with natural ease, the kind that came from generations of money and breeding—from his mother's side of the family, at least. "Well, I sincerely hope your visit will be one of an extended nature."

Lucy's late father hadn't been titled, but he had been a wealthy landowner, so she had spent her life mingling with Arthur's kind, and she was instinctively leery of him. "Polo?" she guessed, then took a sip of her drink.

He inclined his golden head. "Of course. And more to my taste, rugby. I helped form the Northern Rugby Football Union."

"Congratulations."

"Thank you. I used to be able to convince Jonathan and Miles to join in on the fun. Although I must admit," he added in a faux-conspiratorial whisper, "that once Miles showed his face on the field, we had a distinct advantage. He scared the other teams witless."

"I am beginning to form a most singular opinion of Lord Blackwell."

"Oh, not at all. He's merely been . . . toughened by his experiences in the war."

Lucy found it rather odd the oldest son and heir to an earldom would enlist for military service. That role usually fell to the second son.

"Have you never met him?" Arthur asked as they continued their meal, the conversations flowing around them in different directions. "He can be rather alarming. But not to worry. His scar didn't actually come from a duel with a jealous husband—I don't think."

Lucy paused with her fork halfway to her mouth. "You're his cousin. One should think you would sing his praises." She softened her remarks with a smile, her words delivered with a hint of feigned flirtatiousness. She had played this kind of game more times than she could count.

"But I do! I do sing his praises. I would hate for you to be frightened, though, especially as you are his guest. And the rumors about him—they are mostly not to be believed."

Lucy glanced up at the others at the table, who were now listening in. Candice Charlesworth arched a brow at her brother and took a sip from her glass. "Arthur is merely envious of our cousin. Strong as an ox, wealthy as Croesus, and titled to boot. I shouldn't believe much of anything my brother says, Miss Pickett."

Arthur looked at them in silence for a moment before laughing. "Candice is indeed a tease. Would that God had blessed me with a younger brother rather than a sister."

"Arthur, what a thing to say!" Aunt Eustace chastised her son with a scowl, and he laughed again.

The entire group tried for levity that felt, to Lucy, forced. She studied Jonathan as conversation resumed and noted that not only was he not laughing, but his mouth was clamped shut and he was flushed from his forehead to his neck. Aunt Eustace said something inane, and Jonathan looked at her for a fraction of a second before forming his lips into a smile.

Lucy maintained idle chatter with Arthur and cast a quick look at Kate, who watched her husband with a brow creased in concern and pushed the food around on her plate, eating very little. The meal progressed, and conversation remained light and inconsequential. There was an undercurrent, however, that Lucy felt. It was as though a thread ran through the entire group, taut and uncomfortable.

By the time dessert rolled around, Lucy had formed some opinions. Aunt Eustace was full of herself, and there was very little space for anyone else in the room, metaphorically and physically. Arthur was handsome, charming, and likely a very shallow rogue with an agenda of his own.

Candice had a quick wit that occasionally bordered on cutting. She had attended school in London while Lucy and Kate had been in Switzerland at finishing school. They had all graduated two years prior, and Lucy wondered if Candice would soon panic at her single state. Her declaration upon meeting Lucy that she was the earl's "spinster cousin" spoke volumes. Most of the girls Lucy knew were already either betrothed or married; some even had a child or two. Candice was clearly feeling the pressure.

Following dinner, Jonathan and Arthur dispensed with the ritual seclusion in the den with a glass of port and instead joined the women in the drawing room for a rousing game of loo. Lucy was up two hands when she noticed Kate beginning to droop in her chair. Her heart tripped, and she looked at Jonathan, who was also watching his wife. Lucy caught his eye and raised a brow. Jonathan nodded and shoved his chair back.

"I do believe it's time for my wife and me to retire," he said to the group with a smile. "Of course, you are all free to continue the game without us. And Mrs. Farrell has informed me that your customary rooms in the north wing overlooking the back gardens have been readied for you."

Aunt Eustace sniffed and muttered something under her breath that sounded like a complaint about the view. Jonathan maintained his smile as he helped Kate from her chair.

"Will you remain with us, Miss Pickett?" Arthur asked Lucy.

"You must," Candice added. "It is entirely too early to turn in."

"I would love to," Lucy lied with a smile. "I do agree—the night is young."

Candice beamed at Lucy and offered her the same devastating smile her brother possessed. Candice was as beautiful as Arthur was handsome. They looked enough alike to be twins; the principal difference—aside from gender—was the dark strawberry strands woven through Candice's sandy-colored hair. Lucy looked at Eustace and concluded the children must have taken after their father in appearance.

Aunt Eustace surveyed the card table with open disdain. "I suppose we ought to finish." She turned to Jonathan as he and Kate made their way to the door. "You must tell Miles that I am utterly vexed he is never in residence when I visit."

"He'll likely return tomorrow," Jonathan said over his shoulder. "I suspect you'll have a chance to tell him so yourself."

Aunt Eustace harrumphed but refrained from further comment, and Lucy's heart thumped at Jonathan's pronouncement. After the couple left the room, Lucy paired up with Candice and dealt another hand. As the game continued, Candice and Arthur became more competitive. Expressions turned grim and conversation ceased to flow as easily as it had when Lucy and Arthur had been paired together and he had been doing his best to charm her. She glanced at the players around the table with a fair amount of amusement. It was loo, for heaven's sake. Furthermore, Candice and Arthur seemed to have come by their competitiveness honestly enough. The look on Eustace's face was enough to have Lucy biting the insides of her cheeks to keep from snickering outright.

Pleasant family.

Lucy felt a momentary pang for her own. It had been a happy household. She and Daniel were thick as thieves despite the fact that he was seven years her senior, and she'd never felt the loss of her father, who had died just before she was born. Her mother was all things practical and nononsense, and her paternal grandmother was nurturing and affectionate. It had been an idyllic childhood, and when compared to the people sitting around the table and playing whist as though England's national security depended upon the outcome, she was grateful for the personalities that comprised her family unit.

She frowned as she looked down at the cards in her hands. Kate had lost her parents to illness and had spent enough time with Lucy's family when she was young that she had become like a sister to Lucy. And now she was ill, and Lucy was at a loss to explain it. She suddenly lost all interest in the Charlesworths, and it took every ounce of her good breeding and polish to finish the night properly and not retire to her bedchamber before the others.

Eustace finally yawned and declared the evening done. Candice drew an arm through Lucy's as they left the drawing room and stepped into the hall where they passed Mr. Arnold, who was turning down sconces for the evening.

"I don't mind telling you, it's absolutely delightful to have another woman my age about the house. I do hope you'll be staying with us for some time," Candice told Lucy as they strolled toward the main staircase.

"Kate is wonderful, of course, but she and Jonathan are all agog for each other and seem to have time for nobody but themselves."

Lucy smiled at Candice, who pouted very prettily indeed. "I imagine that must be very trying. I know I am frustrated when people don't have the time of day for me."

Candice cast an assessing glance at Lucy as they began climbing the stairs. "It is just that my life is so frightfully dull," she finally said. "You cannot imagine how wonderful it is to leave Charlesworth House for any length of time. Stammershire is provincial, the people gauche." Candice glanced over her shoulder, then pulled Lucy closer to share a conspiratorial whisper. "Although my mother seems to like them well enough. She is convinced that if we can manage to host just the right dinner ball, she will be as popular as she was when she lived at home as the daughter of an earl."

"And what do you think?"

"I think she is wasting her time. Nobody dares venture so far north anymore with Scotland just over the border. And as I said, the people who live in town are hardly worth the effort of fine food and entertainment."

"I suppose it is fortunate for you, then, that your mother enjoys visiting Blackwell on a regular basis."

"You've no idea." Candice's face was resolute.

The Charlesworths' bedchambers were on the opposite side of the hall from Lucy's, and after reaching Candice's door on the second floor, she parted company with a promise to take breakfast with the family in the morning.

Lucy made her way down the dark hallway, which was punctuated with wall sconces that gave off a low level of light. When she entered her bedroom, she switched on a lamp by her bedside and listened for the hum that signaled the connection to the Tesla control room.

Lucy changed her clothes with a fair amount of twisting and turning. Life was definitely easier with a maid. Kate had offered hers, but Lucy's mood was just somber enough that she didn't care for company.

She slipped a long, white nightgown over her head, adjusting the cuffs at her wrists. The fire in the hearth was banked and the room's temperature pleasant enough, but her feet were cold. Locating her slippers in the wardrobe, she put them on and sat in a chair near the fire. She curled her feet under her and leaned back in the comfortable chair, noting with pleasure the hot teapot that had been placed at the side table near her elbow. Pouring herself a cup, she gently blew over the top of it and took a cautious sip.

Closing her eyes with pleasure, she swallowed the herbal brew and relaxed. She replaced the teacup on the tray and began pulling pins from her hair, eventually shaking out the mahogany mass and allowing the curls to fall down her back. Sighing, she massaged her head with her fingertips; the pins had been tight, and the release was sublime.

Lucy enjoyed the glowing coals of the hearth as she finished her tea, finally replacing the cup and saucer on the side table and rubbing her eyes. She feared her mind was twirling with too many thoughts to get any rest, but once she switched off her lamp and lay down, the comfortable bed lulled her into a blessedly relaxed state.

She couldn't exactly define what it was that roused her from sleep. The room was dark with only moonlight streaming in from the turret window. And there was a woman at the foot of her bed, watching her.

Chapter 5

Kate?" Lucy's voice was scratchy and her vision blurred. She blinked, trying to focus.

The woman was dressed in a gown of deep red, and although she seemed real enough, there was a slight translucence to her that gave her an eerie, ethereal glow. The apparition remained silent.

Leaning up on one elbow, Lucy squinted carefully at the woman before sucking in her breath and scooting back against the headboard with a *thunk.* "You're not Kate," she finally whispered, heart pounding.

The expression on the woman's face was flat, emotionless. She was pretty, with dark hair like Jonathan's. She also seemed to have his nose, her features a more feminine version of his. Lucy had seen her before, in the portrait gallery. "Marie? Lady Blake?"

The woman continued to stare, unblinking, at Lucy's face.

Lucy's heart thudded in her ears, and she struggled to control her breathing when the figure put a hand on the tall post attached to the footboard.

The bed moved. Infinitesimally but noticeably.

The woman shoved at the bedpost again, and Lucy fought to smother a scream. She scooted to the far side of the bed.

"Wha . . . wha . . . ?" she gasped.

Marie's nostrils flared slightly, and with flashing eyes, she shoved the bedpost one last time and crossed the room to the door, which she promptly walked through.

Lucy blinked. Trying to muscle the experience into something that made sense to her was proving difficult. She lay absolutely still for one long minute, then two, breathing as though she'd run a mile. The room was as silent as a tomb except for the quiet ticking of the clock above the mantelpiece. After what seemed like hours but was in reality only minutes, she sat up slowly and put a hand to her forehead.

"Warm tea," she whimpered. "I need warm tea."

She pulled herself out of bed on legs that trembled and stumbled. She found the wrapper that matched her nightgown in the wardrobe and thrust her arms through, missing several times before finally tugging it into place. She tied the white ribbon into a bow at her throat with trembling fingers and wondered why she bothered.

Horribly rattled, she finally took a deep breath and slowly approached the footboard, placing her hand on the post where Marie's had been. Giving it an experimental push, her heart thumped once, *hard*, when she realized it took a fair amount of effort to move it the way Marie had. It was an extremely heavy piece of furniture. The frame was solid oak; there was no give to the connecting points, no squeaking hinges.

Lucy stood at the bedpost for a long moment before turning to pour herself a cup of tea, which was now cold, and the cup rattled against the saucer before she had the wherewithal to set it back down.

"The kitchen," she murmured aloud. She could make some tea in the kitchen.

Frightened to move yet too frightened to stay, she eased herself out of the door and looked down the long hallway to be sure a beautiful woman in a red dress wasn't wandering about. Closing the door behind her, as if that would do any good, she made her way noiselessly down the carpeted floor, hoping that Marie was busying herself with Aunt Eustace and had no further plans to rattle Lucy's bed.

The house was eerie in the dark. Lucy amended that thought: it was eerie in the day as well. But with all the living occupants safely abed, the notion that otherworldly creatures roamed the halls made the long shadows and creaking noises all the more macabre.

Finding the kitchen deserted, Lucy set one of the wall sconces to low light and hunted for a stash of tea and a teapot. Locating both and firing up the stove, she sat on a stool near one perfectly polished countertop while the water heated. Her heart still thumped more rapidly than she was accustomed to, and she checked the tea canister for the third time to be sure she wasn't going to drink something loaded with a stimulant that would send her flying to the moon.

She needed a book. Reading would soothe her nerves and help her forget she'd seen a ghost, which she was now forced to admit, existed. The library was down the long hallway. She would drink her tea first and then stop there before heading back to her room.

When the teakettle whistled, she strained the liquid into a cup and looked at it. It was cold in the kitchen, and the single lit sconce on the wall could hardly be considered cozy; she didn't want to stay there. Changing her plans, she emptied the cup into the white stone kitchen sink, and, holding the tea canister in one arm, she took the steaming pot instead. She would return it in the morning.

She made her way to the library, entering quietly through the one double door that stood ajar. A soft glow of lantern light shone from within, and as she moved farther into the enormous room, she inhaled the wonderful smell of cedar wood and old books.

She closed her eyes briefly and calmed her furiously beating heart, only to have the silence shattered by a loud, masculine start of surprise and the sound of splintering glass. Her eyes flew open in horror, and she stared at a man with fury stamped across his face.

The earl of Blackwell.

She would have known him anywhere. He had features similar to Jonathan's, only his jaw was more angular, his entire appearance more harsh. And he was much taller, much more . . . everything. It didn't take her long to assess the scene. She must have caught him by surprise, which caused him to drop his drink. Liquid puddled at his feet on the stone hearth amidst chunks of thick, broken glass.

"I apologize, my lord. I wasn't aware anybody was here." Lucy swallowed and began backing toward the door.

The earl looked at her for a long moment, his ice-blue eyes eerie and bright even in the darkened interior. He approached her steadily, his movements sure and unhurried, and she turned to run from the room.

"Stop."

Perhaps it was the tone or the fact that she had been frightened enough for one day, but the one-word command gave Lucy the backbone to turn and stand her ground. She was not a servant or 'ton; she was a guest in the home. She refused to be bullied. It had often been her downfall—her patience was nearly limitless, but it eventually ran out.

By the time the earl reached Lucy, she had had to crane her neck back to continue meeting those eyes. His broad shoulders blocked the view of anything else but him, and she was given no other alternative than to maintain her false sense of bravado while her very last nerve was stretched to the snapping point. She felt herself trembling. What a wretched family! Obsequious and insulting relatives? First an angry ghost and now an angry lord? Jonathan was the only pleasant one in the entire bunch.

Blackwell was dressed in black trousers with black riding boots spattered with mud. His discarded overcoat was slung over the back of the sofa, his unbuttoned vest was black, as was his cravat, which was undone and hung loosely about his neck. He'd rolled back the cuffs of his snowy-white shirt, which was the only contrast on an otherwise intimidating male with black hair.

A thick scar ran the length of his profile on the left side of his face. It extended from his temple, across the cheekbone, and down to his jawline just beyond the corner of his mouth. The flickering lamplight showed that it continued under his chin and down across the front of his neck, where it eventually disappeared under his shirt.

She frowned and drew her brows together, studying his face.

"Do you have something you would like to say?" he murmured, his voice deep, strained.

She spoke before giving any real thought to her words. "Your scar isn't nearly as fearsome as others suggested." Her voice trailed off as she realized the extent of her social gaffe. Not only was she wandering about in the wee hours of the morning in nothing but her night clothing, but she had also just insulted the lord of the manor and her cousin's brother-in-law. She was usually much more circumspect.

"Who are you, and what are you doing in my house?" His tone was benign enough, but a muscle worked in his jaw.

She lifted her chin a fraction. "My name is Lucy, my lord. I am Kate's cousin."

"And she has invited you for a visit."

"Yes. And I appreciate your gracious hospitality." She thought she heard him grinding his teeth.

"I take it your visit will be a short one."

Mercy, he was large. He had to have known he was intimidating her. He was a peer of the realm, and as such would adhere to social graces, which did not include taking such liberties with uncomfortably close proximity. Society was thankfully past the day when time spent alone in a room with a gentleman meant swift and definitive social ruin, but it was nighttime, after all, and he was standing much too close. She felt heat radiating from him—or perhaps it was her own flushed face.

"My cousin is ill, and I intend to remain until I am convinced she is well again."

"She has an army of servants and a husband who can care for her."

"Forgive me, but your brother knows nothing about illness or healing. And Kate informed me that the one doctor Mrs. Farrell contacted attempted to bleed her with leeches. I find that barbaric and ridiculous."

"I suppose you are a medical professional yourself, Cousin Lucy?" He withdrew a white handkerchief from his pocket and slowly wiped the liquid from his sloshed drink off his fingers.

Uncertainty again lost to anger, and she welcomed it. "I am a botanist and well versed in botanical aids. As you don't seem inclined to provide for the family who lives under your roof, it is going to have to fall to someone else." She had the satisfaction of seeing his expression slacken momentarily before he narrowed his eyes at her.

"I provide very well for those under my roof, and I take exception to the fact that you would insult me in my own home. Your cousin did not seem to be suffering overmuch the last time I saw her, now that she has taken on the role of lady of the manor."

"If you knew her in the least you would realize *that* is the last role in the world she wants. I don't care if she becomes queen, I would rather she be healthy," Lucy shot back and gestured in frustration, only to realize she still held the tea canister and hot teapot. It bumped against his arm, and he looked down at it and then back at her.

He seemed absolutely flummoxed, and had she not been angry and still a bit terrified, she might have smiled.

"I have brought a friend with me—a doctor—who will see to Kate in the morning," he ground out. "And in the meantime, I'll thank you to remain in your room during the nighttime hours."

Her face felt hot again in spite of her resolve to remain unaffected. "I do not usually make a habit of wandering the house at all hours, especially in this ensemble," she said, hearing the stiffness in her tone. "I was . . . I wasn't resting well and needed some warm tea, and I thought I might find a book of poetry or a novel to calm my nerves."

He glanced down at the pot in her hand. "How much tea were you thinking of drinking?"

"Enough to put me to sleep."

He worked his mouth and seemed to be searching for something to say. She dropped a quick curtsey and said, "Good night, my lord. Again, my apologies for disrupting your . . . quiet." She'd almost said "brooding" but caught it on the tip of her tongue just as it was preparing to fly out.

She turned and made for the door as smoothly as she could, praying she wouldn't trip and ruin a grand exit.

Miles stared after the retreating figure, his head spinning. When he had lifted the glass to his lips, the apparition of a woman had given him such a start that he'd dropped the brandy, spilling it over his hand in the process. She had been startled—likely horrified—to have come upon him. When he read the conflicting emotions on her face, he had been assured she was flesh and blood, not a spirit.

He disliked being surprised, and woven through his anger were threads of fear. He'd unleashed it on her without saying much of anything—knew it had hit its mark because he had read it clearly on her face when she'd turned to flee. And when he'd invaded her personal space and saw her breathing quicken and her pulse point pounding at her throat, he'd wanted to reach out and shake her for making him uncomfortable in his own home. But she had stood her ground, dared to insult him and his methods of caring for his family, and hadn't retreated, gasping in fear or fainting as his own wife had done on more than one occasion before her death.

Thoughts of Clara never did him any good, and he felt his black mood deepen. He made his way back to the hearth and sank into the chair closest to the fire. Leaning forward, he braced his forearms on his knees and buried his head in his hands. It had been a wretched night at the end of a wretched weekend.

He had seen Marie.

She'd been furious, the way she had occasionally been on the mortal side of life's veil. He had never known someone with such a fiery personality, and he was grateful to realize it had accompanied her into the next life. She was still herself, and he found himself oddly relieved. The fact that she was lingering around the manor was unsettling, however.

That evening marked the first time he had seen her. Jonathan had told him Kate suspected there was a spirit about and that it was likely Marie, but he had scoffed at the notion. The last thing he wanted was a Medium wandering the halls, lighting incense and intoning gibberish. Now that he had seen his sister with his own two eyes, wearing the very dress in which she'd breathed her last, he was forced to admit he'd been wrong in dismissing Jonathan's observations. He knew of the existence of ghosts—he'd seen enough on the battlefield to acknowledge the reality of them—but for his sister to reappear in all her beautiful fury had stopped him cold.

She hadn't said a word, merely looked at him as he'd entered his suite after telling Marcus, his valet, that he didn't require any help. The sight of her had stolen the breath from his lungs, and he ached. He and Jonathan both had adored Marie—they were the elder and younger bookends to her vibrancy and life—and when she'd . . . gone, the gaping hole she'd left behind had been excruciating. It still was.

After Marie's death, Miles had kept himself busier than was probably healthy, and Jonathan had Kate, but in the quiet hours when he couldn't escape his own thoughts, he was forced to consider the most horrifying thing of all. And it was the reason he'd not enlisted Oliver's help in searching for her murderer.

Miles was a werewolf, and he might have been the one who'd killed her.

Chapter 6

Lucy returned the teapot and canister to a confused Mr. Grafton the next morning before she made her way to the breakfast room. She had slept longer than she'd intended to, which shouldn't have surprised her. After leaving the library and its surly master the night before, sleep had been a long time coming. And she hadn't retrieved a book from the library, which had been her goal in the first place.

She noticed Lord Blackwell as soon as she entered the room. He had a presence about him that would have been overwhelming in an opera hall. He was dressed entirely in black, again, the only contrast the white shirt that showed beneath his suit coat and vest, and a perfectly placed charcoal-gray cravat. He should have looked every inch the gentleman, yet he seemed rather predatory—even larger in the light of day. He stood just inside the door and spoke to a man who looked vaguely familiar to Lucy. An image of him hovered on the fringes of her memory.

Blackwell met her eyes, but he might have been a statue for all the inflection she read there. She turned her attention from him with a concerted effort and noted the absence of Kate and Jonathan, but the presence of the three Charlesworths, two of whom looked beautiful and one who looked surly.

She studied the men standing by the door, trying to determine why she knew the guest; he glanced at her, then looked more fully at her face.

His mouth turned upward in a wide grin, and he approached her with quick, long-legged strides.

"Miss Pickett! What a surprise to see you here. I don't suppose you remember me?" He offered his hand, continuing before she could reply. "Samuel MacInnes. Daniel and I were in the same company during our time in India, along with Blackwell." He gestured with a thumb over his shoulder. "I met Daniel during our pre-deployment training and visited your home with him just before we shipped out."

"Dr. MacInnes, of course!" Lucy returned his smile. "Thank you for bringing Daniel home safely. My mother was beside herself the entire time he was gone."

"Please, I insist you call me Sam."

Lord Blackwell shifted slightly, and Lucy noted his approach from the corner of her eye.

"Are you Daniel's wife, then?" the earl asked her, frowning.

Samuel MacInnes chuckled. "I'm fairly certain he would have mentioned a wife, Miles. This is his sister, Lucy."

"Yes." Lord Blackwell studied her face—looking for a resemblance, perhaps? "I'm glad to know the connection," he said, stiff and formal as though the confession was painful for him. "I hold your brother in very high regard."

"Daniel is a very likable fellow."

Lucy studied the pair of men with interest. Samuel had referred to Lord Blackwell casually, without deferring in any way to his rank or title. Samuel was a wealthy doctor but untitled. She wondered if Daniel enjoyed the same ease with them.

For a moment, she was irrationally defensive of her brother. He was wealthy beyond measure with his airships; the money had bought him status with society, but there were those who still considered him gauche. New money, as others had also viewed their father. That people looked down their noses at Daniel set her teeth on edge. They likely looked upon her the same way, but she didn't care a fig about that. She had her friends, her social life, and had been popular in school. She was happy and had little use for snobbery anyway. She didn't care for the good opinion of those who would judge either her or Daniel by their ancestry.

Mr. Grafton's head assistant spoke from the doorway. "Breakfast is served."

As the party seated themselves around the table, Mr. Grafton's automaton servers delivered the first course from the sideboard.

Lucy found herself seated between Arthur Charlesworth, who smelled pleasantly of cologne, and Samuel MacInnes. Aunt Eustace had been angling to sit next to Blackwell, so when Samuel beat her to the vacancy, Lucy breathed an internal sigh of relief. Blackwell occupied the head of the table, and across from Lucy were Candice and Aunt Eustace, who seemed to occupy two spots all by herself. The hostess's seat opposite Lord Blackwell was conspicuously vacant.

"So, Dr. MacInnes—Sam," Lucy said, hoping to engage him in conversation before Arthur could begin, "what is it that occupies your time now that you're home from the war?"

"I have a medical practice and perform surgery at the hospital in London. I also like to make time to visit with friends and family when I can."

"Perhaps you have better luck finding Blackwell at home than we do," Aunt Eustace interjected. "My only two nephews, and only one of them is usually in residence."

Samuel cleared his throat, and Lucy looked to the head of the table. Lord Blackwell continued his meal without even seeming to notice that Eustace was in the room.

Interesting. Jonathan was clearly irritated by the woman, as was Kate, but the elder brother simply dismissed her.

"Of course, when my brother was alive," Eustace continued, "we were always assured he would be here to spend time with us. His only relations. His untimely death certainly changed the tide of familial affection."

Arthur stiffened beside her, and Lucy wondered what the woman was implying. Untimely death? Aunt Eustace clearly had an ax to grind with the new earl because Jonathan and Kate were nothing if not warm and inviting to her despite their obvious distaste.

Blackwell finally raised his head and scrutinized the woman with such a cold stare that Eustace visibly shrank back in her seat, mumbling something Lucy couldn't hear. Lucy couldn't say that she blamed her; those blue eyes were deadly. Candice angled her head over her plate, but not before Lucy saw something suspiciously resembling a smirk. There was also a flash in the young woman's eyes—something calculating—that she had smoothed over by the time she resumed her meal.

Arthur exhaled quietly and pushed his food around a bit before setting the fork down and opting for a drink of juice instead.

Samuel remained silent, but Lucy noted his white-knuckled grip on his knife as he spread jelly on his toast. She glanced up, and he looked at her askance with a wink that was probably meant to reassure but was at odds with the rest of his somber expression.

Lord Blackwell continued his meal, the only evidence of any emotion showing on the side of his face where the jagged scar stood out in stark relief against his complexion, which had darkened a shade. A muscle in his jaw flexed as he cut a piece of ham and speared it. Arthur had implied that the scar had been the result of a duel with a jealous husband, but as she considered it in the light of day, she came to a conclusion: Either the earl's opponent had used a ridiculously dull blade or the scar had come about through an entirely different accident. It was not the result of a clean slice.

Conversation resumed, stilted at first, but eventually flowing back into a normal rhythm. Dr. MacInnes and the earl discussed former associates from their regiment, and Arthur leaned into Lucy. "He never wanted the earldom, you know. The suggestion that he might have killed his father for it is absurd. My mother certainly does not mean to imply it."

Lucy squinted at him. Was there no end to the backhanded defense of his cousin? Why on earth did he keep telling her such things? Truly, if Arthur sought to protect or improve the earl's reputation, he'd do a much better job by keeping his mouth shut. Against her better judgment, and to satisfy her curiosity, she murmured, "Is that why he sought out a commission in the army?"

Arthur nodded and then amended the gesture, saying, "Well, I can't be certain, but that is what I presume. He doesn't explain himself to anyone."

"And had he died in battle, the title would have passed to Jonathan," she murmured.

"Indeed," Arthur said, dismissing his mother's crassness. He picked up his fork and resumed his meal. "Lady Blackwell, his mother, provided her husband the heir and the spare."

"And the old earl had but one sister, your mother."

"Correct."

Lucy bit her lip to check her next comment. *No other relatives but your family. And you stand just behind Jonathan to inherit.*

Miles left the dining room without bothering to engage in niceties. He motioned for Sam to follow him to the observatory, his mood foul. He didn't trust his aunt as far as he could throw her. Simply sharing the breakfast table with her had been enough to turn his stomach.

And as for the lovely Miss Pickett—she was the only bright spot in the room, and he didn't appreciate it. She had been dressed in the height of fashion, her tight black outer corset laced atop a white blouse and dark green skirt. The entire outfit had emphasized her frame to perfection. She had worn small, black pearl earrings—he'd noticed those because of the way the curve of her jaw flowed gently to the graceful line of her neck. The deep brunette curls looked as soft as silk, piled artlessly atop her head whereas last night in the library the whole of it had cascaded down her back, uninhibited by pins and ribbons.

He rarely made a point of noticing a woman's appearance, much less her attire. But he could hardly be faulted; he was a man, after all, and Daniel's sister had been graced with a figure that would tempt a saint.

He had watched her as she viewed the whole breakfast spectacle with the slightest hint of a smile on her face. If she were anything like her brother, she would be an astute judge of character. She clearly recognized his relations for the ridiculous lot they were, and the way his cousin Arthur had leaned into her side for intimate conversation had set his teeth on edge.

They all needed to leave. The whole lot of them, including Miss Pickett. Especially Miss Pickett. That he had noted so many ridiculous details about her was beyond irritating.

"In a hurry, old man?" Sam called out from behind him.

Miles stopped outside the observatory, realizing his thoughts and his pace had run ahead of his friend.

Sam joined him, a bit winded, and together they moved to the center of the room where a large wooden desk sat near a huge telescope that faced the glass-paneled ceiling. On the far side of the room was a makeshift bed next to a table that held a contraption Miles both depended upon and hated.

"You having to charge more frequently?" Sam asked.

Miles nodded.

"Well, as I mentioned before, the new apparatus is nearing completion. It will make your current beauty a thing of the past." Sam sat at the desk and flipped open a book. He turned several pages before stopping to display an intricate design he had drawn himself. His attention to detail had always been impeccable, and his mind often traveled at a rate that was, at times, dizzying for Miles to follow. "This is what it will look like."

Miles looked over Sam's shoulder. "I shall have to take your word for it. I see gears and pins, but am lost much beyond that."

"Here is what I've changed." Sam pointed to the top of his diagram with a pencil. "I added one more cog up here—just a small one—but I think that might make the difference. It distributes the burden more evenly among the others, making the whole of it more efficient." He looked up at Miles. "The added piece makes for a smoother revolution and takes some of the stress off the larger components."

Miles rubbed the back of his neck as he studied the piece. Now that

Sam had pointed out the difference between this drawing and the one he'd presented on his last visit, he saw where the adjustments had been made and the logic behind them.

"I really would like to go with you to the lodge next time so that I might observe—"

Miles shook his head and moved away from the desk. He thrust his hands deep into his pockets and looked out the windows to the land below. His land, as far as the eye could see. Tangled, twisted, overgrown lands, haunted with an aura that constantly had him on edge. "Never. It is not worth the risk, you know that. I've gone so far as to have Mrs. Romany and Poole lock me out of the lodge at night."

Sam was quiet, and Miles eventually faced him, resting his back against the window. Sam had stretched out in the chair, his long legs sprawled in front of him, and he tapped the pencil against his notebook with narrowed eyes. "And yet we managed in India."

"Exactly. So you shouldn't need to witness anything further."

"I wouldn't exactly say I was witness to anything there—that any of us were. I want this mechanism to work, Miles, but I can't do it if I don't understand exactly what we need."

"You've studied my father's failed mechanism, not to mention the one you implanted in me after battle. Even from my limited experience, I can see that your design is already a vast improvement over the old one."

"I need to be able to measure your vital signs during—"

"I can't guarantee your safety, and I could never live with myself if something were to go wrong." Miles felt anger tight in his chest and an alarming burning sensation behind his eyes. He needed to calm himself. The stress on his heartclock increased when he was angry, which was, unfortunately, nearly every waking moment.

"I am beginning to wonder if you even care about our success. If you have a death wish, my lord, you ought to have just crossed enemy lines when we were in battle."

Miles looked evenly at his friend. "How very droll." In truth, there were times he wished he *had* stepped in the path of a ray gun or missile during his time at war. Jonathan could have taken on the mantle of all things Blackwell and Miles would be resting comfortably in hell, which was surely where his kind went.

"If you do not allow me to help you, your days are numbered. Your heart apparatus will not be able to sustain the constant stress. Your father had issues with his heartclock, and with your added . . ."

"My added what? Condition? Such a delicate way to describe it."

Samuel crossed one booted foot over his knee, still tapping the end of his pencil against the notebook—a sign Miles recognized that the metaphorical cogs in Sam's head were churning and spinning.

"Which generation was the last known to also share your . . . *condition*?" Sam asked. "Some time ago, I would presume?"

Miles closed his eyes and leaned his head back against the window. "My father."

When Sam didn't respond, Miles opened his eyes. Sam's mouth had gone slack. "Your father was a shifter? A wolf?"

Miles nodded.

"How long have you known?"

"Since my eighteenth year."

"How did you discover it?"

"I saw it."

Samuel closed his mouth and slowly sat up in the chair. The tapping of the pencil had ceased altogether, and had Miles not been feeling so incredibly weary, he might have had made a joke at his friend's expense.

"Did anyone else know? Anyone at all? Family?"

Miles thought of his extended relatives with disgust. "Heaven forbid, no. And I've never told a soul. I doubt my mother was even aware, although she must have at least suspected."

The pencil tapping resumed. "And Randolph has secured himself a position on the PSRC. Does Oliver suspect him of sending the notes? Randolph did disappear suspiciously from our barracks once at the same time you went into the hills to shift. He could be setting you up for blackmail, and if that fails, he'll send the Committee to your door." Sam paused. "Have you considered telling Jonathan?"

"I don't intend to ever breathe a word of this to anyone. There are exactly four people in this world that I trust, one of whom is my brother, and I would never burden him with this. As the age of majority has come upon him and gone, I must assume he will not fall victim to it." He smiled without humor. "The condition."

"Possibly." Samuel pursed his lips. "Or perhaps not. We simply do not know enough about it. Do you have access to old family histories? Journals? As many generations before your father as you can find?"

Miles nodded. "In the library archives. The older volumes are under lock and key. My father insisted upon it, and I've never bothered with them."

"I had intended to stay until morning, but think I will impose upon you for at least an additional day." Samuel paused. "Dig out the old diaries. I'll look at them tonight."

Miles nodded slowly. "Thank you, Sam. For your efforts, your time. Heaven knows I do not deserve it."

"Yes, you do. You saved my life in battle more than once. And even if you hadn't, our bond is thicker than blood. I do not do this out of some noble sense of duty. I would see you happy, Miles, and living a full life."

"I fear you may be wasting your time," Miles murmured and turned back to the window. He looked down over the side lawn and saw his sister-in-law and her cousin strolling toward the stables in smartly turned-out riding habits.

Kate was traditional in her attire, while Daniel's sister wore a daring pair of skintight breeches and knee-high riding boots. She laughed at something Kate said and placed an arm around her cousin's shoulders. She was full of energy. Alive. Happy. She had made it very clear that she was at Blackwell to help her cousin. There was an air of confidence about her that suggested she probably conquered everything she set her mind to.

Lucy Pickett would be the one at a social gathering to lead up a rousing match of cricket or croquet. From the looks of her, she'd probably also hold her own in target practice with a ladies' model ray gun or in a three-legged race across the lawn with a partner.

Miles was the sort who brooded on the sidelines like the predator he was. The rumors swirled and spun, grew larger each season. Clara's and Marie's deaths had only put a big black underscore on what was already a declining reputation. Oh, he would certainly never be snubbed. He would always be invited to every social event the country could invent. It was considered a coup by the ladies of society to have him in attendance at their balls and soirees. Some ladies, ruled entirely by greed and status, thrust their young daughters in his path in hopes of a good match. He had no patience for it, nor any inclination to ever marry again. And if society knew the truth of what he really was, they would bar the front door and scream.

Jonathan was his heir, and assuming his brother and Kate had children, the line would continue on into the eternities, making his ancestors and his father very proud. For his own part, it was an empty, hollow victory. After his mother had died, his cold, aloof father had become even more cold and aloof, secretly gambling away the estate. When the "condition" had come upon Miles, he had known his fate was sealed. It was not for him to have a normal life; the fiasco that had been his marriage to Clara was proof enough of that.

He watched Miss Pickett's trim figure as she neared the stables. She moved with the grace of one entirely comfortable in her own skin. She was the perfect reminder of everything that was light and good. Of everything he was not.

Miles shook his head. "I do not believe I am destined to live a full life." He turned back to Sam. "Are you certain you wouldn't rather enjoy the guest suites?" He gestured to the expansive room with its domed glass ceiling. "It does get cold up here."

Sam shook his head with a wry smile that didn't quite meet his eyes. "I like sleeping where I can see the stars. Since India I've not done well through the night in enclosed spaces."

Miles felt a wave of self-recrimination. He'd been so consumed with his own troubles he'd not thought to ask after Sam's welfare. The war had been hard on them all. "Where do you sleep at home?"

"On the floor next to the balcony." He smiled, and this time the humor reached his eyes. "Gives my valet fits, but he knows by now not to say anything." Sam waved a hand in the air as if to clear it of the conversation. "Besides, I'm becoming intimate with the constellations. One could do far worse."

Chapter 7

Dear Daniel,

How are you, I am fine, and etc. etc. I must dispense with frivolities and come directly to the point. I am visiting Kate at Blackwell Manor and have some concerns. What do you know of Blackwell, himself? I mean to say, I am well aware that you and he are good friends, but this house seems to have its fair share of secrets, and I wonder if you would be willing to shed light on anything about the man or the family beyond what we read in the society pages. Did you ever meet Marie Blake? What was your opinion of her? It appears she died a most tragic death. As you are often privy to gossip and juicy tidbits from your passengers, have you heard anything at all relating to her demise? Knowledge is power, and I am in desperate need of both.

Also, Kate is ill. I am not certain what to make of it at this point, but I am doing my best. I will keep you and Mamma and Grandmamma abreast of any further news regarding her. You will, of course, read between the lines—I am concerned. I would think she is being poisoned if not for the fact that everyone is served from the same platters and nobody else in the house exhibits her same symptoms.

You'll be pleased to know that your friend, Dr. MacInnes, is visiting Blackwell and sends his regards. He and Blackwell spend time together sequestered on the third floor. Kate doesn't know why, but as I am infinitely curious, I would dearly love to know the nature of their business. But, truly, it is none of mine.

I will close now, so that I might send this letter out with the daily post. You'll understand my reluctance to telescribe you with any of this. I cannot very well have a copy of the transmission left behind in the archive room for all and sundry to read. You and I both know that nothing is safe, even under lock and key. And on a related note, I do still have the location of your pocket watch. When you can determine where it's hidden, you may claim it. I must say I am disappointed in your lack of success thus far. I found my strand of pearls in a matter of days.

Your most affectionate sister,
Lucy

Lucy tossed and turned, finding it nearly impossible to fall asleep and remain there for any length of time. The storm that raged outside seemed to be encamped directly over the house; lightning flashed mere seconds before the thunder sounded, and she wondered if the house would see an interruption of the Tesla service before the elements finished their tirade.

The day had been pleasant enough. She and Kate had gone riding for a good hour after breakfast, and, after lunch and Kate's brief nap, during which Lucy had written to Daniel, the two of them had answered correspondence in the form of wedding felicitations that had continued to pile up despite the fact that Kate and Jonathan had been married for two months.

Lucy also took some time that afternoon to familiarize herself with the library. The magnificence of it took her breath away. The last time she had seen it had been in the dark of night, and given her encounter with the surly Lord Blackwell, she had hardly taken note of the room's splendor.

The library was two stories high, open in the center with spiral staircases winding up to the second level on either side of the room. The main area in the center was outfitted with three separate seating areas: one to the left at the hearth; one near the enormous wall of windows that housed cushioned window seats and a set of French doors, ten feet in height, that led to the patio outside; and one final furniture grouping to the right of the room that included a chaise longue, a pair of Queen Anne chairs, and a large writing desk. With the exception of the windows, the walls surrounding the room were lined with books of every size, shape, and subject.

While Kate had settled into a comfortable chair near the fireplace with an Austen, Lucy wasted no time in finding the area devoted to the botanical sciences—up the staircase to the right. She owned copies of a few of the titles she found, and she was delighted to see several rare volumes she'd been wanting to get her hands on for ages.

She lost track of time, blissfully whiling away the hours making notations in her own journals and adding details to her meticulous observations about certain herbs and their properties, especially as they might relate to counteracting the Vampiric Aid.

Later, at supper, she, Kate, and Jonathan had entertained the Charlesworths without the benefit of his lordship, who had gone out for the evening with Samuel MacInnes. Aside from a comment about a possible vamp attack in town, which Lucy made a mental note to examine further, there had been nothing compelling in the conversation, and Lucy had found herself wishing Lord Blackwell had been there, if only to have provided some entertainment with the lovely Aunt Eustace, who had been at her surly, caustic best.

Lightning flashed again, illuminating Lucy's room in a blinding glow. She squeezed her eyes shut, still seeing the light behind closed eyelids. A shutter banged somewhere overhead, and Lucy opened her eyes to the room, which was once again encased in darkness except for the scant light that shone through the turret windows in the corner.

She thought she felt a breeze—just a slight ruffling of air, really—but it made no sense in a room with closed windows. She rubbed her eyes and shifted her position in the bed, looking for a more comfortable spot, when her gaze caught on the woman who stood, still and silent, at her footboard, watching her.

Marie Blake was again resplendent in her red evening gown, her eyes focused on Lucy, her expression hard. The apparition narrowed her gaze, and Lucy's heart tripped in her chest.

She didn't much relish the thought of the woman shaking her out of bed, so she scooted closer to the side to make a quick escape. To where, she didn't know, and her heart beat furiously as Marie continued to regard her with a certain amount of venom in her expression.

"Lady Marie," Lucy whispered and winced as the lightning flashed, followed by an earsplitting crack of thunder that made her jump. "I . . . that is . . . I'm not entirely certain . . ."

Lucy's voice trailed off as a long, red furrow appeared across Marie's cheek and down her neck, spreading across the expanse of her chest and the bodice of her dress. As Lucy watched, horrified, the ghostly wound slowly widened and began dripping blood.

A small, inarticulate sound escaped Lucy's throat as another scratch appeared, this time beginning on Marie's forehead and tearing across her nose, dripping dark red as it traveled down her face and onto her chest beside the first wound.

"She was torn to shreds," Kate's voice echoed in Lucy's head as she stared at the vision before her with eyes wide, wanting to look away but unable to. *"It looked as though she'd been attacked by a wild animal."*

Marie's gaze remained riveted on Lucy's face, even as blood trailed into her eyes.

Lucy exhaled, nearly forgetting to draw another breath. Lightning cracked again, and Marie slowly moved toward the door. She paused, looked back at Lucy, and inclined her head toward the hallway.

She is insane if she thinks I'm going to follow her! Lucy stared at the apparition, mouth agape.

Marie stood poised at the door, trickles of blood soaking black through the fabric of the dress. A row of three scratches appeared on Marie's arm, and Lucy realized that if the vision continued, she would see all of it in its gory mess—Marie Blake, torn to shreds by a wild animal.

The thought propelled her out of bed, and she stumbled to the wardrobe for her outer wrap with one eye still on the door. Perhaps if she hurried, Marie could show her whatever it was she wanted her to see and then maybe she would leave. Maybe the grisly wounds would stop appearing.

Or maybe the ghost was leading her to her own bloody end.

"Right, then," she whispered as she fumbled with a pair of slippers. She approached the door with dread, not wanting to come any closer to the apparition than was absolutely necessary. Her eyes burned with unshed tears that she blinked back. If she managed to survive the night without fainting, or worse, it might well be a miracle.

Marie glanced back at her, and Lucy stood straighter. Her legs felt weak, and she was so very cold. She set her expression firmly, trying to look fierce, and wished for all she was worth that the moisture in her eyes would evaporate. Quietly exhaling, she watched Marie pass through the closed door.

She reached for the latch with a hand that shook so badly she had to steady it with the other. Opening the door, she saw Marie standing in the hallway, waiting. To Lucy's immense relief, the blood was gone, the woman's appearance unmarked.

Marie traveled the length of the hallway, around the corner, and to the front staircase as though she were flying—which, Lucy reasoned, she probably was. By the time Lucy reached the landing, she was nearly at a run. She headed down the stairs to keep Marie in sight, fighting the instinct to run the other way, one hand trailing along the banister, the other clutching the skirts of her nightgown and robe. The clock in the main entryway struck one o'clock as she rounded the corner and then headed north on the main level.

The hallway was dark, and Lucy wished she'd thought to grab a Tesla torch. As it was, she had to rely on the glow emanating from the woman in front of her. She saw Marie enter the portrait hall and was still several doors away when she struck a solid object at the library entrance.

The object had arms that snaked around her waist and dragged her into the large room before she could so much as blink. Gasping for air that had escaped her from the collision, she pushed against a solid wall that must have been the outer casing of a 'ton.

"Stop," the figure ground out, and Lucy looked up at a face that was inches from her own.

"Lord . . . Lord . . ." She felt light-headed. Perhaps she was going to faint after all.

Blackwell stared down at her, gripping her upper arms. "Miss Pickett, what in *blazes* are you doing?"

"No, please," she bit out, straining toward the door. "I must follow . . ." She was terrified and confused, the room reeling around her as if the whole experience were nothing more than a bizarre dream. A loud crash sounded from down the hallway, but it was followed so closely by a blinding flash of lightning and an explosion of thunder that she wondered if she'd heard the first noise at all.

Blackwell cursed and winced at both the light and sound. He dragged her with him across the expanse of the library to the far wall, where the bank of windows showed the black of night and the relentless pounding of rain.

"Who opened these?" he growled as he pulled a lever on the wall near the corner, activating a mechanism that hummed quietly to life and pulled the enormous drapes across the windows, effectively shutting out the storm.

Lucy had opened the drapes earlier in the day with Kate. The thought of sitting in the magnificent room without enjoying the view—admittedly, a messy view—of the patio and gardens outside had seemed ridiculous. She was not about to admit to her actions now.

The earl's grip was bruising her arm, and she winced. "Lord Blackwell," she said, taking a deep, shuddering breath and trying to pull herself together, *"please."* To her eternal mortification, one of the tears she had been holding at bay finally escaped and rolled in a solitary path down her cheek.

Lord Blackwell looked down at his hand as if only then realizing he still held her captive. He released her, and she rubbed her arm, looking at the library doors and wondering if she dared go back out into the hallway and then to the portrait gallery. She wiped her cheek on her shoulder, willing herself to keep her composure.

"Miss Pickett," he said again, one hand thrust into his pocket and the other plowing through his thick, black hair, "I demand to know why you insist on prowling my home when all other reasonable beings are asleep. Despite my friendship with your brother, I'm nigh unto throwing you out on your ear. Are you stealing from me?"

"Stealing?" Lucy tore her gaze from the doorway. She swallowed when she realized how close he stood to her—towered over her, really—with the ragged line of his scar prominent in his anger. A scar not unlike the first one she'd seen on his dead sister's ghost. Her breathing still came in uneven gasps, as though she'd been running a great distance.

She put a hand to her forehead and closed her eyes, wishing desperately for a cup of tea. What were the odds that Marie still waited for her in the gallery? And furthermore, now that she was away from the apparition, did she really want to go and find her? There was something comforting about being in the presence of a living, breathing human, even if he was almost as frightening as the haunting spirit.

"No," she finally said, opening her eyes and looking up at Blackwell. "I am not stealing from you. I may not be titled, but I come from a fair amount of money; I do not need yours in the least. And what," she said, feeling the beginnings of outrage creeping into her system, "were you thinking, dragging me in here? Could you not see I was otherwise occupied?"

He gaped at her, opening and closing his mouth before echoing her statement. "Otherwise occupied? Lady, you were tearing through my house like a madwoman! I heard you rushing down the stairs and couldn't, for the life of me, figure your reasoning other than that you were up to no good. This marks the second night you have been wandering my house, and I demand to know what you're about. Kate's relative or no, you will not remain here if this continues."

Lucy glared and set her shoulders. "Lord Blackwell, this household is not one of order. My cousin is not well, and I've hearing rumblings about some ridiculous 'Bride's Curse' that, before I arrived, I would have considered the height of idiocy. And as if that weren't enough, I have been visited"—she ground out the word, unable to believe she was admitting it—"by what appears to be a spirit bent on communicating *something* to me, and I have no idea what it might be."

He had watched her closely throughout her tirade, and when she paused for breath, he raised one brow.

"I am well aware," she raised a hand to forestall him, "that such a thing seems ridiculous, but—"

"What spirit?"

She stopped. "I'm sorry?"

He inched closer to her, and she fought to keep from retreating. His eyes, holding hers, were unblinking, piercing. "You said you have been visited by a spirit."

She nodded. "Yes."

"Who is it?"

"My lord, I—"

"Describe the person."

Why she was reluctant to tell him, she couldn't say, but when she realized he wasn't going to let the matter drop, she let out a small sigh. "It was your sister, my lord."

Miles looked at the petite woman before him, trying to maintain a neutral expression while feeling like she'd hit him in the stomach with a mallet. He hadn't imagined it, then. Marie was here, and apparently every bit as tenacious as she had ever been.

He noted Miss Pickett still rubbing at her arm where he'd squeezed the life out of it, and he felt a pang of remorse. He could no longer attempt to ignore that she was still fighting tears. It wasn't anything about her expression—it was the luminescence in her eyes, the moisture that pooled there, hovering.

His mother would be mortified by his lack of civility. It had been so long since he'd bothered with it that he wasn't certain he remembered even the basics. He was fairly sure that accosting a young woman, a guest in one's home, was hardly proper. She was trembling, and he briefly closed his eyes with a shake of his head. "Please." He gestured toward a chair near the hearth where a few coals still glowed. "Sit."

She looked at him for a long moment before finally moving to the chair and sitting on the very edge of it, her trembling still visible, although from the set of her chin, she was likely trying to squelch it. She blinked a few times, and to his immense relief, he saw she no longer seemed on the verge of tears.

He retrieved a blanket from the arm of the sofa and, unfolding it, wrapped it about her shoulders before stooping and adding two more logs to the fire. After blowing on the embers, he straightened and brushed the dirt from his hands, glancing again at the young woman who watched him with an expression that could only be described as wary.

Miss Pickett was alarmingly pale and still shook beneath the blanket.

"Here," he said. Motioning for her to stand and step aside, he pulled the chair closer to the fire.

She cocked a brow at him but remained silent, retaking her seat with a nod of thanks. He had to admire her pluck. Clearly terrified, she still had a sense of confidence about her. She was one of few. His own wife had been horrified by his very presence. He frowned. Marie had found Clara ridiculous and had been angry that he'd married such a "ninny."

"I would ring for some tea, but there's nobody about." His tone sounded gruff to his own ears. "Even the 'tons are down for the night."

"I don't need any tea."

"You could probably do with a good shot of brandy."

"I don't drink spirits." She laughed, utterly without humor. "Spirits," she muttered as though to herself. She glanced at him and motioned with her hand. "Spirits, you see. We were just discussing . . ."

"Yes. I see the irony."

She nodded, refraining from further comment, and rubbed her forehead as if it pained her. He felt something resembling an ache in the region of his chest. He didn't know how to comfort her; he didn't know how to comfort anyone.

He cleared his throat. "Miss Pickett, I wish I could explain—"

"She was trying to tell me something."

He blinked. "I beg your pardon?"

Miss Pickett drew her eyebrows together, gazing into the fire. "She seemed very insistent that I follow her." She looked up at him, and Miles had the distinct impression she was gauging his reaction.

"And where was she leading you?"

"Well, I might know the answer to that question had I not been dragged in here."

He squinted at her. "You were willingly following a spirit." He paused. "Are you a Medium, then?"

"Most definitely not."

He almost smiled at her tone. "So you are a skeptic."

She shook her head and looked away. "I *was*."

"Miss Pickett, you were running at full speed. And I'm gathering from your reaction now that you were afraid."

She frowned. "Perhaps I am more afraid of you."

"You wouldn't be the first," he muttered.

Her expression softened, and he hardened his. He didn't want or need her pity. "Did Marie say anything to you?"

She shook her head. "No," she sighed, "she . . . uh . . ."

"Yes?"

"The first night, she shook my bed. I thought she was angry at me."

Miles frowned. "The first night?"

"She appeared in my room last night—just before I met you. In here, oddly enough."

"Ah, yes. With an entire canister of tea and a boiling teapot."

"She didn't say anything then, either. But tonight was different. I wasn't sleeping well—the storm woke me—" Miss Pickett gestured as thunder cracked, almost on cue. "And suddenly, she was just there."

"You said it was different."

Miss Pickett winced and shivered once, the movement noticeably more pronounced than before. A myriad of expressions crossed her face, belying thoughts that she likely would rather have kept to herself.

He scowled. "What is it you're not saying? Out with it, if you please. I have no patience for games."

Her eyes narrowed, and her jaw set as she met his direct gaze, holding it. "I am not playing games. And you, sir, are a cad." She rose from the chair, took the blanket from her shoulders, and shook it once. Folding it neatly, she placed it on the arm of the chair and turned to him. "Good evening."

He stared at her with his brows raised as she walked toward the door with sure strides, not faltering even once although he'd clearly seen that she wasn't yet collected.

"Miss Pickett." He was suddenly irritated, although he couldn't say if it was at her or himself. He followed her, gathering his suit coat from a chair as he passed by. "I'll see you to your chambers."

"You needn't bother," she said clearly over her shoulder. "I found my way down here, I can find my way back up."

He followed her anyway, keeping his distance. Her even, measured stride carried her through the front hall, up the wide, sweeping staircase, and around the corner to the right on the second floor. When he reached the landing, he followed her path and peered down the long hallway of the north wing. He saw her wrap her arms around her middle and quicken her step until she was almost sprinting.

With equal parts self-recrimination and loathing, he waited quietly in the shadows until she was safely in her room, the door closed and locked behind her. For all the good it would do. He thought of Marie and was amazed that Miss Lucy Pickett had stayed beyond that first night.

And Marie? What was she attempting to convey? The thought chilled him as he slowly made his way toward the south wing. The ache he felt at missing his sister warred with the wish, becoming ever more urgent, that she would leave. No good could come of her continued visits, and the fact that she had settled her attention on Miss Pickett, a self-proclaimed skeptic, was perplexing.

Miss Pickett had said she would remain as long as Kate wished it, or until she was convinced Kate was well. While Miles knew he could have her forcibly shipped back home, he wasn't certain even he was so crass. Let her stay. Let her try to heal her cousin and commune with the dead. It wasn't as though his life was pleasant anyway. Why not add a little more chaos to the mix?

His only concern was Blackwell Manor itself. It was all he had, his only legacy, the one thing he would pass on. All he could hope for was that Jonathan might someday tell his children a story of his childhood and of his older brother, who hadn't always been a monster.

Miles entered his suite and saw that Marcus had banked the fire and left a light glowing on a side table. Fighting the urge to slam the door shut, he closed it quietly instead and made his way to the window. The thunder had quieted, but an occasional spear of lightning flashed in the distance, visible through a crack in the drapery. The rain still fell steadily against the glass.

Removing his cuff links, he lifted the curtain aside and caught his reflection in the black expanse of the night. The glass, slightly wavy, distorted the image of his face, and he stared for a long moment before clenching his jaw and dropping his hand, the fabric falling silently back into place.

Chapter 8

When Lucy descended for breakfast the following morning, she did so with steps that dragged. Her eyes were red and sore. She had cried herself to sleep, half terrified she would receive another visit from Beyond. She was exhausted and had awoken with a blinding headache that had her wincing in pain.

As she neared the last few steps on the main staircase, she spied Kate, who was deep in conversation with Mrs. Farrell. Lucy made an effort to perk up. Nobody but his lordship needed to know she'd spent time the night before with his crazed sister and, more scandalously, him—again—in her nightgown.

Kate and the housekeeper spoke in hushed tones, and as Lucy approached, she slowed her step. Kate glanced at her and beckoned while Mrs. Farrell continued speaking.

" . . . was already put back into place by the time I entered. Although it's likely inconsequential, I thought I'd mention it."

Kate nodded. "Thank you, Mrs. Farrell. I wonder if I ought to tell his lordship . . ."

It was all Lucy could do to remain silent and not interrupt the conversation to thank Mrs. Farrell for her efficiency and tell her that Kate would handle the matter—whatever it happened to be. Mrs. Farrell seemed genuine enough, fair and professional, but there were many a housekeeper who weren't, and the last thing Kate needed was a household that undermined her authority. *Be decisive with the staff, Kate.*

"I shouldn't see why Lord Blackwell need bother himself with it," Mrs. Farrell said, looking at Kate as one might a daughter, and she patted her arm and offered her a quick smile. "I feel you should be kept abreast of all happenings in the residence, as the lady of the house."

"Of course," Kate said. "Thank you again."

Mrs. Farrell tipped her head in acknowledgment and deference and, with a nod to Lucy, left the front hall.

"What is it?" Lucy asked.

Kate waved a hand. "Nothing, really. One of the paintings in the portrait hall fell to the floor last night."

Lucy's heart thumped. "Which one, did she say?"

Kate looked at Lucy, her expression scrunched. "Why?"

Lucy looped her arm through Kate's and began walking slowly with her toward the dining room. She looked around to see if they were alone. In an undertone, she gave her the briefest of details about her nocturnal visit.

Kate's mouth dropped open, and she stopped walking. Lucy nudged her forward with a little shake. "Which is why I find myself wondering," she murmured to Kate, "which portrait ended up on the floor."

"I'm afraid we will never know." Kate frowned. "Mrs. Farrell's new 'ton assistant, Alice-Two, was the one who righted the portrait, but apparently she then went to the kitchen and hasn't moved since. She's being reprogramed as we speak. Even if we were to examine the record of her behavior on the tin itself, it wouldn't tell us which portrait she picked up. Mrs. Farrell has had the worst luck with her assistants; this makes for the third one this month."

Lucy frowned, wincing at the stab of pain to her forehead. "Is there an issue with the 'tons programming?"

"I'm not certain. After the programmer Mrs. Farrell was paying to come in from town made off with a matching pair of silver goblets, she has taken to programming her own staff. Though I personally think she may not fully understand even the basics of the task."

Lucy glanced at Kate with a smile as they neared the dining room. "'Alice-Two,' is it? Dare I assume 'Alice-One' was the last assistant?"

"Yes." Kate laughed. "Although we merely referred to her as 'Alice.'"

"Of course."

"Mrs. Farrell says she's tired of coming up with new names for the staff."

"So might we see an 'Alice-Fifteen' sometime in the future?"

Kate laughed again, and Lucy was glad of it. There was a sparkle to her eyes, the truest sign of her cousin's genuine happiness, although there were smudges beneath them that still gave Lucy pause.

She surveyed the dining room as they entered, wincing at the bright light that streamed through the windows and straight to the back of her skull. Of all days for the sun to finally show its face . . . She hoped to be able to claim a seat facing the door.

A quick glance around the room showed all of the usual diners in attendance. "How long do the Charlesworths usually stay?" she whispered in Kate's ear.

"Too long," came the muttered reply. "Jonathan says their visits are rarely less than a week or two."

Arthur Charlesworth excused himself from Jonathan and Samuel MacInnes and made his way to Lucy and Kate. Where was his lordship? Not that she cared, precisely. It was only that she found it rather unfair that she should be well enough to attend breakfast after the ruckus last night, but he had yet to show his face.

"Dear ladies," Arthur said with a courtly bow and that devastating smile. "And how are you both this fine morning?"

Lucy murmured something she hoped was appropriate as across the room Jonathan laughed loudly at something Dr. MacInnes was saying. If she didn't have a good, bracing cup of tea soon, her head was likely to split down the middle. She closed her eyes briefly and allowed Kate to carry the conversation with Arthur when Lucy felt the air in the room . . .

change. She didn't have to turn to the door to know that Blackwell had joined them.

His head was pounding, and he would have dearly loved to remain in bed for the day with the curtains drawn. Miles was contemplating making his excuses and doing just that when he saw Miss Pickett standing with Kate and Arthur, the latter of whom was falling all over himself in an apparent attempt to charm them.

Miss Pickett eventually looked over her shoulder at him and made eye contact before turning her attention back to Arthur. She hadn't even nodded to him, and all things considered, he couldn't say that he blamed her. She'd called him a cad, and she'd been right. He deserved to be called much worse. He hadn't been sensitive at all to the distress she'd clearly been feeling.

She was pale, he noticed as he walked into the room and made his way to Jonathan and Sam. She also winced slightly when Arthur barked out a laugh at something Kate said; he pitied Miss Pickett indeed if her head was pounding with as much pomp and circumstance as his own.

"I'm sorry?" he said to Sam, blinking.

"I said it's good of you to join us. I didn't think you were going to—you're rarely late to breakfast."

"I'm not late." He tugged on his cuff and straightened the cuff link. "The food has yet to even arrive from the kitchen."

As if on cue, Mr. Grafton entered with his 'tons following behind carrying warm dishes that they placed carefully on the sideboards. Miles was relieved at the interruption, truth be told. Eustace had been making her way to him from across the room. She was likely going to pester him about the fact that he never visited her at Charlesworth House.

He almost smiled at the look of disappointment that crossed his aunt's face as the small, conversing groups gathered around the table and settled in for breakfast. Arthur stood behind Miss Pickett's chair and scooted her in before performing the same service for Candice, who sat to Miss Pickett's right. Miles looked again at his houseguest, who was undoubtedly suffering from fatigue, but he was struck by the beauty in her face. A man could certainly do worse than gaze at her throughout the course of a meal.

She was . . . different, though. Normal women did not run around strange houses, following ghosts hither and yon. Any woman with an ounce of common sense would have stayed in her room and screamed for help.

Feeling infinitely more weary than he was willing to admit to anyone, he turned his attention away from his good friend's sister—another reason he shouldn't look at her for any prolonged amount of time—and placed his napkin in his lap. When he raised his head, a movement to his right caught his eye. He sucked in his breath when he saw Marie for a flash of a second, seated in the chair adjacent his, and then she was gone.

Arthur pulled the chair out for himself, smiling at something Miss Pickett said.

Miles stared at Arthur, or rather at the chair in which his cousin sat, long enough that Arthur looked at Miles, head tipped to one side in question.

"Right, then," he muttered and nodded to Mr. Grafton, who signaled the servers to begin. If Marie's purpose was to slowly drive him mad, he feared she might accomplish it.

"All I know," Eustace was saying to the group at large, "is that this is the second body to be found drained in the last week. There must be a vamp in town, and I don't see why authorities haven't been brought in from London."

"They must be on their way, I should think," Sam said. "One body alone is disturbing, but two can hardly be considered coincidence."

"Where was the body found?" Lucy asked.

Miles cocked a brow but refrained from commenting. The woman certainly had no compunction about inquiring after grisly details. Might explain why she had the courage to go chasing around after ghosts.

"Somewhere in the village, on a back street." Eustace sniffed and scooped up a forkful of eggs. "A maid or some such, but still."

"Indeed," Kate said, and Miles glanced at her with surprise. There was an edge to her voice he hadn't heard before. Maybe having Cousin Lucy for a visit was doing some good. "I don't imagine a maid's family would mourn her loss any less than a noblewoman's."

A moment of silence—just a fraction, really—shot around the table, and Miles's estimation of his sister-in-law rose a notch. She had some spine after all. Lucy, for her part, raised her glass for a drink, likely to stave off a snort of laughter. Even Candice regarded Kate with a cocked brow and a light nod of approval.

Arthur laughed, as of course he would, and attempted to steer the conversation to safer ground by suggesting such unseemly talk was certainly something they could all do without. Sam picked up the cue seamlessly and asked Eustace about the current state of medical care in Stammershire.

Jonathan, for his part, regarded his bride with the same besotted expression he'd worn since their wedding. He picked up her hand and, with a wink, placed a kiss on her fingers.

Lucy stood in the portrait gallery, massaging her temples with her fingertips. She figured she might be able to handle the sight of Marie during the daylight hours and actually wished the woman would appear. *Whose picture did you knock down, Marie?*

Her heels echoed against the marble tile as she slowly walked the perimeter of the room, examining the austere pictures of generations of ancestors: his lordship's parents, a painting of the three Blackwell children when Jonathan had been little more than an infant, and a more recent painting of Blackwell in his military finery, which she had missed during her first tour of the gallery.

Lucy sucked in her breath at the sight of the painting. The artist was to be complimented—the likeness was astounding, right down to the look in his eyes that spoke clearly of his inner discontent. He was a handsome devil; were it not for his mean disposition, people might find him less frightening.

Having a better knowledge of the Blake family's personalities gave Lucy a different perspective than when she'd first toured the room. When she examined the portrait of the former earl as a youth, pictured with a young Eustace, she had to wonder what kind of dreams the young woman had harbored before the realities of adult life had intruded. One detail remained consistent—the young Eustace was pictured without a smile.

A display of three portraits near the window caught Lucy's eye—Marie, Clara, and the three Charlesworths. Lucy had noted them on her first visit but now had time to study the images in detail. Aunt Eustace was seated with her children standing beautifully poised behind her chair. Arthur and Candice were depicted with as much perfection as they possessed in reality. Even Eustace was the image of her former, younger self—with the exception of several added pounds.

Clara seemed to have been the quintessentially delicate maiden. There was a naïveté about her that almost had Lucy's pity. Looking at the image of the fiery Marie next to her, Lucy wondered if Clara had ever stood a chance of success in the Blake household. She would have stepped into a situation where she was expected to be the lady of the manor while living with a sister-in-law who had grown up in the home, who could have possibly been extremely territorial, and who could have eaten her for lunch.

What had Clara's short relationship with Lord Blackwell been like? Lucy rolled her eyes, immediately regretting it as her head throbbed. That man would require a woman who could hold her own with him, someone who wouldn't back down from the bulk of his intimidating stature and the even more intimidating personality housed within it. Heaven help any woman not equal to the task. As she considered the sweet face of the late Lady Blackwell, she figured that heaven probably had.

She turned to leave when she noticed a small chip in the bottom right-hand corner of the frame of the Charlesworth portrait. She touched it with her fingertip, wondering if the frame had had the slight imperfection for long—or perhaps for just a matter of hours. Surely a woman of Eustace's stature, or imagined stature, wouldn't permit such an atrocity for long if she were aware of it. Lucy suspected the vain woman probably visited the portrait gallery with each pass down the hallway.

She looked around the easel, examining the cold marble tiles for telltale signs of disturbance, and was rewarded with the sight of a splintered piece of mahogany that matched the chip missing from the frame. She fit the piece to the frame and nodded, chewing on her lip in thought.

Lucy had distinctly heard a crash the night before, a loud one that had carried clear into the library. Continued examination revealed a slight scratch on the upper right corner of Marie's picture frame. Lucy put a hand to the frame and moved it fractionally. It was heavy. A similar test of the Charlesworth frame proved the same.

Perhaps it hadn't been just one portrait that had fallen over. Perhaps Marie had taken a swipe at two of them, or even all three.

Lucy cast one last glance at the portrait of Marie as she left the room, feeling a connection with the woman that wasn't necessarily welcome. The sight of her face was becoming familiar, and that was an unsettling notion.

Chapter 9

After returning to her room, Lucy telescribed a message to Director Lark that there were rumors of a vampire in Coleshire. She then pawed through her wardrobe until she found a warm, hooded cape that hung almost to the ground. The sun had been short-lived—the heavens had reopened as though making up for lost time. Retrieving her parasol and gloves, she made her way through the house and to the kitchen.

Mr. Grafton was in deep discussion with Kate, who looked slightly overwhelmed at the papers and menus strewn before her on the kitchen butcher block, so Lucy slipped out of the back entrance alone and snapped open her parasol.

The rain immediately pattered on the surface of it, and she pinched the handle between her arm and her body in order to lift her fur-lined hood over her hair and tie the bow loosely under her chin.

A glance to her right showed figures in the greenhouse. They wore the dark maroon uniforms of Mr. Grafton's kitchen help, and she imagined the 'tons were busy, culling the spices and herbs necessary for the day's lunch and dinner. The five of them worked seamlessly as opposed to Mrs. Farrell's maids, who, she'd noticed, tended to clash occasionally.

The brisk walk along the path into the woods was bracing, and Lucy felt her head clear as she breathed deeply. The rain, the foliage, the encroaching autumn—it all combined to fill her with a fresh sense of euphoria. The oppression she'd felt in the portrait gallery slipped away.

The world was silent except for the soft sound of her feet against the earth and the rain on her parasol. A few moments later, she found herself standing outside Marie's garden gate. She hadn't realized that was where she'd been headed. She frowned at the gate and once again, as she had before, tried the handle. Of course it was locked, and she lay her gloved hand against the thick, wooden door, wondering if she should bother Mr. Clancy and retrieve the key.

The rain was steady, though, and there would be better days to examine the garden at her leisure. Angling her head, she could see through a crack in the gate, and she moved closer to it. The green of the interior blended together, and she strained to bring it into focus when a face appeared on the other side of the gate.

She gasped, stumbling back several steps. It had been Marie—of course—who else would be in her garden?

"Honestly," she whispered, her breath running shallow in her lungs. "Were you this terrifying in the flesh?"

A slight rustle behind her—no more than a shift in the wind, really—told her she wasn't alone on her side of the garden wall, either. Thoughts of blood-drained bodies flooded her brain as she whirled around, heart in her throat, to find Arthur Charlesworth standing so close to her that she nearly smacked him upside the head with her parasol spokes.

"Mr. Charlesworth!" She was light-headed with all the shock and gasping and wondered if she might actually faint.

The gentleman reached forward and steadied her arms while avoiding the swinging umbrella with a laugh. "My goodness, Miss Pickett! I did not mean to give you such a start. Are you well?"

She nodded, pressing her hand to her chest. "I shall be in a moment. How long have you been standing there? You might have announced yourself."

"I only just approached." He placed his hand beneath her elbow. "I saw you leaving the house and wondered if you would enjoy some company. I had no idea you were such a quick walker."

Lucy gathered her scattered wits. If she were a betting woman, she'd wager that he had been behind her for a while. When she'd spun around, he hadn't been walking toward her. He had been firmly planted in that spot.

She glanced at his face, searching for guile or deceit in his features. He was as he always was—genial, charming, handsome. "I believe I'll head back for the house," she said with a light smile. "Will you join me?"

He inclined his head and walked with her, his hand still supporting her elbow. "You seemed most startled. Before you spied me, that is."

She nodded. "I thought I saw something. Likely just a trick of the shadows."

He raised a brow. "Shadows in the rain?"

She twitched her lips into what she knew was a flirtatious gesture, even while she fought the urge to pull her arm free of his grasp. She chuckled instead. "Stranger things have happened, I'm sure. From what I understand, the garden is overgrown and in need of pruning. It must have been an excess of foliage."

"It was Marie's domain, you know. She loved that sanctuary of hers—as if she needed one." The last part sounded to Lucy as though it had come out of his mouth of its own accord. He seemed almost surprised by it himself. He laughed and shrugged. "One needed a gilded invitation to join her in that place. Such a shame it's gone to ruin."

It sounded to Lucy as though Cousin Arthur had not been welcome in the garden, but she kept her opinion to herself. Perhaps it was the depressing reality of Marie's garden, coupled with the dreary weather and the tangled undergrowth in the woods, that made Arthur seem more shiftless than he actually was. Just because Marie hadn't liked her relatives when she was alive didn't necessarily make them sinister.

"Do you miss her, then? It must have been painful to lose her, as young as she was. And on the heels of Lady Blackwell's passing."

He nodded, brows drawn in thought. "Of course I miss her—I miss her terribly. Marie was . . ." Arthur looked into the distance as they strolled through the darkened, tangled woods. "Alive. She was vibrant. Mercurial. She knew exactly whom she liked and whom she did not. And Lady Blackwell—sweet Clara." He shook his head. "At the time, townspeople and even some of the staff here began to whisper that it was the old Bride's Curse come home to roost."

"I've heard that mentioned once before. What, exactly, is this curse?" It was dark in the tunnel of trees, and there were places where a stray branch or twig tugged on Lucy's cloak, like bony fingers. She shivered and pushed back her hood. Not having the full benefit of her peripheral vision was disconcerting.

"It's nonsense, really. Three generations ago, the Blackwell family had five sons, each of whom brought home a bride—who died within a month, maybe two, of the wedding. It was only through the family's daughter that the family legacy continued. She had a son who inherited the title from his grandfather."

Lucy frowned. "I can imagine why the family would have believed they were cursed."

Arthur nodded. "As the family continued, the curse became nothing more than a legend. But now—well, legends linger in the memory, and I'm afraid Clara became the latest victim of the Bride's Curse." He looked at Lucy. "Do you believe in such things?"

"Not as a rule. I do not much care for things that have no explanation."

"But, Miss Pickett, there are many things in this world that have no explanation."

"That may be true, but to the best of my abilities, I study the matter until I can explain it."

"A bluestocking, then?"

Lucy glanced at him. He was all charm and friendliness. "I believe in the rights of women."

"As you should, most definitely. I find it . . . refreshing."

"And I find your enlightened opinion refreshing." She smiled at him, thinking that too much more refreshing conversation would find her losing her breakfast. She didn't trust the man as far as she could throw him.

He laughed, and they emerged from the thick entanglement that guarded the pathway. Lucy realized it was the first time since her arrival that she could honestly say she was glad to see the manor. "To market, to market, to buy a fat pig," she murmured.

"Home again, home again, jiggety-jig," he finished for her, and she tipped her head in acknowledgment. "And this is where I must leave you," he said as they neared the courtyard. He released her elbow, and Lucy resisted the urge to rub it clean. "I'm off to the stables to check on my stallion. He threw a shoe yesterday and stumbled a bit in the process."

"I do hope he is well." Lucy continued on her way to the house, acutely aware that Arthur watched her leave.

Once in the kitchen, Lucy unwound her scarf from her neck. She lightly shook her parasol outside the open kitchen door before closing the door firmly.

"Lady Kate is in the ballroom," Mr. Grafton told her as he whisked something in a large bowl. "I was instructed to tell you to join her as soon as you return."

"The ballroom in the south wing?"

"The very same."

Lucy was surprised. Had the lord of the manor lifted his edict about mere mortals traipsing through his territory?

Mr. Grafton glanced up from his mixing bowl. "I gather they are practicing for the upcoming festivities at Charlesworth House. Mr. Jonathan says he has two left feet."

Lucy smiled and made her way to her room, where she shrugged out of her cloak and gloves. She straightened her clothing before the vanity and pinned a few errant curls back into place. Looking around the room, Lucy furrowed her brow. Marie could certainly come and go as she pleased; there was no help for that. Still, Lucy locked the door behind her and pocketed the key.

She quickly made her way to the south wing. It wasn't long before she heard the strains of music floating down the hallway, and she paused at the ballroom's large, arched double doorway. Kate was moving in time to the music with her husband, who seemed to be doing well enough despite a few fumbles.

Lucy felt her throat tighten with both joy and a measure of fear as she watched her cousin, graceful and beautiful, in the arms of the man she loved. There was something amiss in the big house, something that threatened Kate's future. Lucy knew that nothing would compel her to leave Blackwell Manor until she was certain Kate was safe.

Lucy glanced left, down the dark hallway to the large pair of black doors in the distance that led to his lordship's chambers. What he did in there, Lucy couldn't begin to imagine. Probably boiled toads and kept small animals in cages. He must be out of the manor; Lucy didn't imagine Jonathan and Kate would have been willing to make use of the ballroom otherwise.

"Lucy!" Kate called from inside the room and motioned with her head. Jonathan stumbled and nearly took his wife to the floor. Kate laughed and patted Jonathan's face as he stammered his apologies and eventually cast Lucy a rueful smile.

"Now you see why my practice is imperative," he said as Lucy entered the room. "I have never been one for dancing, and I do not wish to embarrass my poor wife. Or wound her in the process."

Kate crossed to the Victrola and stopped the music. The last strains echoed through the cavernous room. A chandelier of immense proportions hung suspended from the ceiling on a copper chain that was the circumference of Lucy's waist. On the far end of the room was a stage for musicians and large windows that overlooked the back of the property. A set of glass French doors led to a large balcony that circled the perimeter outside. Lucy imagined the place as it must have looked in its prime—all aglitter with guests, food and drink, and comfortable seating out on the balcony where lovers could look at the stars on a warm summer night.

What remained now was a cold shell. The room was still beautiful, with its ornate décor and appointments, but it was in need of a good dusting, and the frescoes on the walls would benefit from a light refreshing. Lucy examined the whole of it with a critical eye, unconsciously making a mental list of everything that needed to be done.

"You're fixing this room, are you not?" Kate asked as she approached.

"Am I so transparent?"

"Very."

Jonathan followed Lucy's gaze and nodded. "It is in sore need of some repair. When my mother died, my father locked it up, and we haven't hosted a ball here since. Every now and again we would sneak in as children, but unfortunately, nobody ever sees it these days."

Lucy placed a hand on his arm. "Oh, Jonathan, it is a lovely room. What a wonderful thing it would be to see it used to its full potential." She smiled. "I am envious. How I would love to have a ballroom this grand at home."

Kate nodded. "Lucy is ever so organized. She throws the most amazing gatherings."

"'Bossy' is probably a more apt description than 'organized,'" Lucy said. "And entirely too much for my own good. But I've interrupted you." She made her way to the Victrola. "You two keep dancing. I'll start the music again."

Jonathan pulled Kate back into his arms, and she smiled at something he said. Lucy felt her heart melting. Fighting a sigh that would have been both melodramatic and entirely nauseating, Lucy started up the record player and placed the needle upon the spinning disc. The sweet strains of a waltz again filled the air, and Lucy folded her arms, unconsciously swaying to the hypnotic rhythm as she watched the young couple.

She wanted to freeze the moment. Everything was perfect; Kate was well and dancing with her handsome prince. Time would continue its forward march, however, and it was futile to wish otherwise. Life would probably have been much simpler had Jonathan been a farmer.

The moment was spoiled as movement at the double doors caught her eye, and her heart tripped at the sight of Miles Blake, Lord of Blackwell, looking none too pleased.

Chapter 10

Miles stopped at the open doorway and took in the scene in stunned anger. He couldn't have been clearer in his instructions that nobody was to enter the south wing without his express permission.

Though as he watched Jonathan and Kate spinning around the room, he had to admit that his brother's skills on the dance floor seemed to be improving. Jonathan had never been one for dancing or anything else that required any degree of coordination.

He looked to the source of the music only to see Miss Pickett watching him as though *he* were the one intruding instead of them. The woman was beautiful, even in her anger. She likely had her share of suitors. Why she hadn't been snapped up before now was a mystery he didn't care to contemplate. She was probably impossibly choosy. Demanding. There was an air about her that any man might find impossible to match.

Miles considered marching over to the Victrola and scratching the blazes out of the record, just to make a point, when Jonathan spied him and his face lit up.

"Miles! You must join us!" Jonathan looked at Lucy, and Miles saw the plan the instant it formulated in his brother's head. "Lucy needs a partner!"

Miles glanced at the woman in question.

Her smile was tight. "Oh, no, I'll just watch. I do not require practice."

"You are already so well accomplished, then?" Miles said, unable to help himself.

Her chin went up a notch, and he saw that Kate and Jonathan had slowed. Did Kate think he would tear down her cousin in front of witnesses?

"Actually, I am, my lord," Lucy said. "Very well accomplished."

"Then you shall have no problem taking a spin about the room." He approached her slowly, hands in his pockets, figuring he looked as unthreatening as he ever would. When her eyes widened slightly, he was forced to revise his assumption, and he steeled himself for the repulsed look that was sure to follow.

Rather than the stammering, horrified refusal he expected to see in her pretty features, her eyes narrowed.

Miles hid his reluctant surge of approval with a smirk. He was gratified that she had to look up to maintain eye contact with him. She deserved it, after all. Her arrival had disrupted his peace of mind, and he didn't feel an ounce of remorse over his lack of propriety as he inched closer.

"Are you asking me to dance, my lord? Because I have yet to hear it phrased as a polite question. After all, you've no idea if my dance card is already full."

Was she flirting with him? He studied her face, struggling to fit her into an acceptable mold. Women did not dance with the Beast of Blackwell Manor, not willingly, not unless they were prodded by their mothers who sought to trap him into an eventual proposal. And those kind were easily discernible—the wily ones were all things polite and coy, but they always held part of themselves back, as if the task at hand were unpleasant but necessary. And the fear was always visible. Always. Even when they tried to hide it.

Miss Pickett held his gaze with a certain amount of anger, but no guile. She had money, he sensed she made her own status, and she needed nothing from him. Feeling an inexplicable and utterly irrational urge to shock her, he noted her bare hands and stripped his gloves from his fingers, one by one, tossing them on the floor near the Victrola. He extended his hand to her, wordless, and waited.

He didn't take kindly to rejection—it was why he never willingly extended himself. It didn't matter that Jonathan and Kate were the only two witnesses; if she openly spurned him, he would feel it. These days, he didn't like feeling much of anything, and the fact that she held such power over the moment did not sit well with him.

Without glancing down even once at his hand, she placed her own in it, and he breathed an inner sigh of relief. Still no sign of fear on her face, no reluctance, just . . . a challenge. Very well. He was good at challenges.

***

Lucy fought to keep her eyes from drifting shut at the sensation of his hand upon the small of her back. She had known from the moment he approached that she would dance with him. This close, he smelled of something wonderful, something she couldn't define, something that made her want to nuzzle her nose against his neck, kiss away the scar.

With a fair amount of alarm, she squelched the idea and focused on keeping her footing. She hadn't lied—she was a very good dancer. She was also fairly accomplished at the pianoforte, the harp, and the violin. She sewed in beautiful, neat stitches and was quite exceptional with a drawing pen and sketchbook. She had been gifted with an intelligent brain and a quick wit. She conversed well with people from all walks of life and could play a mean game of croquet.

What Lucy had never experienced, however, was a prolonged exchange with a man of substance, one whose personality seemed a match for her own. Boys, she handled well enough. She flirted easily and could entertain their interests on a surface level. But she had yet to feel the thrill of a genuine challenge from a man who played at a deeper and much more dangerous game.

This man was not a boy.

And, oh dear. His lordship was addling her brain. His strong hand at her back—his other completely enfolding her own—and his nearness had her scrambling for something to say. Lucy never lacked for something to say.

She felt his gaze on her face as they stepped neatly together around the room. He was an exceptional dancer, which caught her by surprise. For someone so big, she would have thought he would be clumsy, or at least tentative. But he led her with sure movements, the slightest pressure of his hand on her back here, a gentle pull to the left there. There was no hesitation, no sense of inadequacy, no stammering compliments about her beauty or the daring honor of her brother, who had voluntarily fought for Queen and country.

She felt flushed and looked beyond his shoulder, which was a feat in itself as he stood a good head and a half taller than she. There was no way on earth she would have backed down from his inelegant request for a dance, but once in the midst of it, she wondered if she would be the one to instigate inane chatter.

Maintaining the same rhythm, he cut the length of his strides by half and gently, subtly, pulled her body closer to his. He kept up with the pressure until she finally looked at his face, her brows raised high.

"Perhaps you are unaccustomed to behaving with propriety." She was trying for tart but afraid it came out rather breathless instead.

"I behave with propriety when it suits me." His reply was a deep rumble, which she felt as much as heard.

"You are exempt from the rules by which the rest of us must live, then."

"Have you not heard? I am an earl."

Arthur Charlesworth had mentioned that his lordship hadn't wanted the earldom, and hearing the bitter tone in his voice now, she wondered if it was true. For one who had never wanted the position, Miles Blake wore it extremely well.

She forced a smile. "Yes, and the last thing I heard on the matter was that even earls are not above the Queen, who behaves with decorum herself."

He gave her a look she interpreted to mean he had a multitude of things he'd like to say on the matter, but he finally settled for what she defined as a jaded half smile. "And do you still have the same impression you expressed the first night you intruded upon my solitude in the library?"

She cast her memory back to that night. What had she said? Her confusion must have shown on her face.

"You said my scar wasn't nearly as fearsome as you'd heard. Or something along those lines."

Oh, mercy. "I was in a bit of a state."

"Couldn't sleep, you said."

"Yes. Nocturnal visits from the Great Beyond have that effect on me, I'm afraid."

A muscle worked in his jaw as he appeared to be searching for the right thing to say. She fought an absurd urge to run her finger along his jawline and down his throat along the white path of his scar. For the love of heaven, what was wrong with her?

"Miss Pickett," he finally said, looking away, "I must apologize—"

She shook her head. "You are indeed an earl, but I hardly expect you to be able to control the otherworld."

He dipped his head in acknowledgment. "I am not . . . content . . . with things I cannot control."

"I don't imagine you are."

The corner of his mouth turned up in the first genuine almost-smile she'd seen on him. She cocked a brow at him and gave him an almost-smile of her own. He slowed, again, sobering, his eyes holding hers. She swallowed and unconsciously bit her lower lip before sternly chastising herself for behaving like a child.

His gaze flickered to her lip and then back up to her eyes, the hand holding hers tightening slightly. She felt the fingers of his hand on her back splaying, pulling her closer until the space between them was reduced to scant inches.

Kate laughed at something Jonathan said, and Blackwell blinked, the spell broken. He resumed their former cadence, but his eyes focused on nothing in the room but her. Lucy felt heat suffusing her face, and her left hand tightened reflexively on his shoulder.

So *this* was what it was like.

She had never understood how an all-consuming passion could sweep and overrule all sense of wisdom and rationale. The most baffling part was that she didn't even like the man. He was rude and heavy-handed. Surly and defensive.

And he smelled divine. As if he sensed the direction of her thoughts, he lightly traced the side of her hand and forefinger with his thumb before pulling their extended arms fractionally closer. Almost as though they were a well-oiled machine that he tightened by small degrees.

She'd seen men admire her before. But never like this. Never with such focus, as if he wanted to devour her whole. Drawing a shaky breath, she said, "You Blakes are an intense lot, aren't you?"

"You have no idea," he murmured. "You really are not afraid of me, are you."

"Should I be?"

"Oh, yes. Yes, you definitely should be."

Her corset suddenly felt too tight, and she resisted the urge to pull her hand free and fan herself with it. She opened her mouth to reply, to attempt something light and flirtatious, and found she couldn't form a single, coherent thought. As she looked at his ice-blue eyes, they seemed to darken slightly, the pupils widening. He broke the gaze with what sounded like a muttered curse. He closed his eyes briefly, opening them to focus instead on something over her head.

The last strains of the waltz faded, and they stopped dancing. He slowly relinquished his hold of her, and she immediately felt the loss of heat. Still holding her right hand, he bowed over it and then straightened. "Thank you for the dance, Miss Pickett."

She dipped instinctively into a curtsey, caught by surprise at his sudden show of manners. "A pleasure, my lord."

A rustle at the door drew her attention, and she removed her hand from his as Arthur and Candice entered, laughing with each other and looking impossibly beautiful. Lucy heard a slight sound from his lordship—disgust? a long-suffering sigh?—and flicked her eyes to his face only to see it was as impassive as ever. She was learning that he kept his emotions well in check. Unless he caught someone running around his house in the middle of the night, that is.

She turned her attention back to the siblings. Arthur approached with a smile as Candice looked at Kate with her brows pinched in a slight frown. "Kate," Candice said as she reached the pair. "You look lovely, as always, but tired, perhaps? Sit on the divan by the windows while I continue your tutoring of my cousin, who has regrettably always had two left feet."

Kate laughed at Jonathan's wounded expression, and Lucy felt a stab of guilt that she hadn't noticed Kate's weariness. Arthur tucked Kate's arm in his. "Allow me," he said with a glance and a smile at Lucy.

Arthur gently escorted Kate to the windows overlooking the back of the estate and settled her comfortably on the divan with murmured comments Lucy couldn't hear, but Kate smiled at the man and they shared a laugh.

"Miles, do start the music again, won't you?" Candice called as she playfully slapped Jonathan on the shoulder and positioned his arm at her waist. "You will be dancing with your new bride before a multitude of guests in but a few weeks' time. You wish to embarrass her?" she said to her cousin. "Besides, it shall be as when we were young. It will evoke pleasant memories."

Blackwell put his hands in his pockets and remained rooted to the spot beside Lucy. "Pleasant for whom?" the earl muttered, and Lucy glanced up at him to see his jaw visibly clench.

It was as Lucy had suspected—there might have been tolerance, but no deeply held affection between the cousins. When Miles made no move to start the Victrola again, Lucy positioned the needle at the beginning of the spinning record. As the music sounded through the room, Arthur left

Kate and crossed to Lucy, where he sketched a deep bow and extended his hand.

"I must dance with the most beautiful woman in all of England," he murmured, and Lucy unconsciously glanced at Lord Blackwell's stony visage before placing her hand in Arthur's.

They quickly settled into a comfortable rhythm, and Lucy found that Arthur was every bit as graceful as his lordship. She knew, however, that should Arthur attempt to pull her close, to try heating her blood with an intense gaze that bordered on scandalous, she would leave him alone on the dance floor.

"Of course you would dance like a dream," Arthur said, and she felt his fingers spread upon the small of her back as Blackwell's had only minutes earlier. How odd that she found it irritating when, by all accounts, *he* was quite likely the most handsome man in all of England.

As he swung her in a wide, elegant sweep, pulling her close against him, a loud screech filled the room. Lucy stumbled to a stop and looked over her shoulder to where Blackwell stood at the Victrola, holding the record in his hand. She pulled away from Arthur, relieved to have a reason to do so.

Blackwell looked at Arthur as he smashed the black disc against his thigh. The shattered pieces skittered onto the floor, settling around the lord's booted feet. "Out," he barked, the sound echoing against the high ceiling. "I do believe I was very clear about this section of the house."

Lucy glanced at Jonathan, who regarded Blackwell with anger clearly stamped on his features. "Of course," he finally said to his brother and made his way to Kate, who stood with wide eyes.

Arthur placed his hand on Lucy's elbow, but when she didn't move, he released her and instead silently made his way to the exit with Candice, followed by Jonathan and Kate. Jonathan paused as though to say something to the earl, but then moved on with his arm around Kate's shoulders.

Lucy stood where she'd stopped dancing, willing her feet to move forward but unable to do anything except look at Blackwell, who had turned his attention to her.

"What?" he growled and walked across the shattered bits of black that crunched under his feet. "What do you wish to say?"

Lucy cleared her throat and met his hot gaze as he neared. "I do not pretend to understand—"

"Correct," he interrupted. "You most certainly do not."

"Nor will I presume to tell you how to behave in your own home."

"I should hope not."

"You are a grown man. I believe you can discern that for yourself. If you'll excuse me." She stepped around him, her shoes echoing on the floor as she left Blackwell standing alone in the room.

Chapter 11

The mood that evening in the card room was surprisingly festive, especially given Miles's behavior in the ballroom earlier. His relatives would likely be in attendance for another few days, but with Jonathan and Kate to dilute the madness—not to mention Miss Pickett—he hoped to be able to ignore the Charlesworths. Provided Miss Pickett, Jonathan, and Kate would forgive him for acting like a cad. Arthur and Candice he rather hoped he had offended.

He shook his head, still unable to pinpoint what had possessed him to destroy the record and throw everyone from the ballroom. The last thing he consciously remembered was Arthur pulling Miss Pickett closer to his fair-haired self—the rest was rather a red haze. If she were going to regard his cousin with the same breathless awareness with which she'd regarded *him,* he hadn't been about to watch it happen.

It helped that Sam had extended his visit for one more day, and Oliver Reed had telescribed that he would arrive the following morning. Miles was eager for an update regarding Oliver's investigation into the threatening notes Miles had received. Having his friends at the manor did much to help his flagging sense of hope, which had become nearly nonexistent in recent months.

Miss Pickett smiled at something Arthur said, and it hit Miles like a punch in the midsection. He had thought of nothing but her since their dance, and he wondered why he tortured himself now. He rarely, if ever, socialized after supper, and when he'd announced his intention to join the family and guests after supper rather than retire to his own quarters, Jonathan's look of surprise was undisguised.

"Beautiful woman," Sam said, taking the seat beside Miles near the hearth.

"Which one? There are three."

"Daniel's sister. She is very much like him in temperament, I believe. It's more pronounced now than when I met her before. She was charming then, but young. Now she looks very much . . . not young."

"I should hate for Daniel to see your visual assault on his sister." Miles fought a sudden urge to plant a fist in his friend's face.

Sam glanced at him before turning his attention back to the card table across the room. "Do not tell me you are unaffected by her charms."

"Charms? She is too assertive, that one. By far."

"And how would you know? I doubt you've spent more than thirty minutes, total, in her company."

Miles raised a brow. "And you have? Are there clandestine assignations transpiring beneath my roof?"

"Can't say I wouldn't mind a few," Sam murmured and took a sip from the tumbler in his hand.

Miles looked at Miss Pickett and felt tension vibrating through him. He thought of her in dancing his arms. She had been petite and soft. Perfect. His teeth clenched as he watched her laugh at his idiot cousin and swat his arm. Who was he trying to fool? That idiot cousin was likely much better company for a young woman of any sort than Miles would be on his best day.

He ran a hand through his hair and closed his eyes, pinching the bridge of his nose with his thumb and forefinger. His life was far too complicated to bring a woman into it.

"Are you ill?" Sam asked him.

Miles rubbed his eyes and turned to his friend with a sigh. "No more than usual."

Sam watched him with eyes that invariably saw far too much. "You've not spoken at all of Marie."

Miles looked into the fire crackling in the hearth. "What is there to say?"

"You know I would lend a listening ear."

He nodded stiffly. "If I should need one, I'll be certain to use you for it."

Sam was silent for a moment. "She was the apple of your eye, and often your confidant."

Miles looked at his friend for the space of a long heartbeat. Had Sam not heard the clear dismissal? "And?"

"Had you told her? Of . . . things?"

Miles's smile felt more like a grimace. "Of my condition?" At Sam's nod, Miles sighed. "No." He paused, weighing his words. "She has been here."

Sam wrinkled his brow.

"Recently."

Dawning comprehension crossed Sam's features, followed by a slow exhalation of breath. "Do you know why?"

Miles shook his head. He chose not to add the fact that Miss Pickett had been the recipient of most of Marie's attention.

"I know of a Medium. She's young, but her mother has told mine of her budding talent."

Miles shook his head. "Not yet."

"Why the wait?"

"I don't know. I'd rather discover Marie's purpose myself. If I cannot, then I will consider your Medium's references."

"Good enough. I've not seen her for a couple of years, but town gossip from my mother's weekly letters suggests Miss Hazel Hughes is quite proficient." He paused again. "Bear in mind, though, that from what little I've heard of such things, it may not be wise to delay the process. The sooner you address matters with an effective Medium, the sooner the issues are resolved. I hear those on the other side—especially those who are exceptionally restless—can make life uncomfortable if they feel they are not being understood."

"I am aware of this." Miles's tone was sharper than he intended. He wanted to handle Marie on his own terms. The last thing he needed was for a professional to tell him what he feared he already knew about the truth surrounding his sister's death.

The card game drew to a close, and the players began to stretch and stand. As Miss Pickett and Kate moved away from the table and slowly wandered toward the door, Miles stood and followed.

"Miss Pickett, I have a question for you of a . . . a botanical nature. Might I have a word?"

She turned in surprise, her mouth slightly open, before composing her features. "Of course."

"I wonder if you would join me in the library. I've come across a book I'd like to show you."

Kate looked at him with brows raised sky-high, but she gave Lucy a subtle shrug and kissed her cousin's cheek. "Good evening, then."

"You rest." Miss Pickett ran her thumb lightly across Kate's cheek. "You're pale." She lowered her voice as they moved into the hallway. "I ought to have insisted you go right upstairs after supper."

"You know I hate to miss a party." Kate kissed her again and turned to look around Miles for Jonathan, who followed closely behind.

"Sleep well, Kate," Miles surprised himself by saying, and those within earshot seemed equally so. Since Kate's mild rebuke of Eustace the other day, Miles had found himself seeing her as though for the first time. In truth, she was a vibrant woman, and he wanted her to be well and whole for his brother's sake, if not her own.

Miss Pickett fell into step beside him as they made their way down the dark hallway to the library. She looked back over her shoulder once, and he saw her brow crease as she visually followed her cousin's progress until she rounded the corner.

"I will have Sam examine her tomorrow," he said gruffly.

Miss Pickett looked up at him, her eyes wary as they passed a sconce that gave off paltry light. "I cannot, for the life of me, determine the nature of her illness," she said, her voice quiet.

As they entered the library, he led her to the hearth and made a show of pulling a book from the mantel and opening it for her. Should any prying relatives have followed them down the hall, they'd see exactly what he'd suggested.

As he flipped through the pages, he leaned closer and murmured, "I must apologize, firstly, for my actions earlier in the ballroom."

She held up a hand with a slight shake of her head. "As I said, I do not understand all that has gone on under this roof in recent months. It is little wonder you might find yourself . . . well, on edge."

He nodded. It was gracious of her, and he knew it. Nobody in polite society of any layer behaved as brutishly as he had, and he was fortunate she even chose to be in the same room with him. Feeling uncomfortable, and feeling frustrated because he was uncomfortable, he closed the book, set it on the mantel, and moved quickly to the true purpose for their visit in the library.

"I clearly have no botanical questions for you. I sought your company to ask that you please keep me apprised of any nocturnal visits you may experience. I do not want the rest of the household to be aware of this recent . . . circumstance."

She looked up at him. "May I ask why? What do you intend to do about it?"

He wished he knew. "I suspect my sister has something to say. I wish I could explain why it seems she has singled you out for her attention, but I'm in rather unfamiliar territory."

Miss Pickett studied him for a long moment until he was nigh unto squirming—an anomaly he hadn't experienced in years. She finally nodded. "I will share whatever I know. And I suppose if the pattern continues, I'll simply see you here in another four hours or so." She offered a small smile that faded quickly. "Incidentally, the other night when I was following Marie, she went into the portrait gallery and knocked over the pictures of herself and the Charlesworths. Possibly the picture of late Lady Blackwell, too—I'm not certain."

"She knocked over . . ." He blinked. "You know this for a fact?"

The look she gave him would have quelled a lesser man. She explained about having heard a noise, learning a 'ton had righted the portraits before being reprogrammed, and finding chipped picture frames. The more she spoke, the more concerned he grew. He knew little of spirits and their capacity on the other side. As Miss Pickett went on to describe the scene she'd witnessed on Marie's second visit—how her appearance revealed the graphic nature of her death—he felt cold to his extremities. Perhaps the household required the services of a Medium sooner rather than later.

"And should I require your assistance?" she asked. "Where am I to find you?"

In my room was on the tip of his tongue, but he held it back—just barely—when he realized the implication. "You have a telescriber, I assume?"

"Of course."

"And you know where to find the connector? It is to the right of the bed, behind the nightstand."

She nodded, then dropped her gaze from his face to his chest.

"Am I suddenly too frightening to look upon?" He forced the safety of cynicism back into his tone.

She lifted her face, boldly examining his scar before meeting his eyes. "You do enjoy hiding behind it, do you not?"

He narrowed his eyes. "Hiding behind what, pray tell?"

"Your supposed disfigurement. Which is laughably benign. I rather think you foster the image and create the accompanying persona to keep the world at bay."

She was too perceptive for comfort. His breath stuck in his lungs, and he forced it out on a laugh that was more of a scoff. It was deliberate, and he knew she would hear it. "And how is it that you know me so very well, Miss Pickett?"

"I know my brother, and he is an excellent judge of character. He claims exactly three close friends, one of whom is you, my lord. And as much time as he spent with you in the war, enduring the most unpleasant of circumstances, I imagine his opinion of you would be sound. Ought I to revise my own?"

She held his gaze, which he knew for a fact was intimidating on a good day. Several sarcastic, cutting responses passed through his mind before he finally felt his lips quirking slightly into his second genuine smile of the day. "I'll leave that for you to decide."

She tipped her head in acknowledgment. "Very well. Might I suggest, then, that you resist the urge to become prickly if a person doesn't stare continuously at your face. That's rude. And in any case, perhaps I was merely admiring the cut of your suit coat."

"Were you, now?"

"I am a woman, am I not? And it is what we do, is it not? We are consummate studiers of and experts on fashion. I would hardly be doing myself any favors by ignoring that which I was born to observe."

He leaned his shoulder against the enormous hearth. "Do you mean to tell me, Miss Pickett, that your primary focus in life is fashion? Do not insult my intelligence."

"I am attempting to be all that I ought. Just today, Mr. Charlesworth asked me if I am a bluestocking. I should hate to offend this household or seem too outrageous."

"Now you are being ridiculous. Aside from the fact that my cousin is an idiot, we seem to be avoiding the reality that, for all your outward calm, you seem rather flustered."

"You do not know me nearly well enough to ascertain whether or not I am 'flustered,' my lord."

He raised a brow. Was she blushing? "Oh, yes, Miss Pickett. I do believe you are indeed flustered."

"I can assure you, what you mistake as flustered is merely a growing sense of irritation."

He smiled again. "May I walk you to your room?"

She frowned, her brows drawing together. "If you must."

"I can certainly remain here, if you'd rather."

"No, no. I suppose I am rather . . . apprehensive."

"I regret that this household makes you in any way uncomfortable. That any of us would." It came out sounding stiff, which was not what he intended. He escorted her through the doorway and into the hall.

The look she gave him was one of chagrin. "My apologies. Your home is lovely, your staff very kind. I . . . well . . ."

"Are you afraid?" What a stupid question. His angry sister—his angry *dead* sister—had awoken her from sleep twice now, the second time with blood dripping down her face. She must be terrified. Not to mention the fact that he'd given her a fine display of his own temper on more than one occasion.

Miss Pickett shook her head but wouldn't meet his eyes.

"You have only to telescribe—or call for Jonathan. He is just down the hall."

"I'll not awaken them," she murmured as they climbed the stairs to the second floor. "Kate needs her rest." She looked as though she wanted to say something else but stopped.

"My telescribe name is 'Blackwell.' I'll come straightaway if something happens." He rather hoped something would happen. The sooner he could ascertain Marie's motives, the better for all of them.

Miss Pickett nodded, and they walked in silence, passing the Charlesworths' guest rooms before stopping at hers. She withdrew a key from her pocket and unlocked the door. He swallowed, briefly closing his eyes. How unfortunate that a guest in his home would feel the need to lock her belongings away. Or attempt to keep someone out.

She looked up at him, her expression unguarded. Her eyes were huge in a face that was suddenly pale. She *was* afraid. But what could he do? Suggest she sleep in his suite?

"If you are reluctant to be alone, I can arrange for one of the maids to join you—human or 'ton, whichever you prefer."

She shook her head and visibly straightened her shoulders. "I shall be fine. Thank you."

He gave her a slight bow, and she dipped into a curtsey he knew was as ingrained in her as breathing. She closed the door between them.

He stood for a few moments outside her locked door before slowly making his way down the hallway toward the south wing.

Chapter 12

This time when Lucy awoke, it was different. There was the hint of a breeze, but cold—painfully so—and dank. Lucy's heart began to race before she even opened her eyes. That she had fallen asleep at all was a miracle, but the strange house seemed determined that she not find respite in slumber.

She opened her eyes slowly, aware of a suffocating blackness. The heavy draperies at the turret had been drawn, but she hadn't closed them. She'd intentionally left them open because the night was clear and a blanket of stars had shone through the mullioned glass.

A whisper floated across the floor. A footstep? It wasn't Marie. Marie was direct. The being that watched her now was anything but.

She held very still, listening to a silence so quiet it roared. There was nothing. No movement, no telltale signs of life other than her own occupying the dark space. Why was it so cold? Even with the fire having died, she knew something was wrong. Ever so slowly, she inched her arm toward the nightstand and toyed with the idea of turning on the small lamp. Her hand touched her telescriber instead, and she closed her fingers around it.

A slight suggestion of noise. A hiss of something that sounded familiar but which she couldn't place. Metal?

Her decision made, she waited for one heartbeat, two, and then flung the heavy blankets aside, sliding from the bed onto the cold floor. Something landed on the bed behind her, and she made a mad dash for the door. She reached out with her free hand to feel the wall as she crashed against it.

Sliding to the right, she found the door and then the key, which she'd left in the lock. She turned it and yanked the door open just as something brushed down the back of her head and clutched her nightgown. Her breath coming in gasps, she wrenched away into the hallway and twisted around, looking behind her with wide eyes at a shadow that remained just that. There were no sconces lit. Were it not for the windows at the end of the hallway, which themselves were covered by curtains that allowed only a sliver of light through the gap between them, it would have been as dark as her bedchamber.

She forced her legs to move, stumbling in her haste and nearly sprawling upon the carpet that muffled the sound of her footsteps. The only sound was her gasping breath as she ran, frantic, to the landing overlooking the main hall and then around the corner and into the south wing.

A whisper? A noise behind her?

Her own gasps precluded any sound her pursuer might be making. She felt it—felt something there. She wasn't alone. She looked back as she ran, seeing nothing but darkness and shadows and her long, tangled curls in her face. The movement threw her balance off, and she stumbled sideways. She hit the side of the unforgiving wall, sucking in her breath at the sharp pain that shot through her shoulder.

Nearly there. She was nearly there.

She flew to the massive oak doors and smacked her palm flat against the solid wood.

Reaching for the large brass handle, she twisted it and cried out in frustration and fear. Locked. Of course it was locked. Looking behind her again while still pulling frantically on the handle, she thought she heard laughter, so faint it might have been nothing. Her knees buckled, and she pounded on the door again, bracing herself against the oak as her legs threatened to give way altogether.

The door opened with a vengeance, shoving Lucy away and sending her flying. She sprawled on the floor, robbed of both breath and coherent thought. She reached upward, nearly mad with fear, as Blackwell grasped her arms and hauled her against him.

"What is it?" he said in her ear. "What is it?" He shook her, and she clutched a fistful of his shirt with her free hand. The other still held tight to her telescriber as though her life depended on it. She looked into the shadows of the long hall but saw nothing. Heard nothing.

"I . . . something . . . someone . . ."

Blackwell followed the direction of her eyes before hauling her into his suite and closing the heavy door behind them. Still holding her tight with one arm, he turned the key in the lock and then guided her toward a sofa facing the fire, its embers still glowing on the hearth.

When she didn't release her desperate hold on his shirtfront, he sat down with her.

"Miss Pickett," he said, his hand covering her fist on his chest. "Miss Pickett."

His voice seemed to come from far away, and Lucy stared into the fireplace and shook her head. If her heart didn't slow, she was afraid it would beat its way out of her chest.

"Lucy."

She turned to face him, finally feeling her wits return. "I am so very sorry," she whispered, taking a deep, shuddering breath.

"Was it Marie?" His voice was low, soft. His hand massaged softly up and down her back, and she felt herself begin to relax by degrees.

She shook her head, looking at his face as she slowly tried to loosen her fist on his chest. Bit by bit, she straightened her fingers until her hand lay flat, nestled under his.

"Someone was in my room," she murmured, breathless, searching his blue eyes, which were bright, even in the dim light. "I promise you, I am not mistaken. He . . . I . . ."

Blackwell shook his head slightly, his thumb trailing along her fingers. "I believe you."

Lucy took another deep breath and slowly exhaled, feeling her shoulders relax. Still, her hand stayed under his, flat against his chest. "By the time I reached your door, there didn't seem to be anyone behind me anymore," she whispered. "I assumed you would think I was imagining things."

"Miss Pickett, in the short time I have known you, you have shown yourself to be a woman of sound mind and common sense. If you say there was someone in your room, then there must have been."

Lucy looked down at the telescriber still in her left hand. "I was going to send you a message."

She felt the rumble of his chuckle under her hand. "And you did."

"I am so sorry—I was a bit worried . . ."

"Worried?"

"Nervous, I suppose."

"Nervous?"

She closed her mouth and let her eyes roam across his face, which was so very close to her own.

"Why did you come here first?" He whispered so quietly that she felt the question rather than heard it.

"I didn't want to awaken Kate," she murmured, drained from the desperate flight yet suddenly very much aware of everything about the room—the last of the dying embers casting a slight glow, his chest rising and falling steadily beneath her hand, his hand atop hers tightening fractionally.

"Arthur's room is in the north wing." He shook his head ever so slightly, his eyes never leaving hers. "You didn't even give it thought."

He was right. "No, I don't suppose I did."

"What am I going to do with you?" he whispered.

He was warm and so solid. She wanted to sink against his side and close her eyes. She did close her eyes but resisted the rest. Releasing a small sigh, she straightened her back and slowly pulled her hand from beneath his. He wrapped his fingers around it, holding it firmly for the space of a heartbeat, two, and then allowed her to reclaim it, placing it in her lap, where it suddenly felt very cold.

"Here." He pulled a blanket from the arm of the couch, his other arm still around her with his hand on her back. He wrapped her securely in the blanket, though she found it woefully inadequate in comparison to the warmth of his body.

Blackwell rose and made his way to the hearth, adding kindling and bringing small flames back to life. The only sounds were the snapping of twigs as he fed the growing fire and the clock on the wall that quietly ticked away the seconds. With a shudder, Lucy drew her knees up to her chest and pulled the blanket around her legs, wrapping herself in a cocoon.

"Now, then. Tell me what you remember." He sat on the couch, though not nearly as close as before. She swallowed an unwanted sense of disappointment. The man was autocratic and entirely too grim. She would do well to remember it.

She looked at the front of his shirt, which was horribly wrinkled from her poor treatment of it, realizing for the first time that he must have hastily dressed when he'd heard her at the door. His feet were bare and his hair was tousled, as though she'd roused him from sleep.

"I apologize, my lord, I—"

"Enough of that." He waved a hand in abrupt dismissal. "Tell me everything you remember. What did you see?"

She winced. "That would be the problem. My room was completely black. The curtains had been drawn—but not by me. And it was cold."

"The fire had died out."

"Yes, but I felt a breeze, almost as though the door were open, but it was shut and locked tight. The key was still in it."

"Did you hear anything? What roused you from sleep?" His voice was deep, quiet.

"A rustle of fabric, just the slightest of sounds—and metal against metal. Rather like a knife or sword being unsheathed." She swallowed, suddenly identifying the sound that had propelled her from her bed.

Blackwell leaned forward, bracing his arms on his knees and looking into the fire, his expression blank, as serious as it always was. "No sign of my sister's spirit?"

She shook her head. "I knew from the moment I awoke that it wasn't her."

"How?"

"She does not hide herself from me. She is bold. Direct." Lucy frowned, trying to articulate her thoughts. "The room itself felt different."

"Are you not frightened by her, then?"

"Oh, yes. I am loath to admit it, but she frightens me a great deal. Forgive me, sir, but there is something about her that is . . . intent. Angrily so."

He shook his head. "Nothing to forgive, Miss Pickett. You are honest, and that is what I require."

The clock on the wall sounded three times, and Lucy realized how very weary she was. Still wrapped tightly in the blanket, she leaned sideways until she rested against the back of the couch. The thought of returning to her own bed had her shuddering.

Blackwell glanced at her. "Are you still cold?"

"I am warm enough. Thank you."

"What are your intentions?"

"My intentions?"

"Surely you do not wish to remain in this house."

Lucy shook her head. "My wishes are of no consequence. I cannot leave until I am assured that Kate is well. If I might impose on your hospitality further, I feel I must remain."

His lips quirked into a smile, and she had the distinct sense he was mocking her. He sat back against the couch, closer to her, and met her gaze directly. "And since when do you require permission from me?"

"It is the polite thing to do."

"And would you leave if I asked you to?"

She regarded him for a moment. "I suppose I would. But I might just drag my cousin with me."

"She has a husband now, and a place here."

"Something is wrong with her. I've known her all my life; we are as close as sisters. She is never ill."

"Have you considered that she may be with child?"

Lucy raised a brow at his direct question, amazed that he could even ask it without so much as a flinch or a stammer. But he was a man who ruled the roost and made no apologies. "It was the first thing I considered. She has assured me that such is not the case."

Blackwell's face remained impassive, giving nothing away. "I cannot have you returning to your room tonight," he finally said. "When it is daylight, I will program one of the 'tons to remain in your room to keep you safe."

"That is not necessary, my lord. I shall simply send for my ray gun."

"You have a ray gun?"

She nodded. "When Daniel returned from the war, he insisted I obtain a concealed weapons permit."

He stared at her before responding. "Why on earth did Daniel feel you would need a concealed weapons permit?"

Her sudden wave of sadness was a surprise. Daniel kept everything light, bobbing on the surface, but there were undercurrents of darkness to her brother that had never been part of his personality before he had spent time in India. And he wouldn't allow Lucy to help him. "He is no longer the carefree young man who entered the service."

Blackwell nodded once, and Lucy wondered what he was thinking. He didn't seem inclined to share, and she didn't pry. When he finally answered her, he did so with a sigh. "I cannot have you sleeping with your ray gun under your pillow."

"I am very accomplished with it, I assure you."

"That may be. But supposing whoever seems bent on doing you harm cannot be stopped with conventional weapons?"

"If that is the case, I fail to see how a 'ton will be able to defend me."

"A 'ton will be much stronger than you are. It will put my mind at ease."

"And my weapon will put my mind at ease."

He glanced at her. "Why did you not bring it with you? To Blackwell Manor, of all places?"

She sighed. "I had taken it from my luggage when I returned home from the Continent, and in my haste to see Kate, I forgot to repack it. I've not carried it long enough to miss it when I'm without it."

"You may certainly send for it if you wish. In the meantime, I will program the 'ton."

As he seemed firmly fixed on his solution, she didn't respond. She wasn't keen on the idea of anything watching her sleep, even a non-sentient metal contraption. She rubbed her eyes. Her energy had worn down, and although her thoughts still tangled and tripped over each other, her body was showing signs of her exhaustion. Her eyes drifted closed. She would rest for just a moment.

"You will sleep in my bed for the remainder of the evening."

Her eyes flew open.

He scowled at her. "I shall sleep out here."

"I will not keep you from your own bed, sir. I can sleep right here on this sofa."

"We'll not argue the matter, Miss Pickett. I doubt I shall sleep much anyway."

"I would feel horribly guilty. You should be in your own bedroom. I'm fine now, in fact. I can return to my own chambers." Though how she would make herself relax again in her bedroom knowing someone wished her ill seemed impossible.

He stood and held out a hand to her. "Come."

She unfolded herself with a wince and stretched her legs, the blanket falling from her shoulders. She stumbled along behind Blackwell as he pulled her around the sofa, away from the door leading to the hall.

"But—"

"Hush." Blackwell led her into an adjoining room with long strides that she had to rush to match. Still holding her hand tightly, he switched on a lamp, the low glow giving just enough light to dispel some of the darkness in the large room. There was a seating area around a cavernous fireplace, another door on the other side of the hearth that led to what she assumed was likely his wardrobe and washroom, and on the far wall was a gargantuan bed.

She cocked a brow at it, taking in the substantial frame of the four posts that rose high into the air and the heavy drapes that were pulled back and secured to them.

He shook his head with a slight eye roll as he caught the direction of her gaze. "It came with the title," he muttered.

"It is very grand." She tamped down a smile.

"It is very ridiculous. But comfortable. I trust you will rest well." He pulled her to the side of the bed, and she wondered if he thought she would resist. Truthfully, the last place she wanted to go by herself was her own room. That he was insisting she remain with him was, while a bit awkward, a relief.

The top of the mattress hit just below her rib cage. "Might you have a step stool?" She was mortified by the thought of clambering up on the bed while he watched. She supposed she could ask his lordship to give her a boost, but the very thought had her cheeks feeling hot. For all that she felt she was fairly worldly and knowledgeable, she was afraid she was swimming in waters that closed well above her head.

She glanced at Blackwell's face, which was cast in shadows, the hard lines returning and his brows drawn over ice-blue eyes.

He was irritated, and she felt a pang of remorse. "Truly, my lord, I can sleep on the sofa. Or in my own room."

With something that sounded suspiciously like a growl, and before she could even begin to ascertain his intentions, he grasped her by the waist and threw her into the air atop the mattress. Her breath left her lungs, and she stared at him with wide eyes.

"Sleep. You look as though you need it."

Gone was the tender rescuer and back was the aristocrat—demanding, directing, expecting nothing less than total compliance. If she weren't so horribly exhausted, she might jump off the bed merely to prove a point.

She'd grown up without a father, and Daniel had always been her friend and confidant, not an authority figure. It was beyond her realm of experience to acquiesce in blind obedience, and when she had come across people who expected it, she typically twisted the situation to her advantage, maintaining an upper hand.

As it was, however, the mattress was as soft as she imagined a cloud to be. She shifted, feeling self-conscious as he stood there, waiting as she maneuvered herself beneath the heavy down comforter that smelled pleasantly of him and settled in.

Lucy couldn't help but blush, her mortification complete. "I have acted as a child tonight, my lord. Your generosity is beyond the pale, and I thank you for it."

He watched her for a moment longer, hands on his hips, shirt open at the throat, and his thick, black hair anything but tamed and in place. "Rest, Miss Pickett. I suspect we shall have a full day ahead of us in a few hours. And immediately following breakfast, I wish to speak to you in my den."

There was something ridiculous about the stilted conversation, especially given the fact that she was in his bed and looking at him from his own pillow. "Very well."

A muscle worked in his jaw, and he was silent for a bit. "Sleep," he finally said and left the room in a few long-legged strides, closing the door behind him.

Chapter 13

Miles spent the bulk of the early morning hours in his sitting room, staring at the fire and thinking about the woman asleep in his bed. The ghost of his murdered sister lingered, and someone in his household had attempted to harm a guest, yet all he could concentrate on was the guest herself.

His own sleep had been fitful at best when he had heard her frantically beating on his door. Shoving his legs into his trousers as he ran, by the time he reached the door he could hear her crying, terrified, on the other side. When he had shoved the door open and sent her sprawling, his mouth had gone dry at the sight of her. Scant moonlight filtered in through a high window, illuminating her mahogany curls, long and uninhibited, cobalt eyes, huge and terrified, and her long legs as the nightgown billowed around her on the floor.

When she had raised her hand in supplication, he had come undone. Without a second thought, he'd hauled her into his suite. She had come to him for protection in a moment of sheer panic, not knowing him well at all, and yet it had been instinctive. She hadn't gone to Arthur or Jonathan, hadn't screamed out for help. She had run the better part of the length of the house with terror at her back. What was it about her that not only kept her from fearing him but made her flee to him for sanctuary?

And who in blazes had tried to hurt her while she slept?

He supposed she might have misheard something, might have imagined something, but he'd told her the truth. He didn't doubt for a moment that she was of sound mind. The fact that she had been so desperately afraid last night when only a few nights before he'd witnessed her bravery firsthand as she had run after Marie's ghost told him that she perceived this most recent threat to be very real.

The clock chimed six, and he leaned his head back against the chair, his legs propped on an ottoman. The staff would be up and about soon, and he needed to get her back to her chambers before anyone realized she'd spent the better part of the night in his. With resignation, he rose and made his way to the bedroom.

He turned a few lamps on low, the familiar hum of the Tesla coils filling the air on the initial spark. As the lights warmed, he started a fire to chase away the chill. Finally, realizing he could no longer avoid the inevitable, he made his way to the bed. Would she be lying in the same spot where he'd left her? He imagined she'd look like a peaceful child with her hands tucked beneath her cheek.

The reality had his lips twitching in spite of himself. She was sprawled on her stomach, her hair wild and tangled about the pillow, obscuring her face like a curtain. A faint outline of her legs, one knee bent, was visible under the thick comforter. An arm hung over the side of the bed, the lace-edged cuff framing her hand. Her breathing was deep and even, and he hated to disturb her.

"Miss Pickett," he whispered. The valet's room adjoined his, and he didn't want Marcus, discreet though he was, to know she was with him. "Miss Pickett."

She didn't move a muscle, did not even twitch. He reached forward and picked up a handful of hair, lifting it to the side and brushing a few stubborn, clinging strands away from her face. He fought the urge to pull her into the shelter of his arms and keep her there forever. What was wrong with him? He pulled his hand back, shoving it into his pocket. This one was definitely beyond his reach.

"Lucy," he murmured but received no response. He leaned down next to her ear and repeated himself.

Finally, she stirred. Her eyes opened slowly, and as he moved back, he saw the exact moment when the confusion cleared and she remembered everything. He was stunned when she looked at him with a dawning sense of awareness; she wasn't the least bit afraid. Wary, perhaps, but as she lifted her head and scraped her hair back, he recognized a look that he hadn't seen from a woman since he had first grown into his lanky body, when he had stretched and filled out, becoming a handsome and reckless young adult.

Before the incident that left him scarred. Before the war. Before everything.

He stepped back and tore his gaze from hers, focusing instead on the ridiculously huge and ornate headboard. Clearing his throat, Miles wondered what had happened to the jaded earl who had gone and left a vulnerable man in his place. It wouldn't do. Not at all.

"You must return to your bedroom," he said quietly, "before anyone else is about. You still have roughly thirty minutes before the servants begin working on this floor."

She pushed herself fully upright, rubbing her forehead and then her eyes. "Thank you," she murmured. "Thank you for everything."

He took in the gentle lines of her tired face, the hair that tumbled down over her shoulder. It was soft, like silk, and he wanted to bury his hands in it.

"Go," he said, motioning with his shoulder, his hands still in his pockets. "We shall speak after breakfast."

She studied him closely before she blinked once and donned the expression he recognized as the one she reserved for polite company. It was the civilized Lucy, the one who easily conversed around the dinner table and who didn't, for a moment, doubt her own abilities. It was nowhere near the Lucy he'd held trembling in his arms mere hours before. Her vulnerability, sentiment, and longing were gone.

He tried, but couldn't avert his eyes as she slid out of bed, landing with a wobble before straightening her gown.

"My lord." She bobbed a brief curtsey. It was ridiculous, really, but for the best. Any hint of intimacy they had shared had been effectively squelched.

When she reached the door, he said, "Do not touch anything in your room but that which is absolutely necessary, and leave a note for the maids to wait until tomorrow to clean. I want to take a look before anything is disrupted. I ought to have gone earlier, but if I do so now, I'm likely to be seen leaving your room."

She nodded and left. Without allowing himself to linger on things best left alone, he applied himself instead to wondering how someone had gained access to her room. She'd said the key was in the lock on the inside of the door. If someone had attempted to unlock it from the outside, the key would have clattered to the floor. And from her description, it seemed as though she had awoken to the slightest of sounds. To a rush of cold air.

He closed his eyes, cursing his stupidity.

Of course.

With a sense of urgency, he dressed quickly for the day without bothering to ring for Marcus, throwing his ensemble together with habits born from years of experience. He left his suite, still tying his cravat, and made his way down the staircase that branched off just outside his wide, double doors.

Once on the main level, he headed to the conservatory on the first floor. The room was encased in shadow, the filmy curtains at the windows allowing little light. Walking to the far wall, he lifted a tapestry that had been in the family for six generations. It was horrid—a garish wolf pack in the act of devouring prey—and he had never liked it. Behind it, the stone was bare, and he ran his hand along the wall until he found the spot where a slight indentation gave way beneath his fingers.

The wall swung noiselessly inward, tapestry and all. He shook his head. He hadn't been in this passageway since he was a boy, hiding from his mother, who insisted he practice the harpsichord. Then, the hinges had squeaked horribly, and it was the noise that had given him away. Now, someone had gone to the trouble of insuring they were well-oiled. As far as he was aware, nobody ever went into the passageways anymore. There were no children about—hadn't been for years—and they were the only creatures likely to find joy in their exploration.

The smell and temperature of the place reminded him of another fact about the numerous passageways: they were notoriously cold. And this particular one connected the conservatory on the main level to Miss Pickett's room on the second floor.

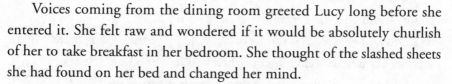

Voices coming from the dining room greeted Lucy long before she entered it. She felt raw and wondered if it would be absolutely churlish of her to take breakfast in her bedroom. She thought of the slashed sheets she had found on her bed and changed her mind.

She had washed and dressed quickly upon returning from Blackwell's chambers. Following his instructions to the letter, she touched only those things she couldn't avoid and had styled her own hair in a simple, loosely braided bun at the crown of her head. Scribbling a quick note for the maid to leave the room undisturbed, she'd locked the door and made her way downstairs on legs that still trembled.

"Oh, Miss Pickett!" Candice beamed when Lucy made her entrance into the breakfast room and rushed toward her, taking both of her hands. "It will be so very grand! His lordship's bosom friends will be joining us for the ball at Charlesworth House!"

Bosom friends? Lucy glanced around the room and saw immediately who had captured the young woman's attention so thoroughly. Oliver Reed stood next to Samuel MacInnes, looking as commanding in real life as he did in the portrait of him she'd seen among Daniel's things. When Samuel noted her gaze, he smiled and elbowed Mr. Reed's arm. The gentlemen approached her and Candice, and she clearly heard the other woman's indrawn breath.

The men were like panthers prowling among the lilies. The home was polished and perfect, the occupants within it proper and socially accept-able, and Mr. Reed and Dr. MacInnes seemed slightly misplaced. The two friends had an air about them that spoke of a leashed energy. She'd noticed it in her brother after his return from India. It was the same aura she'd sensed in Blackwell. Restless. Ruthless. Determined.

She smiled and extended her hand as Sam made the introductions. "Oliver Reed, Miss Lucy Pickett. Daniel's sister."

Mr. Reed took her hand, and she inclined her head when he mur-mured, "A pleasure." He was a man who wore his clothing well—no fuss or frills, everything tailored, nothing wasted. His eyes were a tawny gold color, his hair a darker brown. He wore it short—shorter than the current fashion—and she was certain he couldn't have cared less.

Blackwell entered the room, drawing her attention. Was there a slight pause in his step, or had she imagined it? He turned his attention to Mr. Reed and approached, a wide, genuine smile crossing his face. She sucked in a breath of her own and wondered if Candice heard it.

The three shook hands and clapped one another's backs in typical manly fashion.

"Thank you for the invitation to stay," Mr. Reed told Blackwell. "I'll likely be back and forth between here and London, but I'll stay for as long as I can. And your aunt has graciously asked that we join you all at the celebration honoring your brother and his new bride."

Lucy watched Blackwell's face, feeling strangely intimate with the man despite the barrier he had slammed between them that morning after he'd woken her. He wasn't interested, and frankly, she couldn't for the life of her imagine why she should care. She'd run to him for help, but he was the lord of the manor, after all, and it only made sense.

Blackwell chatted easily with Mr. Reed and Dr. MacInnes, for a mo-ment looking as he might have if his life had been less complicated. She was disrupted from her thoughts when Candice, who still held tight to Lucy's arm, sighed again. "It will be absolutely lovely," she said, repeating the sentiment that seemed to be her hallmark. "Nothing ever happens in our sleepy little village."

Lucy patted Candice's arm. "You should make it a point to have a stay in London. So much is going on there that before long you'll be glad to go back home."

Candice's eyes narrowed fractionally as she watched the men converse. "I have spent time in London." She turned to Lucy, her eyes liquid, bright. "It didn't go well."

"I'm sorry to hear it. I shall give you my address. We have a small town house, and if you would like, please visit me sometime. It's not nearly as grand as all of this, of course, but it is lovely. I am frequently in residence because of my work."

"You are so very kind." Candice glowed. "I do wish we had gone to school together. I believe we would have been the best of friends."

Lucy smiled, trying to keep her attention focused though her thoughts were across the room. "I'm certain of it."

Mr. Grafton entered, and just behind him, Kate and Jonathan. Kate looked well this morning. For that, Lucy was grateful.

The guests arranged themselves at the table while the 'tons placed large serving platters on the sideboard and removed the coverings. Candice chose the seat next to Lucy, while Arthur secured the one across from her. He inquired about her health, wondering how she'd rested and commenting on the beauty of the morning. Lucy nodded at all the right places and answered his questions without much thought. She was preoccupied with the man at the head of the table and the state of her room upstairs.

Breakfast passed uneventfully, Aunt Eustace strangely quiet and the earl's friends charming and entertaining. The whole affair was excruciatingly formal, and Lucy wondered how the mood might have been if only Blackwell and his friends dined together. She felt like an intruder wandering into a tableau that didn't concern her, one where she was not entirely welcome.

As the guests discussed their plans for the day and then left the table,

Blackwell made eye contact with Lucy and motioned his head toward the hallway. "I'll meet you in an hour," he said to Sam and Mr. Reed. "Until then, please make good use of the stables."

Lucy told Kate that his lordship had some questions for her of a botanical nature, and while her cousin raised a brow, she didn't press the matter. Blackwell reached her side and indicated for her to precede him from the room. As she turned to leave, Arthur materialized.

"And where are you headed?" he asked.

Blackwell spoke before Lucy could. "One of the horses is showing signs of an illness. I've asked Miss Pickett to share her botanical knowledge with me in hopes we might find a solution."

Arthur wrinkled his brow. "Do you not have a veterinarian on retainer?"

"He is useless." Blackwell placed a hand at the small of Lucy's back and propelled her from the room.

"You need lessons, my lord," she murmured once they were alone.

"I'm sorry?"

"There are ways to handle people that prove more effective in the long run."

"I find my way to be most effective. And quick."

Lucy lengthened her stride to keep up with Blackwell, who had crossed the main hall and was moving into the north wing on the main level. She motioned to the room adjacent the library as they moved past it. "Is that not your den?"

"We are going elsewhere."

"Elsewhere?"

Another turn of a corner had them before a set of double doors Kate had pointed out as the conservatory, which she had said was little used, if ever.

Blackwell gave Lucy a long look before he finally twisted the handle of one of the doors and pushed it inward. Motioning for her to enter the room, he followed her and switched on the sconces that flanked the entrance.

A grand piano sat in the corner to her right, with wrought-iron furniture painted white and upholstered in various shades of spring green
placed in multiple seating arrangements about the room. The walls were
papered in a light-green toile, and a large, plush carpet anchored the room
at the center.

A harp graced the far left corner, and seated next to it, a cello on a
stand. A delicate crystal chandelier hung from the center of the ceiling,
and a window seat against the far wall would be the perfect spot to sit
with a sketchbook or novel.

"This is lovely," she murmured, taking in each detail with a cultured
eye.

He grunted, glancing at her. "You are surprised."

"It is very . . . feminine. Serene. Someone with subtle taste decorated
this room."

"My mother."

Lucy looked at Blackwell, trying to read his tone, which was far from
revealing. If anything, it was conspicuous in its lack of inflection. "Did
she play many instruments?"

He nodded. Placing his hands in his pockets, he looked around the
room. "Everything in here. Plus the flute. She insisted Marie and I learn a
little bit of everything as well."

"Do you have a favorite?"

He gave a light shrug. "I suppose I enjoy the piano and cello equally."

"Very different instruments. Perhaps to cater to your mercurial moods."

Blackwell glanced at her sharply, and she regretted that she'd tipped
her proverbial hand. She'd decided when leaving his suite that morning
that she would not let on that he had bruised her feelings. Or perhaps
it was her pride. They had shared a few intimate moments in her terror
the night before, and she supposed she'd been hoping on some level for a
deeper sense of familiarity, a less stilted formality. There was also the fact
that being around him did strange things to her insides, and it was an
insult to her ego that he was apparently not also similarly affected.

He narrowed his eyes, scrutinizing her for a long moment that had her wanting to fidget. *Enough, already!* "So, my lord," she said. "Why have you brought me here?"

Blackwell still watched her with ice-blue eyes that she feared saw everything. He finally blinked, his expression flat, and motioned with his head. "I brought you here to see this."

He moved to the wall and ran his fingers alongside a tapestry. Intrigued, she followed and stood beside him as he pressed what must have been a hidden mechanism, because the tapestry swung open to reveal a dark, recessed enclosure. She gave a small start of surprise at the revelation. "Is it a priest hole, then?"

Blackwell shook his head and reached into his coat pocket for a small torch that he flicked on, illuminating the darkened area. Stairs led upward, and she rubbed her arms absently at the cold air that escaped the opening and flooded into the conservatory. Realization dawned, and her mouth fell open as she looked up at the ceiling, her mind's eye seeing directly to the floor above.

"Yes," Blackwell said and, placing a hand on her arm, pulled her into the passageway with him. "Up," he told her and followed as she lifted her skirt, ascending the narrow stone staircase.

Chapter 14

The stairs curved, and the passageway turned as they continued upward until they reached a small landing. Blackwell's torch illuminated a door, and he felt alongside the seam between the door and the frame, searching for what she assumed must be another triggering mechanism.

Lucy's skirts billowed around his legs, and she felt his thigh against hers. A combination of tension over the dank smell, which brought back the horrors of the night before, and the man's proximity had her nerves stretched to the breaking point.

A *click* echoed through the passageway, and she looked up. His face was cast in shadow, barely visible in the dim light. He moved down a few steps and pulled her out of the way as he reached up to nudge the door with his fingers. She grasped the edge of it and pulled it toward them, immediately registering the rush of warm air. Stepping back to the small landing, she entered her bedroom with Blackwell close behind her.

"This would be why your door was still—" Blackwell broke off as he walked around Lucy. He stared at her bedding, which lay in ruins with large slashes and a profusion of eiderdown feathers. His jaw clenched visibly with the subtle movement of his scar. "I cannot believe I insisted you return this morning without at least the company of a 'ton." He paused. "Miss Pickett, you must leave the manor."

"I cannot go," she said quietly. "I will not leave Kate, and she will not leave Jonathan. Something isn't right. I've heard rumblings about a curse and—"

"What curse?" He looked at her, and she fought to keep from retreating a step.

"Some silly Bride's Curse. I mentioned it to you before. I've no doubt it's rooted in nonsense, but I admit I'm growing concerned."

"Oh." Rubbing the back of his neck, he frowned, drawing his brows together. "It is nonsense. Who told you of it?"

Lucy watched him closely. "Arthur."

His nostrils flared slightly. "I suggest you ignore everything he says."

"Why is there no love lost between you?"

His answering expression was flat. "Do not pretend to suggest you can't comprehend the reasons."

She shrugged. "He's harmless enough. Would probably make someone a suitable match." She was well aware that on some level she was baiting him; it was perverse.

Blackwell studied her before finally answering, "Yes, I suppose he probably would."

She fought a scowl at his easy capitulation and followed his gaze back to the torn bedding.

"Miss Pickett, are you not in the least afraid? Your brother would have my head if he knew you were in danger under my roof, and he would be completely justified. Perhaps I should suggest Jonathan take his bride to Paris for an extended holiday."

Lucy shook her head. "I've already tried. Kate feels their honeymoon was vacation enough and wants to familiarize herself with the staff." She paused. "Kate is passive. She lacks a strong hand. Running a household of such magnitude is proving to be a challenge for her, I believe."

"This household runs like clockwork. She needn't do anything."

"I know this, and I believe she does as well. I think she may feel she should prove herself worthy of her station. She is not the countess, but

she is the lady of the house, for all intents and purposes, since you are—"
Lucy nearly bit her tongue.

"Since I am . . ."

She closed her eyes briefly, wondering when she had ever been so
tactless.

"Since I am single? Without a wife of my own? I did try. She seemed
to prefer death to my company."

Lucy cocked a brow, her emotions a swirling mass of mortification,
pity, and exasperation. "What are you suggesting, sir?"

"I am suggesting nothing."

In the end, compassion won out, and she moved closer, though she
folded her arms across her chest to keep from reaching out to him. He
wouldn't appreciate the overture. She decided the wisest course of action
was to redirect the conversation.

"Well, then, as I am a guest of your brother and his wife and refuse to
leave, might I request a chamber that doesn't adjoin another via a dank,
eerie passageway?"

Blackwell lifted the comforter and let it fall back to the bed with
a flurry of small, downy feathers. He looked at her for a long, measured moment. "There are guest rooms in the south wing. I've had Mrs.
Farrell ready one for Oliver. I shall have another made up for you, and
I shall also install a lady's maid so that your reputation might remain
unsullied."

"That is very thoughtful of you, but I do not mind remaining here
in the north wing if another chamber is available. I know you guard your
privacy well. I regret intruding upon it last night."

"Do you?"

Lucy blinked. She hadn't expected that. To be coy or feign innocence?
If he had been a man of Arthur's ilk, she would have been comfortably in
her own element. As it was, Blackwell seemed like a cobra ready to strike.
"Of course. I woke you from sleep and then took your bed. I doubt you
got any rest at all, and I am to blame."

"I did not get any rest, and yes, you are most definitely to blame."

"Well, then, I suppose I owe you a favor."

"Go home."

"Anything but that."

"You are determined to stay."

Lucy nodded.

"Very well. Tomorrow morning I must visit a few tenant families, and in the past, these visits have met with a more favorable outcome if I have a woman along to soften my fierce exterior. You will come with me. As a favor to me."

Her lips twitched. "Any woman will do? What sort do you usually recruit for these appointments?"

"Marie always went with me. I haven't been on any visits since her death."

Lucy, her arms still folded, tightened her fists. Conversations were so much easier for her with people who appreciated sympathy. She swallowed past the sudden lump in her throat. "I would be honored, then."

He nodded once. "In the meantime, I shall have Mrs. Farrell arrange for new sleeping arrangements for you and see that your things are packed up and moved."

"I can pack them myself." Lucy moved to the wardrobe, waving a dismissive hand.

"You'll not stay in here alone."

She glanced over her shoulder as she opened the wardrobe door. "It is broad daylight. Alarming occurrences seem to happen only at night, here." A rustle at the bottom of the wardrobe caught Lucy's attention, and she lifted the hems of several dresses to see the slithering black body of a snake before she stumbled backward in surprise.

"What is it?" Blackwell's eyes widened as the serpent's head poked out from the yards of fabric. "Be still," he snapped at her unnecessarily. She stood rooted to the spot, hardly daring to breathe.

Lucy stared at the reptile, hoping the spots appearing before her eyes were not a warning of pending unconsciousness. She abhorred snakes, had since she was a child, and had suffered a bite that had left her feverish for weeks. From the corner of her eye, she caught Blackwell's slow approach before his torch flew through the air and smashed the head of the reptile against the base of the wardrobe with a sickening, soggy thud.

"I don't mind spiders so much," she said, inhaling and exhaling with more rapidity than was probably wise, "but snakes do rather terrify me."

Blackwell was as white as a sheet. She saw the moment when fear metamorphosed into fury, and he rushed toward her, propelling her toward the door with an arm about her shoulders. "You will not—will *not*—stay in this room."

"I need to get my things," she said, fumbling to withdraw a key from her pocket.

"I will have someone else retrieve your things."

He unlocked the door and pulled her through to the landing overlooking the main hall, past bewildered servants—human and 'ton alike—and down the long hallway into the south wing. He finally stopped at the doors to his suite where he pulled his own key from his pocket and shoved it into the lock, the fingers of his other hand biting into her shoulder. He opened the heavy door and guided her through it, finally glancing down at her face and loosening his grip.

"I appreciate your thoughtfulness." Her fear had her feeling positively weak. "But my notes and journals are in there. They are very important to me, and I'd rather not have anyone pawing through them. We didn't lock the door when we left, and I'm sure it seems silly, but there are some rather sensitive observations in my journals, formulas I am working on . . ." She was babbling and couldn't seem to stop herself. "I realized this morning that I'd left the room unlocked and unattended last night when I . . . came here . . ."

"You were distressed. It's to be expected."

"Yes. Well." Lucy took a deep breath. "I don't much care for snakes."

"Nor do I."

"Clearly. You made quick work of it. Thank you." She shuddered involuntarily, remembering the sound of the torch smashing the creature's head.

"It was a black adder, if I'm not mistaken. They are highly venomous." Blackwell nodded to the left of the large sitting room. "There's a hallway branching off that way." He moved toward it, and she followed him. "This is the countess's quarters. As you can see, it's a fair distance from mine, although still in the same suite, and there are maids' quarters adjoining the main bedchamber."

Lucy looked at him in some shock, not trusting herself to speak for a moment. "This was your mother's room, then."

He nodded.

"And the late Lady Blackwell's."

A muscle worked in his jaw. "Yes."

"Lord Blackwell, I would never dream of imposing in such a way. You'd rather I not be here at all, and to install myself in your late wife's chambers—it hardly bears contemplation."

"Miss Pickett." His tone was measured. "I would not have offered it if I hadn't intended for you to accept it. You insist on staying in my home—very well. But it is my wish that you remain here, where nobody will dare another attempt on your life. As I said, I will assign you a maid, and she can use the adjoining room. Have a gaggle of them in there if you'd like."

Lucy peered through the open door of the countess's chambers. The room was dark—the drapes closed, the furniture covered. "It is most generous, sir. And with any luck, I shall soon find something of use for Kate. I will examine the herbs in the greenhouse today and do a bit more research in my botanical journals. The key to her health is somewhere, I simply need to find it."

"We still don't know why someone would try to kill you. Twice." He muttered almost to himself.

"I am certain some might find me vexing."

He looked at her with eyelids half closed. "That does not even warrant a response. Who have you met or interacted with since your arrival?"

"The three Charlesworths, and Kate and Jonathan, of course. And

Mrs. Farrell, Mr. Grafton, and Mr. Clancy. Martha Watts. And a host of maids and 'tons. Also Dr. MacInnes and Mr. Reed."

"What have you told people of the nature of your visit?"

She shrugged. "Nothing, really. Only that I am here to spend time with my cousin. I did mention to your relatives that I believe Kate may be ill."

He frowned. "They may be irritating in the extreme, but I'm hard pressed to believe any of those three might be inclined to kill you. What would they gain?"

"Nothing." Lucy spread her hands. "Perhaps there is a malfunctioning 'ton in the household. When I was at school, one of our 'ton maids turned three girls' bedrooms upside down before she could be stopped. Her punch card had aged, and the hardware couldn't read it properly. Rather than cleaning, she destroyed the place."

Blackwell nodded. "We had a similar malfunction with one in India. Blasted thing turned its guns on us. I suspect Daniel may have mentioned it—that was how he received the shoulder wound."

She stared at him. "Shoulder wound?"

Blackwell was silent for a moment. "He didn't tell you."

Lucy clamped her lips together and looked into the darkened room at nothing in particular. "No. No, he did not."

"I am . . . I apologize. He clearly meant to keep it to himself, likely so as not to worry you or your mother."

Lucy shook her head. "That stubborn . . ." She wrung her hands, a habit she'd not succumbed to since finishing school had polished it out of her. "I *knew* it."

Blackwell cursed under his breath, and Lucy glanced at him. "You needn't worry, my lord. I shall not give you up to him. I shall encourage him to tell me on his own."

"You expect him to tell you everything?"

"He used to!" She frowned. "Though he's not been the same." Lucy flushed. "I feel as though I lost a friend when he went away to fight and I've yet to get him back."

"You care for him very much."

Lucy's eyes burned with tears that caught her by surprise. "Yes." She turned her head, embarrassed.

"Come," Blackwell said and held out his arm. "I must speak with Mrs. Farrell."

Chapter 15

I must admit, I'm surprised to see you opening the south wing." Oliver looked askance at Miles. "Why the change? Are you no longer worried about unintentionally harming someone?" Oliver poured himself a drink at the sideboard in the third-floor observatory before joining Miles and Sam in the comfortable chairs around the hearth.

Miles shook his head and leaned back against the chair, closing his eyes. He was so very tired. "I'm worried now more than ever, but I'm fairly certain nothing will happen here. If I make my usual trip to the hunting lodge at least a day in advance, nobody will be in any danger. It's been years, and I think the pattern is well-established. I've yet to see a variation, even in extreme circumstances."

"A variation might have been nice in India." Sam crossed one booted foot over his other knee. "The enemy wouldn't have seen it coming."

Miles opened his eyes a fraction and looked at Sam. "You know very well I can't control it."

"You don't know if you can control it because you've never taken the opportunity to find out. What better way than with one of us?" Sam looked at Oliver, who nodded in agreement.

"There is no worse way to find out. I'll not entertain the topic again." He turned his attention to Oliver. "You said you had a promising lead?"

Oliver nodded. "Several of the notes seem to have originated from the mid- to northern regions. Except the last one—I've traced it to Scotland."

Miles blinked. "Scotland?"

"Yes. And I'm hoping you have another note for me. You should, if the writer continues his pattern."

Miles was quiet for a moment. "I did receive another one."

"Where is it?"

"The hunting lodge."

"Did you leave it there?"

"In a manner of speaking."

Oliver raised a brow.

"I burned it."

Oliver's mouth dropped open fractionally. "Why on earth would you burn it?"

Miles braced his elbows on his knees, massaging his temples with his hands. "I was angry, Oliver. I am livid that someone dares to play this game with me."

Oliver turned his attention to the fireplace, his brows tightly drawn. Sam remained wisely silent.

"Well," Oliver finally said, "should you receive another, and I must assume you will, I'd like it sent to me immediately. I don't care where I am—telescribe me and I will give you my location."

Miles nodded. "There's something else." He glanced at his good friends before fixing his gaze on the majestic view outside the large windows. He winced, thinking of Lucy. He gave them what he knew of her history upon arriving at Blackwell, leaving nothing out. He was worried for her safety and didn't have the luxury of attempting to solve the problem on his own.

"I returned to the chamber with her after instructing Mrs. Farrell of the change and helped Miss Pickett gather her papers and books. She was most concerned about them."

Sam nodded. "She should be. The Botanical Aid Society has her exploring theories about counteracting Vampiric Assimilation Aid."

Miles's gut churned with something he couldn't define. "She didn't tell me," he finally muttered. "When did she say this?"

"The other afternoon. I had heard rumors about it in medical circles, that there were a few women on the Botanical Aid Society's research team. Lucy was in the greenhouse, and I happened upon her while taking a stroll after lunch. I asked her, and she confirmed it."

"*Lucy*, is it?"

Sam regarded him before his mouth twitched at the corner. "Yes. She's given me leave to use her Christian name. Am I to assume she's not done the same for you?"

Miles narrowed his eyes. "What are your intentions?"

"My intentions? Blackwell, I have no intentions. I enjoy the lady's company."

Oliver made a noise that sounded suspiciously like a snort, but when Miles looked at him, the man was the picture of innocence. The chime of a clock on the wall signaled the luncheon hour and dispelled the awkward moment.

The day was cool, but not uncomfortably so, and for once the rain had decided to abate. Lucy stood at the threshold of Marie's garden dressed in warm brown breeches and knee-high boots with a cream-colored blouse and brown satin outer corset. The whole of the ensemble was topped with an overcoat that had been tailored to her trim frame. Her fingers were cold despite the leather gloves, but that was nothing new. Unless she wore furred mittens, her fingers were often cold.

Mr. Clancy stood beside her at the gate, perusing the sight before them.

"I don't suppose you have any 'ton servants at your disposal?" she asked.

He nodded curtly. "Aye, I might. How many do ye want?"

Lucy considered the state of the garden, which wasn't so overgrown as to be hopeless, but it was certainly more than she could manage herself. "Five should do the trick, don't you think?"

"I'll have them started up straightaway. They've been down for . . . a while."

Lucy figured they'd been down since Marie's death. "They are still programmed for grounds keeping, then?"

"Aye. I didn't turn them back over to the main house, just put them away for a time."

"How many do you have?"

"Eight."

Lucy moved along the path into the center of the garden. It smelled divine, and she took a deep, appreciative breath, eyes closed. Multitudinous forms of flora mingled to form an olfactory cocktail that had her senses reeling. It was no wonder Marie had loved it so much.

When she opened her eyes, she saw Mr. Clancy observing her with eyes that watered. Before she could ask him if he was well, he turned and left the garden without saying a word.

Lucy thoughtfully watched the empty gate before turning her attention back to the plants. Withdrawing a small black notebook from her cloak pocket, she began making notes. The mesh netting that hung down from her top hat and framed her face warred with her ability to focus on the paper, and she impatiently folded the veil up and out of the way. Sometimes function required fashion take a backseat, a fact with which her school mistresses would have never agreed.

She quickly sketched the garden. With five 'tons helping her, she could easily divide the work and be finished in perhaps a week, maybe less. And the repetitive nature of the manual labor would give her time to mull over Kate's condition and some possible solutions. She'd tried several different herbal concoctions, but each had alleviated only one or two of the symptoms at a time and not the root cause of the illness. Sam had examined her, and he was baffled as well.

Lucy frowned as she moved deeper into the garden, pursing her lips in thought. Perhaps Kate was suffering from an ailment of fatigue. Sam had told her of other cases similar to her cousin's where the afflicted slept sixteen hours a day and it still wasn't enough rest. Except Kate had begun experiencing some nausea as well. Each time Lucy felt she was narrowing in on a solution, Kate developed another odd symptom or complaint.

Also in the back of her mind was Director Lark's answer to her message about the recent vampire killings in the village: The matter was under investigation, but all leads had run cold. It left Lucy feeling unsettled, anxious.

Lucy walked to the wrought-iron gazebo. Ivy grew so thick it draped walls around the whole of it, rendering the interior significantly dark. It was eerie and cold—cold in a way that the rest of the garden wasn't. Lucy had placed one boot on the bottom step, if only to prove to herself that she wasn't afraid, when a yell from the gate arrested her progress.

"Stay out of there," Mr. Clancy shouted. He made his way quickly across the garden, and when he reached Lucy, his face was flushed with exertion. "Do not enter that place," he said, his voice as rough as gravel.

Lucy stepped back onto the ground. "Mr. Clancy, I should very much like to clean it up, to straighten it so that it might be a place of enjoyment again. That beautiful bench inside is completely filthy and covered with dirt and moss. With your permission, I'll restore it to its former glory."

The gardener's gaze hardened more, though she wouldn't have thought it possible. "I've given ye all I'm going ta," he ground out. "Stay out of that gazebo or I'll have it torn ta the ground. I just may do it anyway."

"No, don't. I will leave it be, I give you my word."

Mr. Clancy finally relaxed by degrees: his shoulders dropping, the angry red splotches receding from his cheeks, his expression smoothing. He again resembled the mellow, gnarled old man she'd come to recognize, as opposed to a rage-fueled, gnarled old man.

Lucy moved away from the gazebo that seemed to cause him such consternation. In the back of her mind, she wondered at his reasons for keeping her out of it. Was it because it was Marie's and he couldn't bear the thought of anyone else setting foot in it? Or was it because he was afraid?

"The 'tons are connected to the Tesla station in the garden shack." Mr. Clancy scratched his chin while examining the sky. "They need two hours to fully charge, but there's no telling about the weather."

Lucy nodded. "Mr. Clancy, I've been wondering about some of the herbs in the greenhouse. Mr. Grafton doesn't know where they've come from, and there are a few I've never seen before. Are they yours, by chance?"

The old man drew his brows together. "No, I don't set foot in that place. Grafton—he be verra territorial about it."

"I think I shall take a few samples and set about identifying them. Perhaps I'll do that now while we're waiting for the 'tons to charge."

"Aye, then. Ye'll find me at the garden shack."

With a smile, and making a concerted effort to not look at the gazebo, Lucy left Marie's garden. She quickly made her way along the twisting path, breathing an unconscious sigh of relief when she spied the imposing view of the back of the manor.

Crossing the lawns to the greenhouse, she slipped inside. Withdrawing her plant identifier from her pocket, she walked down the aisle to the back corner where she'd seen the odd plants the first time she'd entered. She stooped down to examine the lower shelf and frowned. Someone had moved the plants in question and replaced them with two pots of basil.

She stood and turned, looking on each shelf above and below the basil pots, wondering if she'd been mistaken about the location of the strange herbs. She took her time walking the greenhouse from back to front, carefully scrutinizing each plant and herb from the large to the small, her brows pinched.

Lucy placed a hand on her hip and narrowed her eyes at the greenhouse in general. Who had she spoken to about the herbs? Mr. Grafton, Mr. Clancy, and Blackwell. One thing was certain—the plants she sought were most definitely gone from the greenhouse.

Perhaps it meant nothing.

Chapter 16

Miles awoke with a start. He wasn't a light sleeper—had never been, really, and even if he had, the war would have drilled it out of him quickly enough. The slightest noises often roused him with alarming results: his heartclock pounding, blood pumping furiously. This evening was no exception. He sat up in bed and stilled his breathing, straining in the silence to hear anything out of the ordinary.

Nothing.

He was likely hyperalert. Even in an unconscious state he must have been well aware of the fact that Lucy Pickett was asleep in his suite. In his dead wife's bedchamber. That was surely the problem. She must have stirred in her slumber, and he heard every movement; compliments of his "condition," he was not unlike the proverbial "Princess and the Pea," who was sensitive to the slightest detail.

With a grunt of disgust, he left the bed and pulled his robe from a bedside chair. Shoving his arms into the sleeves, he exited the bedroom and made his way through the large sitting room and to the countess's chamber doors. They stood tall and closed. Hopefully locked.

He'd been very specific in his instructions. Miss Pickett was to lock her hallway door, the double doors leading to the balcony overlooking the back lawns, and the door inside her dressing room that led to his dressing room.

Lightly tapping her door with the back of his knuckles, he leaned in close to listen. If he didn't hear anything within the next thirty seconds, he would assume all was well and leave. Thirty seconds turned into a full minute. He knocked again. It wasn't long before he heard movement on the other side of the door, followed by the click of the lock sliding back.

The door opened a crack, and a thread of light spilled across the hallway. Lucy peered up at him, blinking. "Is something wrong?"

Miles stared at her, his mouth going dry as he remembered how she'd felt in his arms. "I thought I heard something." He suddenly felt very foolish. "You are well, then?"

Lucy rubbed at her temple and then brushed her hair off her shoulder and away from her face. "I believe so. If there was a noise, I didn't hear it."

Miles nodded. "Good. Very good."

"Yes."

"You haven't seen . . ."

"Your sister?"

Miles nodded again.

"No. Not yet, anyway. Perhaps you've effectively scared everyone off, mortal and spirit alike." Lucy smiled and rubbed her eye. Her fingers were slender, the nails perfectly shaped and tended. There wasn't a detail about her that seemed amiss. Even the tendrils and curls that fell around her face, mussed from her sleep, seemed to fit her, didn't make her any less polished or cultured. He thought of the way he'd found her in his bed only that morning, sprawled and disheveled, and smiled.

"Are you well, then, my lord?" Lucy asked him.

"You should call me Miles. We are suite mates, after all."

"Which is precisely why I should continue to address you properly."

Miles frowned. That hadn't gone at all as he'd expected. He'd been fully prepared for her to give him leave to call her "Lucy" as she'd done for Sam. "Well, then," he said. "I bid you good night. Tomorrow following breakfast we will make our visits to my tenants after making a quick stop at the apothecary. Lock your door."

She paused before nodding once. "Good night."

"Good night." He waited until he heard the lock turn before returning to his own bedchamber. He tried not to think about the fact that Miss Pickett was far more distracting than his wife had ever been. Of course, Clara had made it abundantly clear she wanted absolutely nothing to do with him. How she'd figured they would ever conceive a child, he didn't know. On their wedding night she'd cried and cowered, and he hadn't used even a modicum of patience to allay her fears. Instead, he'd left her alone and decided to give her time to grow used to the idea that she would have to lie with him at least once if they were to produce an heir, but before a month was out, she was dead.

His mood suddenly dark, he closed his door with a little more force than was strictly necessary.

⚙

"You must go, I insist," Kate said to Lucy the next morning.

"If you are unwell, I should stay." Lucy placed the backs of her fingers against Kate's brow. She was warm, but not alarmingly so.

"Nonsense. Go with Blackwell. If he's requested your company, it must mean he likes you. I shall be fine. Jonathan stepped out for a moment and will be back with some tea. Says he wants to brew it himself."

Lucy frowned. "Does he not trust the kitchen help?"

Kate shrugged. "I believe he's growing leery of everyone."

"Again, I think the two of you should leave. Go on holiday for a while."

Kate shook her head. "Travel, with my nausea? The very thought makes my stomach turn. No, I shall stay put and fight whatever malady plagues me."

Lucy thought of the strange herbs in the greenhouse that were suddenly gone and wondered for the hundredth time if Kate were being poisoned. Leaning forward, Lucy placed a kiss on Kate's forehead and squeezed her hand. She made her way from the bedroom to the main hall where she descended the stairs and headed for the kitchen.

"Miss Pickett," Mr. Grafton said in surprise, "we are nearly ready to serve breakfast. Do you need something?"

Lucy eyed the man, rethinking her impulse to take Kate's cause to the staff. She knew close to nothing about the people who resided under Blackwell's roof with the exception of Kate herself. For all she knew, the rumors were true and Blackwell had killed his wife and sister. Kate might simply be the next in line.

That makes no sense, though. To what end?

Lucy spied Jonathan and joined him with a quick smile at Mr. Grafton. "Just checking on Kate's tea."

Jonathan glanced up, his face grim, and the smile he gave her was strained. "Nearly ready," he said. "I'm giving her a rather weak brew and some plain toast with a bit of jam and butter."

Lucy patted his arm, pondering two things: If Jonathan were harming Kate in some way, he would certainly know by now that Lucy was not about to be put off or sent home, and if he were innocent and truly the loving picture of a spouse he appeared to be, he might find comfort in the fact that he had an ally.

"I'll remain here for as long as it takes," Lucy murmured to Jonathan. "We will find a solution to whatever ails her."

Jonathan glanced over his shoulder and then back to the teacup, where he stirred the liquid slowly. "People keep speaking of the curse," he whispered, barely moving his lips. "I worry that Kate will hear it."

"Nonsense. I do not place stock in such things. Nor does Kate."

"Nor do I. But there are those who do."

Lucy shrugged. "So let them."

Jonathan set the spoon down and reached for a saucer. Placing it and the teacup atop a tray, he glanced at Lucy. "I should hate for Kate to be burdened by the rumors. She is feeling badly enough as it is. She doesn't need the staff gossiping about her."

"Staff will gossip regardless of the issue. If it isn't this, it will be something else." She gave him a small smile and patted him on the arm.

Jonathan finished Kate's tray and climbed the servant's stairs just off the kitchen to the second floor. What a singular man, he was, Lucy thought. He served his wife as a personal maid would without giving it a second thought.

As she made her way down the hall from the kitchen, she saw Blackwell standing at the breakfast room doorway.

"There you are," he said. "You are late." He watched her, his brows drawn.

"I am not late; breakfast has not yet arrived from the kitchen." As she drew closer, she noted fine lines around his eyes and a faint smudge of darkness beneath them. "And you didn't sleep well."

He paused as though weighing the words of a possible response. "I trust you did?" he finally said.

She nodded. "Blissfully. Thank you for providing the peace of mind."

He smiled, although it clearly lacked humor. "Seems like a commodity that ought to be a given when visiting the home of a relative."

"I've told you I do not judge you harshly over that which you have no control. You've shown me every courtesy."

Blackwell lowered his voice. "I've discreetly questioned some of the staff. None of them claim to have any knowledge of the snake in your wardrobe or how it came to be there."

"Someone is seeking to frighten me off. I must have made an enemy somewhere along the line."

He frowned, inching infinitesimally closer until she could smell his aftershave and that indefinable *something* that seemed to draw her to him against her better judgment.

"You oughtn't to go about alone."

"I do not know whom to trust," she whispered, giving voice to an unconscious fear.

"Trust me," he murmured. "Or Jonathan." A glance at his face revealed clear tension.

"Nobody else? Not even Mrs. Farrell or Mr. Grafton? Martha Watts, the stable mistress?" Her mouth lifted in a smile. "They seem innocent enough."

He didn't share the lightness of the mood she was trying to create. "Yet your cousin lies ill, and you are nearly killed twice."

She sobered and drew in a breath. "I trust you."

He shook his head slightly. "Probably not wise," he muttered.

Lucy raised a brow. "You only just told me that you are but one of two people who are certain to not wish me harm."

He looked at her for a long moment before finally offering his arm. "Mr. Grafton is coming with breakfast. Let's eat so we can be on our way."

Breakfast followed the same pattern as it had every other morning at Blackwell Manor, with the notable absence of Kate. Lucy's nerves stretched taut as she tamped down her worry over her cousin and replaced it instead with thoughts of riding around Blackwell lands with one very irascible earl who set her pulse pounding and kept her slightly off-kilter.

He disappeared into his den immediately following breakfast after giving her instructions to meet him in ten minutes at the stables with her warmest outer clothing but not necessarily a riding habit. What the others might have thought of the fact that she was going out with him, she could only speculate. Arthur had looked positively sulky, Aunt Eustace angry, Candice contemplative.

Samuel told Oliver he wanted to show him his progress on his most recent mechanical project in the observatory, and Lucy fought the urge to ask if she might see it later as well. Candice had pouted about the fact that the three gentlemen seemed to spend so much time in that "infernal observatory," which was hardly the thing to do in a house full of mixed company and cherished guests. The comment had served to pique Lucy's curiosity that there was something not only scientific but also apparently fairly secretive in nature happening on the third floor. She considered methods for manipulating an invitation out of Dr. MacInnes.

Mr. Arnold retrieved Lucy's heavy cloak and gloves from the cloakroom just off the front hall entry. She exited the house and walked around the side toward the stables, which were situated down a gradual slope lined with grass. She pulled her fur-lined hood over her head in the cooling air and tucked a few errant curls away from her face.

A quick glance inside the stables told her that Blackwell was either out of sight at the back of the enormous room or he hadn't yet arrived from the house.

Martha Watts called out to Lucy, giving a quick nod with her head. "Miss Pickett, his lordship's waitin' for ye around the other side in the autocar garage."

Lucy thanked the woman and walked around the stable to the connected garage at the back. A variety of polished and smooth conveyances and auto-propelled craft stood in orderly rows, ready for the lord of the manor. A few more were in various states of disassembly as a handful of 'tons worked to repair damage and replace worn parts.

She caught sight of Blackwell speaking with one of the mechanics, who was bent down and tightening a bolt on one of the double-seater auto-propelled Travelers, which resembled an open-horse carriage.

"Good as new, she is," the man said with a grunt as he stood and wiped his hands with a rag. "Replaced the broken cogs myself."

Blackwell nodded. "Good man. I trust the roof is repaired?"

"Yessir, m'lord. I just finished oiling the hinges."

Blackwell looked up as Lucy approached. He extended a hand to her as he flipped the carriage stairs down with one foot. "Do the same for the other double-seater," he said to the mechanic as Lucy took his hand and climbed into the conveyance. "I want them both in working order at all times."

"Yessir. And, m'lord?"

Blackwell turned back to the man as Lucy settled in and arranged her skirts. "Yes?"

"Mr. Charlesworth asked to use one o' 'em later this afternoon. Didn't say where he was goin'."

Blackwell's dark brows lowered in a fierce scowl as he climbed into the driver's seat on Lucy's right. "He is not to use anything in this garage. It is enough that he makes use of the stables."

"Very good, m'lord."

Lucy looked askance at Blackwell as he fired the motor to life and maneuvered the Traveler out of the large double doors and into the yard. Lucy was impressed. After the initial wind up, the engine settled into a low purr that allowed for comfortable conversation.

"Well, then," she said to Blackwell, who handled the Traveler with practiced ease, "where are we headed?"

"We will first stop at the apothecary in town—I have a few items to retrieve, and I thought you might see if anything sparks your interest for Kate—and then we will visit four families."

Lucy pulled the collar of her cloak up against her neck. "You said they are tenants. Have they been on the land for generations, then?"

"Yes." Blackwell glanced at her and adjusted the heating mechanism. She felt a warm surge of air against her feet, and the seat beneath them increased slightly in temperature until she was quite comfortable.

"Oh, that's lovely. We can ride with the top down and still stay warm. The heated seats must be a new feature, yes? I thought I was abreast of recent developments. Daniel likes to remain informed, and he shares his knowledge of new gadgetry and conveniences with all and sundry."

She thought she detected the hint of a twitch about Blackwell's lips before he turned his attention back to the path in front of them.

"I do enjoy the fresh air," he said as they left the front drive and began the twisting journey through the wooded miles between Blackwell Manor and town. "Unless the weather turns, we should be fine."

They lapsed into a comfortable silence as the Traveler carried them under the gnarled trees that served as a canopy for several miles. "Not nearly so intimidating in the daylight," she murmured as she turned her gaze upward and detected patches of sky through the limbs.

"A sentiment that holds true for many things."

She looked at his profile, catching her breath at the delicious contrast of his olive-toned skin against the black hair. "That is true. Although there is a certain allure to the mystery."

He caught her eye with one brow raised. "You are one for adventure, then? You prefer danger to safety?"

"Mmm, no, but I do prefer the unique over the ordinary. Do you travel much?"

"Around Britain, a fair amount. But beyond the war, not much else. My mother took Marie and me to the Continent once when we were very young."

"Did you enjoy it?"

"I did. I haven't thought of it until now."

"I do so enjoy seeing how other people live. My home is full of things I've collected. My mother despairs of ever reclaiming the parlor for herself." Lucy smiled at the thought of her family and made a mental note to telescribe her mother upon her return to Blackwell.

A slight breeze blew across the open body of the Traveler, carrying with it that familiar scent that belonged uniquely to the earl. She tipped the brim of her black top hat, angling it against the wind and tugging the tulle down just below her eyes. She shifted fractionally closer to him. Just to remain warm, of course.

Blackwell leaned forward to flip a switch on the front control panel, and Lucy placed a hand on his arm. "Oh, no, do not raise the top on my account."

"You are certain?"

He left the switch alone and rested his hand on his thigh while steering the conveyance with his other. His broad shoulder subtly shielded hers, and she fought the urge to rest her head against him. "Most definitely," she said. "I find I am rather enjoying the breeze."

Chapter 17

Miles was more than grateful Lucy didn't want him to put the top of the Traveler into place. He was warmer than he'd ever been in his life at the feel of her arm just beneath his. The knowledge that he could shift his hand mere inches and place it comfortably on her knee had him considering loosening his tie and unbuttoning his collar. The lady was either incredibly brave or incredibly naïve.

They eventually wound their way out of the wooded tunnel and reached the outskirts of town, passing the airfield on their left.

"My brother's ships." Lucy pointed at two airships bearing the Pickett logo that were docked in place, awaiting passengers and cargo. Daniel's fleet stood head and shoulders above his competitors. They were sleek in design, quick in travel, and plush enough to satisfy even the most discerning customer.

"He's done well," Miles said with a nod. "You must be very proud."

"I am." Lucy turned her face to his, her smile slipping. "He's worked so hard. Too hard."

"Sometimes it's easier to remain busy," he said quietly. "Too much thinking can be dangerous."

"I want to fix him." She turned her gaze back to the road, but to his gratification, she didn't pull away physically.

"Unfortunately, some things cannot be fixed. Or they take an incredibly long time."

"I can fix anything." She smiled at him, holding his gaze with those incredibly blue eyes. "Well, perhaps not anything. *Almost* anything."

He fought his own smile. Those muscles were rusty from disuse, and he was vaguely uncomfortable with it. Open up too much to this woman and he would find himself in a world of hurt. "Name something impressive you've been able to fix."

"Hmm." She tapped her lower lip with her fingertip. "I arranged a social for the Botanical Aid Society last year that fed and entertained nearly five hundred people."

"You attended finishing school. I should hope you would be able to accomplish such a feat."

"With only a twenty-four-hour notice."

That gave him pause. "But the plans had already been laid, yes?"

"No. The organizer fled the country to avoid embezzlement charges. It was only after he was gone that we realized he not only had done nothing to prepare for the social but also had taken all of the money with him."

"Well, then, I stand corrected. That is indeed an impressive accomplishment."

"You, sir, are mocking me."

"Not at all."

"I should like to see you perform such a miracle."

He snorted. "I would hire someone else to do it. Problem solved."

"Yes. You would hire someone like me to do it. Doesn't take much talent to hand over a fistful of cash."

"I'm curious, Miss Pickett—I've heard through the rumor mill that you are quite well-known in scientific circles as an excellent researcher. I wonder why you wouldn't list those accomplishments first before something more mundane. Ordinary." He glanced at her and was surprised to see a slight flush to her cheeks.

"I do not like to boast."

He laughed out loud, and it caught him entirely off guard.

Her answering expression spoke clearly of outrage, whether real or feigned he was uncertain. "I am most modest!"

Miles attempted to rein in his mirth when he realized she was genuinely distressed. "You *are* modest," he said as they made their way into the town's center. "Modest about that which I would think you should be most boastful."

He felt her gaze upon his face and glanced at her out of the corner of his eye. "What is it?"

"You've been engaging in the rumor mill about me?" One perfectly arched brow lifted.

He opened his mouth to sputter a litany of denials, then clamped it shut and gathered his thoughts. "I seek to know about those who spend time under my roof." He pulled his emotional cloak firmly about himself. "Forewarned is forearmed."

Her lips quirked into a smug smile, blast her, and she turned her gaze forward again. "If you were curious, you need only have asked."

It was with no small amount of relief that Miles spied the apothecary shop and pulled the Traveler to the waiting spot near the front door. He secured the vehicle and helped her alight, his fingers tightening fractionally, unintentionally, on hers before releasing her hand.

The handful of people inside the shop monopolized the attention of the harried apothecary, and Lucy turned to the wares displayed on shelves along the back wall. "I believe I will purchase a few things while we're here," she said as he followed her.

He observed her closely as she read labels on bottles, tracing her finger along some and whispering to herself. She had lifted the veil on her top hat upon entering the shop, and her cheeks were becomingly pink from the cold outside air. Lightly running one finger underneath her nose, she sniffed and squinted at a small label while retrieving a white handkerchief from her cloak pocket. He shook his head. He was intrigued simply watching the woman wipe her nose.

He didn't register the whispering coming from the corner until he noticed that Lucy's attention was no longer on the shelves. She had turned to the pair—likely a mother and daughter—who cast furtive glances in his direction and then looked hastily away as he made eye contact with them.

"Did you have something you'd like to say?" Lucy said to the pair, her voice even and quiet.

"I beg your pardon?" the older woman said, her face darkening by degrees until she was decidedly blushing.

"It's only that I heard you whispering about His Lordship, the Earl of Blackwell, and I wondered if you desired an introduction."

Miles leaned casually against one shelf, his hands in his pockets, and watched a woman defend him for the first time in his life.

"I, well . . ." the woman stammered. The younger woman looked at Lucy with her mouth hanging open.

"I mean, he's right here," Lucy said. "And I'm a guest at Blackwell Manor—we are practically related. I would be more than happy to conduct the formalities."

Lucy's profile showed a pleasant expression, her mouth a genial smile. Her eyes, however, told a different story altogether. He wasn't sure if it was the slight tightening at the corners that spoke of her true mood or the fact that she watched the women unblinking, boldly.

Silence stretched uncomfortably for one heartbeat, two, and then the woman found her voice. "Oh, no, I wouldn't dream," she murmured.

Lucy waved her hand. "It is no bother, truly, especially as you seem to be a woman of some quality and bearing. Upbringing."

The younger woman swallowed visibly and nudged her companion, who threw a final look at Lucy, a mortified glance at him, and the two made their way past him and out of the shop.

"Can't even manage a curtsey." Lucy shook her head. "Must have been raised in a barn."

"I didn't hear what they were saying," he admitted, feeling nearly as stunned now that the scene was over as the two women probably did.

"It doesn't bear repeating. They were ignorance personified. Oh, look, I do believe it's our turn."

The apothecary approached and bobbed a quick bow. "Apologies, my lord, for the delay. I have the items you telescribed for, just behind the counter."

"Excellent." Miles glanced at Lucy—she had turned her attention back to the bottles lining the shelves—and followed the man to the front of the shop. Other people had entered, and a path cleared itself as the small crowd moved out of his way.

He was accustomed to it, had told himself early on that it was their deference to his title, but he knew the truth, and it somehow never got any easier. People avoided him because he was large, his expression was always fierce, and he had an ugly slash of a scar running down the entire side of his face. There was no hiding it. It was there for the world to see, and the world generally didn't like it. The rumors that had circulated since Clara's and Marie's deaths had only intensified the degree to which people gawked and whispered.

Miles paid for the small box of medicines the apothecary handed him as Lucy approached the counter, a few bottles in hand.

"Do you happen to have any Burgmary in stock?" she asked as she placed her selections on the countertop and opened her reticule.

"Nay, miss, not today. I should have some next week. Would you like me to send you a message when it comes in?"

"That would be lovely." Lucy gifted him with a smile that had the older man blushing. The apothecary busied himself wrapping Lucy's purchases, stammering something about sending a message by telescribe to the Tesla Room at the manor.

Miles sucked in a breath and, with a slight shake of his head, turned from the counter, deciding to wait for her by the door. He was as affected by Lucy as the old man was. Any more charm from her and he'd be writing sickening sonnets and singing beneath her balcony. Which was actually quite near his own.

Blast.

It was definitely time to remove himself. He was drawn to her, and it did not bode well. For all that she seemed unafraid of him, gently flirted, even, she was not a woman with whom one dallied and then left on mutually good terms. She was a lady with polish, intelligence, grace, and wit. She was a happy person, content with her identity. He had no business finding himself attracted to her for any reason other than the most superficial, and nobody could fault him for that. She was beautiful.

She was also Daniel's sister.

A woman in line behind Lucy glanced at him as he waited, and then made a comment to the gentleman standing next to her. Lucy completed her purchase, gave the couple behind her a quick remark in low tones that he couldn't hear, and then made her way to him at the door. Deliberately placing her hand upon his arm, she thanked him warmly for holding the door open and stepped out of the apothecary shop.

Lucy fumed but hid it well. She knew she hid it well because she knew how to behave. It seemed the entire town of Coleshire lacked manners. It was true that she'd half believed the rumors about the Earl of Blackwell before she'd met him; she'd had no cause to believe otherwise. Claiming an acquaintance with him, however, had changed things.

People looked at him as though he were Beelzebub himself. The entire apothecary shop had stared and whispered, and he hadn't heard a word of it. Either it didn't bother him or he had grown so accustomed to it that he didn't notice the rude behavior. *The lot of you are ridiculous!* she had wanted to shout. *And cruel.* The man needed a champion, even if he didn't realize it.

Dark storm clouds gathered overhead. Blackwell handed her up into the Traveler and glanced over as he settled in beside her.

"Hand me the box," she said and gestured to the package he'd purchased. "I'll hold it for you." He gave it to her, and she balanced it on her lap with her own bag. "It's a good thing we stopped. I was able to buy some things to mix in a brew for Kate that Mr. Grafton doesn't have in the greenhouse. What are your purchases for?"

As Blackwell started the Traveler's engines, the first few drops of rain began to fall. With a slight frown, he flipped the switch for the convertible roof, and the partitions slid and clicked into place like a large fan unfurling. It settled around the front and side windows, which Blackwell rolled up with the twist of a crank. In a matter of moments, the vehicle was secured.

"Two of the tenants we are visiting today have chronic illnesses that require medication. I try to visit at least twice a year to deliver it and see to their general welfare." He seemed almost sheepish at the admission.

Her lips quirked. The Beast of Blackwell Manor was bashful. "That's very magnanimous of you, my lord."

He glanced at her as the vehicle warmed to a comfortable degree. "It surprises you." He paused, his head slightly tipped. "It should."

"That's ridiculous. I'm not surprised in the least." Although she would have been a week ago.

"What is it, Miss Pickett, that sets you apart from the rest of the world?" He guided the vehicle away from the shop and down the road.

"In what manner?"

"Are you not afraid I murdered my wife? My sister?"

Well. That was certainly blunt. Lucy looked at his profile, which was clear and strong. Very much like the man himself, and she wondered if he would thank her for saying so. Throwing caution to the wind, she opted for the truth.

"You are not, at your core, as you would have people believe. You've been sorely misjudged, and you foster the harsh exterior as a means of self-preservation. You are an enigma, a contradiction."

Blackwell's expression was flat. "My, but you are a dramatic one."

"Not in the least. You are abrupt and at times even rude, certainly to those for whom you have no patience, and you dare the world to mock you to your face. And yet you adored your sister, love your brother, and worry over the health of my cousin. You have taken every measure to be sure I am safe in your home. I believe I've mentioned it before, but I value my brother's judgment. Daniel would not be associated with one who had it in him to murder in cold blood."

Blackwell's jaw clenched as he turned his attention back to the road. The raindrops fell more quickly, splattering on the front window and necessitating the use of the Traveler's window-cleaning blades. "You do not know what I am capable of."

"Forgive me, my lord, but why would you trouble yourself to warn me if you were full of nefarious intentions? It does not stand to reason, and you strike me very much as a man of reason."

"People sometimes behave in ways that are beyond their control."

"You fancy yourself a lunatic, then? Or perhaps you have an illness that renders you incoherent? A babbling, raging menace?"

"You mock me, Miss Pickett, after your fine demonstration of defense at the apothecary?"

"I do not mock you. I do not believe you are prone to behavior you cannot control."

He smiled, but his expression would have appeared less menacing had he scowled. "You are naïve."

"Perhaps. But not about this."

His lips tightened. "As much as you would like to believe it, the world is not always a pleasant place."

She narrowed her eyes. "I am not a fool, my lord. My work itself stems from a need to combat a depravity that turns my stomach."

"And yet you continue with no thought of your own safety because you insist on trying to fix a world that doesn't want to be fixed," he bit out.

"Perhaps your corner of the world doesn't want improvement, but I daresay the families of the two recent vamp victims in town would have appreciated the intervention of what I hope to discover." Her temper flared, and Lucy reminded herself that she was a paragon of patience.

He shook his head. "That Daniel allows this is beyond reason. Do you never wonder if you are being followed? Pursued? Those vamp attacks occurred only after you arrived at Blackwell."

The hold on her temper snapped. "Daniel doesn't 'allow' me anything. I am an adult woman in my own right, and I have worked tirelessly for my current station. And as for the assumption that I have vampires on my trail—that is absurd. I am one research botanist. If I thought for even a moment that my presence would bring others harm, the last place I would go would be anywhere near my family."

He was quiet, and she fumed in silence. Societal views on women's roles were shifting, and it wasn't an oddity that she'd had training beyond finishing school or that she held a position of respect in the world of science. But old attitudes tended to remain in place, and Blackwell was not the first to question Daniel's actions as it concerned her own choices.

She forced herself to relax and take a deep breath as they traveled into the village outskirts, passing small homes along the way. When they reached Blackwell land, she was gratified to see the residences in good condition, neat and tidy, well-tended.

Blackwell pulled alongside one of the homes and paused, eyes on hers, before finally switching the engine off. Rather than speak, he exited the vehicle on his own side, held a hand out for the medicine, and then motioned for her to exit as well. She placed her hand in his and stepped out into the cold rain, gasping slightly when he pulled her forward toward the porch overhang and out of the weather in the blink of an eye.

His heavy scowl was in place, and she was tempted to admonish him for it before the tenants opened the door but decided she'd snapped at him enough for one afternoon. And as for apologies, well, he clearly needed a lesson or two.

Chapter 18

Lucy worked in Marie's garden with several grounds-keeping 'tons. It had been a relief to return to the manor after delivering medicine with Blackwell; conversation on the way back had been stilted at best. She was seeing significant progress now in the garden, which made her happy.

Mr. Clancy approached from the gate with a note. It was a request for her presence in the main house, and she frowned at the paper. She had established a good rhythm with the 'tons and hated to be interrupted. Mr. Clancy insisted he would stay in the garden and continue supervising.

Following the request on the note, she made her way to Blackwell's study, where she found the earl and Kate, along with a young woman Lucy had never met. When Blackwell indicated a vacant chair in the seating around the hearth, she took it without acknowledging him.

"This is Miss Hazel Hughes, and she is a Medium, an expert in her field," Miles said. "As activities of late concern all of us, I believe a discussion is in order so Miss Hughes will be better apprised of the situation."

Kate gasped. "Lucy, you didn't tell me!"

Lucy closed her eyes. She wished Blackwell would have given her some kind of warning he was bringing in a Medium.

"I didn't want you to worry, Kate," she said. "But it seems help is at hand!" She deliberately turned her attention to Miss Hughes. Lucy judged the woman to be roughly her same age and wondered that such a young Medium was already considered an expert in her field. People sometimes questioned Lucy's own work, however—*Present company included,* she thought with a sniff—and she decided to set her initial reaction to the side.

Hazel Hughes wore the latest in fashion and a lovely, elaborate hat adorned with lace, feathers, and flowers and a pair of stylish goggles perched on the brim. Her thick hair was beautifully curled and coiffed, the color of dark honey. Her eyes were a striking shade of gold and green and showed a fair amount of—apprehension? A frightened Medium? Perhaps she was intimidated by Blackwell. He did have that effect on people.

As Hazel cleared her throat and began to speak, Lucy stole a glance at Blackwell. His focus was on Lucy, and she held his gaze without flinching. The fact that he had shown a compassionate nature when they had visited the four tenants even after the awkward exchange in the Traveler only served to further her contemplation. He'd provided medicine for ill women and children, for heaven's sake. What was she supposed to do with that?

" . . . see the spirit when she appears," Hazel was saying.

"I haven't seen her," Kate said, "but I know she's been in my chambers on more than one occasion—there have been flashes, and the sense that someone is there."

"She has been in my chambers, too," Lucy said.

"Have you seen her fully formed or just a sense of her?" Hazel asked Lucy.

"Fully formed." Lucy swallowed. "Miss Hughes, I do not know exactly when Marie may show herself again to me, but I'm more than happy to have help interpreting her. What is your usual method when you perform this service?"

"Well," she began, "I suppose I should remain here for a few days—I believe that's how it's done."

An awkward silence settled in the room. Lucy was the first to recover her voice. "So this would be your first time, then?"

"I was under the impression you came highly recommended," Blackwell said to the young woman, who blushed to the roots of her hair. Lucy shot him a look of reproach, but he didn't so much as glance her way.

"I come from a long line of Light Magick users," Hazel told him. "Each generation has been skilled at Medium work, and I am . . . told . . . I possess the traits necessary for"—she swallowed audibly—"communing with the deceased." Hazel clasped her gloved fingers in her lap, twisting them and gripping them before straightening her spine slightly.

Blackwell closed his eyes and pinched the bridge of his nose with his thumb and forefinger.

Lucy bit the inside of her cheek and made a decision. "Miss Hughes, the late Lady Marie visits me at night. I would be happy to share the suite of chambers I occupy so that you'll be close by when she arrives. There's a room adjoining mine that I believe would suit you quite well."

Lucy felt Blackwell's stare but didn't make eye contact with him. What did the man expect? Somebody had to take matters in hand, and if he was too irritated to do it, Lucy would deal with it herself. If he had issues that there would be yet another woman in his precious south wing, he had best learn to resolve them.

"Miss Hughes," Kate said, "I have often heard of Mediums who can call spirits to them. Is this something you do?"

Hazel nodded, but her hesitation spoke volumes. "I am certainly willing to try."

"So," Blackwell interjected, "you would come to this house under the pretense of expertise and then insult me with weak expressions of what you *might* be able to accomplish?"

Hazel Hughes colored significantly again, and Lucy's heart turned over. The young woman had been thrown into something far beyond her capacity.

"Miss Hughes, I will not be requiring your services, and, furthermore,

I intend to—" Blackwell started, but Lucy cut him off by quickly rising from her seat and making her way to him. She placed her hand on his arm and tugged.

"Lord Blackwell, I have remembered an urgent matter I was to have brought to your attention. Walk with me, please, while I explain. Miss Hughes, I shall return straightaway."

Blackwell looked at her, his eyes fairly sparking with anger and the promise of retribution. Feeling far less bravery than she exhibited, she lightly shoved the man to propel him from the room. When her efforts met with all the effectiveness of trying to fell an oak tree, she looked up at his face with her eyes narrowed.

A muscle flexed in his jaw, and he gripped the hand she'd placed on his forearm. She thought he might thrust it from him, but he instead pulled it firmly through his arm and made his way from the den with large strides she struggled to match. He walked straight ahead, anchoring her to his side. In silence, he pulled her into the library, where he shut the wide double doors behind them and turned to face her.

"What in the *world* possessed you to speak for me?" he ground out. "I will not have that charlatan spending one night under my roof, let alone in my *suite*."

Lucy took a deep breath. "Listen here, Blackwell. As long as my cousin is living in this home, I plan to help her present a façade of gentility and polish to the world in the name of this family. I'll not have her living under a cloud of scandal and suspicion merely because she is now tied to your name by marriage. You were behaving like an absolute oaf, and it seems to me that Hazel Hughes deserves a chance to try her skills."

"Her skills?" he exploded, throwing his arms wide. "What skills? She has none!"

"You do not know that!"

Blackwell spat out a curse beneath his breath, brushing past her to a sidebar along the wall where he poured himself a substantial drink. "Dr. MacInnes's *mother* suggested her because Miss Hughes came highly recommended from *her* friend, who also happens to be Miss Hughes's mother!"

"She said it herself—she comes from a long line of talent. If she truly has the gift, we will know by tonight. If not, you may send her on her way with your blessing."

"Oh, well, I thank you for that, Miss Pickett." He took a long swallow of the amber liquid and slammed the empty tumbler on the bar. "Is there anything else in which you'd like to instruct me before I go about the rest of my day?"

She wondered if steam escaped her ears. "As a matter of fact, yes. You may not have wanted the earldom, but it is yours. Regardless of your feelings about your responsibilities, you have the memory of your mother to consider. At least behave as though she were watching. Which she may very well be!"

Lucy spun on her heel and yanked open one of the library doors only to find three female 'tons listening at the keyhole. They jumped back in surprise, and Lucy stared them down as they scattered before she turned back to Blackwell. "You may consider having some of the staff reprogrammed. For 'tons with bland personalities, they are awfully nosy."

She returned to the den where she caught Miss Hughes at the door. "Please, do stay," Lucy said to the young woman, whose eyes were bright with unshed tears.

"His lordship is absolutely correct," Miss Hughes said and attempted to move past Lucy. "I am here only because—" She cut herself off and chewed on her lip, inspecting something on her glove.

"Miss Hughes, is it true, about your lineage?"

Hazel nodded.

"Have you made any efforts to work as a Medium?"

"No. My mother . . . suggested . . . this would be an excellent opportunity to begin my career and carry on the family tradition. She is . . . difficult."

"I see no reason you shouldn't at least make an attempt. Stay the one night, and if you are dissatisfied with your performance, you will have the reassurance of knowing you made a noble effort. And you'll be able to report to your mother with a clear conscience."

Miss Hughes shook her head slightly and finally lifted her gaze to Lucy's. She looked as though she wanted to say something further but merely nodded. "Very well. Thank you for placing your trust in me."

"Think nothing of it. We shall settle you in the room by mine and see what we can't conjure up tonight, yes?"

It might have been Lucy's imagination, but she thought Hazel looked slightly green at the suggestion.

The large clock in the hallway struck midnight, and Lucy sat on the sofa by the hearth in the library with a very tense Miss Hughes. Lucy had made a point of telling anyone within earshot that they were not attempting to conjure Lady Marie until the following night so that she might ease Hazel into the task tonight without an audience.

"Suppose you tell me what you know of spirits before we begin," Lucy said.

Hazel brightened and sat back on the sofa. "I know plenty. I have a very good memory—never forget anything I read. What sorts of things would you like to know?"

Lucy spread her hands. "I know next to nothing about ghosts. I wasn't even certain they existed before I arrived here. To begin with, why can I not speak to Lady Marie? Or she to me?"

"Most spiritualists will tell you that there are only certain people who can commune with the dead. It is a gift that seems to be bestowed rather than learned."

"And can Mediums actually hear spirits speak?"

Hazel nodded. "Yes, they converse as easily as you and I are right now."

"And what is it that most spirits seem to want? Why do you suppose

Marie Blake still lingers at this house? And why would she be spending so much time with me when I clearly cannot converse with her?"

Hazel's brow pinched in a frown, and she glanced at the doors leading to the hallway. "I have heard rumors only, of course," she said in an undertone, "and I hesitate to suggest anything unfair about his lordship or the family . . ."

"I suspect that those who died here recently did not succumb to natural causes," Lucy told her. "So whether or not the rumors you've heard are true, there is indeed something unsettling about recent events. Please do speak freely."

Hazel chewed on her lip as she looked into the flames gently dancing in the fireplace. "Spirits who have met a violent end often seek out those they feel might have the strength to help them, and they are allowed a certain amount of time in this realm to attempt to find justice for what is usually an untimely demise."

"How much time?"

"Between six months and a year. Sometimes longer, depending on the circumstances, which is why there are some structures that seem to be haunted for years, even decades. There must be some reasoning behind the differences in individual instances, but nobody that I know of has been able to discern it. And each visit is only allowed to last a finite amount of time."

Lucy frowned, thinking. "That would explain why Marie doesn't linger. I've wondered why she disappears when she seems so clearly determined to tell me something." She paused. "Both Clara and Marie have been dead for six months exactly."

Hazel looked at her. "If his lordship's sister is going to make her message known, she may be running short of time."

"Why isn't the late Lady Blackwell lingering here as well?"

"Did she die before her time?"

"I suspect as much, although I'm not certain."

"Do you know much of her personality?"

Lucy nodded. "Some."

"Typically, the intensity of an individual's personality will determine whether or not the spirit will remain here to seek justice. If she was a fairly passive woman, it's likely she accepted her fate without argument and has moved on."

"Ah. I believe Lady Clara was very much the passive sort. Lady Marie was very much . . . not." Lucy paused. "She moved my bed."

Hazel's eyes widened. "Oh, my. She is a strong one, then."

"I do not care for the sound of that."

"Spirits rarely do physical harm to the living."

"Nor is that very reassuring."

Hazel smiled a bit. She was very lovely, Lucy realized. It was the first lighthearted expression she'd seen cross the young Medium's face.

"Do you suppose you might try to conjure Marie right now?" Lucy said.

Hazel nodded with a small sigh. "I will try." She stood and walked a few steps to the hearth, removing a piece of jewelry from her pocket. She fastened the chain around her neck and settled the talisman against her chest. With a slight shrug at Lucy and a dubious quirk of the brow, she closed her eyes and whispered something, slowly raising her arms above her head.

Lucy looked on with a fair amount of apprehension as her heart sped up. The one benefit, should Marie actually appear, would be that Hazel would be able to understand her. Unless, of course, Hazel wasn't equipped with necessary Medium skills and Marie took offense.

Hazel's voice was constant as she murmured a low chant, and the air around the room grew tranquil, serene. Lucy had had the misfortune, once, of being in the presence of a Dark Magick user, and the sensations she had felt were thick and suffocating; the memories of it still made Lucy's skin crawl.

This was different, much to her relief. Lucy was so at ease and relaxed that if Marie appeared, she figured she'd offer her a seat for a pleasant chat. Wind and rain pelted the windows outside, but the crackle of the fire and the spell that Miss Hughes wove about the room was peaceful and warm. Hazel's face was upturned, and she seemed to glow from within. She might not be able to commune with the dead, but she could definitely do something.

A flash of black burst through the glass windows high above and flew through the room. The violence and the sound shattered the night, and Lucy gasped and ducked her head. The creature dove at Hazel, who had opened her eyes but seemed disoriented, transfixed. She was thrown into the large hearth, her head smashing against the brick as she landed in the flames.

With a horrified scream, Lucy lunged across the table and pulled Hazel from the fire, rolling her around on the thick rug and smacking the small flames that licked at her back. Shielding Hazel with her own body, she buried her head in the young woman's hair as the darkness again swooped down from above. Lucy felt something sharp rake down her back before a roar from the doorway sounded, and the glass in the windows shattered a second time.

Chapter 19

Miles took in the scene with a rage that was surpassed only by a nauseating sense of fear that gathered thick in his throat as he crossed the room to the two women crumpled on the floor. He pulled first at Lucy, whose pale pink corset and ruffled white shirt were sliced across her shoulders. Angry red lines seeped blood onto the delicate fabric.

She glanced at him with huge eyes as she ran her hands over an unconscious Miss Hughes.

"She hit her head," Lucy said, her voice shaking. She placed her hand at the back of Miss Hughes's head and pulled it away to reveal a liberal smear of blood. "And she was thrown in the fire, although I believe her clothing took the brunt of it. I pulled her out right away."

Miles caught sight of Lucy's other hand and grasped her wrist, examining her palm. It was a pale shade of red that would soon become darker, more inflamed and blistered. "You've been burned," he said through clenched teeth.

He made his way to the telescribe connector on the wall and attached his telescriber with a hand that trembled slightly. Barely trusting himself to speak with any sense of calm, he punched in a message for Sam to come immediately to the library with his medical bag.

Gusts of wind and rain howled through the broken windows, and he looked up at the jagged pieces of glass where something large and fast had flown into the room. With a litany of curses, he slammed his hand against the crank that controlled the heavy drapes and walked back to Lucy while the mechanism pulled the material closed, muting the storm outside.

Lucy looked at him as he knelt by her side and placed two fingers on Miss Hughes's throat, relieved to feel a thready pulse in the Medium's neck.

"She was attempting to conjure Marie," Lucy said quietly, holding the hem of her skirt against Miss Hughes's head.

"With what? Black Magick?"

Lucy scowled at him. "No. Far from it."

"Marie did not do this," he said. "It was not her presence in this room when I entered."

"No," Lucy agreed. "Most assuredly it was not your sister. I know who it was. Or rather, what." Her expression was as grave as he'd ever seen it. "It was a vampire in black mist form."

She glanced up as Sam entered and squatted down next to Miss Hughes. "A vamp? Then we must treat your back immediately. We will need a mix of Abelfirth and Chromaxium. We shall have to rush you to the airfield and head straight for London—I don't have any with me."

Lucy moved her hand and bloodied dress away from the young Medium's head. "I have some upstairs."

Miles stared at her, slack-jawed, as did Sam, who temporarily stilled his hands. "How on earth do you have a supply of anti-vamp?" Sam asked. "It's all I can do to secure some, and even then I must jump through a series of hoops that make it nigh impossible."

"I am part of the research team. I told you this." Lucy must have finally registered the pain of the burns on her palms because she cradled them to her chest. "While team members' identities aren't secret, it's still not common knowledge. We are at a certain amount of risk from those entities who wish to see us fail."

"Namely vampires." Miles felt his anger surge again. "Why does Daniel allow this?"

It was the wrong thing to say, and had he more of his wits about him, he would have bit his tongue before he made the same mistake twice. Lucy arched a brow, and Sam muttered something under his breath that sounded suspiciously like "Idiot."

"Are we discussing this again?" Lucy said. "Daniel is not my keeper, nor am I a slave." She sat back on her heels and winced. Sam glanced up at her, and Miles saw his jaw tighten fractionally.

"We must apply the anti-vamp immediately," he said as he examined Miss Hughes's back where her clothing had burned away. "Have a 'ton bring it down, Miles."

"No," Lucy said and struggled to her feet. Miles stood with her and caught her elbow when she stumbled. "I can't have just anyone rummaging through my things. I'll do it myself." She paused, looking at Miss Hughes. "Will she be well?"

"I hope so," Sam said, grim with intense concentration. "Where is Oliver?" Sam asked Miles as he reached for something in his medicine bag.

"Bow Street requested his help in London." Miles also wished for Oliver's command in dire circumstances, his connections with law enforcement. "He should return in a day or two."

"Help Lucy," Sam said as he thumbed back one of Miss Hughes's eyelids and shone a light in her pupil.

Lucy's face was pale, and a light sheen of sweat had appeared across her forehead. She wobbled on her feet.

"Hurry," Sam barked.

Miles picked her up, wincing inwardly at her gasp of pain as he tightened his arms around her wounded back. Turning on a burst of speed he knew he might have to explain later, he moved to the door. He could only hope she was too distracted to notice that he moved much faster than he ought to be able to.

He made short work of the stairs, grateful he'd charged his heartclock that afternoon. He fumbled with the lock on the suite door and then made his way to her room, where he set her gently on the bed and turned on the nightstand light. She was shivering, and he felt a stab of alarm to see a sheen of tears in her eyes.

"Oh, for the love of heaven, do not cry."

She nodded to her trunk at the end of the bed. "The key is in my portmanteau." She curled over, cradling her hands in her lap.

A vampire had infiltrated his home, and his fury burned low and hot. When bloodless animals had begun appearing in town weeks ago, his reconnaissance around the grounds had yielded no results. Now one of the vile creatures threatened the few things he held dear.

He pawed through Lucy's bag until he found a small key ring tied with a delicate pink ribbon. It looked ridiculous in his large hand, and as he fitted the key in the lock, he reminded himself again that he had no business spending time in her company. That he had installed her in his own suite was unforgivably selfish, but the thought of her anywhere else in the house was unthinkable, especially now.

He carefully lifted out boxes and containers of various herbs and medicinal concoctions from the trunk and set them on the floor. He'd realized earlier that day when she'd held her ground with him and put him in his place that she was probably the one woman on earth who could handle him. He'd seen her interest in him spark in her eyes more than once, but she didn't know he was deadly, and that would change everything.

But he would take advantage of every last moment of her company, even if it meant keeping her at arm's length. It would have to be enough to know she was in his house. He would torture himself as long as he could stand it, drinking in the sight of her without touching her.

He glanced up at her, his heartclock increasing as she moaned in pain. If he couldn't help her, and quickly, she wouldn't be around much longer for him to adore. He found himself angry that she would put herself in danger. And for what? The ghost of his sister? Her cousin's health? Did she never think to guard her own?

"It's in the blue glass container at the bottom. The label says AVS."

"AVS?" He continued shifting jars and boxes around.

"Anti-venom serum." Her breath came out in a gasp, and he ground his teeth in frustration.

"Here it is." He clutched the jar, making his way to her side. "How is it administered?"

"We do not have time to dilute it." She tried to straighten but couldn't. "Shake the bottle to stir the contents. Then apply it to your handkerchief and press it lightly to the wounds."

Following her instructions, he pulled a handkerchief from his pocket. "What happens if it isn't diluted?"

"It hurts more."

He hesitated.

"Do not fear—it isn't as though I will succumb to an overdose of the medicine." She squeezed her eyes shut. "I am ready."

He cursed under his breath and sat next to her on the bed. He looked at the cloth, damp with medicine, and shook his head. He braced an arm across her body and, with a hand on her shoulder, pulled her to him. He held her tightly as he pulled back the stiff edges of her torn corset and the shredded fabric of the soft white shirt underneath. A row of four long gashes began at the base of her neck and ran midway down her back. Blood still dripped but was beginning to coagulate, even as the skin around the cuts was turning an alarming shade of gray-green that deepened by the minute.

He pressed the cloth to the back of her neck. Her gut-wrenching cry stabbed into his soul, and he was almost relieved when he felt her slacken and then lose consciousness from the pain. He paused only long enough to be sure she still breathed and then made quick work of dabbing the solution along each and every mark. The medicine bubbled where it made contact with the wounds, and while the gashes didn't disappear, the horrible discoloration began to slowly abate.

Lucy stirred, and he willed her to stay unconscious, wondering if she had something in her bag of tricks to alleviate pain. As she moaned and released a huge, shuddering sigh, he rocked her slightly back and forth.

"Shhh," he whispered. "I have you."

He looked down at her burned and bloodied hands still cradled in her lap. "Lucy," he murmured, his lips against her hair, which was hanging in pins and disarray, "do you have a salve for burns?"

She nodded weakly, and his heart turned over at the sob she tried to stifle. "In the trunk. It will do well enough—anything else I'd have to mix."

"Good. I'm going to help you lie down on the bed, on your stomach."

She nodded, but when she straightened her back, she sucked her breath in and shook her head. "I'll sit," she managed.

He moved to the trunk, his frown so fierce it made his head ache. Finding the burn ointment, he returned to Lucy and applied it liberally to her hands, not bothering to first clean the blood away. If she objected, she kept it to herself as first one tear and then another rolled quietly down her cheek.

"You should see if Sam requires assistance," she murmured. "I fear Miss Hughes was seriously hurt."

As though her words made the man himself materialize, Miles heard a series of knocks on the outer suite door—a pattern he'd not heard since the war. "Do not move," he said to Lucy and hurried through the sitting room, running a hand through his hair.

Miles opened the door to see Sam scribbling on a piece of paper. His friend glanced up after a moment and handed it to him. "I need to take Miss Hughes to London immediately," he said. "I've scribed ahead to the airstrip. They have an emergency airship at the ready. Miss Watts is bringing the Traveler to the front door—I'll have it returned."

Miles waved it aside. "We'll retrieve it. How is Miss Hughes?"

Sam shook his head. "I'll know better when I get her to the hospital. I've written instructions for Lucy's care." He pointed to the paper he'd handed Miles. "Scribe me immediately if her fever spikes above the red line. She should have a thermometer with her other medicines."

Miles nodded. "Travel safely."

"I will scribe as soon as Miss Hughes's condition is stabilized." Sam clasped Miles's hand and then jogged quickly down the hallway, where he was swallowed up by the dark.

Reading the paper as he returned to Lucy's bedchamber, Miles noted some dosages for a combination of medicinal herbs Sam had labeled "pain relief." It had to be better than the burn ointment. He quickly examined Lucy's medicines, all of which were labeled in her neat, precise hand, setting aside the ones he'd need. The lady herself remained hunched on the bed, exactly as he'd left her, drooping with fatigue. Her eyes were closed, her breathing shallow, as though inhaling too deeply was an impossibility.

Miles found the proper ingredients and a mortar and pestle and followed the instructions Sam had left for him. He crushed the prescribed herbs to a fine powder and then added them to a small amount of water from the pitcher at the dry sink.

"Lucy," he murmured, "you must drink this."

"What are you giving me?" she whispered, looking as though she'd lived through a battle. Her eyes were swollen, her expression drawn in pain, and her clothes were bloodied and torn.

He tipped the cup to her lips, gently tugging on her chin. She pulled back slightly and then sniffed the drink, relaxing and allowing him to pour it slowly into her mouth. "You need to bathe and change your clothes," he said when she finished drinking. "I shall awaken Kate."

Lucy shook her head. "No, please. She will be terrified, and I'll not have her weakened further. She will blame herself."

"The blame lies not with her." He pinched his lips together, feeling equal parts recrimination and self-loathing. "I bear full responsibility." He paused, and as much as it pained him, he pushed forward. "Miss Pickett, you must leave. Your life is in danger, and I should hate very much for you to come to further harm."

"You're very kind," she said softly, blinking slowly. He could only assume the pain reliever was taking effect. Mercifully, it must have also included a sleeping agent.

"Kindness has nothing to do with it," he muttered. "I shall fetch a 'ton to help get you changed," he said, more to himself than her, and her eyes shot open again.

"No. Frankly, my lord, I do not trust anyone but you and my cousin. Mrs. Farrell complains daily about complications with the 'tons. The medicine on my back must dry in the air, at any rate. I shall sleep as I am." Her eyelids drooped again, and she tipped to the side.

Miles carefully laid her down and positioned a pillow under her head, pulling what pins he could see from her hair and setting them on the nightstand. He untied and loosened the frothy, ribboned laces on her dainty, pale pink boots. Her beautiful skirts were ghoulishly smeared with Miss Hughes's blood, and it made for a horrific contrast. Placing her boots on the floor, he drew the comforter around her, careful to leave her back exposed, but tucking it in under her elbows and around her legs.

He turned the light down and stood watching her for a long moment as her breathing eventually deepened and her body seemed to finally relax. He rubbed his hand across his face and down the back of his neck, wondering what was happening in his home and, more to the point, his heart.

Chapter 20

Lucy spent the better part of the following week in the countess's
bedchambers, healing as quickly as could be expected. She had
convinced Blackwell to tell the others she had merely fallen ill.
How he had managed to explain away the mess in the library she didn't
know. Her only concern was that Kate not be worried or unduly alarmed
by anything. Lucy had given Jonathan instructions via Blackwell to treat
Kate with a variety of teas and herbs, and to their collective delight, they
seemed to be working well.

Lucy managed intimate tasks on her own. Her toiletries and bath-
ing were difficult at first, but she insisted on total secrecy concerning the
events of that fateful night. If the vampire who had attacked was near
or—heaven help them—disguised in the household itself, she was determined to play a careful game of strategy. She and Blackwell would behave
as though nothing untoward had happened, and then she would take the
opportunity to surreptitiously examine the details around the home and
grounds. She had made a study of the vile creatures, and that she hadn't
been aware of one so threatening and close by was a testament as to how
worried she'd been about Kate's health. It was also proof of the Vampiric
Assimilation Aid's effectiveness—an added impetus to speed her research
efforts.

Blackwell had situated a 'ton lady's maid in the adjoining room but, at

Lucy's request, had deactivated her and removed her programming chip, which gave Lucy a measure of security. Her reputation was secure because the household believed the maid to be with her every moment, even when the earl was in the room, but Lucy didn't have to worry that a faulty 'ton would try to kill her in her sleep.

Blackwell treated her wounds, applying new rounds of medicine—greatly diluted—and cloth bandages. She was healing beautifully and very near her usual energy levels by the week's end. She was almost sorry that the quiet, intimate communication she had enjoyed with Blackwell would come to a close; Blackwell spent much of the day with her, seeking to divert her attention from the discomfort of not only the vampire wounds but also her burned, blistering hands.

For his part, he seemed thrilled to have a reason to avoid spending time with the Charlesworths. And the day after the attack, he apologized for his boorish behavior in the Traveler, and Lucy readily forgave him.

She received a letter from her brother, Daniel, who told her that he considered the Earl of Blackwell to be above reproach and the most loyal of friends, but that he had no intimate knowledge of the extended family. Daniel said that he missed her and looked forward to the time when they would be at leisure to enjoy one another's company, and that he hoped it would be soon. He would be forced, however, to rely upon her sense of punctuality to guide him because he was still missing his pocket watch.

Oliver Reed returned from London and remained at the manor for several more days, and, at Blackwell's request, she'd told Mr. Reed everything she remembered about the night of the vampire attack while he listened carefully and scribbled in his notebook. They played short games of checkers and longer games of chess. The two men taught her to play poker and vingt-et-un, showing remorse for having done so only after she began to beat them.

Each evening when her eyelids grew heavy, Blackwell waited until she changed in the dressing room and then tucked her into bed as one would a child. The more she found her health returning, the less childlike she felt around him. She knew their private cocoon of pleasant time spent together was drawing to a close when he started shoving his hands in his pockets and backing his way to the door before bidding her good night.

One week melted into two, and Lucy grew restless at being confined, despite her enjoyment of Blackwell's company. When her energy was nearly at full strength, she began visiting with the rest of the household, catching up on gossip and delighting over Kate's improved health. The Charlesworths' ball was still three weeks away, and Kate had been thrilled when Lucy agreed to remain at the manor and travel with them northward for the celebration.

Lucy and Kate spent a fair amount of time in Marie's garden with Mr. Clancy, who seemed to be taking a grudging liking to the cousins and their work in restoring the garden. Now instead of grunting and scowling at Lucy, he only grunted. He was on hand to help and always had the 'tons fully charged and ready.

The work progressed beautifully as Marie's sanctuary took shape before the onset of winter. The air developed a decided nip, and flurries of snow drifted and threatened but had yet to fall in earnest. The air was filled with the sharp yet pleasant smell of burning sticks and weeds, and Lucy relished each sensation, grateful to feel alive again. Mr. Clancy still insisted that the gazebo remain untouched, and Lucy respected his wishes even while wondering if he would ever acquiesce and give her a pair of pruners.

The relatives eventually left to return home and ready Charlesworth House for the upcoming ball. The entirety of Blackwell Manor, it seemed, breathed a collective sigh of relief. Oliver Reed also took his leave, his work requiring him to return to London; he would meet up with them later at the ball. Lucy had found the detective's dry sense of humor delightful and missed him when he left.

There were no more visits from ghosts or attacks from vampires. If what Hazel Hughes had said was true, Marie would have to know that Lucy wasn't in any condition to help her after the vampire attack, which, she assumed, was the reason for the ghost's absence. Miss Hughes herself was reportedly doing well in London and was nearly healed from her injuries.

While Lucy regretted the attack on Miss Hughes, she was grateful that she now better understood the nature of ghosts. They had also learned, interestingly enough, that Miss Hughes did possess some sort of gift, which Lucy hoped might bring the young woman a measure of peace with her meddling mother.

Life at the manor settled into a comfortable, albeit temporary, routine.

One late afternoon she came upon Blackwell in his suite's sitting room, going over some papers. He sat with his arms braced on his knees and his head dipped down in what she could only read as defeat, which she found disquieting. She approached from behind, catching a glimpse of the small note he held tightly in his fingers. *I know your secret,* the note read, and it stopped Lucy cold. Standing behind him, she wondered if she should make her presence known or try to sneak back out.

The decision was made for her when Blackwell suddenly turned his head. "You ought to announce yourself."

Rather than take offense, she circled the sofa and sat next to him, watching as he pulled his anger and cynicism back over his features.

He couldn't hide entirely, however; it was in his eyes. He was agitated, clearly, but beyond that she read fear. Despair.

"Is there anything I can do for you?"

He closed his eyes. "No," he said, pinching the bridge of his nose. He set the papers on the coffee table facedown. The small note she'd seen was underneath the stack. "You should leave. Leave this place."

Her heart twisted. "I plan to, soon. Kate seems to be on the mend, and after the ball, I shall return to London."

Blackwell raised his head, those expressive eyes showing a fraction of regret for a moment. He nodded. "It is for the best."

What had she expected? That he would beg her to stay? And why did she care? She'd known the man less than a month, and during that time, she'd given him a ridiculous amount of inconvenience. He looked incredibly exhausted. If only he hadn't seemed so vulnerable, she might have been able to harden her heart to him.

"I leave for the hunting lodge in the morning," he said. "I am glad you were able to help Kate. She seems to be feeling well. I am also pleased for your recovery and offer my apologies that it was necessary in the first place."

She studied him, weighing her words carefully. "You needn't carry all of your burdens alone, you know."

He smiled at her, but it was sad. "I cannot ask another to share them." He winced and put a hand to his chest.

"What is it?"

"Nothing. I must spend some time upstairs in the observatory."

"Would you like some company?"

"Definitely not."

Lucy bit her lip and then stood. "Martyrdom favors very few people, Lord Blackwell. And you are not one of them."

"What are you suggesting?" His tone was weary. Resigned.

"That there are those who care for you who would gladly ease your load."

"And I would not burden any I care for with it." He gathered his papers and made his way to the door. He paused, looked back at her as though he wanted to say something else, but then opened the door and left.

Miles staggered the last few steps into the observatory and into the reclining chair next to the heart machine. He opened his chest panel and plugged his heartclock into it, breathing a sigh of relief that he'd not passed out before reaching the third floor. Sam had told him the frequency with which he would need to regenerate would increase. He'd nearly waited too long.

As soon as he finished, he would pack his bag and head for the hunting lodge. The last two weeks he had spent with Lucy had set his heart down a path he had sworn he would never travel. Her injuries had filled him with fear for her life, and being with her while she recovered had been the sweetest torture he'd ever known.

He had watched her as she'd charmed, finessed, and brightened everyone around her as she regained her strength. Even the staff. Nobody was immune to her efforts, and she performed them with grace and seeming ease. Thoughts of their dance in the ballroom plagued him regularly, and he was constantly forced to think of something—anything—but the memory of holding her close in his arms. The diversions never lasted for long, though, and she had him strung tighter than a bow.

The sooner he left, the better. He could handle seeing her at Charlesworth House. It was one more time, after all. She was dangerous to him because she made him hope for things that could never be. Fate was cruel, and he resented the fact he'd been given even a glimmer of hope for a normal life. The best thing he could do for her would be to divert her attention elsewhere.

That ridiculous Arthur had shown a marked interest in Lucy. As much as it pained him, Miles vowed to do everything he could to encourage it. He was more suitable for a lady of quality and bearing than Miles could ever be.

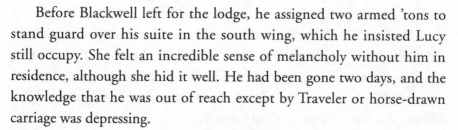

Before Blackwell left for the lodge, he assigned two armed 'tons to stand guard over his suite in the south wing, which he insisted Lucy still occupy. She felt an incredible sense of melancholy without him in residence, although she hid it well. He had been gone two days, and the knowledge that he was out of reach except by Traveler or horse-drawn carriage was depressing.

If the man had his way, he'd spend the rest of his days alone while his family and friends moved forward. But why? Why not find a suitable match and remarry? It couldn't all be blamed on the scar. *She* found him attractive; surely there were other women in society who would have jumped at the chance to be Lady Blackwell. There was something else—she knew it. What that something was, unfortunately, remained undefined even though she used her best skills of persuasion on select members of the staff. It wasn't as though they seemed to be hiding something—rather they seemed to be as much in the dark as she was.

The next morning, Lucy made her daily trek upstairs to Kate's bedchamber. A feeble voice bid her enter, and it was with a sense of dismay that she saw Kate in bed, looking nearly as pale as the white sheets around her.

"I wasn't feeling well after dinner last night," Kate said as Lucy dragged a chair to the bedside. "I had breakfast sent up, but I can hardly stomach a bite."

Lucy looked at the tray on the nightstand. The bulk of the ham and eggs still remained on the plate. She felt a crushing sense of hopelessness that Kate wasn't yet cured. "Oh, Kate. Are you certain you cannot eat more? You need your strength."

"I am afraid, Lucy," Kate whispered and grasped her hand. "I am so desperately afraid. I do not want to die. I overheard Mrs. Farrell telling Mr. Grafton that the late Lady Blackwell showed symptoms similar to mine before she fell ill and died."

Lucy lifted a brow. "Kate, surely you are not putting stock in that silly curse."

"I don't know!" The quiet wail tore at Lucy's heart. "I do not know anything anymore!"

Lucy rubbed Kate's hand gently, her mind spinning. She glanced down at Kate's fingers, noting with alarm that her cousin was losing weight even in her extremities. An elusive thought at the back of her mind surged forward, and she looked closer, this time at Kate's fingernails. Each nail showed faint ridges from side to side.

Lucy took a deep breath, and then two. "Wait here, dear. I shall return straightaway." She grabbed the food tray and left the room, storming her way down to the kitchen. She slammed it on the butcher block with rather more force than she'd intended and stared at Mr. Grafton. "What are you putting in her food?" she demanded.

Mr. Grafton stared at Lucy, eyes wide. "Miss?"

"Kate's food. Or is it her drink? If you tell me now, I will attempt to make things easier for you in the long run."

"Miss Pickett, I have no earthly idea what ye're talkin' about!"

Curse it all, she needed to talk to Blackwell. She considered using the Tesla Room to wire him at the hunting lodge, but she'd heard Jonathan say once that the Tesla Room at the lodge was outdated and not always reliable. Besides, whatever she scribed from the manor would leave behind a record for anyone to read.

Kate's fingernails showed evidence of the late stages of poisoning. And given the fact that Mrs. Farrell equated Kate's current symptoms with Clara's, Lucy wondered how much resistance she would encounter over a request to disinter Clara's body for proof that the late countess had been murdered. Poisoned.

Her thoughts a swirling mess, she turned her attention to Mr. Grafton. "Kate and Jonathan are going on a short holiday, and when they return, nobody is to prepare Kate's food unless I am present and watching the process. And I want to know who has access to the food from the time it leaves this kitchen until it finds its way into Kate's mouth. I do hope I am clear."

The portly cook stared at her with a slack jaw.

"Do I have your word, sir?"

He nodded. "Aye, miss. You have me word."

Lucy returned to Kate's room and opened the door, prepared to ask after Jonathan's whereabouts only to see the man himself hovering at Kate's bedside, his face a mire of confusion and worry.

"A word with you, if you please?" Lucy said to Jonathan.

Jonathan kissed Kate's forehead and joined Lucy in the hallway.

She closed the door softly and drew in a breath. "She is being poisoned, Jonathan."

"I beg your pardon?" He looked at the closed door in bafflement and then back to Lucy. "How do you know? We've considered every possibility, and there are many times when I make the tea myself."

"Have you always delivered it yourself?"

"Ye—no, actually. There have been times when I've prepared something for her and handed the tray off to a 'ton for delivery. These are not programmed to make decisions on their own, so I had assumed it was safer than trusting a human staff member."

"Do you remember which 'tons?"

Jonathan squinted in thought. "Robert, I believe, and Charles."

"I will look into it. In the meantime, I would strongly suggest you take Kate on a holiday. It doesn't have to be far, perhaps just to Bath or maybe London for a time. Enough to get her system cleaned out." Lucy had to trust that she was doing the right thing. If Jonathan was the problem, she was handing Kate a death sentence.

Jonathan's eyes filmed over, and he blinked away tears. "I will take her to Bath. What have I done to my sweet wife, bringing her into this house?"

"We will find our answers," Lucy said and patted his arm. "I'll look into the 'tons. You get Kate out of the house. Today."

"I must tell Miles. He is likely gone for another two days. I could telescribe to the hunting lodge—"

Lucy shook her head. "We don't want to tip our hand. I just did with Mr. Grafton, and I'm wishing now that I would have cooled my temper. We certainly do not want the person or people doing this to be aware of our knowledge. I want to know who's behind it so we can eliminate the threat. It's my fondest hope that you two will enjoy each other's company for many years to come."

Jonathan frowned. "Miles really must be informed."

"I will find a way to alert him, I give you my word. Don't let Kate eat another morsel until you leave. If she needs tea, brew it yourself and deliver it personally."

Jonathan nodded and reentered Kate's bedchamber.

Lucy briefly closed her eyes and placed her palm to her forehead.

Usually the problems she fixed were so much simpler. And the stakes were never so high.

Lucy climbed the back stairway to the servants' quarters on the third floor. She searched the 'ton docking stations quickly until she located the two designated for Robert and Charles, specifically. A quick scan of the log posted next to the stations showed they were both in the outdoor shop for repairs, along with one of the house maids.

Lucy rushed down the stairs and out the front door, past a baffled Mr. Arnold who called after her about her coat, and headed for the stables. Martha Watts directed her to the repair shop at the rear of the garage, but warned her that the repair team was gone for lunch.

"So much the better," Lucy muttered as she entered the room. The three 'tons she had been looking for lay inert on repair tables beside a handful of replacement parts and gears. She worked quickly, removing the programming tin from Robert first. She slid it into her telescriber and scanned through a long series of code that directed the 'ton's behavior, looking for anything out of the ordinary. Some lines down, she found what she sought, and it made her heart constrict painfully in her chest.

"Sporadium," she whispered. It was the herb she'd been unable to identify in the greenhouse. Robert had been programmed to put trace amounts of the herb into Kate's tea. Lucy exhaled, her breath coming quickly as she pocketed the card and turned her attention to Charles's programming tin. Now that she knew the code to look for, she found it quickly. Charles had been similarly programmed.

Lucy kept that tin as well. She checked the house maid, but its programming card was normal. She looked out the window at the rainy, fog-shrouded ether that wrapped itself around the manor's black stone edifice. Kate drew closer to death the longer she remained in that house.

Chapter 21

"Mr. Clancy, please. The second Traveler is malfunctioning, and I must reach the hunting lodge before nightfall. The stable boys will listen to you. Miss Watts said that if you will approve it, she'll let me take one of the horses and a carriage." Lucy stood at the door to the old man's cottage and shivered in the waning light and steady rain. She'd been waiting all day for the Traveler to be fixed, and she was determined to see Miles that evening.

Mr. Clancy looked at her before replying. "What be your business at the hunting lodge, then?"

Lucy squirmed. "I need to show his lordship something very important."

Mr. Clancy raised an eyebrow at her and said nothing.

"Something that may explain more fully the death of his wife," Lucy huffed. "And also about the nature of Kate's illness."

Mr. Clancy's expression remained neutral, so bland, in fact, that she figured he wasn't going to help. Then he brushed past her, heading for the stables and garage. Surprised, Lucy had to trot to keep up with him. She snapped open her waterproof parasol as the rain increased its intensity.

"I'll have them send you with one of the mechanical horses," he told her. "There's a nasty storm brewin', and he'll serve you better than a natural horse."

"Thank you so much, Mr. Clancy. Somehow I will find a way to repay the favor."

Martha greeted them at the stable doors. "Yeh twisted the old man's arm, I see."

Mr. Clancy scowled at her and requested that a mechanical horse and carriage be readied for Lucy's use. She hugged the man quickly and then dashed into the house for the bag she'd packed. Kate and Jonathan had already left for Bath, and knowing that Kate was out of the house, and hopefully out of danger, allowed her the luxury of turning her mind to other things—things that required his lordship's attention.

By the time Lucy had grabbed her belongings and dashed back out to the stables, the enormous horse and small covered carriage were ready. Martha stood by the contraptions, and when Lucy approached, she fired off directions and admonitions regarding its usage.

"Yer control panel is here, just in front, and unless you do somethin' stupid, he'll obey you nice."

Lucy glanced at the darkening clouds overhead. The wind had a bite to it that penetrated her heavy cloak, and she looked forward to the warm interior of the carriage. "And the horse will perform well in adverse weather?"

"O' course. He's been coated with anti-rust, and the outer casing protects the inner workings. Mr. Clancy programmed the directions to the lodge, for yer ease, and set the speed at three-quarters of maximum. Should reach the lodge in about three hours." Martha handed Lucy a tin punch card and gave her a curt nod.

"Thank you. I shall take great care of the equipment."

Martha placed Lucy's overnight bag in the small boot at the back of the carriage. Locking it securely, she patted it once and then handed Lucy the key. "Godspeed, then."

Lucy climbed into the carriage, closing the door behind her. Taking the tin Mr. Clancy had programmed, she placed it into the program slot and waited thirty seconds while it processed. Then, with a slight lurch, the mechanical horse moved forward and took her away from the stables, down the front drive, and out onto the main road.

The horse traveled at a quick pace, unencumbered by the rain that was falling in steady sheets. The carriage interior was warm, but chill seeped in through the windows and doors. She had mentally dubbed the wooded patch of land between the manor and town "the tunnel," and while she was in it, the darkness closed in significantly. She switched on two outer lamps—one on the big horse's forehead and one on the front of the conveyance, although that one did little more than illuminate the horse's huge metal backside.

At her side, she'd attached a small purse which contained the very objects that necessitated visiting Blackwell in person and risk facing his wrath. Her nerves were strung tight, and she told herself repeatedly to keep her emotions in check. She leaned against the plush seat and tried to relax, secure in the knowledge that the programmed punch card would take her safely to her destination. All that was required of her was patience.

Now that she had a moment to sit and do nothing but think, she realized how tired she was. Leaning her head against the side cushion, she allowed herself the luxury of closing her eyes, telling herself she would sleep for just a little while.

She awoke to darkness. The world beyond the beam of light cast by the carriage's headlamp was black. Perhaps even more alarming, however, was the snow that fell hard and fast, the gusting wind temporarily blowing the flakes violently sideways. Squinting out the front window, she saw the back end of the horse, which was stationary, with copious amounts of steam escaping its right flank.

With a muttered curse, she drew her cloak's hood into place and opened the door, pushing against the wind and making her way outside to examine the horse. "You're supposed to be in tip-top condition," she muttered to the animal as she walked around to where steam poured out in a steady blast.

Not an accomplished mechanic in the least, she went to the front of the animal and opened the panel on its chest. The cold made her fingers clumsy, and the metal sheet slipped closed. She struggled to open it, though once she found herself looking at the buttons and wires within the control panel, she had to admit she had no idea what to do with any of it.

She closed the panel, securing it back into place, and climbed back into the carriage. Her options were few. She could remain in the carriage and hope someone would find her once they'd realized she'd gone missing—but who would do that? Mr. Clancy and Martha knew where she was going, but nobody else did. Why would they think to go out looking for her? Or telescribe the lodge to see if she'd arrived? It wasn't as though Lucy was their daughter.

Or she could take the tin programming card, slip it into her own telescriber, and go the rest of the way on foot. In a storm that was looking to turn itself into a raging blizzard. And because she'd slept for part of the journey, she had no idea how far she was from the lodge. Checking her pocket watch, she calculated the time she'd left the manor against the time she was to have arrived at the hunting lodge. It was an hour shy of midnight.

How long would the power charge of the carriage hold out? If it hadn't been hooked to a Tesla Connector to charge for long, she could well find herself sitting in the cold and dark soon.

With a frown and not a little bit of unnerving fear, she pulled the tin programming card from the control panel inside the carriage and slipped it into her telescriber, which she'd had the foresight to charge completely, thankfully. It didn't pinpoint her location—it couldn't unless she were connected to an actual Tesla Connector, and the odds of finding a Tesla Booth in this forest were laughable—but she ought to be able to at least determine how much ground the horse had covered before breaking down by checking the carriage's wheel-rotation calculation.

She looked closely at the control panel until she saw the switch. Flipping it, she waited until a small piece of paper was ejected. She read it carefully; she was two miles away from the lodge. As if helping her to make the decision—to stay or to go—the carriage lights began to flicker and the heating mechanism shut down. The resulting silence in the absence of the steady hum of the machinery was so complete that it roared.

Taking a deep breath, she exited the carriage, unlocked the boot, and pulled out her overnight bag. Popping her umbrella open and angling it against the driving snow, she consulted her telescriber. Mr. Clancy's directions were clear, a map appearing alongside written coordinates.

The road stretched before her, but she was unable to see more than ten feet beyond herself. The map showed a fork in the road, which she had to assume the horse had already taken while she was asleep.

What am I doing?

Less than a month ago, she'd been living her well-ordered life. Now she found herself risking life and limb for her cousin and an irascible earl. Putting one foot in front of the other, she began her journey into an abyss of darkness and snow.

The first mile was slow going in the face of the storm. The only sound was the wind whistling eerily through the trees and brushing up against her parasol, which was proving to be largely ineffectual. A distance that would normally have taken thirty minutes at an easy pace stretched into a good forty-five.

Her cloak grew heavier under the onslaught of snow that melted into the fabric and left her drenched. She had abandoned her hat to the carriage, which was just as well. Even with the parasol, her hair whipped clear of the pins that had held it in an elegant coiffure hours before. Trying to keep her hood in place required more energy than it was worth when a sudden gust of wind flipped her parasol inside out and sent it flying up into the trees.

She tugged at the hood of her cloak, trying to hold it in place with both hands. She was beyond the point of trying to protect her hair. All she wanted was to be able to see where she was walking without getting an eyeful of wind and snow.

Lucy periodically consulted her telescriber, constantly reminding herself that after the fork in the road, there was only one path leading to the hunting lodge, which was situated along the coastline. If she remained on the main path, narrow though it was, she would reach the hunting lodge within the hour. She hoped.

Her fingers and toes were so cold that they hurt, and she found herself wishing they would go numb.

I could sit for just a moment, she thought. *Rest.*

But just as her knees tried to buckle beneath her, she spied a flash of red on the path in the distance.

"Wait!" she called out, unconcerned that whomever or whatever the thing was might not wish her well. "Please help me." Her voice was little more than a croak, snatched away by the wind as soon as it left her lips.

She struggled forward, her feet burning in pain, and feeling a deep, throbbing headache taking root behind her eyes. Keeping the figure in red in her sight, she followed it, even hurried to try to see what it was. The minutes seemed like hours, and still the red beacon stayed before her, like a lighthouse in a storm.

"Marie?" Lucy whispered as she drew closer to the person who seemed to have stopped and waited for her.

It was indeed Marie. She looked familiar in her red gown, her hair blowing slightly in the wicked breeze but otherwise unaffected by the raging elements. When Lucy came within fifty feet of the specter, Marie again moved forward. Lucy supposed that the angry ghost might well lead her right off the edge of a cliff, but at that point she hurt too much to care one way or the other.

"*No,*" she moaned when Marie disappeared. Moving as quickly as her sore feet would allow, she made her way to the last place she'd seen Marie.

Coming out of a clearing, she spied an expanse of flat ground—likely a lawn—that sprawled before a building that was darker than even Blackwell Manor had been on the first night of her arrival. Trees lined the path leading to the front door, and while not nearly as large as the manor itself, the hunting lodge was impressive in its own right. There was no light coming from inside. She had to assume that if the earl was in residence, he was probably asleep.

She stumbled down the length of the path, moving as automatically as if someone had placed a punch card into her brain. Her only thought was to get inside and sit by a fire for the next two years. She forced her feet to climb the stairs. She dropped her bag next to the front door and lifted the metal knocker with fingers that could hardly function. The loud sound of metal on door broke the silence. It was the only sound, however. Nothing moved inside the lodge, despite repeated assaults on the door with the knocker.

She tried the door but it was, of course, locked. Even if Blackwell wasn't here, she had to get inside the building or risk freezing to death. Leaving her bag on the porch, she descended the front steps and made her way around the side of the house, hoping to find a servant's entrance. Trees planted alongside the building snagged at her hair—clearly there wasn't an entrance to be found there. She fought the urge to crumble at the base of one of the trees and fall asleep.

A low growl split the night, and she whirled around, looking behind her. A chill ran down her spine, and she felt her heart beat so rapidly she wondered if it would expire from exhaustion. The growl came again, closer, and she spun forward, terrified. Running the length of the building, heedless of the brambles, thorns, and branches that ripped at her hair and clothes, she reached the back and spied a door.

The world slowed as she lunged for the entrance, moving as though stuck in a mud that refused to give an inch. By the time she reached the back door and pulled on the handle for all she was worth, the growl was nearly at her heels. She looked over her shoulder, terrified, as an enormous wolf stalked her, watching her every movement.

It was a huge animal, entirely black but shot through with strands of silver. The eyes were ice-blue and seemed to glow in the dark.

Her calm having long since fled, she banged on the back door with her fist. "Blackwell!" she screamed. She drew in another shuddering breath as the wolf moved inexorably closer, its intense regard never wavering. *"Miles!"*

Lucy stumbled back from the door, moving slowly, keeping the wolf in sight. There were trees to her back, and a quick glance in that direction showed undergrowth and foliage. The creature would likely navigate it better than she could, but her only other option was to stand and be mauled. She'd rather take her chances with one desperate attempt at escape.

She turned and dashed through the trees, stumbling and crashing, falling and staggering to her feet and all the while hearing growls that turned to snarls. A quick look over her shoulder proved a waste of energy as the wolf blended with the darkness of the thicket. The eyes, though. She saw them clearly enough.

She continued her maniacal flight, stumbling again, but this time when she shoved herself up from the ground, she took a step and met nothing but air. Her last conscious thought was that her family would be so horribly sad at her death.

Lucy awoke in a darkened room, the only light coming from a small lamp on a bedside table. As she squinted and tried to rise on one elbow, she heard a clucking sound, rather like a mother soothing a small child.

"Rest, yet," the woman's voice said. "Ye've had a nasty fall." The accent was pronounced, but Lucy couldn't place it.

The woman moved closer to the bedside and laid a hand on Lucy's brow. "And ye're warm again."

Lucy heard the sound of water hitting a basin as though being wrung from fabric. She felt a cloth placed on her forehead, and the woman gently pushed her shoulders back into the mattress.

"Where am I?" she tried to ask, but it came out as little more than a whisper.

"Ye're safe. Just rest."

She fell into a fitful sleep, dreaming of wolves, of curses, of having to bury Kate in a grave next to Clara and Marie.

When she awoke again, her relief that she'd been dreaming was quickly replaced by the realization that her nightmares only mirrored her current reality.

She shifted into a sitting position and gasped with pain that was so profound she saw stars. She clasped her right arm to her ribs and found bandages wrapped around her torso. Looking down at herself with a wince, she realized she was wearing her nightgown and that her suitcase had been placed at the foot of the bed on a bench.

The light in the room was still dim, but the curtains on three large windows were open enough to allow a glimpse of daylight to shine through. The sky beyond the windows was white, and the snow outside continued to swirl and fall in what resembled a large collection of eider-down feathers.

The bed she currently occupied was a large affair, not so very different from the earl's quarters back at the manor. A seating area near the hearth and an impressively huge rack of antlers hanging on the wall above the fireplace completed the décor of what was clearly a very masculine room.

Taking further stock of her injuries, she realized that besides the wrapping on her ribs she also wore splints on both her left wrist and her right ankle. She clenched her teeth against the pain that throbbed from the injuries as she tried to get comfortable. Fluffing the pillow up behind her back, she gingerly reclined and rested her head against the headboard.

She reached her right hand to her head and felt an enormous goose egg beneath her hair. She remembered flashes of sensations: tumbling down the side of a steep ravine behind the hunting lodge and smashing into rocks and trees that slowed her descent by degrees while doing a fair amount of damage.

Lifting her hair to one side and leaning more comfortably against the pillows, she felt a soreness around the skin on her neck and touched it with her fingertips. Perhaps her cloak had snagged on something and rubbed her skin raw.

She took as deep a breath as the tight bandages would allow and frowned. If her ribs were broken, the bandage wasn't going to be of much use. One of her friends at school in Switzerland had suffered a fall, and the attending nurse had insisted that tightly wrapping the wound served no purpose other than to deny the patient the ability to breathe.

Lucy released the top few buttons on her nightgown using only her right hand, as any movement with the fingers on her left had her gasping in pain. It was slow going, but she eventually had given herself enough of an opening to reach inside and unwrap the tight binding around her torso. While she couldn't draw a deep breath even without the dressing, she did feel a modicum of relief.

She had nearly all of the buttons of her nightgown done up again when there was a quiet knock on the door. "Come in," she croaked out and looked at the nightstand for the teacup of water she remembered from before. Someone had helped her take a few sips. A woman with an accent . . .

The door opened to reveal Lord Blackwell looking at her with a carefully blank expression.

Chapter 22

He closed the door quietly behind him.

Lucy looked a mess, she was certain, although she hadn't yet spied herself in a mirror. Her hair hung down in tangled masses, and she pushed some of it away from her face, wincing, and wondered if there was a spot anywhere on her body that wasn't bruised or broken.

Perhaps even more alarming, however, was the expression on Blackwell's face. He didn't give away even the slightest clue as to what he was thinking, which was more than a little unnerving.

Blackwell pulled a chair to the bedside and sat back in it, crossing his long legs at the ankles and linking his fingers over his midsection. He watched her with unblinking eyes, and Lucy wondered if he were measuring his words carefully. It would be a first, that much was certain. He was dressed casually in shirtsleeves and black trousers, his ever-present black riding boots the only spot of polish. She was beginning to think that the only person she'd seen so consistently without his vest, coat, and hat was her brother.

"You wanted to see me?" Blackwell finally asked.

Lucy closed her eyes. Mercy, she hurt. Feeling ridiculously young and dramatic, she nodded and opened her eyes. She tried to speak but could only croak. Tears burned and threaten to fall. She reached for the teacup on the table, realizing belatedly that the fingers on her left hand likely wouldn't be able to grasp it.

Seeing her intention, Blackwell leaned forward and picked up the cup. Placing it carefully in her right hand, he sat back in his chair while she took a few cautious sips of water.

"I did want to see you, my lord," she said, her voice sounding marginally better. "It is a matter of some importance, or I would never have imposed on your privacy. I know you guard it well."

"It didn't occur to you to have someone accompany you?"

Lucy sighed, placing her arm around her ribs and holding her left side with her right hand. "I do not know whom I can trust other than Mr. Clancy, and even then I wonder. He and Miss Watts are the only two people who know my destination was your hunting lodge. Everybody else thinks I headed back to London while Kate and Jonathan are at Bath."

A muscle worked in his jaw, and he pinned her so completely with his heavy stare that she wished he would find someone else with which to be angry. "Do you realize you were nearly at death's door when I found you?"

She struggled to maintain his gaze. "I apologize for the inconvenience my mishaps have caused you."

"Your mishaps? Mishaps?" He shook his head. "I found your horse and carriage down the road two miles. You walked all that way in a blizzard and then fell fifty feet down a steep embankment. Much longer outside in the cold and you would have died from exposure. I'm amazed the fall didn't kill you."

She licked her lips and took another sip of water. "How did you know I was there, that I had fallen?"

He broke eye contact, looking at the lamp on the table rather than at her. "I have eyes and ears everywhere," he finally said and brought his ice-blue gaze back to her face. He leaned forward and braced his arms on his knees. "Miss Pickett . . . Lucy—for the love of heaven, may I call you Lucy? I've saved you from a ghost *and* a vamp attack. I've seen your naked back, and this marks the second time you've slept in my bed."

Her mouth twitched at the corner. "Yes, you may address me by my given name."

"Very well, then. Lucy, what the blazes were you thinking?"

She took another faux deep breath, wincing in spite of her resolve not to display any discomfort before him. "Kate and Jonathan are at Bath."

"You mentioned that."

"I convinced Jonathan he needed to get Kate out of the manor and away to safety."

His eyes narrowed. "Why?"

"She is being poisoned."

The man took the news in stride, she had to give him that. She'd been unsure of his reaction. She had thought he might not believe her.

He kept his expression carefully neutral. "And how did you arrive at this conclusion?"

"Her fingernails. They are beginning to show stripes that signal poison in the system." She paused. "I have a horrible request of you. One that I suspect may result in my immediate ejection from this lodge."

"I cannot imagine what that would be."

"I suspect Lady Clara was also poisoned. I'd like to have a look at her fingernails."

He stared at her, his mouth slack. "You want to disinter my late wife?"

"I am aware of the ghoulish nature of my request. I realize it may not be possible—you would need access to the Gravelocker's code, which can take weeks to obtain approval for, but—"

"I have the code," he interrupted. "I assume you have good reason to request such a thing?"

She nodded. "I pulled punch cards from two of the 'tons at the manor. Someone had programmed both of them to add small amounts of an herb to Kate's beverages—the same mysterious herb I found in the greenhouse when I first arrived at the manor. She's been on the mend the last two weeks, but as I considered it after the fact, I realized it was because those two 'tons were out for repairs. The punch cards, however, were never examined or replaced."

He remained silent as he watched her, shaking his head once before rising from his chair and pacing the room. After a couple of circuits, he stopped at the foot of the bed. "Who would do this?"

"How long have you had Mr. Grafton's 'tons?"

"Years. A decade, at least."

"And who would benefit from your wife's death?" she asked him softly.

He shook his head and resumed pacing. "It makes no sense at all. If someone were after my title, I should think *I* would be the one drinking poison." He stopped again at the foot of the bed. He stared through Lucy, his mouth dropping open slightly. He closed it with an expression of un-guarded pain. "Marie."

"Marie?" Lucy echoed. "Forgive me, but why on earth would Marie want Clara dead? Envy? Perhaps because Clara was stepping into a role that Marie felt was hers?"

Blackwell shook his head and ran both hands through his hair. "She wasn't envious of Clara. She was disgusted with Clara."

"But why?"

He returned to the chair by Lucy's bedside. "Clara was frightened of me. She never, we never even . . . She was a timid, frail thing, and she couldn't stand to be in the same room with me, let alone the same bed. Marie despised her for it."

"You told your sister that your wife had refused you?"

Blackwell's expression darkened. "No, I did not share such things with my sister. But Marie had good rapport with the staff, every last one. She received the information from Clara's maid and, of course, came to me in a cold fury. She wanted me to annul the marriage, find someone who would at least be willing to give me an heir."

"But would she have gone to such drastic measures as poisoning Clara?"

"I don't know." His hands again plowed through the thick hair, and her heart turned over at the sight of his distress. "I wouldn't have thought her capable of such malice. She was . . . She was a force to be reckoned with, but now I'm left to wonder if she was thinking unclearly and I was too absorbed in my own misery to realize it."

"Whether she did or did not commit murder is not a reflection on you. It is not your guilt to carry."

"I knew Marie better than anyone. I ought to have seen it."

"Perhaps, but perhaps not." Lucy's ankle throbbed, and she shoved the covers down with her one good hand, pulling her leg out and propping her ankle atop the bedding. All thoughts of modesty and propriety flew from her head as a stabbing pain shot thorough her ankle and into her foot.

Blackwell rose and reached across Lucy for another pillow, which he folded and propped under her foot.

"Thank you," she murmured. He was close enough for her to lean forward and nuzzle his neck, and she closed her eyes against the temptation. Her heartbeat increased and she felt light-headed. She almost laughed at the absurdity of it all. She had traveled through a blinding storm, made a nuisance of herself, had taken his bed yet again, and asked to dig up his wife's dead body to examine her fingernails. A kiss on the neck when he'd clearly shown he wasn't interested in such intimacy would likely shoot him through the roof.

Lucy refocused her thoughts. "We must consider the fact that, while Marie may have hated Clara, Marie herself met an unfortunate end the day after Clara passed. Forgive me for intruding on painful memories, but if my vision of Marie is true, her wounds were not self-inflicted. Kate told me Marie had a way with animals, even wild ones. The theory that she was randomly attacked by a large cat seems unlikely."

"What are you suggesting?" His voice was tight as he took the teacup from her hand and refilled it with water from a pitcher on the nightstand.

"I am suggesting that perhaps Clara and Marie both met their ends at the hands of the same person." She took the cup from him with a nod of thanks.

Blackwell studied her until she felt . . . warm. "Now do you see why you must leave?"

She raised a brow but regretted the movement. Even her face hurt—her face, for heaven's sake. "I am not the lady of the manor, and thus not in any danger of being poisoned. The devil himself couldn't drag me away at this point. I want to see my cousin safe in her own home. I want to exact justice for Marie—and Clara. We must know how she died in the event of criminal charges."

And I want to fix you, to make you smile. And take you on a very long, extended holiday across Europe . . .

"Lucy." He walked to the middle window and pulled the curtains all the way open. "Still the storm rages," he said softly. "I'll not move you to-day—you must rest—but when this is over, I'm contacting your brother. Perhaps you'll heed his advice."

"Blackwell, I am not a child." She eyed him steadily as he left the window and returned to her bedside. "I am staying with you until these things are resolved." She paused. "You need me, and unlike the rest of this pathetic country, I am not afraid of you. I can help you."

He smiled, but it seemed sad. Resigned. "Because you fix things? Am I another of your projects? I shall save you the energy and trouble—I cannot be fixed."

She ignored him. "When we have determined who is behind the mayhem, I will leave you in peace, but do not ask me to go one minute before. It will nag at me until the day I die."

"You owe nothing to Clara or Marie."

"Marie has sought me out. She led me here last night when I would have sat down in the snow and died." Lucy swallowed. "I owe her everything."

Miles looked at her for the space of several unnerving heartbeats before finally nodding. "Very well. But I insist you tell me everything that transpires and that you do not go off on your own trying to 'fix' this ridiculous family."

"I give you my word. I am not foolish." She looked down at her battered body and couldn't help the small laugh that escaped and then turned into a groan of pain. "Not usually, anyway. But I didn't dare telescribe the information from the manor where anyone could read it."

He nodded. "I'll have Mrs. Romany prepare a light brunch for you."

"The woman who was with me earlier?"

"Yes. She is a gypsy by birth, and from a family who were always welcomed on Blackwell land. I'm having her prepare the adjoining chamber for you as we speak."

"She had the feel of a healer about her." Lucy slid carefully back down under the covers. "Very gentle."

He turned to go.

"Blackwell," she called out, still hearing the scratchiness in her throat. "Thank you. I don't know how you found me, but I am grateful."

"You are welcome," he said, ever the consummate aristocrat. "And I must thank you for risking all to tell me about the chaos erupting in my own home." He frowned. "Do you have the program cards with you? Those you found in the two 'tons?"

She nodded and directed him to the purse pouch she'd worn at her waist the night before.

"Oliver will want to see them." He pawed through the yards of fabric on her discarded dress, which Mrs. Romany had placed over the back of a chair near the fireplace. There was something oddly intimate about watching a man sifting through her petticoats, and her heart thumped hard as he set aside her bodice and her black satin corset that was laced liberally with pearls.

Finally pulling the purse from the dress, he held it up, and she nodded.

"They're wrapped in felt," she told him.

He opened the small clasp on the delicate beaded purse, his large, tanned hands appearing all the more masculine in contrast. He retrieved the bundle in question and snapped the purse closed, placing it on the nightstand next to her. "Should you need your things," he said.

"Are you remaining here for the day?"

"Yes. The roads are impassable, even for the Traveler." He paused, looking at her intently. "I want your word that you will not leave your room once night falls."

She managed a rueful smile. "I don't believe I'll be going much of anywhere in the immediate future." She paused. "Why do you come here so frequently?"

"I enjoy hunting."

"Yes, I see the impressive rack hanging over the mantel."

"Exactly," he said, although the slight flare of his nostrils as he examined the antlers spoke of his true feelings.

"Did you take that one down yourself?"

Blackwell shook his head. "That was my father's trophy. It has hung in that spot for as long as I can remember."

"So what prey do you enjoy hunting?" She shifted gingerly and fluffed the pillow beneath her head.

He turned his gaze from the antlers on the wall to her face. "This and that."

"You do not enjoy hunting at all. So why, then, escape monthly to a hunting lodge? And why keep that ridiculous rack?"

His brows drew together. "It is tradition," he muttered.

"You are the earl now," Lucy said on a yawn. "You can make your own traditions."

She closed her eyes and felt herself slipping into a welcomed state of rest. Everything hurt. The last conscious sensation she had was the feeling of a warm hand upon her forehead, followed by a cool, wet cloth.

Chapter 23

Lucy slept away the better part of the day. By the time she awoke, feeling moderately refreshed, the outside world had turned dark. Mrs. Romany had made her a delicious meal and had sat with her while she ate before helping Lucy into the adjoining bedchamber, which was significantly more feminine in décor. The old woman quietly knitted, her gnarled fingers managing the needles with an ease that spoke of years of experience. She told Lucy that she was employed year-round at the lodge, along with a butler, Poole, and a skeleton staff of 'tons. Beyond that, she didn't say much, and Lucy enjoyed the comfortable silence.

She hadn't seen Miles since earlier that morning when he'd brought her a cane from his father's study. The dinner hour had come and gone, and she'd self-administered some medicinal herbs from a stash in her suitcase. The medicine blunted the harsh edges of the pain, and she felt her flagging energy return by degrees.

After seeing Lucy settled in for the evening, Mrs. Romany had told her she would be in her own room down the hall. Blackwell had also told her that he had business to see to, though when Lucy had asked him what sort of business he conducted at night, he'd completely ignored the question.

Mrs. Romany had lit the lamps in the chamber, drawn the curtains securely against the windows, and built a cozy fire. The old woman cared for every detail that Lucy could have requested, and she snuggled under the covers with an odd sense of contentment. Her eyelids drooped, and she nodded off, hoping to be in possession of a clearer head come morning.

Lucy slept for several hours before she awoke with an urgent need to use the latrine. A quick check of her pocket watch showed that it would soon be dawn, but she knew she wouldn't be able to wait for Mrs. Romany's assistance to travel to the outhouse.

Gingerly swinging her feet to the side of the bed, she slid to the floor, balancing the brunt of her weight on her left foot and her cane. Not bothering to dress, she simply took her heavy cloak, which had dried by the fire, and swung it around her shoulders with a gasp of pain.

She shoved her left foot into a boot, but not her right, and then grabbed a pair of galoshes that she fitted over both feet. She made her way to the landing just outside the door. To her immediate right was a staircase leading down to the main front hall.

Navigating the stairs took some time, and she was breathless when she reached the bottom. The silence in the lodge was pronounced. Given that the lodge wasn't a household full of people, there was no need for bustling staff seeing to their morning duties. Crossing to the heavy front doors, she slid back the dead bolt and swung the door open against the protesting hinges and her protesting torso. Pausing only to lift her hood into place, she stepped out into the falling snow.

Making her way carefully down the stone steps, she turned and looked for the path in the snow that Miles had shoveled earlier. Of course the path was again hidden beneath a blanket of white, and she shook her head as she began picking her way through the snowdrifts. The snow slid into her galoshes and trickled down to her feet in cold rivulets that had her shivering.

The sky was just beginning to lighten by the time Lucy stepped out of the outhouse to begin her return to the lodge. A low-pitched growl sounded to her left. She spied movement not twenty yards away in the trees that surrounded the building.

It was the same enormous black wolf she had seen before. She would know it anywhere.

Cursing the fact that she'd ventured outside without her ray gun, she inched her way back to the outhouse door, wondering if the structure would hold in the face of a wolf attack. It hadn't seen her yet, but before she could hide, the wolf howled and arched its back. The creature's spine, its legs, even its ears seemed to swell and recede as the wolf again opened its mouth and issued a wretched cry.

Horrified, she stood stock-still as before her very eyes the wolf's fur began to disappear, its hind legs extended, and with a loud series of cracks, the wolf shifted into the shape of a man. Leaning heavily on her cane and bracing one hand against the outhouse, she opened her mouth to scream but couldn't make a sound.

The man—she would know him anywhere. She wondered why she hadn't put it together the night before when she'd had a good look at those mesmerizing ice-blue eyes the wolf had possessed.

Miles braced his hands on his knees and coughed, spitting something and wiping his arm across his forehead.

She barely registered the fact that he was naked—had been too stunned to notice anything but the fact that Blackwell was a predatory shifter—and she blinked against the swirling snow, watching as he reached into a metal box on the ground and pulled out breeches and then shrugged into a white dress shirt. He had just finished putting on his boots and was donning his overcoat when he looked up and saw her.

"Lucy!"

Miles began running toward her, and she felt light-headed. She turned to escape—to anywhere, really—when she remembered her battered ankle and nearly collapsed from the pain of stepping down on it.

Miles grew nearer, and she put out a hand in a feeble attempt to ward him off. Her head spun, her body ached, and she realized she would never make it to the lodge before he caught her. It didn't mean she wouldn't try, and in a full-blown fit of panic, she began running for the lodge, ignoring the pain that lanced through her ankle and up her leg, robbing her of breath and all rational thought.

"No!" Her voice was a shaky wail as Blackwell easily overtook her. She shoved at his torso with her broken and bandaged left wrist, her breath driven from her by the stab of pain that erupted from her side at the defensive movement.

"Lucy, stop. You're hurting yourself." Miles grasped her upper arms. Pulling her close to his side, he began walking toward the lodge, and to her dismay, she felt her knees give way beneath her. She couldn't draw a decent breath against her bruised and cracked ribs, and she cried out in a swirling mass of fear, anger, and white-hot pain.

Before Lucy knew what he was doing, Miles had scooped her into his arms and carried her across the distance to the lodge. Once on the porch, he opened the door with the hand that braced her legs. He kicked the door closed behind them, and he carried her up the stairs and into her bedchamber.

Lucy was robbed of breath, of sense, of coherent thought. Miles set her gently on the bed and stepped back, watching her as though he expected her to bolt at any moment. She stared at him, trying to reconcile what she'd witnessed with the man who stood before her.

"Why didn't you tell me?" she finally asked. She would not cry. Most assuredly, she would not cry.

Miles cursed and bent to remove the galoshes from her feet, moving very carefully with her right ankle. "It isn't exactly the thing one goes about advertising," he said as he unbuttoned her cloak and pushed it down off her shoulders.

He left her sitting on the bed and made his way to a sidebar where he retrieved a flask of brandy and a glass. Pouring two fingers' worth of liquid into it, he handed her the glass. "Drink it," he said when she hesitated.

"I don't drink."

"You do today."

Perhaps she was dreaming. Nothing seemed real. The world was slightly off-kilter, and she couldn't reason her way to find the fix. She took a sip and tried not to cough as the liquor burned a path to her stomach. Handing him the glass, she shook her head when he tried to press it back into her hand.

"I want my wits about me," she said, wiping a hand across her mouth, "when I verbally tear you limb from limb."

Miles closed his mouth as he studied the woman before him with a fair amount of shock. She was *angry*? The moment he'd shifted and seen her standing outside, his heart had stuttered alarmingly. He must have carried her into the house and up the stairs by sheer will. His heartclock still worked at a furious pace, and he took a deep breath to calm himself.

"What could you possibly have been thinking to keep such a detail from me?" she asked, eyes narrowed.

"I wasn't aware you needed to know." He reached behind him for a chair and sat beside the bed.

"What is it?" Her eyes widened, and she slipped off the bed, her breath escaping in a rush as she wrapped an arm around her midsection. "Are you ill?"

He waved his hand at her. "Now I shall have to put you back into bed." He caught his breath, relieved to finally feel the heartclock regulate itself.

"You're quite pale." Lucy placed her palm alongside his cheek.

He flinched involuntarily, thoroughly and completely baffled. She had run from him in terror but was now angry and apparently no longer afraid of him. "I do not understand you, Lucy Pickett."

She frowned and turned his face one way and then another, as though she were an examining physician. Finally dropping her hand, she studied him for some time with an expression that gave nothing away.

"How many people know about this?"

He blinked. "I beg your pardon?"

"How many? And have you run afoul of anyone on the PSRC?"

He sighed and closed his eyes, pinching the bridge of his nose. "Possibly."

Lucy folded her arms across her chest and leveled him with a stare that was only slightly diminished in its impact by a wince. "Who knows about this?"

"Oliver, Sam, and Daniel. And one other. Possibly two."

"Aside from me?"

"Yes. Aside from you."

"And who would these others be?"

He shook his head. "I do not know. Someone has discovered it, however, and has become rather a nuisance about it."

She cocked a brow. "Someone who is sending you notes?"

He shrugged.

"Blackmail?"

"Not yet."

She studied him for another moment and then sighed with a brief eye roll. "And you've not confided in your brother. Your heir and the one person who likely cares more for you than anyone on earth."

"What would you suggest I say to him?" He felt his anger rise. "I am an aberration, a flaw in the family gene pool."

She narrowed her eyes a fraction, and he realized she held his future in her hands. What she chose to do with the information she now had could mean his doom. "I insist you allow me to help you."

He bit back a quick retort and instead looked away, focusing on the bedside lamp as though it held something of interest. "Why? I saw your initial reaction, your recoil. I am more beast than man."

"It's true, I was horrified from the *shock*. And you would blame me for that? I, who have never once shrunk from your presence? Who have enjoyed your company? You lied to me!"

He whipped his gaze to hers. "I never lied to you."

"A lie of omission is no less heinous than one of commission. For the love of heaven, I watched as a wolf transformed into . . . *you*. I've never witnessed a complete transformation, and you would judge me harshly for reacting in fear?" She paused, studying him. "How did I come to be in your room after my fall down the ravine?"

"I'm not entirely certain." He pinched his lips together. The woman would pry for every detail when he was accustomed to sharing with no one.

Lucy put a hand to her throat and traced her finger along a particularly red, angry-looking mark. "You pulled me up the side of the ravine by my cloak. As a wolf."

"I don't know." Miles studied her for a moment. Her dark hair hung around her shoulders and framed her face in curls he knew firsthand to be softer than satin. Her deep, cobalt eyes locked with his, and he felt his mouth go dry. "Do not ask me for things I cannot explain." His throat ached with longing for absolution and a physical desire that was rendering him short of breath.

Lucy shook her head. "Has the world been so horrible to you, then? Are there none aside from your friends who wish you well?"

His lips twitched. "Perhaps I do not deserve it. And not from one as beautiful as you."

She flushed and chewed on her lip, likely trying to eliminate the smile that threatened at the corners of her mouth. The light coloring on her cheeks, however, stood in contrast to the pale state of her complexion.

"You must rest," he murmured, rising from the chair. Forcing his arms to innocently lift her back onto the bed, he restrained himself from taking her face in his hands and kissing her senseless. "Your reputation may be in serious need of rescue when you return. The family all know that Mrs. Romany is in residence here, but . . ." Miles shoved his hands deep into his pockets. "You did say that only Mr. Clancy and Martha Watts know where you are?"

Lucy nodded. "I told everyone else I was going to London. If it becomes necessary, Kate will tell the world I was with her and Jonathan in Bath. I am not concerned." As she shifted against the bedding and angled to move beneath the fluffy duvet, a small groan escaped her lips.

Miles lifted the blankets as she settled down into the bed. "Lucy, I am so sorry," he said. "This is my fault."

"No." She shook her head against the pillow. "You were exactly where you ought to have been. I intruded." She yawned. "I apologize that I am still so fatigued. I ought to be up and preparing for the day."

"You had quite a nasty shock, not to mention the fall. Besides, there's nobody about to entertain. Rest for a few hours. I will have Mrs. Romany see to a decent breakfast."

She leaned up on one elbow, gasping at the movement but looking at him with widened eyes. "You have been awake all night long, and here you are making breakfast plans. You should rest as well."

He carefully kept his expression blank as he put his hand on her shoulder, gently exerting enough pressure that she settled back down on the pillow. She had seen him shift from a predatory state and now acted as though she'd witnessed nothing out of the ordinary. She was likely the only woman in all of England who could manage it. His hand seemed overly large against her petite frame, and he tightened his jaw. He still wasn't convinced she would be safe around him. In either form.

Allowing himself one small moment of self-indulgence, he traced his fingertip down her cheek. He desperately wanted to kiss her. "Rest."

"Miles, I feel awful—"

"Say that again."

She frowned. "I feel awful that I've encroached on your privacy, but it really was necessary to tell you—"

He shook his head. "Not that part. The other part."

To her credit, she was quick. Her confusion cleared, and she locked the depths of her blue eyes upon his face. "Miles." She whispered it, the sound traveling like soft fingers down his spine.

"Yes. That part." He watched her for a moment longer and finally turned and left the room before he did something entirely foolish like brush a kiss across her forehead.

Chapter 24

Lucy awoke several hours later to realize that not only had she slept through breakfast, but she'd also missed lunch. It was late afternoon according to her pocket watch, and she was torn between gratitude and mortification that Miles had let her sleep so long.

Glancing around the room, she sat up. With a fair amount of indrawn breaths and grunts of pain, Lucy went about readying herself for the day, largely spent though it was. She managed to give herself a sponge bath at the dry sink with water that had long since gone cold, but she felt marginally better afterward. She brushed through her hair but quickly squelched the idea of attempting a braid. She had the use of only one good hand, and raising the other hurt her side so much she could barely draw a breath.

Rather than trying to manage an entire ensemble, she clumsily struggled into a robe and made her way across the room with the use of the cane. She stood at the top of the stairs for a moment, catching her breath and bracing herself for the long walk down.

It wasn't until she neared the bottom few steps that she heard a piano echoing faintly through the empty house. She followed the sound across the front entry and down a hallway to the right. Passing several closed doors, she wondered if the lodge was ever fully in use. On the rare occasion that a door happened to be open, the furniture in the room was fully draped in white fabric, the curtains drawn tight. She was saddened that the beautiful building was never filled with the sounds of conversation and laughter, the clink of dinner dishes and gentle music in the drawing room, children chasing each other through the halls until finally scolded by an adult.

Someone was indulging himself at the moment, however, and the sound of the piano grew louder as Lucy approached. A door was open, and she peered inside to see a conservatory with drapes drawn and one lone lantern giving barely enough light to illuminate Miles, who sat at the instrument, his shoulders hunched, his face drawn in what was unquestionable pain.

A tumbler sat atop the beautiful, black grand piano, and Lucy bit her lip, wondering which was more worrying—the fact that Miles looked so incredibly tortured or that he'd placed a glass of liquid on the piano where it could easily have been knocked inside the body of the beautiful instrument.

The melody was unfamiliar. It was haunting and mirrored well the emotion that played upon Blackwell's face. Lucy winced as she watched the man—proud, powerful, intimidating. Anguished. Making her way across the floor, she wondered how best to approach without startling him.

In the end, he seemed to know she was there. He lifted his head and met her eyes, his own bright. His fingers slowed on the keys, and as she neared, he reached for his glass with one hand and took a drink, still watching her. He placed the glass back on the piano, but she was too entranced to care. The look on his face had her eyes burning. She wanted to lift the world off his shoulders and send it flying.

She stood by his side and placed the backs of her fingers on his cheek.

"God has sent you to torture me." He closed his eyes and clasped her hand, a light shudder vibrating through his shoulders. "To tease me with what can never be."

Lucy braced the cane against the side of the piano bench and slid between Miles and the keyboard. He looked up at her as she stood between his knees and took his face in her hands, the thumb of her right hand lightly stroking his scar. "Why will you not allow it?" she whispered.

On a shuddering breath, he slowly, gently wrapped both of his arms around her waist and rested his head against her. His hot tears melted into the fabric of her robe and nightgown, and she held his head and shoulders in her arms, feeling a tear of her own escape and trail down her cheek. His quiet sobs broke her heart and hurt far worse than the pressure of his arms against her injured ribs.

"What is it?" she murmured against his hair and stroked his shoulder and down his back. "Why do you fight so terribly hard?"

"There is no hope for me." His eyes remained closed. "I will always be a danger to those close to me."

"That isn't true." Lucy gently ran her fingers through his thick, black hair. "Why do you torture yourself so?"

"I killed Marie," he said, his voice breaking on a sob. "I killed my sister."

Lucy lifted her head and stared down at him. "Miles," she said gently, "there is no way on God's green earth that you killed Marie."

"You believe the best in me, but you would believe the best in everyone. I must face the truth, turn myself in. The estate would be in better hands with Jonathan anyway."

At that, Lucy felt a measure of alarm and nudged his head up until he met her eyes. Her heart twisted at the sight of him, broken and defeated. "First of all," she said, "Jonathan is a wonderful man, but he makes a far better poet than earl. And secondly—" Lucy shifted slightly to sit on the bench next to him. "Secondly, I would wager my life and the lives of my family that you were not responsible for your sister's death. And that has nothing to do with my optimistic heart and everything to do with proven science."

He looked at her blankly.

She sighed. "My uncle is a shifter. A fox. I would not consider myself an expert on the subject, but I do know a few things. The strength of character of the person while human determines the nature of the animal.

If you wouldn't have killed your sister as a human, you wouldn't have done so as a wolf, either."

Moisture clung to his thick, black lashes, and he looked as vulnerable as a child. "A lovely thought, but one I do not have the luxury of believing."

"My aunt was determined to learn all there was about the condition, and I was with her when she invited a specialist to dinner who was, of course, discreet and trustworthy. The doctor was a wealth of information and provided my aunt with several periodicals and medical journals with the stipulation she keep the information to herself. There are documented cases, studies done both in laboratories and in the wild, wherein the nature of the person has been compared to the nature of the beast. Aside from some instincts—most relatively harmless—the 'personalities' are the same. Even in predators, which is why the Predatory Shifter Regulations Committee is ridiculous. If the general populace was aware of these things—scientifically proven, no less—the Committee's entire existence as a body would be not only irrelevant but also criminal. They keep the information hidden with threats and blackmail against the scientific community."

His hands tightened fractionally on her waist. "What you're saying offers me a glimmer of hope that I'm not certain I have a right to claim."

"What do you remember when you shift back?"

"Impressions, flashes of scenes, images," he mumbled and then sighed. "When Clara died, Jonathan scribed me from the manor, so I left the lodge with one night still left to shift."

"What do you remember from the night Marie died?"

Miles closed his eyes, his brows knit. "She was in the gazebo, covered in blood. Her eyes were open. She looked at me . . ." He shook his head. "I should never have gone back to the manor early. I've always made certain to be far away from anyone when I shift. Even during the war I would leave, go off on my own."

"And with Oliver as your captain, you were never reported missing."

He nodded.

"Did you seek out Marie that night?"

"Yes. She had sent me a note," he said with a frown. "Wanted to meet me in the garden. It was nearly midnight. I had planned to shift at the graveyard, but she said it was urgent. Something about Clara. I was hoping to find Marie before I changed."

"Was that an unusual request? Did you make a habit of meeting in her garden late at night?"

Miles shook his head. "No, but then nothing seemed normal that night. The house was in an uproar over Clara's death. There was talk of an investigation . . ."

Lucy bit her lip and placed her palm on Miles's chest, feeling the steady rhythm of his heartclock. "I believe the reason you remember seeing Marie like that is because she was already dead when you arrived. I believe you were framed."

"Convenient."

"Do you remember anything else at all about that night? Other people? 'Tons?"

"I am tired, Lucy." He looked at her through heavy-lidded eyes.

"This is important. Do you remember seeing or hearing anyone else?"

He leaned forward, maintaining eye contact until he finally dipped his face and nuzzled his nose and lips along the side of her neck. "I do not want to talk anymore."

She sighed and closed her eyes, trying to remember what she had considered so important that they discuss. "How much have you had to drink?" she murmured.

"Entirely too much. I suspect I shall have plenty for which to apologize before long."

Lucy felt a warm glow spread from her neck where Miles kissed and gently nipped throughout her entire body to her extremities. Twining her arms around his neck, she burrowed her hand in the softness of his hair as he drew his mouth along her jaw and finally captured her lips.

It was every bit as intoxicating as she'd imagined, and she moaned softly as he carried her along a maelstrom of sensation and emotion that robbed her of breath and rational thought.

He grasped her tightly, and she winced in pain. He immediately pulled back, his eyes glazed and dilated. "I'm sorry," he whispered. "Lucy, I'm sorry."

"It's fine, truly," she managed, trying to slow her breathing and stop the assault on her aching ribs. "I just need to catch my breath."

He touched his forehead to hers, inhaling and exhaling rapidly as he cupped her face in his hand. "I shouldn't drink. Were I a man of honor, I would leave you alone for someone more appropriate."

"Well, then, I certainly hope you are not a man of honor." She smiled.

His laugh rumbled deep in his chest, and she felt it. "I don't envy Daniel the task it must have been to keep you safe."

"Psh. I was obedient to a fault, and very demure."

He lifted his head. "Let's find some dinner. And I do believe I need a cup of coffee. Or three."

In the kitchen, Miles watched Lucy nibble the bread and cheese on her plate and wondered if he were dreaming or merely feeling the buzz that accompanied too many glasses of whiskey. She was here, with him, had seen him shift, and still she offered him compassion without pity. She had touched his face, had kissed him with an ardor that matched his own and left him feeling an odd mix of bewilderment and arousal.

"Why?" he asked her, genuinely baffled. "Why are you here with me?"

She wrapped her arm around her waist as she straightened in her seat. Studying him over the rim of her cup, she took a sip of tea, then replaced it on the saucer and smiled. "I like you. You are handsome and intelligent, and actually quite funny."

He cocked a brow. "When have I ever been funny?"

She wiped the corner of her mouth with a napkin and chuckled. "All the time."

Miles shook his head and took a swig of his coffee. "You're the first to ever say it." He stretched and sat back in his chair. Shifting always left him fatigued.

"Now then," Lucy said, brushing crumbs from her lap. "What sort of condition do you find your heart in these days?"

He paused. "Why do you ask?"

"I know that the larger the animal, the harder the process is on the human heart. Many shifters require heartclock transplants that doctors are unable or unwilling to perform for fear of legal prosecution."

"Did your mother never tell you it is unladylike to possess an over-abundance of knowledge?"

"Thankfully, we live in a modern age and not a century ago." Lucy eyed him flatly. "Besides, I daresay you have no patience for women who cannot think."

"That's true enough. I just would find it infinitely more convenient right now if were you not so . . . well informed."

She raised her eyebrows and tilted her head. "Oddly enough, it seems that I am more well-informed on the subject at hand than are you."

He held up a hand. "Touché. And I have had a transplant already. Two years ago."

She wrinkled her forehead. "On the battlefield?"

"Yes. Well, no. We were in India, but the procedure was not necessitated as a result of combat."

Lucy nodded slowly. "Sam. Of course he would do it for you."

"The official documents state that the transplant was required because of a wound sustained in battle." The memories were hazy and heavy. Anesthetic had been scarce, not to mention any kind of pain reliever after the fact. It had still been a better option, though, than coming home and risking discovery while trying to find a surgeon willing to do the transplant and not ask questions about why it was necessary.

"And how is the device now?"

He hesitated. Sharing information with anyone was such a foreign concept that he found himself fighting long-ingrained habits. He had a hard enough time confiding in his friends. "It is failing."

There was a certain amount of satisfaction in rendering the woman speechless. He smiled in spite of himself.

"Failing?" She stared at him for some time before repeating herself. "*Failing?* What is Sam doing for you, then? I hope he is planning to replace it soon."

"He is working on a prototype that will supposedly work indefinitely without even a hitch. But it isn't a guarantee of success, and there are . . . risks."

"Risks. What kind of risks?"

"You cannot fix everything, Lucy Pickett."

"Knowledge is power. What kind of risks?"

He smiled and leaned forward, clasping her fingers across the narrow table. "The mild sort that suggest a positive outcome is likely."

With a sigh, she rose, still holding his hand, and circled the table. She stood at his side and combed her fingers through his hair, gently pushing it away from his face before placing a light kiss on his forehead.

He linked an arm about her waist, his lips quirked. "Your brother is going to have my head."

"My brother quite likes you. He'll be most happy."

He chuckled. "You are naïve."

"Not entirely." She tilted her head. "There have been enough instances with former suitors to bring out his protective nature, I've seen it."

Miles lifted a brow. "What sort of instances?"

She smiled. "Nothing of consequence."

He shook his head. "I can only imagine your social calendar once you made your debut. And the number of men Daniel had to beat back with a stick."

"I've seen your sister. You must have done some protecting of your own."

He smiled. "A fair amount. She couldn't find a man to match her personality, or more to the point, a man who wasn't afraid of her, but I think she might have eventually. She met Daniel on a few occasions, you know. Mentioned in passing she found him most attractive."

Lucy smiled widely. "Of course she did. And what a handsome pair they would have made."

He paused and placed his knuckles lightly against Lucy's cheek. "I believe this is the first time in months I've smiled when speaking of her. Perhaps it won't hurt forever."

Lucy's eyes dropped to his lips, and he waited, wondering if she would take the initiative and kiss him first. She was tentative, hesitant, but she leaned into him and touched her lips to his mouth. She was sweet and soft, and everything he'd been convinced he would never have. He almost didn't dare believe it still.

"You're playing with fire," he murmured against her mouth and gently nudged her away from him. "In more ways than one. I am not willing to subject you to a lifetime of the potential dangers of living with a predatory shifter."

He found himself smugly satisfied that her eyes were glazed from the kiss, and she blinked, trying to focus on what he was saying.

She shook her head. "We've already discussed that. I'm not in any danger. In fact, you saved my life while in shifted form. We'll be fine. We can go for long walks together." She smirked. "I'll buy a leash."

He was laughing, long and hard, when Mrs. Romany entered the kitchen carrying a basket of cleaning supplies. She stopped in her tracks and stared at him. He realized the poor woman had probably never seen him even smile.

He reached up and tweaked Lucy's nose. "Awfully sure of yourself, Miss Pickett." He was still laughing when a light noise—just a hint, really—penetrated the happiness that enveloped the room.

He grew very still, his hands tightening on her waist. "Shh," he whispered.

The crack of a twig. An animal, perhaps? It came from the back door—the one that led to the thicket and the ravine where Lucy had taken her tumble. Ever so slowly, he eased out of the chair and padded swiftly to the door across the room. Lucy's eyes were huge, her fists clenched, and Mrs. Romany was still as stone. For the first time in his life, he wished that he were in wolf form.

The night outside was black, punctuated with swirls of white snow that blew into the glass before settling against the panes and onto the ground below. A low growl involuntarily escaped his throat, and thrusting his feet into the boots by the door, he turned the knob with a glance over his shoulder at Lucy, her face pale.

He put a finger to his lips, and she and Mrs. Romany both nodded at him in response. He slowly opened the door.

A cold gust of wind and snow tore into the kitchen, nearly ripping the door from the hinges. As he squinted into the dark of the night outside, he smelled something—something entirely familiar, something he knew he would have identified as a wolf but which remained frustratingly elusive to him as a human. And then the scent was gone.

As he pulled the door closed, an object bumped against it, and he looked down to see a small, metal box. If it contained the message he suspected it did, it meant his stalker was changing the routine. Picking up the box, he glanced around outside one more time. Whoever had left it had done a fairly thorough job of masking his tracks.

One notion in particular gave him cause for concern as he closed the kitchen door firmly behind him. As he locked it and closed the shutters over the windows, he had to wonder *what* would have the wherewithal to brave such a storm.

Chapter 25

iles had immediately retired to his chambers. He had placed a kiss on Lucy's forehead and left the kitchen with the box under his arm, telling Mrs. Romany to take care of her.

Feeling more than a little concerned about whatever was in that box, Lucy tried to relax in her room while Mrs. Romany kept her company, knitting in a chair by the fire.

Lucy hadn't pressed the issue of the box, had figured Miles would tell her what was happening in his own time. Which would be fine if she could maintain a good hold on her patience.

Perhaps he'd fallen asleep. As she studied the connecting door between their rooms, she admitted to herself that she wasn't going to get any rest while stewing over what was in that infernal box.

"I'm checking on him," she told Mrs. Romany, who looked up from her knitting with a frown.

"You need to rest."

"I'll come back straightaway. And I'll leave the door open." Lucy felt ridiculously young, much like she had at school when she'd been chastened by an instructor.

Mrs. Romany nodded at her and turned her attention back to her knitting. Biting back a smile, Lucy gave a perfunctory knock on the door and cracked it open to see Miles sprawled on the sofa in front of his hearth.

She made her way across the floor and was nearly to the couch when Miles said, "Why are you out of bed?"

She sat down carefully beside him, hiding a wince. "What's in the box, Miles?"

He glanced at her out of the corner of his eye before turning his attention back to the orange flames in the fireplace. "A note of affection."

"Is that all?"

"No."

She waited, but when he didn't elaborate further, she frowned. Rather than speak, however, she rested her arm on the back of the couch and placed her hand on his head, lightly running her fingers through his hair.

"Why are you here, Lucy Pickett?" He stared into the fire, his expression blank.

"I thought we'd already established that."

"It can lead to absolutely no good for you. Somebody wants to destroy me, and I will not have you caught in the cross fire." The alcohol had clearly worn off. His guard and sense of duty had slammed back into place.

"I don't believe that is your decision to make."

He glanced at her. "You think I cannot make you leave?"

"I think you can try. You can pretend that there is no affection between us, that we have not become friends. You can pretend that you are not attracted to me." She blushed in spite of her resolve to be sophisticated and urbane. "But we both know that all of those things are lies."

He turned his body to face her. Placing his lips to her palm, he lay the lightest of kisses upon it and closed his eyes. When he finally looked at her, his face was bleak. "There is no future with me. If I am not destroyed by my enemies, I will be hunted down by the Committee. And if that doesn't take me, my failing heart will."

"I never met a problem I couldn't fix." She smiled at him, despite the burning in her eyes, the tears that threatened to fall. "And never have I faced one with higher stakes. You need me. And I need you."

He shook his head. "You do most certainly do not need me."

The tears fell, first one and then another. "You treat me as an equal," she whispered. "You do not doubt my intellect or mock my interests. You do not placate me with platitudes or suggest that my studies would be better suited to a man's abilities. I tell you I am searching for a cure to counteract the Vampiric Assimilation Aid and you believe me. Your only concern is for my safety, and as frustrated as it has made me, I also appreciate it. There are men within my own circle at the Society who scoff behind my back, despite my accomplishments." She smiled, although it felt shaky, and wiped at a tear with her fingertip. "So, yes, my lord, I do need you. You are a most singular man, one I daresay is most suited to me. I sincerely doubt I would find your equal, even should I search far and wide."

Miles pulled a white handkerchief from his trouser pocket and gently wiped her cheeks. "Well, then," he finally murmured. "I suppose I must devise a plan."

"You may begin by telling me exactly what you are facing."

He sighed, just a small sound that carried a wealth of meaning behind it. "You've seen one of the notes before, I take it. From someone who, apparently, 'knows my secret.' I take great care to be alone when I shift, but someone is clearly aware of it."

"What else was in the box?"

His voice was low, reluctant. "Last month when I shifted, I waited too long to undress. My shirt was ripped to shreds, and as I was trying to remove it during the process, I sliced my arm open. I bled all over the shirt, of course, and when I returned at dawn to shift back, only my trousers were there. Someone had made off with the shirt."

"And returned it tonight, with another note?" Lucy pursed her lips in thought.

He shook his head. "Only a part of it was returned. A scrap with blood on it."

"This has been going on for how long?"

"This makes the eleventh note. They were arriving monthly until last week at the manor, and now this one."

"And how are they usually delivered?"

"Plain envelope, nothing on it but my name. Usually delivered here to the lodge, but I did receive one at the London town house. And the most recent before tonight went directly to the manor."

"Might we assume your stalker is preparing to act, then? Perhaps the next note will be one of extortion. Money, other assets."

Miles moved to the fireplace, piling two more logs and fanning the flames until the wood crackled in the quiet night. "There was more written on the note tonight," he finally said as he straightened and shoved his hands in his pockets. Leaning one shoulder against the tall mantelpiece, dressed in trousers and a white shirt open at the throat, he was breathtakingly handsome, and she felt her heart trip, wondering how on earth no woman had snatched him up already.

"What did it say?" she managed to ask as she took in the sight of him. Tall. Strong. *Hers.*

"It told me to pass the earldom on to my brother."

Lucy blinked. "Who would benefit from Jonathan being the earl? Besides Jonathan?"

Miles arched a brow. "You believe my brother is behind this?"

She widened her eyes and shrugged. "It's baffling. Perhaps Arthur wants to inherit and is trying to rid himself of both you and Jonathan."

He shook his head. "Why not just kill me outright? Or turn my name in to the PSRC?"

Lucy frowned. "There is that."

"There is a man on the PSRC, a ridiculous fool who fought alongside me and the others. I suspect, although I'm not certain, that he may have followed me one night when I shifted. It was miles away from our camp, but he was in the area the next morning. He doesn't know that I saw him."

"What is his name?"

"Bryce Randolph."

Lucy squinted into the fire, thinking. "It does sound familiar. I wonder if Daniel has mentioned him at some point."

"And then there are my father's former friends."

"I'm sorry?"

Miles shook his head. "My father made promises to two neighboring land owners to sell Blackwell to them. The buyers were then going to divide the land and sell it piecemeal at exorbitant costs, making a tidy profit. New money is taking the place of old, and land ownership isn't the guarantee of wealth and status it used to be."

"If your father was looking to earn money off the land, why did he not just parcel it off himself as the neighbors were planning to do?"

"His health was failing, and he couldn't be bothered with business details. He had opted to take the lump sum and be done with it. Then he died suddenly without completing the transaction."

"And you refused to sell."

Miles swallowed and looked away. "My father had gambled away almost everything, used the land as collateral. When I returned from India, Blackwell Manor was all but lost. Creditors were pounding at the door, threatening to seize this hunting lodge and the London town house as well. I had enough money of my own invested to cover the two properties and Blackwell Manor itself, but the extensive lands where the tenants are located was nearing foreclosure and mandatory sale. I didn't have enough to cover everything."

Lucy's mouth dropped open as her thoughts clicked into place. "That's why you married Clara," she murmured.

His face gave nothing away.

"You've allowed everyone to believe you married an heiress to save the earldom. In reality, you did it to save the tenants from eviction."

"The tenants are happy."

"The neighboring landowners are not."

He nodded.

"Miles, why? Why do you allow people to believe the worst about you?"

"They're going to believe it anyway. I grew weary of the effort it took to convince them otherwise."

She watched him quietly, knowing he wouldn't appreciate any sympathy. "I would like your permission to examine the Tesla Room records at Blackwell when I return. There are details I'd like to examine. Also, I am not nearly tired tonight, and I would love a game of chess."

As dawn approached, Miles stood outside the massive double doors that graced the front of the hunting lodge and stared into the trees at a small, dark shape that stood out against the white expanse of snow covering the ground. His energy had returned in spades; it was amazing how refreshed he felt after plugging into the heartclock machine for a few hours.

Lucy had lasted well into the night, playing several smart games of chess before fatigue eventually clouded her judgment. He had carried her back to her bed, amidst feeble protests on her part, and when he'd heard her deep, even breathing from the next room, he'd made himself comfortable in a reading chair next to the fire and plugged into the heart charger.

She was still resting, and he wasn't surprised. He thought of her now as he made his way across the front lawn, his great coat dragging through the snow. He'd allowed himself the luxury of watching her sleep for a moment that morning, even with Mrs. Romany still in the room and snoring quietly from the sofa. Lucy's dark hair spread across the pillow, eyelashes like fans against her cheeks. She gave the occasional wince as she shifted in sleep, unconsciously feeling the pain of her injuries.

He frowned as he thought of the mad tumble she'd taken down the side of the ravine. He barely remembered it. There were images, impressions, but he was never fully himself when he shifted. The thought that the fall could have killed her was never far from his thoughts, and he couldn't shake the crushing sense of responsibility he felt. If she hadn't been terrified of the wolf, she wouldn't have fallen down the ravine.

He was still several yards away from the black object lying on the ground when he recognized it for what it was and stopped in his tracks. Quietly examining his surroundings, he waited for the space of several heartbeats before continuing, this time more slowly.

It was a trap, one with vicious teeth and strength enough to snap the legs or crush the head of an unsuspecting animal. He'd certainly seen them before, but never on Blackwell land. As he neared the thing, he kept watch, his senses alert, attempting to determine whether or not he was alone near the edge of the woods.

Moving to a nearby tree, he wrenched off a dead branch that he then used to trip the contraption. It snapped the branch clean in half, a harsh metallic sound ringing through the forest. He nudged the trap grimly with one booted foot as a very real fear began to take root. Anger was much easier to handle than fear, though, and he welcomed the surge of rage that quickly followed and coursed through his veins, causing his heartclock to increase in rhythm and exertion.

He could only hope that the wolf possessed an innate ability to sense danger. He didn't recall ever having seen a trap anywhere near the lodge before, and one thing he did know for certain was that the wolf had never ventured beyond Blackwell land. It was as though he instinctively sensed his own boundaries.

He pulled the trap loose from the stake that anchored it deep into the cold ground and lifted it by its heavy chain to eye level. The trap had no qualities to give away the identity of its owner. He searched for a blacksmith's mark and found none. The trap was sinister in both feel and appearance, and the cold of the metal seeped through his warm, lined leather gloves.

He turned back toward the hunting lodge, still holding the trap, and considered the fact that the next time he shifted, he would have to remain indoors. He'd tried that once before and had experienced a sense of frustration unlike any other. He'd shifted back to find the den in absolute shambles. It wasn't the mess that had given him pause, it was the shattered glass that littered the floor and had cut him deeply, leaving him with gashes on his hands and feet. It was then that he'd realized he was a danger to himself closed in, and heaven help anyone around him who might happen to get in his way.

He entered the lodge and made his way with quick strides to the door in the kitchen that led to a small cellar. He didn't need the light—one benefit, he supposed, to his genetic abnormality—and swept his gaze over the food that was stored on shelves and the racks of lamb and pork that hung suspended from the rafters.

Crossing to the far corner, he tossed the trap to the floor where it hit with a clang that was loud against the stillness. Perhaps it was time to accept Oliver's offer of more aggressive investigation into the person—or persons—who meant him harm. What had once been apathy had given way to a fledgling sense of hope for a relatively normal future, and he found himself loath to abandon it after having been without it for so long.

Perhaps it was all just ridiculous nonsense. His father had not been happy, that much had been clear. And according to Blake family history, the wolf had appeared randomly over thirteen generations. Miles seriously doubted that any of his ancestors had ever found real joy or any sense of lasting peace.

For the first time since he had shifted as a young man, he found himself wondering if there was a cure. Perhaps it was time to send for Hazel Hughes—not so much for her abilities, which were clearly odd, but for her knowledge. She might know where to look for answers.

Turning away from the death trap, he returned to the kitchen and shook out of his coat and gloves. Lucy would be awake before long, and it appeared Mrs. Romany was still sleeping comfortably in the room with her. It was the butler's day off, and Miles hadn't bothered to program the few 'tons in residence for some time. It fell to him to find something for breakfast and, while he never felt compunction about finding something for himself to eat, it was awkward in the light of day to fix food for a lady and his housekeeper while lacking any kind of culinary talent. Bread and cheese while half drunk had been one thing. Now he was sober, and he felt ridiculous.

Lucy wouldn't complain, though, he knew that much. But he found himself wanting to be more than adequate. He wanted to be exceptional for her, and there was the rub. Miles Phillip Charles Blake, fourteenth earl of Blackwell, had never bothered trying to impress anyone.

With an irritated sigh, he opened several cupboards and a pantry door before he found some biscuits and jam. He supposed it would have to do. Besides, he had bigger issues at hand. Coupled with the fact that somebody was bent on killing him, he had to get Lucy back home without a soul knowing she had spent the weekend alone with him. And the sooner, the better. He had an uneasy sense that she wasn't safe with him. As much as he would have liked to convince himself that he could protect her, he knew she could easily be caught in the cross fire, and it wasn't a risk he was willing to take.

Chapter 26

Lucy was livid. After breakfast, Miles, with no more than a handful of words, had packed her belongings and hauled them to the lodge's entryway. He told her he had programmed the carriage to take her home to her mother. Only when she'd told him, in no uncertain terms, that she would simply leave her mother's house and return to Blackwell on her own did he reprogram the carriage's destination.

Acquiescing with quiet, although visible, fury, he had taken her telescriber and sent word to the manor that she would be returning and to please have the countess's chambers ready for her arrival. When she'd balked at the high-handedness of the request, he'd quelled her objections with a look that brooked no argument. She wisely kept any further objections to herself.

The circuitous route through London had added an additional two hours to her trip, and she was exhausted.

Upon her arrival, Mrs. Farrell had told her that Jonathan had telescribed from Bath to say that Kate was doing very well and they would leave for the ball at Charlesworth House directly from there. Kate's maid was to pack a trunk that Lucy would take with her for Kate when she left for the ball in two days.

Lucy had been looking forward to the trip with some anticipation, hoping for some time alone with Miles in a covered carriage, but the way he'd been acting since that morning had her doubting he would come near her with a ten-foot pole.

Not one for fits of self-doubt, she nevertheless found herself wondering if Miles was losing interest, if perhaps now that they were no longer marooned in a blizzard his ardor had cooled. He had lived a solitary life before meeting her, and just because he desired her and had shared a moment or two of emotion didn't necessarily mean he planned to have any kind of future that included her.

Well, that was just fine, she fumed as she moved around the countess's chambers, jabbing loose pins back into her coiffure and straightening her gown despite screams of protest from her aching and bruised body. If he didn't care for her company, if he had insisted she stay in this suite out of a sense of personal duty to her safety and nothing more, then she was not going to beg for his affection.

She could, however, finish the task she'd begun upon her arrival at Blackwell. Kate had been poisoned by 'tons who had been programmed to do the deed, and Lucy was determined to uncover who was behind it. Locking the door behind her, per his lordship's instructions, she made her way through the sitting room with the use of the cane Miles had given her at the hunting lodge. When she reached the front stairs, she finally began to feel the welcomed effects of the numbing herb she'd crushed and put into her tea, and she walked with more ease.

She continued her way through the main hall, past the breakfast and dining rooms and through the next door on her right. The hum of the Tesla Room was familiar, and it never failed to leave Lucy with a sense of awe at the power contained in the electric coils.

The logs were kept in neat black books that marched side by side down rows of shelves in the large room. Every week, the paper roll bearing copies of each telescribed message that either came into or left the manor was collected, cut, neatly labeled, and filed away in the books.

Lucy pulled the black ledgers from the shelves that dated back to Kate's arrival at the manor and set them on a waist-high table at the far end of the room. She flipped through the pages, running her finger down the text of incoming and outgoing messages. There were telescriptions to the market requesting deliveries of various foodstuffs, mentions of pending visits from the Charlesworths, Sam, and Oliver, requests for meetings with Miles from members of Parliament and also from surrounding neighbors.

Lucy looked pensively at the books, tapping her forefinger against the paper. On a whim, she returned to the archives and selected two more ledgers dating back six months. She opened the first and walked back to the table, where she continued her perusal to the comfortable accompaniment of the Tesla coils' hum.

She reviewed the telescriptions sent from Clara to her family across the ocean as well as the communications sent to and from Marie. Clara had scribed on more than one occasion that she wasn't feeling well, and Lucy's heart raced as she read the haunting words of a dying woman to a family who didn't seem inclined to offer much support in return. Their answering messages contained suggestions that she stay indoors and away from the cold English air. At one point, Clara's mother had scribed to say that Clara should have the earl contact a physician if she were truly worried for her health. The message was dated shortly before Clara's eventual demise.

Lucy frowned as she turned the next page and saw the message from Miles to the family saying that Clara had passed from an unknown illness.

The obsequious reply from the Americas was that the family was glad to know their daughter would be buried on esteemed Blackwell land and that perhaps a member of the family would visit the grave the next time one of them traveled to London on business.

Lucy looked up in disgust and stared at the wall, deep in thought. What was wrong with the girl's family? As much as she felt pettily jealous of Miles's first wife, her sense of pity overrode any other emotion.

As Lucy read the telescriptions that followed, an ache gathered in her throat. Miles's messages to the Charlesworths and his friends about Marie's death were succinct and devoid of emotion. It was a far more telling sign of his grief than lengthy explanations would have been.

She replaced the transcription books in their proper places on the archive shelves and walked to the door that connected the Tesla Room to the Programming Room. The quiet in the room after the hum of the Tesla coils was marked, and Lucy flipped a light switch on the wall as she closed the door behind her.

The programming tins were as neatly categorized as the telescribed messages had been; neat rows of boxes lined side by side were dated and catalogued numerically. It was a testament to the estate's wealth; the average household sent their 'ton's cards through a buffer, smoothing out the programming bumps and readying them for new instruction. Recycling the tins saved money, but, while it was efficient, it didn't allow for permanent records. When mistakes were made, whether big or small, a quick examination of the programming instructions pointed fingers in the right direction—either the programmer was at fault, or the 'ton itself had malfunctioned.

Lucy made her way slowly along the shelves, looking for the dates in question. "Six months ago," she murmured aloud and stopped when she spied the correct collection of spent tins. Pulling a box from the shelf, she opened the lid and carefully withdrew several cards dated from Clara's arrival at Blackwell. She fed them one by one into the reading machine and scanned the instructions as they appeared on the black screen.

The programming was standard: the name and serial number of the 'ton read across the top, along with a listing of duties to be performed and the duration of each. Ejecting and feeding card after card, Lucy watched specifically for cards that had been inserted into Mr. Grafton's cooking staff. Some of Mr. Grafton's cards and a few for Mr. Clancy's 'tons were notably absent.

She wondered if Mr. Clancy kept his archives in the grounds' Charging Room. It would have been unusual for the tins to be housed in different places on the estate. Families who wanted a record of everything that transpired on their property typically maintained a tidy system in one central location.

Lucy glanced at the numbered tin she had just fed into the machine before placing it back into the box where she'd kept her other hand as a placeholder. She lifted the next several tins, prepared to continue her examination, when she noticed a discrepancy in the numbering. Looking again at the tin in her hand, she looked back at the box to the one she'd just replaced.

She chewed on her lip as her heart began to thump. Flipping through the tins showed a clear gap in serial numbers; they hadn't merely been misfiled. There were a total of five missing programming cards and no way of knowing which 'tons had used them—or to what end.

Lucy scrutinized the dates in question and pulled a pen and small notebook from her pocket. She scribbled the dates onto the page and then continued to flip through the tins, making careful note of missing dates and serial numbers. As she made her way through the box and into the beginning of the next, an alarming pattern emerged.

She carefully replaced the tins and returned to the Tesla Room. She pulled one of the telescribing books off the shelf and leafed through several pages, stopping periodically and jotting notes next to those she'd already made. When she finished, she took a deep breath and examined her findings.

There were programming tins missing throughout the entire month of Clara's residence, and, perhaps more telling, two were absent on the day immediately following her death—the day of Marie's death.

According to the transcription records, there had been a series of guests at the manor during those times that included several players Lucy knew, and a few she did not. The names of those she hadn't met included men Miles had mentioned as his father's former friends who were now his enemies.

And among the names she knew well were Eustace, Arthur, and Candice Charlesworth; Samuel MacInnes; Daniel Pickett; and Oliver Reed.

Mrs. Farrell was present at the manor every day and night, as were Mr. Clancy, Miss Watts, and Mr. Grafton. Any one of them could have gained access to the Programming Room, and Lucy had seen with her own eyes that each staff member possessed at least a rudimentary ability to program.

The one thing that gave her hope when she considered the possibility of telling Miles that one of his friends may well have killed his wife or sister was the fact that Marie had knocked over the portrait of the Charlesworths in the gallery, which seemed to implicate the family.

Lucy frowned as she reflected on Candice's attraction to Oliver; she had certainly seemed fixated on him despite the fact that he had remained largely aloof. Might his aloofness been an act? The possibility that the detective might somehow be involved was chilling. He would have contacts, possible methods of avoiding investigation. She didn't suspect her brother for even a moment.

Of course, there was always Miles himself, but she doubted he had any involvement in the deaths. He could have disposed of Lucy easily enough at the hunting lodge for bringing up questions that might have cast suspicion upon him. Not to mention the fact that it would break her heart to discover he was a murderer. No, that wouldn't do at all.

She supposed she would have to keep looking for the answers. Proving his innocence might be the most important thing she would ever do. Not only for him but for herself.

Miles awoke with a start. As his eyes gradually focused on the flash of red beside his bed at the manor, his heart thumped when he saw his dead sister watching him, her eyes hard. "Oh, Marie," he murmured, his voice thick with sleep. "What do you need from me?"

Her gaze softened, and his eyes pricked with a surprising sting of tears.

She moved slowly toward the door and turned to look over shoulder at him—pausing, waiting. He climbed out of the warm cocoon of his bed and dressed quickly, adding his overcoat when Marie looked at it pointedly.

Miles glanced at Lucy's closed bedroom door before following Marie out of the south wing. Lucy was fully invested in his family drama, and the thought crossed his mind to awaken her, but she was exhausted. He'd seen it in her face at dinner that evening.

Marie moved swiftly down the hallway, turning corners and descending staircases so quickly Miles had to move nearly at a trot. It was no wonder Lucy had been chasing Marie at a dead run that second night when he'd caught her and hauled her into the library.

There had been no further vampire attacks in his absence, either at the manor or in town, and Oliver had sent word that more investigators were on their way to Coleshire to look for new leads. Miles was relieved at the temporary respite, but he still needed to find the person responsible for the deaths of his sister and his wife, and the fact that the murderer was still at large gave him added incentive to keep Lucy at bay. If she were added to the list of growing tragedies . . .

His heartclock tripped at the thought, as though a fist had reached into his chest and clenched it.

Marie glanced back occasionally, eventually leading him out of the house and into the back gardens. She kept moving, past the greenhouse, through the paths of tangled, dead rosebushes, and into the thicket of trees beyond. He thought she might stop at her garden and felt a fair amount of surprise when she glided past it.

He grew increasingly uneasy once he realized where she was going. The pathway beyond her walled sanctuary led through the trees and to a plot of land encircled by a wrought-iron fence with a gate that, he knew all too well, screeched on hinges as though protesting an unwelcome invasion by the living.

The family cemetery was a fairly large affair, as through the years tenants had also been buried there. It was shrouded in trees whose thick, gnarled branches acted as protectors of the dead and a warning to those who might come to disturb.

Marie passed directly through the gate, and as Miles opened it, true to form, the sound tore through the night. He would always hate that sound. It symbolized sadness and grief. He had heard it enough as a child, burying tenants who had been old or ill, but it now reminded him of laying his mother to rest. And his wife and sister.

He hadn't lost any sleep over the death of his father, and he flicked a dismissive and disgusted glance at the man's ridiculously ostentatious headstone as Marie led him past it. That he could walk past the man's grave without a flicker of emotion was a feat that had taken years to master.

Images flashed through his mind. He had been a young man, out late at night, cavorting with friends, attempting to sneak back into the house unnoticed, when he'd come upon his father.

His father, just outside these very gates, naked. That much had stopped Miles cold. And then the horror of watching the man shift—his limbs contorting, his muscles, bones, and tendons snapping and rearranging to accommodate a new form.

Although he didn't remember doing it, Miles must have made a sound that alerted the wolf to his presence—or perhaps it was his scent, carried on the breeze—because once his father had fully shifted, the wolf turned and ran at him. Before Miles had had the presence of mind to flee, the animal had been upon him, knocking him to the ground and taking a swipe at his head. He had turned his face, his scream trapped by the enormous paw pressing down on his chest.

The wolf had paused, snarling and sides heaving, and then darted around the cemetery gates and into the trees, leaving Miles bruised and bleeding profusely from the ragged gash across his face.

Once Miles had begun shifting, he'd assumed he would also be a danger to others because wasn't that the case when he'd come upon his father? Lucy's information that the animal wouldn't do anything that the human wouldn't do suddenly made sense. His father had not been a good man. He had been cold, distant, and cruelly dismissive. It was no wonder such a man had become a wolf and disfigured Miles in a way that changed his future completely.

The images and memories heightened his agitation, despite his best intentions to remain impassive, so that by the time Marie reached Clara's grave, he was on edge, strung taut.

"What is it you wish for me to know?" he said aloud to Marie, who stood, looking at the ground that covered the body of his dead wife. His voice was harsh—he heard it himself—and Marie regarded him with a raised brow, looking so much as she had in life that he caught his breath. She had always disarmed him, pulled him from a sour mood with a sardonic comment, a playful, sisterly slap upside the head. He almost expected it of her now, and he felt his throat clog with unshed tears.

"What is it?" he whispered, aching.

Marie knelt on the ground and placed her hands flat. It was with no small amount of shock that Miles watched her curl her fingers into the frozen earth and begin to pull. Even more profoundly disturbing was the fact that she was actually moving the dirt.

He dropped next to her and placed his hand over hers, only to be caught in a surreal flood of emotion and befuddled logic as his hand passed through hers and onto the ground. Her face was so close to his, so familiar and *there* that he found it impossible to believe she wasn't real.

Marie turned back to the ground and clawed at it violently, dirt and rock pulling up from the grave in small mounds that brushed against his hands and fell to the side.

He looked at her face, a twisted mix of fury and desperation, and he instinctively reached for her shoulders, trying to turn her toward him, to stop her frantic movements.

"Marie, stop," he said as his hands passed through her ghostly form. *"Stop."*

She finally ceased, looking at him with wide eyes, sparked with equal parts anger and sorrow. Her face took on an expression of protest as she suddenly was sucked away from him, as though pulled from behind by an enormous hand. In the flash of an instant, she was gone.

No! Miles hung his head, weary to the bone, and reached for the dirt his sister had overturned with such frantic desperation. With a sense of resolve, he regarded the shack in the corner of the graveyard, covered by ivy and branches. He knew it hadn't been accessed in at least six months—maybe longer if Mr. Clancy had brought tools with him from outside for the recent burials.

He broke the rusty lock on the shed and entered, his eyes falling upon a cluster of shovels in the corner. Grabbing one, he returned to the ground that covered his wife's grave and dug the blade in deep.

Chapter 27

Lucy turned over in bed as the insistent noise of her telescriber on the nightstand pulled her from the deepest sleep she'd experienced in a long time. She grabbed the machine more to silence the racket than to see who wanted her attention so late at night.

She finally, reluctantly, switched on the bedside lamp and squinted at the message.

Balcony

Lucy frowned. The sender screen showed the message had come from the grounds' outbuilding, but there was no name attached. *Balcony?*

She glanced at the double French doors that graced the far side of the room and led out onto the countess's private balcony. Was it Miles? If he needed her, why hadn't he just come to the door?

She climbed out of bed, finding her slippers and padding across the room, shivering. When she reached the doors, she raised her hand to the curtain covering the glass and slowly inched it aside. She couldn't see anything and lifting the fabric higher proved fruitless. There was nothing to see.

Was she foolish enough to actually go out onto the balcony? She shook her head and turned away from the doors, making her way instead to the sitting room. Miles's bedroom door was closed, but without giving it a second thought, she crossed to it and knocked.

She waited for what seemed like a long time, and when he didn't answer, she felt her muscles tense. Turning the knob proved fruitless; the blasted man had locked his door. Well, of course he had. Someone seemed bent on killing him. Her heart thumping at the thought, she wondered if she dared shoot the lock with her ray gun.

Deciding desperate times called for desperate measures, she returned to her room, pawed through her portmanteau, and found the weapon. Within a matter of minutes, she'd blown a hole through both Miles's doorknob and the locking mechanism. Nudging the door open with her foot, she looked into his bedroom only to find it empty.

Rather than feel relief that he wasn't dead, she grew short of breath. Her hand that still clutched the gun felt clammy. Where was he? Was he hurt? Abducted? She rubbed her arm across her forehead and, biting her lip in growing consternation, returned to her bedchamber, barely registering the pain of her sore ankle.

She glanced at the telescriber, which had received another message. It was a repeat of the first. It had to be Miles. Who else would dare telescribe her in the middle of the night? She tightened her grip on her weapon and approached the double doors. Cracking one open, she braced against the bone-deep cold that immediately swept into the room from outside. Fog had gathered, thick and eerie, and she was unable to see more than a few feet beyond the edge of the balcony.

She stood, her gun arm bent at the elbow, and tried to still her breathing, which sounded loud in the dense night. A sound to her left, quiet yet mechanical in nature, heralded the arrival of one of Mr. Clancy's 'tons. The green uniform was visible through the balcony's stone railings, and she tensed, frowning, and straightened her gun until it was level with the 'ton's head.

"A message from Mr. Clancy," the boy told her as he cleared the railing. His black eyes were unblinking. "You needn't shoot," he added. Extending his hand, he presented a folded piece of paper.

She finally took it, her eyes never leaving his face. "Why didn't he telescribe me the message?" she asked him, wary.

"He says it is a sensitive matter that oughtn't to go on the official record."

The young man turned and climbed back over the balcony railing. He was quiet until he must have reached a height that made for a comfortable drop. She heard him hit the ground and then run toward the grounds' shed. He was quickly swallowed by the thickening fog that steadily crept toward the house.

Senses on alert and more than a little afraid, she backed into her room and closed the French doors firmly behind her. Opening the folded letter, she read the few words scrawled on the paper.

His lordship is at the graveyard.

She frowned. Why would Miles be at the graveyard at two o'clock in the morning, and why would Mr. Clancy want her to know? She quickly changed clothing, donning a riding outfit with minimal buttons and ribbons, and checked her pocket watch before putting it in her pants pocket.

She'd only seen the graveyard from afar, and as she placed her thigh holster around her leg and secured the ray gun in place, she wondered how she was going to find it in the dark fog. Grabbing a Tesla torch, she tested it before leaving her room and making her way out of the south wing, exiting the house through the back kitchen door.

The light she shone on the path through the woods didn't penetrate the thick fog beyond a few feet, and the effect was disconcerting. It was as though she were walking into an abyss with no notion of what lay on the other side, and each snap of a twig, each sound of a night creature, was magnified all the more because nothing was visible.

She couldn't run. The lack of visibility hindered her, but so did the pain in her tender ribs and ankle. The combination of exertion and fear had her breathing rapidly, and the stabbing sensation in her side slowed her down despite her determination to reach the graveyard quickly.

What seemed like an eternity was in reality a mere ten minutes, but by the time Lucy reached the looming graveyard gate, she felt as though she'd run all day. She stood for several long moments, catching her breath and wondering what she would say to Miles, wondering what he could possibly be doing.

Shifting the torch to her injured hand and bracing it against her body, she reached for the handle on the gate and clasped it with fingers that were painfully cold. She slipped the latch and tugged on the heavy monstrosity, gasping in dismay at the horrid screeching sound that split the night.

She stood rooted in fear. The thick fog swirled around her, she couldn't see more than a few feet in front of her face, and she had no idea where to go. She wasn't familiar with the landscape. She didn't know where Miles was or if he was even really out there.

Fighting back a whimper, she moved forward, shining the torch ahead of her and knowing full well that if someone meant her harm she was little more than a sitting duck. She was reluctant to pull out her ray gun for fear of accidentally blasting a hole through Miles's chest. She doubted very much that Sam, talented though he was, would be able to repair the damage.

A figure emerged from the fog and bore down upon her like a freight train. She stumbled backward in fear as the shape grasped her by the shoulders before she could draw her weapon.

"Lucy!"

Her breath left her in a rush, and to her horror, she felt her knees buckle. "Miles, I might have killed you!"

He hauled her up against him, and she nearly sobbed with relief— both that he wasn't dead and neither was she.

"Woman, are you *insane?*"

She nodded and bumped her head against his chin. "Yes. Yes, I do believe so."

He held her away from him, and she realized he was soaking wet with a combination of fog-induced dampness and sweat, and he was incredibly pale.

"What are you doing?" She put her hand alongside his clammy cheek. "Miles, you do not look well. What is happening? I received a message from Mr. Clancy that you were here. He went to great trouble to secretly inform me."

Miles clenched his jaw. "He's going to find himself unemployed by morning."

"No, no. Really, I'm sure he meant well. Perhaps he was concerned about you."

"So he sends out a tiny woman with broken ribs who can barely walk?" His eyes narrowed, and they were frighteningly bloodshot. "Tell me what you're doing here." His breathing was labored, though she wasn't certain if it was from anger or exertion.

The graveyard gate's hinges screamed again, and Miles pulled Lucy behind him.

Lucy unhooked her ray gun from her thigh holster and tapped his hand with it. He glanced down at it and cast an unreadable look at her before taking it from her fingers with a slight shake of his head. Inching slowly to the right, he backed her up against the trunk of a large, gnarled tree, shielding her from whatever was coming.

Lucy heard the familiar whirring of 'tons moments before Miles let out a string of curses. She moved out from behind him and saw Mr. Clancy and four of his groundsboys approaching with shovels and large clippers.

Mr. Clancy looked at her somewhat sheepishly before turning to Miles. "Stephen was supposed to tell her to meet me at the greenhouse," he said gruffly. "I would never have had her walk all this way by herself."

Miles looked first at Lucy and then at the gardener before finally managing to speak. "What are you doing here?" he barked at the older man.

"Miss Marie said you needed help," Clancy answered as he shuffled closer. His eyes were suspiciously bright, and Lucy's heart broke to remember how close he'd been to Marie. "And so I came. With help."

Miles looked at him and then the groundsboys for a long moment, a muscle working in his jaw, before he nodded once. The fog combined with the light from the Tesla torch, giving Lucy another good look at the earl's face, which was nearly gray.

"What have you been doing, Miles?" she demanded.

He didn't respond, but, with a curt nod, he grabbed her hand and turned deeper into the graveyard. He stepped around headstones of varying heights, and she followed carefully, her suspicions confirmed by the time they reached their destination.

The earth next to Clara Blake's headstone had been partially dug. A lone shovel sat off to the side as if tossed there in a hurry. Lucy must have interrupted Miles when she opened the gate. "Why didn't you tell me you were doing this tonight? It was my idea, and I didn't mean for you to have to do this alone—I would have—"

"Marie led me here," he interrupted, his voice low.

He tucked Lucy's ray gun into his waistband and retrieved the shovel.

Mr. Clancy put his hand on Miles's arm. "Let the boys do the rest," he muttered. After a significant pause, while the old man stared at Miles's face, he added, "You'd best sit a spell."

Lucy spied a bench nearby, one of several conveniently placed for the bereaved to commune with their dead, and motioned to it with her head. To her relief, Miles followed without argument and sat next to her with a quiet exhalation of air.

"You need to plug in, don't you? Is it portable? Can I bring it to you?" She knew he wouldn't appreciate the fussing, but she was fighting a sense of desperation that clogged her throat. If only Sam were still at the manor.

"I have time," he told her. "When we finish here, I'll go up to the observatory."

"That's where you keep it. I wondered." The length of his thigh touched hers, and it struck her as the ultimate irony that such a strong, vital man was at the mercy of a clockwork mechanism no bigger than his fist.

They looked on in silence at the tableau before them. The 'tons dug down into the earth with far more strength than most humans would have been able to manage. It wasn't long before the shovels scraped against something solid, and, with one hard thump of her heart, Lucy realized they'd reached Clara's coffin.

Under Mr. Clancy's direction, the 'tons dug around the large box. Threading ropes beneath it, they maneuvered the coffin to the surface, revealing the locking mechanisms on the side. Lucy watched in trepidation as they set the coffin next to the gaping hole in the ground. Mr. Clancy looked over at Miles.

Lucy felt him tense beside her. She wanted to tell him it was unnecessary, that they didn't need to open the box. It didn't matter anyway, did it? Whether she'd been murdered or had died of an illness, either way she was gone.

Except it did matter. Someone was poisoning Kate, and someone had already murdered at least one person, possibly two. They needed to know the truth.

"Stay here," Miles finally said, looking at the coffin. "You don't need to see this."

"Yes, I do. You don't know what you're looking for."

He studied her face, his expression blank. She would have given anything to know what he was thinking. He didn't say anything but stood and grabbed her hand, leading her to the grave.

Mr. Clancy motioned to the 'tons, and they all stepped back as Lucy and Miles approached. The coffin's locking mechanisms were a complex configuration of dials and knobs that required a series of passwords to disengage. Resurrectionists were notorious for digging up bodies for necromancers to use to create zombies—and never for purposes other than the most nefarious—and so coffins in the modern age were locked, sealed and buried for eternity.

"Who else set the locks with you?" Lucy asked Miles. By law, both a relation and a certified Gravelocker were required to input a secret code.

"Marie."

Lucy nodded. She didn't have to ask him if he knew her passwords, nor was she about to question whether or not Marie had been a certified Gravelocker.

He knelt next to the coffin, and using one of Mr. Clancy's large clippers, he cut the chains that held the outer casing over the locks.

Tendrils of fog swept along the ground and drifted into the air. Lucy moved closer to him, less afraid of cracking open a coffin than of the encroaching eeriness of the night.

Miles spun the dial on the left, clicking in the numbers and letters of his password. He paused and glanced up to his right, visibly tensing. The air around them had changed, crackling with a dark intensity that had Lucy's stomach churning.

She looked into the fog-enshrouded night, squinting but seeing nothing, hearing nothing.

Mr. Clancy inched to Miles's side. "We'd best be about finishin' this, then," the old man whispered.

Miles nodded, his eyes still canvassing the area just beyond their vision. His attention still focused on the fog, he extended his hand toward Lucy, and when she took it, he pulled her down close to his side. "Stay right here," he murmured. He took her ray gun from his waistband, and, putting a hand on her thigh, placed the gun back in the holster. "If I have to leave, use one of the 'tons as a shield. Do not hesitate to fire this," he finished with a slight shake of the holster.

Cursing under his breath, he returned his focus to the locks on the coffin while occasionally glancing into the night. He made quick work of the first lock, multiple dead bolts sliding back with a click and whir of gears. He spun the dial of the second lock and clicked the correct digits into place. The locking mechanism released as the first had, and Miles stood, bringing Lucy with him.

They backed up a few steps, and Mr. Clancy gestured to two of the 'tons, who approached either end of the coffin with crowbars and began to pry it up. Lucy glanced at Miles, and her breath caught in her throat at the look on his face—a combination of anger and distress—paired with a ghostly pallor. She closed her eyes briefly as she heard the lid lift before turning her attention to the ghoulish task at hand.

Stiffening her resolve, Lucy stepped forward to examine the dead woman's remains. She caught a glimpse of a body dressed in white lace and a beautiful veil, hands crossed atop her midsection, an embroidered handkerchief placed lightly in her fingers. She was going to have to get much closer to examine Clara's fingernails, and she welcomed the comfort of Miles's hand at the small of her back.

Miles took the Tesla torch from her trembling hand and shined the light on Clara's still form. The air around them was quiet. Not a breeze wafted, no natural sounds of small creatures at night.

The violent shove that came at them from behind sent Lucy sprawling headlong atop the body and Miles flying to the side.

Chapter 28

Lucy fought the screaming pain in her side as she shoved herself upward, bracing herself against the sickeningly rotted shoulder of the dead woman. The decaying bones beneath her splinted hand cracked in protest.

The air left her lungs in a great whoosh, and she struggled to draw a decent breath. The coffin teetered on the edge of the gaping hole next to it, and for a horrified moment, Lucy was certain she was going to plunge into pit along with the coffin and Clara's remains.

Lucy registered the 'tons at either end of the coffin as they righted it. She couldn't see Miles, but she heard his roar and saw a blur of activity as she lifted her head. There was a loud hiss and a snarl, and then he was pursuing their attacker into the fog.

"No!" she tried to call out, but it emerged as little more than a whisper.

Hands pulled her from behind, lifting her roughly up and away from the body. In a last fit of desperation and coherent thought, she grabbed the torch, which had landed next to Clara's head. Knowing she would likely see the gruesome image of the dead woman's face for the rest of her life, she fought a dry heave as she moved the torch to illuminate Clara's hands.

"Wait," she managed as the hands that lifted her squeezed her midsection. "Wait!" She threw a glance over her shoulder to see Mr. Clancy's grim face. "Let me look!"

Without stopping to gauge his reaction, she turned back and grabbed at one of Clara's hands. Positioning the torch directly above the stiff fingers, she took a good, long look at the fingernails.

The process of decay had taken its toll, but the telltale striping was unmistakable. Her heart lodged in her throat, and she again felt herself on the verge of vomiting. Her horrified cough quickly turned to miserable retching sounds. The image before her might well be Kate in another six months if they couldn't find the person responsible for killing the family.

Mr. Clancy pulled her fully out of the coffin and released her as she collapsed to the ground. She lost whatever dinner remained in her stomach, nearly choking on the pain the stress caused her broken ribs. She heard the old man release a litany of curses and growled epithets as the loud sound of the coffin lid slamming shut rang through the night.

Lucy wiped her mouth with the back of her hand. She looked at Mr. Clancy, who sat next to the coffin, his arm atop the lid, examining the remains of two of his 'tons who lay scattered on the ground. The other two 'tons stared at him in shock, their programming clearly lacking in commands for counteracting any sort of physical attack. At least they'd had the wherewithal to keep the coffin from falling back into the hole.

There was only one creature with enough speed and strength to wreak such havoc in a matter of moments. Lucy pictured Miles chasing after a vampire in the dense fog as a man and not a wolf. He would be killed—she knew it. They would walk the grounds the next day, and they would find his body, his throat torn out, his eyes staring, unseeing, into the sky.

Lucy wrapped her arm around her waist as the sobs came, unbidden, her ribs on fire with each violently drawn breath.

"We must find him," she cried out to Mr. Clancy, who looked at her with a sense of resolve.

Using the coffin to give himself leverage, he pushed to his feet and made his way to her side, where he unceremoniously hauled her up and threw an arm awkwardly about her shoulders. He propelled her away from the coffin toward a small shack, where he stopped and pulled a telescriber from his pocket.

The old man opened a control panel positioned on the side of a tall pole at the back of the shack and withdrew a long cord, which he plugged into his machine.

Lucy tried to still her churning emotions, but her heart pounded and her teeth began to chatter. The violent beating of her heart only served to remind her that Miles had already been walking a thin line before the attack—he needed to plug in to his recharger immediately.

Placing a hand to her forehead, tears streaming down her face, she met Mr. Clancy's grim gaze as he punched the buttons on his telescriber. "I am sending for Martha Watts," he said. "She will bring stable boys to help clean up and look for the master."

"And she can be trusted to be discreet?" Lucy managed to ask through her tears.

"Aye." He nodded once, curtly, and finished his message. They waited for a moment, and his telescriber, still plugged into the Tesla pole, chimed a response. "She will be right here," he told Lucy. He looked at her as he disconnected his telescriber, the softening in his old eyes unmistakable.

"How did you speak with Marie?" Lucy whispered.

Mr. Clancy shrugged as he shuffled toward her and took her arm, leading her back to the bench next to the grave. "I just knew."

"Has she visited you before?"

"Nay."

"Have you communicated with ghosts before?" Lucy asked, still crying, unable to stop.

"A bit. When I was younger."

Lucy laughed, hearing the half-crazed note in her own voice. "All this time, and you could have told us what she wanted."

"She didna come to me, lassie. Not until tonight."

"Silly woman," Lucy said, trying for levity and failing miserably. "She wasted her time with me." She hugged Mr. Clancy's arm and choked on a sob.

"Nay," the old man answered in his gravelly voice. "That girl never made a move she didna mean."

Martha Watts arrived at the graveyard with a speed that eased Lucy's worry immensely. She'd brought with her a large horseless carriage and several 'ton stable boys, who, following Mr. Clancy's instructions, gathered the pieces of the destroyed 'tons. Under Miss Watts's direction, two of the 'tons went about the business of reburying the former countess. They straightened the body, adjusted the veil, and placed her hands carefully over the midsection again.

Miss Watts motioned toward Lucy, summoning her to the side of the coffin. "We'll have to lock it ourselves," she said. "I'm a certified Gravelocker, and, as you're Kate's cousin, you're the closest we have to a family member." Bending down, she spun the dial on the left, inputting a code and setting the locking mechanism. She touched her thumb to a small square to the right of it, a procedure introduced in recent years to prevent only one person from securing both locks. She pointed for Lucy to do the same thing on the right.

Lucy knelt slowly next to the box and spun the dials, inputting her mother's initials and Daniel's birth date, then placed her thumb on the identifier. The password was easily enough deciphered, she supposed, but she was too weary to care. When she finished, she placed her palm against the side of the coffin and leaned her forehead on it.

"That was horrid," she whispered into the night, hoping Clara might somehow hear. "I am so incredibly, absolutely sorry." She finally stood, and Miss Watts looked at her with something akin to sympathy.

"You should sit," she said and took Lucy by the arm to the carriage. She opened the passenger door and all but shoved Lucy inside, holding up a hand when Lucy meant to protest.

"Clancy has sent three of the boys to find the master," Martha told her. "They will bring him back."

Lucy leaned her head against the seat as Martha fired up the carriage motor and cranked the heat mechanism. It wasn't long before the seats were wonderfully warm, and Lucy began to feel some of the chill dissipate.

"Good?" Martha asked her with a nod.

"Thank you." Lucy closed her eyes. She must have dozed, because when the carriage door suddenly opened, she was startled and disoriented.

"Found him a mile up the road near the river," Mr. Clancy grunted as he helped one 'ton shove a half-conscious Miles into the carriage next to Lucy.

She moved aside to make more room and helped position the big man against the seat back and grasped his face in her hand.

"Miles," she breathed, horrified. "Wake up. Please wake up."

His head rolled listlessly to the side, and she placed her ear against his chest. The tick of his heartclock was slow and barely discernible. He breathed shallowly in and out, and his skin was frighteningly cold.

"We must get him to the observatory," she told Mr. Clancy and Martha. "Hurry!"

The ride back to the manor was rough as Martha took corners and bumps at breakneck speed. The black of night was beginning to shift to light, though fog still clung thickly to the ground. Lucy clenched her jaw so tightly it hurt as she braced Miles against the ruts in the road that nearly sent him flying from the seat. She doubted anyone in the house knew about Miles's condition, much less the fact that he regularly charged his heartclock in the third-floor observatory. She had to get him into the manor unseen.

"Stay with me," she murmured to Miles as he bounced violently against the side of the carriage and emitted a low groan. Lucy made a careful examination of his neck, relieved to find a notable absence of bite marks. She wrapped her arms around his body and clung tightly to him, bracing her foot against the opposite seat for leverage against the vehicle's erratic movements.

The carriage eventually slowed and geared down as the pathway smoothed and turned a corner. Martha had taken them directly up the front drive. Lucy closed her eyes and threw a prayer heavenward that the staff were still sleeping. She looked out the window and saw Martha at the front door with a large key, which she inserted into the lock. As she opened the door, two 'tons jumped down from the carriage top and opened the passenger doors.

"The third floor," Lucy told the boys.

They nodded as they pulled Miles from the carriage and braced him, one under each arm. They managed him as easily as an adult would a child, except for the fact that the earl was significantly taller than they were and his feet dragged on the ground.

"Why upstairs?" Martha asked Lucy as she quickly closed the front door and locked it, glancing around the empty front hall.

Lucy paused. "He is ill. His treatment is up there."

The older woman looked at her with narrowed eyes. "I've known his lordship since he was just a boy. He's a good man, that one is, and there's naught I wouldn't do for him."

Lucy nodded, feeling oddly guilty at being privy to a secret that Miles had shared with very few people. She tried to tell herself that the lord of the manor hardly need share his personal information with his staff, but as she looked into Martha's eyes, she knew the affection was real, that the woman's worry transcended class.

"Dr. MacInnes has been helping him," Lucy said, winded as they continued to the third floor. "He seems very hopeful." As consolation went, it wasn't much, but it was the best she could offer.

They reached the observatory, and Lucy moved ahead to open the door, but it was, of course, locked tight. She rattled the knob in frustration and looked at Miles, who hung limply between the two 'tons.

"Blast it, Miles!" She turned back to the door and smacked it in frustration.

Martha edged her out of the way with one brow cocked, whether shocked by Lucy's unladylike language or by her use of the master's Christian name, she didn't know. The older woman tried a series of keys, none of which worked on the lock.

Miles's breath was light and shallow, his face gray.

She drew her ray gun from the holster and shot away a locking mechanism for the second time that day. The door inched open, and Lucy shoved her way into the room, holding the door wide for the 'tons, who dragged Miles in.

Lucy examined the space, crossing to a mechanism on the table next to the bed. A heartclock charger. She'd seen one before but had never tried to work it herself. Motioning for the boys to place Miles on the bed, she ran her fingers over the machine, familiarizing herself with its components.

She glanced at Martha. "They should probably leave," she murmured.

Martha nodded at Lucy and left the room, taking the stable boys with her. That the door wouldn't lock now was unfortunate, but Lucy dismissed it as she located the machine's wiring and power crank. Confident she could at least get him hooked up properly, Lucy turned to Miles with a deep breath.

He lay so still. She bit her lip as she placed her hands at the top of his shirt and ripped it clean to his waist, sending expensive buttons flying. She caught her breath at the sight of his chest. The skin around the panel that hid the outer components connected to the heartclock was bruised and black. She hadn't seen the mechanism up close before, but she was fairly certain that the bruising was fresh and not necessarily normal.

She grasped the cords hanging from the charging machine and gently touched the skin around the panel with her fingertip, seeking for the opening. She caught her breath as her probing caused blood to pool onto her finger and soak into the splinted bandage on her hand. As she examined closer, she saw what appeared to be claw marks, as though something or someone had tried to rip the heartclock from his chest.

When she opened the small panel, she noted that the area around the charging mechanism was pooled in blood, and even as she watched, the claw marks began taking on a gray-green hue.

Lucy needed Sam, needed him desperately. She couldn't even be sure if the outer hookups on Miles's chest were still connected to the mechanism inside. She attached the wires anyway, carefully securing them to their corresponding receivers. Stretching around to the other side of the charger, she quickly twisted the crank several times and then threw the switch that set the cogs and gears in motion.

Before long, a gentle whirring filled the space, and as she watched, the chest panel moved infinitesimally with the charge that she hoped was making its way to the heartclock housed inside Miles. Finding a stack of clean white towels in a small drawer in the table, she snapped one open and gently placed it under the wires and around the wound where blood pooled and seeped.

She had to retrieve the anti-venom from her supplies, but she first glanced around the room and was relieved to find the telescribing connector not far from the bed. She pulled her telescriber from her pocket and, with shaking fingers, sent a message to her brother.

> Daniel, if you are in London,
> you must bring Sam MacInnes
> to Blackwell immediately.

Air travel was much faster than ground.

Chapter 29

Miles squinted against the bright light as he slowly opened his eyes. The light was actually nothing more than the glow of a bedside lamp—his bedside lamp, he realized as he looked around and recognized his bedchamber. A warm fire crackled in the hearth, and he felt surprisingly rested.

He winced at a pain in his chest as he shifted in bed. One of the large sitting room chairs had been dragged next to the bed, and in it, Lucy lay curled up, asleep. He studied her as memories flooded his brain. Something had attacked them while they were attempting to examine Clara. He had chased after the thing . . . and that was the last he could remember.

Lucy's dark hair was unbound and hung over the arm of the chair in long, curled waves. She was partially covered with a light blanket and wore a dress that looked as though she'd spend more than a few hours sleeping in it. His mouth lifted at the corner, and he slid to the edge of the bed to reach for a pitcher of water and a glass. He poured himself a drink and wondered how long he'd been out of commission.

He took stock of himself, noting the fresh bandage across his heart and the light trousers someone had dressed him in. He doubted very much Lucy could have managed it on her own, although he would have liked to have seen her inevitable blush. Placing his hand on his chest, he noted significant soreness but otherwise enjoyed a surprising sense of well-being. When he tried to define it more fully, he realized he couldn't feel the mechanism clicking. He was also breathing easily, effortlessly. It had been a very long time since he'd felt . . . normal.

With a frown, he held still. What on earth had happened? He slid from the bed and walked to the windows, where he lifted the drapes aside and looked out at the darkness beyond. Cold rain hit the glass in a steady thrum, and, as he watched, turned to snow. The clock on the mantel showed the hour at ten. He returned to the bedside, where he knelt beside Lucy's chair.

He reached for a lock of hair and rubbed it between his fingers. She awoke and looked at him with a moment of confusion before her expression cleared. Her eyes filmed over, and slowly, gently, she reached around his shoulders with her arm and drew closer to him. She rested her face against his neck, and he felt the hot trail of her tears slide down his skin.

"Shhh," he whispered and cradled her head with his hand. When had he developed such a tender streak? It would ruin his reputation for certain.

Lucy eventually pulled back and sat up in the chair, wiping her face with a handkerchief she withdrew from the sleeve of her dress. She laughed a little, flushing. "I've made good use of this over the last three days. Think I've cried more since being here than I have in years."

"I did tell you to leave," he said and lightly pinched her foot. "Three days?"

She nodded and sniffed, wiping at her nose. "The Charlesworths have even postponed the ball for your sake."

"What happened?"

"The long and short of it is that Sam got his hands on the new heart-clock. And not a moment too soon."

He stared at her, stunned. "He performed the transplant? Here?"

She nodded. "Upstairs. Daniel flew him in."

"Are they both still here? Have you had some time with your brother, then?"

Lucy nodded. "We talked at some length while you were upstairs with

Sam." She smiled. "Poor Daniel. I do believe he was trying to keep me distracted with tales of piracy in the high skies." She then told Miles everything that had happened from the time of the attack in the graveyard.

He shook his head. "I don't remember anything beyond running after the thing into the fog."

"It was a vampire—the thing tried to rip out your heartclock. I had to use anti-venom on the wound before Sam even arrived. The vamp knocked me into the coffin, sent you sprawling, and took out two of the groundsboys."

"Knocked you into . . ." His mouth dropped open. "I didn't realize." He shook his head. "Lucy, I am sorry—I do not know what to say."

"It was hardly your fault," she said and rubbed an eye. "I will say, however, that it isn't an experience I wish to repeat."

Miles stifled a groan and rested his forehead on her knee. He felt her fingers in his hair and closed his eyes. "I would assume you were correct in your supposition about Clara?"

She was silent for a long moment, and Miles lifted his head. Sorrow creased her brow, and she nodded. "I'm so sorry. She was most definitely poisoned."

Miles took her hand and placed his lips on her knuckles for a kiss before he lay his head against her knee again. "What a wretched end," he said, his heart heavy. "And although I wouldn't wish it on an enemy, I cannot even say there was any love lost." He looked up at Lucy. "I am truly the beast others believe of me."

"You did not kill her, Miles."

"I brought her here. I married her for her money."

"I agree, it is a tragic ending to a young life. You cannot, however, pretend that alliances between families aren't forged every day for money and titles. Because yours was not a love match does not make a beast of you."

Miles shrugged, and they sat in silence for a time. "This must end," he finally said. "All of the madness. It has been a pall over this house long enough."

Lucy turned the heavy key in the lock on Marie's garden gate and slipped inside, hoping Mr. Clancy wouldn't somehow know she was there without him. The man had an uncanny ability to know what was going on even when he was nowhere near the place. She regretted the necessity of deceit but knew he would never allow her access to the gazebo otherwise.

She was absolutely exhausted. In the past month, she had been infected with vampire venom, suffered broken ribs, a badly sprained ankle and wrist, and had been shoved into a casket with a decomposing corpse. The fact that she temporarily needed a cane to walk should be the least of her complaints, although she felt positively ancient each time she moved around with it. Thankfully, breathing was less painful than before, a good sign that her ribs were on the mend.

The air was cold—painfully so—and tendrils of fog clung to the ground and obscured the far corners of the garden, the gazebo included. She hadn't told Miles what she was doing—she hadn't told anyone. He was at the manor preparing to head north for the Charlesworths' ball, and Lucy had figured she might never get another opportunity to examine the gazebo by herself.

There was something that pulled her to the gazebo time and again, though she had respected Clancy's wishes to leave it alone. There hadn't been a single instance that she'd been inside the walls of Marie's garden when Lucy hadn't felt a very real impression to enter the place. And at the lodge, Miles had mentioned that he saw Marie in the gazebo itself.

It was as though Mr. Clancy ignored its existence and noticed it only when Lucy pointed it out to him. She had pieced together that it had been Marie's favorite spot in the whole world, but as it was also where she'd been found butchered, Mr. Clancy was torn. He wanted to get rid of it, but it had been her refuge; destroying it would destroy the memory of her.

The air around her felt charged, eerie, and trying to tell herself that there was nobody else in the garden was proving difficult. A glance over her shoulder gave her little reassurance. The gate was completely obscured by the fog, which seemed an entity unto its own.

"Nonsense," she murmured and continued on her way, the frozen ground crunching under her boots. The gazebo finally materialized before her, and she eyed the thick tendrils and twisted sticks of dormant ivy that made for an impenetrable enclosure, the once-green leaves now brown and crumbling.

Silence hummed in her ears as she carefully picked her way to the entrance. Despite the lack of healthy foliage, the interior was still substantially darker than the outside world. Placing one foot at the bottom step, she navigated the stairs on an ankle that was beginning to throb.

Taking a deep breath, Lucy looked into the gazebo and squinted as her eyes adjusted. There was something there, something toward the center. Frowning, she fumbled in her pocket for the small Tesla torch she'd brought from the house and looked up at the canopy of densely packed vines that closed out the light.

She switched on the torch and cast the beam across the stone floor where it caught on a bright red dress that had become altogether too familiar. Her heart in her throat, Lucy inched closer, only to stumble back in horror at the graphic scene.

The vision was of Marie, prostrate on the ground, with huge gashes across her midsection and face. Her blood seeped with sickening speed across the fabric of her dress, and Lucy felt light-headed at the brutal sight of Marie's torn throat and chest, the blood across her face obscuring her once-beautiful features.

Lucy's stomach lurched, and she felt her eyes burn with the sting of tears. "Why?" she whispered and inched her way backward until she came up against the wall of vines and tendrils encircling the gazebo. "Won't you please tell me what you need?"

To her horror, Marie's fingers twitched, her outstretched arm pointing at something on the floor. The open, sightless eyes flickered, following the line of her arm. She moved her forefinger fractionally at something only she could see.

Lucy, the torch in her hand wobbling so severely she feared she'd drop it, moved forward slowly, gripping her cane. Perhaps she could use it to defend herself. But defend herself against what? A ghost? The victim of a violent crime? Marie was not the problem.

Lucy kept the beam of light focused on the twitching fingers and fought a wave of nausea. The vision of Marie didn't look like a ghost—the sight of her seemed so incredibly real that Lucy doubted her sanity. As she neared the delicate hand, she crouched down close enough to examine the floor but far enough away to at least give herself the impression that she could leap out of the way if need be.

Marie's hand was slender, her fingers graceful, and she had clearly not succumbed to death without a fight. Her forearm was a mass of cuts and blood, her fingernails chipped and broken. Marie clenched her fist, all but her forefinger, which pointed directly at Lucy's boot. Shining the light carefully around her own foot, Lucy set down her cane and brushed aside the dead twigs and leaves that covered the marble floor.

One tense minute became two, and just as Lucy was about to cry out in despair, her fingers brushed across something that caught the light and shone dully against the debris. As she pulled it from the leaves and settled it into her gloved palm, her heart thumped in recognition.

It was a button belonging to a stable boy's 'ton uniform, clearly engraved with the Blackwell crest. Marie must have ripped it from her attacker during the struggle.

"Oh, Marie," Lucy breathed, feeling a chill settle deep into her bones. "It wasn't Miles or even a vampire. A programmed 'ton did this to you."

Thoughts tumbled in her head, and she glanced at the dead woman, only to find the marble floor empty, as if Marie had never been there.

Chapter 30

Miles stood in the wheelhouse and looked out over the darkening countryside as Daniel's personal airship carried the small entourage to the Charlesworths' country home near the Scottish border. While it had been good to see his friend again, Miles realized Lucy definitely had the right of it—Daniel was harboring a heavy heart beneath a practiced and casual façade. Miles never had been one to pry, however, and after stewing for some time about Daniel's welfare, he finally decided the man would come to him if he needed help.

"I should tell you," Miles said to Daniel as his friend consulted an instrument and made a course correction, "I plan to seek your sister's hand."

Daniel looked at Miles, his face impassive. "I was hoping you'd do the honorable thing, especially after ensconcing her in your personal suite."

Miles frowned and opened his mouth, searching for the right words with which to defend himself.

"Never seen you speechless, Blackwell," Daniel said, chuckling. "And you may as well know that I've already told Lucy I approve of you as a suitor, should that be the direction you decide to take." He looked out at the darkening sky. "She is very . . . Lucy is exceptionally bright. You are aware of the work she does for the Botanical Aid Society?"

Miles nodded. "I have hope she will continue in that vein. She is valuable to their efforts of late, though I know her work puts her at great personal risk." He shook his head. "She is obliged to carry her own supply of anti-venom."

"Which is why I am comforted at the thought of her being with someone who can provide adequate protection, keep her safe."

Miles shook his head. "She has come to more harm in the past month than I believe she ever has. Nevertheless, I intend to employ any measures necessary to protect her."

Daniel glanced at Miles, one brow raised. "Including trying to keep her from her work? I'm afraid that would not end well."

Miles ran a hand through his hair. "I would not try to keep her from it. She may, however, have to subject herself to the inconvenience of an armed guard."

Daniel's mouth twitched. "I wish you good luck."

Miles cast his friend a caustic glance as Daniel laughed.

Reaching into his pocket, Miles closed his fingers around the 'ton uniform button Lucy had handed him earlier that afternoon. It exonerated him, true, but it also meant that someone in his household had programmed one of the stable boys to kill Marie. The button was the last thing her mortal fingers had touched, and he couldn't decide if he wanted to keep the thing or hurl it far into the ocean.

He resented the Charlesworths and their blasted ball and all that went with it. He felt more than ever that he ought to be at Blackwell Manor, scouring programming tins and interrogating the staff. Lucy had convinced him that it would look extremely suspect if he not only didn't attend his only brother's wedding celebration—which had been postponed for *his* sake—but also went on a rampage, accusing all and sundry of killing his sister. There was wisdom to her suggestion that they act as though they hadn't discovered anything at all, that their chances of finding evidence against those responsible would be possible only if the guilty party didn't know they were looking.

Her words before they left echoed in his head: *I think we can safely say that there is a vampire among us, and it is someone we know.* But as much as he tried, he couldn't make sense of the riddle. Who would program 'tons to poison Clara and Kate and kill Marie in such a way as to suggest an animal attack? And could it be the same person who was aware of his status as a predatory shifter? Who knew his secret? Who was insisting he step aside and hand the earldom to Jonathan?

Miles rubbed his hand along his face, feeling the familiar ridges of the scar that had made his life at times unbearably hard and yet seemed to have no adverse impact on Lucy, who sat in the passenger section of the airship with Sam. Miles was as baffled by her affection for him as he was by the odd questions that seemed to arise every day—questions he was afraid might keep eluding him until it was too late.

Of one thing he was certain: the only person who would benefit from the earldom passing to Jonathan would be Jonathan himself, and Miles would exhaust every last possibility before allowing himself to even begin suspecting his brother of plotting against him. He was afraid that would prove more than his heart could handle—newly transplanted or no.

Lucy took in her surroundings with an eye for detail. Charlesworth House, while not as grand as Blackwell Manor, was certainly beautiful in its own right. The building, situated in a hamlet near the border that nestled along the coastline, spoke of an understated charm, from the wide windows that graced the main level to the widow's walk against the third-floor turrets.

A flurry of activity flowed from the conveyances that had driven them from the airfield to the front steps where 'tons made quick work of delivering the guests' travel trunks to their respective rooms.

"Welcome!" Aunt Eustace filled the doorway, temporarily blocking the warm light that spilled from within the house and lit the darkening night. "I am so glad to see you've arrived intact! When you telescribed that you would be arriving by airship, why I nearly suffered a fit of vapors!"

Lucy leaned forward to receive Eustace's kisses, which were delivered to the air on either side of her cheeks. "I daresay airships are safer than ground travel. Wouldn't you agree, Lord Blackwell?" Lucy said when Miles didn't seem inclined to answer his aunt.

Miles flicked a flat glance at Lucy before turning his attention to Eustace. "Most certainly," he said as Eustace clasped him to her ample bosom. "And we arrived hours before we would have, otherwise," he finished as he broke away and flared his nostrils slightly in Lucy's direction.

"I insisted," Lucy said to Eustace. "I didn't want to miss a moment of the festivities."

"Yes, yes!" Eustace guided Lucy into the house where a squeal of delight echoed from the high ceiling in the foyer.

Candice flew down the stairs and grasped Lucy's hands, pulling her forward in an ebullient hug. "What a delight you're here early!" she said, her eyes shining in her beautiful face. "I've made certain to place you in the chamber nearest mine so we won't lose a moment of fun!" Her gaze widened when she spied Daniel. "Oh, hello, what a pleasure it is to see you again."

Lucy cast a confused glance at her brother and motioned him closer. "Miss Candice Charlesworth, my brother, Mr. Daniel Pickett. Owner of Picket Airships."

Candice placed a hand on her chest. "We've met once before. When we happened to visit Blackwell at the same time." She fluttered her fingers at Daniel, who clasped them with a light bow.

"A pleasure," he said, although Lucy was fairly certain it was anything but. Her brother despised clinging, simpering debutantes.

The young woman's gaze remained on Daniel, and Lucy figured her brother would find himself cajoled into more than one dance at the next day's ball. Candice embraced Lucy again and squeezed tight in her excitement. Lucy winced and stifled a groan as she caught Daniel's eye over Candice's shoulder. He shot her a look that promised future retribution.

"Candice, really, do give the lady some room to breathe." Arthur entered the hall with a smile. "Clearly, we do not often host celebrations." He reached Lucy's side, and when she took his offered hand, he bowed over it with a soft kiss on her knuckles.

Lucy felt the warmth of Miles's hand at the small of her back, and she knew as Arthur straightened and looked over her shoulder that Miles was sending his cousin a very thinly veiled message. His hand slid around her waist to rest comfortably on her hip, and Arthur's gaze flicked to it before he brought his attention back to Lucy's face with a smile.

"I do hope you will save a dance for me," he said. "We were interrupted last time."

Lucy fought to keep the smile fixed to her face as she felt Miles tense. Arthur couldn't have been clearer in his intentions than if he'd thrown a glove at Miles's feet.

"Well, then!" Candice broke the awkward moment and pulled Lucy toward the center of the hall. "Let us all make our way to the parlor. Winston has made some delightful refreshments for us to enjoy. And Mr. Pickett, do not even think of trying to escape. You simply must join us."

"Where are Kate and Jonathan?" Lucy unbuttoned her traveling coat, handing it off to the butler, who balanced a growing heap of outerwear to hang in the cloakroom.

Candice's brow creased. "They are resting. I'm afraid Kate was tired from their travels."

The hall was full of servants running to and fro, delivering luggage and taking orders from Eustace. Lucy felt a light ache settle behind her eyes. "Kate hasn't seen Daniel for several weeks. I'm sure she will want to join us," she told Candice.

Arthur shook his head with a frown. "We extended an invitation earlier, but Jonathan was firm that we leave Kate in peace. Jonathan mentioned he was feeling a bit under the weather himself."

Something wasn't right.

"What is it?" Miles's voice was low, next to her ear.

She smoothed her expression when she noted both Candice and Arthur watching her closely. Sam had made his way to them and, glancing first at Lucy and then at Miles, turned his attention to Candice. "The parlor, you said? Excellent! I am absolutely famished."

Candice beamed at him and took the arm he offered, and they led the way to the evening refreshments while Lucy wondered if Kate's problem was due to those who lived at Charlesworth House or the husband who'd brought her to it.

Daniel touched her arm and motioned upstairs. "I'll find her. If there's a problem, I'll send immediately for Sam."

The night passed uneventfully, which allowed Miles to breathe a sigh of relief the next morning at breakfast. Lucy had insisted she would not retire for the evening until she had a chance to visit with Kate, even though Daniel had joined the group in the parlor after scouting the guest rooms on the second floor and had told Lucy that Kate was well enough, if not a bit tired.

When Jonathan had offered to take the bedchamber designated for Lucy so that Lucy could stay by Kate's side, Miles had been beyond grateful. After all that had happened, there was no possibility he would allow Lucy to sleep alone in her own chamber. He had been prepared to cause a scandal by sleeping on the floor of her room with the door open if need be, but Daniel had shot daggers at him with his eyes, and Sam had talked him out of it. Jonathan's solution had been perfect, and their hosts seemed to accept the reasoning that Lucy and Kate needed to catch up on all the latest gossip.

Oliver was to arrive within the hour, and Miles was glad for the support from his friends. His impatience at the intrigue his life had encountered was at its zenith, and he wanted nothing more than to make Lucy officially his before God and country, take her home, and not receive visitors for at least a week.

It had been an odd realization as he'd awoken that morning and dressed for the day that he'd been thinking of Lucy as his bride for quite some time; he had just never acknowledged it to himself. The fact that he'd put her in the countess's chambers ought to have been his first indication that his subconscious was traveling down roads he wasn't even aware existed. And now that he was healthy with the new heartclock and knew that Lucy held him in tender affection despite his obvious flaws, he had allowed himself to dream of a future with her.

As soon as the last breakfast morsels had been swallowed, Lucy had been spirited away with Kate, Candice, and—heaven help them—Eustace to prepare for the "Event of the Year!" He rolled his eyes at the thought. He needed some air. Charlesworth House had always been stifling to him; even as a child, he had dreaded the mandatory familial visits to the place.

Perhaps he had absorbed his mother's reaction to her sister-in-law. Miles had always known his mother was ill at ease with the Charlesworths, although he had never discerned the reason. He supposed his aunt's cloying company was reason enough. Even still, his mother had been lovely and vivacious. A more mature, polished version of Marie, really. And Eustace had always seemed to resent the fact that her brother and family retained the home in which she'd been raised but not allowed to inherit.

Miles made his way down to the main floor and exited through a back door to the grounds outside. He drew his collar against the cold, the winter air having fully descended upon the northern climes. He walked along a path that twisted through tall shrubbery until the house was out of sight.

He knew that before long he would find himself in a maze, a groomed, life-sized monstrosity where he and Marie once spent several terrifying hours lost as children. Their mother had finally found them— or rather, they found her by listening to the sound of her voice. It wasn't unlike the way Lucy had found him in the maze of his own misery and how she'd led him into hope and light. His mother would have liked Lucy, he decided. It was fairly clear that Marie did.

They would survive the infernal ball, he would have Oliver place every resource at his disposal to discover the identity of not only the murderer but the one who stalked him, and he would have a life with Lucy or die trying.

Kate sat at the vanity in the bedroom, and Lucy toyed with a curl that had fallen from her cousin's coiffure. Biting her lip, Lucy looked at Kate's reflection in the mirror and fought with her emotions, trying to keep the worry from her face. Kate was pale, alarmingly so, and under her eyes were dark smudges that face paint didn't entirely disguise.

"It is the curse," Kate whispered as she stared at her reflection. "The Bride's Curse." Her eyes widened, and she met Lucy's gaze in the mirror. "You mustn't fall in love with Miles! You will be next, Lucy!" She turned in her seat and clasped Lucy's hand. "I've seen how you are together. He adores you; it is in his eyes."

Lucy shook her head and forced a bright smile. "Silly. There is no curse. Someone wishes you ill, and we are going to discover who that person is before we leave this place. You are certain you felt well in Bath?"

Kate nodded, her eyes filming over. "I felt nearly my normal self by the time we left to come here."

"And you ate dinner here last night?"

"I wasn't hungry. I had a cup of tea."

"And who served it to you?"

"Jonathan brought it up from the kitchen."

Lucy frowned. "Who made the tea, do you know?"

Kate shrugged. "I don't think he did it himself. He was also feeling ill last night."

"Have you noticed anything odd about the 'tons? Their behavior?"

Kate shook her head, clutching Lucy's fingers tightly. "Other than a scramble to reprogram one that had gone faulty. The problem must be spreading from Blackwell." She offered a weak smile.

Lucy narrowed her eyes in thought. "And you arrived early yesterday afternoon—two hours before you were expected . . ." She shook her head and knelt down, rubbing her hand softly across Kate's knuckles. "We can leave now, Kate, this very moment. I'll take you home, and we will get you well."

"I can't," Kate whispered. "I cannot leave Jonathan. He is my life and I, his. Let us get through the ball tonight and then in the morning we will discuss the future. It is probably time we consider moving to Jonathan's property in the country."

"Something is very wrong in this family, Kate." She didn't tell her cousin that she suspected whomever was poisoning her was also likely a vampire in hiding. A tear slipped from Kate's eye, and Lucy thumbed it away, her resolve settling firmly in place. "We leave tomorrow, my dear, come hell or high water, and you and Jonathan will move from Blackwell Manor."

Lucy stood and straightened her skirts. The dress she'd chosen to wear to the ball was a beautiful satin-and-velvet affair, ice-blue in color and trimmed with delicate pearls. It was a suitable counterpart to Kate's lovely white ensemble that, to Lucy's alarm, hung more loosely on Kate's frame than it should.

A maid came bustling into the bedroom after a perfunctory knock at the door. "The folks are gatherin'!" the young woman said as she drew the drapes over the darkening evening sky and stoked the fire. "And don't ya both look lovely! Will ya be goin' down right away, then?"

Lucy looked at Kate, who mustered a smile. "You wait here," Lucy told her. "I'll find Jonathan. He should escort you down."

Kate clasped Lucy to her in a tight embrace.

Lucy willed herself not to cry. "We will fix this, Kate," she whispered. "I will not leave you until you are safe."

Kate nodded, her head bumping against Lucy's. Lucy kissed her cheek, and, with a quick squeeze of her shoulders, left the room in a rustle of fabric, her shoes clicking on the floor. She made her way to Jonathan's room and knocked; he answered, fumbling with his cravat and looking harried.

"May I?" She smiled in spite of herself.

"I detest these sorts of things," he told her with a scowl. "I am here only for Kate's sake. Were it not for her image, I would have politely declined."

Lucy reached for the ends of Jonathan's cravat and began folding and twisting it into submission. "You're a good man," she said.

"I do try," he said. Lucy nudged his chin higher for better access to his neck.

The family resemblance to his brother was uncanny, but Jonathan had a softer edge to his whole being that reflected his gentler nature. She wondered about the terms of the shape-shifting legacy, and whether or not it affected more than just the oldest son. She assumed Kate would have told her if Jonathan were a werewolf, but perhaps not.

She wished there were telltale signs of Vampiric Assimilation Aid use. A vampire she could spot easily at thirty paces. One using Assimilation? That was the beauty of the drug for the user and the detriment of it for everyone else. The undead appeared as alive as the living.

If she had to go strictly by her feelings and intuition, she would comfortably state that she didn't believe Jonathan to be the one trying to kill Kate. Besides, she figured he could have killed Kate easily in Bath, had that been his intention. He could have told them that Kate had fallen ill and died and that he had been helpless to prevent it.

"There." She smoothed the cravat down against his dress shirt and gave it a final tap. "Kate is waiting for you." She paused. "I believe it would be in her best interest to leave in the morning. She doesn't look well."

Jonathan nodded, his face grim. "I am concerned. It is like she has fallen ill just from being in this house."

Lucy looked down the hallway and back again at Jonathan. "Keep her away from these people," she murmured.

Jonathan stared at her before nodding once. "You've also been hurt," he said with a nod at her splinted wrist. "I urge you to take care yourself."

"Of course. Now then, your bride awaits. Place a smile on your face for her sake."

He managed one, albeit weak.

The corners of her mouth twitched in response. "That will have to do. I don't suppose I need to suggest you remain attached to her side at all costs?"

Jonathan took a deep breath and turned, saying over his shoulder as he walked, "I fully intend to."

Lucy watched from the shadows as Jonathan knocked on the bedroom door and then bowed when Kate opened it. She heard her cousin's laugh and then watched as the couple walked toward the main staircase, Jonathan's arm firmly about Kate's shoulders.

Lucy remained in the empty hallway for a moment, formulating a plan. Kate had fallen ill upon her arrival at the house the day before, and, to Lucy's knowledge, the family were the only ones in residence. Sam had arrived with her and Miles, and Oliver had arrived only that morning. She felt some relief at being able to cross Miles's friends off her suspect list.

That meant that at some point as the evening progressed, Lucy needed to examine three bedrooms in secret. She had a vague notion of what she might be looking for, but she wished she didn't feel as though she were charging headlong into something about which she knew precious little.

"Where are you now, Marie?" she muttered quietly, half expecting the woman in red to appear. "I could use your help." When she didn't appear, Lucy sighed heavily and made her way down the hall. How she was going to escape the notice of not only her hosts but Miles as well was anyone's guess. She would put in an appearance, make an excuse of some sort, and then do a little exploring.

Of one thing she was certain—she wasn't going to leave Charlesworth House until she knew who was poisoning her cousin.

Chapter 31

Miles stood just outside the ballroom entrance, every muscle and sinew tense, his nerves stretched raw. There was something in the air, something not quite right, and he was frustrated by his inability to pinpoint it. He'd never believed there would come a time when he wished he could shift, if only for a moment, to see if he could detect the problem with more accuracy. But running through his brother's wedding celebration as a wolf might put a bit of a damper on the occasion for the happy couple, so it was probably a good thing he was unable to shift at will.

He looked at the couple in question, who also stood in the hallway, waiting to be announced to the gathering crowd. Kate was clearly unwell. She leaned against Jonathan and tried to smile but looked as though she'd rather dissolve into tears. Jonathan held her close, now and again closing his eyes and placing a soft kiss atop her head.

Lucy had the right of it. She'd mentioned it to him earlier, and he completely agreed—Jonathan and Kate needed to get far away from everyone, even Blackwell itself.

And speaking of Lucy—Jonathan had said she was on her way down, but she'd yet to make an appearance. His blood hummed, both in worry and anticipation.

Oliver approached from inside the ballroom and joined Miles at the doorway. "When this is finished and you return to Blackwell, I am post-ing guards at your property perimeter. We will see this thing finished one way or another."

Miles nodded. Oliver had sent the scrap of bloodied shirt and the note, along with the box they'd been delivered in, to his lab and was awaiting final analysis on the soil sample found inside the tin. It might prove useless. Odds were it was simply dirt from the hunting lodge, but there was a possibility it might show the origin of the box itself. If it had come from Scotland, Oliver had warned, it was time for a trip farther north. Miles had readily agreed; he was tired of the cat-and-mouse game, especially now that his health had returned, and with a vengeance.

Miles's breath caught in his throat as he spied Lucy making her way down the sweeping staircase in a gown that seemed designed to show off her every asset. She was exquisite, from the curls of dark hair piled atop her head to the stunning blue of her eyes, from the graceful line of her throat to the creamy expanse of skin that was covered enough for propri-ety's sake but showcased enough to make a man's mouth water. The skirts were full and flowing and hid a pair of legs he'd seen in breeches and knew all too well were perfection itself.

He glanced at Oliver, who stared at Lucy before recovering himself and closing his mouth. Oliver offered a shrug and the hint of a smile and then clapped him on the shoulder. "Good luck, old man." He returned to the ballroom with a chuckle.

She approached him, moving gracefully, if a little slowly, and he men-tally shook his head at the look on her face. As if she wanted him and only him. What he'd ever done to deserve her, he'd never know, but he wasn't about to let it stand in his way. All thoughts of encouraging her interest in Arthur had fled, and he wondered why he'd ever been fool enough to consider it.

He held out his hand, and she placed hers in it. He glanced at the bandage wrapped around her wrist with a wince, hating that it had been his fault she'd been wounded in the first place.

"I had it rebandaged to match the ensemble," she said and placed her fingertip under his chin. Drawing his attention to her face, she smiled and rose up on her toes. He obliged her willingly and leaned forward to place a kiss on her lips that was entirely too chaste. The fact that she'd instigated it, however, was statement enough to any who happened to see it. She'd staked her claim, and he knew now what her intentions were. She wasn't of loose moral fiber, and he had every intention of making an honest woman out of her now that she'd dared to actually kiss him in public.

He smiled at her, for a moment the stresses of the past weeks melting away, and he pulled her close, against his better judgment. Wrapping his arm around her waist, he placed his other hand at the back of her neck and tipped her head, his thumb tracing the delicate line of her jaw. Her palm lay flat against his chest, and she smiled through a light blush that only added to her beauty.

"My lord, you will cause a scandal," she whispered.

"On the contrary. I intend to make you my bride."

Her eyes flickered to his lips and then to his eyes. "And I intend to allow it."

"I am very glad to hear it. Society generally frowns on abduction and forced marriages these days." He was less than an inch from her mouth when Jonathan cleared his throat. Miles glanced up to where Kate, Jonathan, Eustace, and the footman gaped at them, speechless.

Eustace's face was turning several alarming shades of purple, and she began to sputter. "I will not have such . . . such . . ."

Miles held up a hand. "Miss Pickett has just agreed to marry me, and I sought to seal the occasion with a kiss. There is no scandal, no cause for alarm. The wedding, in fact, will take place in a matter of weeks."

Lucy's head dropped against his chest with a light groan. She was an accomplished woman who walked through society with popularity and style. Of course she would want more time to plan an elaborate wedding. Miles glanced down at her and added, "Well, a month, perhaps."

"Lucy, is this true?" Kate's happy squeal was the most vibrant emotion the young woman had expressed in a long time, and Lucy squirmed in his arms, but he didn't release her.

"Yes, I, well—" Lucy managed. "I believe the timing might be a subject for debate, but it is indeed true." She looked askance at Miles with a light shake of her head. "But this is your night, Kate." Lucy shoved away from Miles and placed her hand through his arm. "We'll enter and then you can be announced."

She tugged at Miles, and he moved, finally, slightly awed and ridiculously happy at what he'd just set into motion. The only downside to the moment was his last view of his sister-in-law's pale face as they entered the ballroom. He wondered if Kate would have the stamina to survive her own wedding celebration.

Lucy applauded with the rest of the people in the crowded ballroom as Kate and Jonathan entered and were officially presented. Eustace was in her element, thrilled beyond words, although she did manage to spew forth quite a few, overjoyed to be allowed the honor of hosting the wedding celebration for her *dear* nephew and his *beautiful* bride, who was such a *boon and a blessing* to the house of Blake. If people thought it unseemly that the family celebrated in such a big way given the fact they had lost two family members a mere six months earlier, they wisely kept it to themselves.

Lucy watched Kate closely, torn between baffled excitement that she was suddenly an engaged woman and constantly trying to assure herself that Kate was not about to collapse and die on the spot. Kate had eaten very little, and only after Lucy had insisted on taking a bite or sip of everything that Kate put in her mouth.

Candice Charlesworth clamored for Oliver's attention, and Oliver, for his part, seemed politely irritated. And Candice wasn't the only one who sought the favor of the handsome detective. More than a few eager women crowded for an introduction despite the fact that he held no title. Lucy mentioned as much to Miles, who rolled his eyes.

"I can count at least five over there who would love nothing more than to end up in his chambers by the end of the evening. They like to make the rounds."

Lucy quirked a brow. "Do they, now? I suppose you would have first-hand knowledge of their intentions?"

He glanced down at her. "Are you jealous?"

"I might be."

"Then, yes."

Lucy elbowed him and took a sip of punch. It was sickeningly sweet, and she fought back a grimace. Miles leaned close to her ear, not quite touching her but close enough that she felt his body heat. "There's not a woman in all the world that can hold a candle to you, Lucy Pickett," he murmured, and she felt it vibrate clear into her heart.

She turned her head, well aware that he was scandalously close and found she didn't much care. Stretching up to whisper to him, he turned his head to allow her better access, and she pursed her lips, blowing lightly across his ear.

He coughed and then chuckled, capturing her gaze with his own. He was still standing much too close. "You play a dangerous game, my sweet." He traced her neck with the tip of his finger.

A movement out of the corner of her eye caught her attention, and Lucy looked to see Arthur standing near them. "I understand congratulations are in order," he said. Lucy wondered what the younger man was thinking beneath the impassive expression.

Miles straightened to his full height. "We are not announcing anything yet," he told his cousin in an undertone. "This evening is for my brother and his wife."

"Of course, of course." Arthur smiled. "And I would do nothing to lessen it. I might, though, request a dance with your beautiful intended. We are to be family, after all."

"Indeed," Lucy said, and Miles placed a hand at the back of her neck. If she didn't already know he spent three days of the month as a wolf, the low growl she heard from him might have come as a surprise.

"You will tread carefully," Miles said to Arthur. "Lucy has been hurt and is still healing."

"Ah, yes. An accident in London, was it not?" Arthur reached for her hand.

She handed her glass of punch to Miles and moved forward, missing the feel of Miles's warm hand as soon as she stepped away. Smiling to hide her sudden sense of unease, she said, "Yes, I'm afraid I can be quite clumsy. Took a nasty fall down a flight of steps at my town house."

"Well, then, I shall handle you with the utmost care." Arthur placed his hand at her back to draw her into the pattern of a waltz, moving gently and in small steps. "I regret I was unable to spend more time with you myself before my cousin pursued your hand," he said. "But such is the nature of life, I suppose. One must act swiftly to achieve one's ends."

A couple passed close by and jostled Lucy into Arthur, who caught her up against him and attempted to take the brunt of the contact. Lucy glanced over her shoulder to see Candice laughing as she swung in a wide arc with Oliver.

"Your sister seems to be enjoying herself," Lucy said, breathless as she righted herself. "And it might be my imagination, but she seems to have taken a fancy to Mr. Reed."

Arthur looked at the couple in question, a brow raised. "Who would know what she ever intends? Candice is . . . a force." He turned speculative as they regained their former stride in time with the music. "She has often reminded me of Marie. They are similar in temperament."

"What of Marie?" Lucy watched his reaction. "Do you not find it rather odd that she died so violently, and only a day after the late countess? I suppose I really ought to familiarize myself with the family's history now that I shall be part of it, wouldn't you agree?"

Arthur looked at her before answering. "Are you afraid?"

"Not in the least. Curious, perhaps."

"I wish I had definitive answers for you." He shrugged lightly. "We cousins have always spent time together, although I wouldn't necessarily say the relationships have been close. Certainly not like you and Kate.

But there were . . . changes . . . I noticed in Miles as he aged. And then of course, after the war. But even given that, I have been surprised at his demeanor over the last year."

Lucy paid close attention to both her dance partner and the room as a whole, noting the crush of people dancing and socializing—Eustace would be on cloud nine for weeks—and Miles, leaning his shoulder against a pillar, watching her without apology. A waiter passed by him, and he placed Lucy's glass of punch on the 'ton's tray without taking his direct gaze from her face. She felt very warm, and it had nothing to do with the temperature in the room or the company of her dance partner.

"What do you mean by that?" she asked Arthur as they turned and Miles was no longer in her line of sight.

"He was angry, of course. Before he was deployed, he was usually irritated, but never what I would call callous or cruel, which he certainly seemed to be when he returned home. He married the late Lady Clara but didn't seem happy. He was cold, rude to everyone. Candice tried very earnestly to bring him out of his shell after Clara died, but he dismissed her as if she were rubbish. Highly uncalled for, really."

"I daresay he was grieving. For Clara and Marie."

"But to spurn her every overture? He didn't even pretend to appreciate the attention she paid him. She certainly tried for much longer than I would have, were I her. I knew she had always fancied him, but thought she'd outgrown it. I finally told her that he was beyond consolation, that she shouldn't exhaust herself any longer in wasting her energy trying to show affection to someone who had no interest in being civil."

Alarm bells sounded in the back of Lucy's mind, and she struggled to keep her face passive. "What was the nature of the attention she paid to his lordship, would you say?"

Arthur regarded her with shrewd eyes that she feared missed nothing. "You needn't feel envy, Miss Pickett. He truly had no interest in her romantically, despite her overtures through the years."

"But you do feel that such might have been *her* goal?" she pressed.

He was silent as he guided her carefully around several spinning couples, the strains of the music winding down. As they slowed to a stop near the balcony doors, Lucy looked into the thick of the room to see Candice herself speaking in earnest to Miles, who seemed to be searching for someone—Lucy could only assume it was her.

She bobbed an absent curtsey to Arthur and turned to make her way across the room when Arthur caught her arm and spun her slightly, throwing an arm about her shoulders. "You look so very flushed, Miss Pickett," he said and opened the balcony door, hustling her out into the cold night air.

"What are you doing?" she snapped at him as he closed the door behind them and led her a short distance down the veranda.

"Miss Pickett." He stopped and took her shoulders in his hands. "As much as I can honestly say that my cousin had no romantic interest in my sister, I must also tell you that I am afraid there is something not quite right with him. He has secrets; I am sure of it."

Lucy's heart beat faster, and she clutched the man's lapels. "What do you mean? What sort of secrets do you suspect him of having?" She had to get back to the ballroom. She was certain Miles hadn't seen them leave, and as much as she would have liked to handle the situation herself, she knew she was no match for Arthur—even if she were at full strength.

Arthur shook his head, scowling. "He is elusive. He spends an inordinate amount of time at the hunting lodge, but it is a well-known fact that he doesn't care to hunt. He is disagreeable, most unpleasant. He will not even confide in the family about how he came by that infernal scar!" He shook her shoulders lightly. "Do you not see? He is no good for someone as genteel, as beautiful, as you."

Before Lucy knew what he was about, Arthur had lowered his head and crushed his lips to hers with bruising force, his fingers biting into her upper arms. She twisted and squirmed, trying to extricate herself. If he continued, she might have to scream, and she did not want to ruin Kate's special night.

Arthur continued his assault, and she tried to draw a breath, feeling a sharp pain in her broken ribs. To her dismay, she realized that even if she so chose, she wouldn't be able to draw in enough air to bring forth a scream of any magnitude.

"Mr. Charlesworth," she managed as she turned her head to the side. "Stop! Stop now!"

"You would give yourself to him?" Arthur ground out as he clasped the back of her neck in his hand, his other hand still gripping her upper arm. "He is a beast of a man, disfigured! I have money, connections! You're not thinking clearly, Lucy."

Black spots danced in front of her eyes as she tried desperately to breathe. With her last ounce of energy, and with as much strength as she could muster, she brought her knee up to his groin. The attack was blunted significantly by her layers of fabric, but it was enough that he grunted and bent forward, releasing the grip on her neck.

She twisted away, still trying to break free from the iron grip he had on her arm. "Let me go," she gritted through clenched teeth. She beat on his wrist with her opposite fist.

The flurry of motion was too much for Lucy to follow. She found herself staggering to the side, released from the crushing fingers.

Miles held Arthur over the side of the balcony by the throat.

"No," she gasped. "Miles, no. You'll kill him and be investigated," she managed between breaths, "much more closely than we would like."

Miles stared at Arthur, his arm a band of steel, unwavering, as the other man wriggled like a fish on a hook. "If you come near her again, ever," Miles bit out, "I will beat you into a bloody mess that your own mother will not recognize."

Arthur's eyes bulged, and his movements grew less frantic.

"Miles!" Lucy pulled on his free arm with a sickening sense of dread.

Miles threw his cousin outward, against the stone stairs below the balcony, which, to Lucy's relief, was not a life-threatening drop. She looked over the side to see Arthur moving, albeit slowly.

She put her hand to her corset, convinced she would never again be able to fill her lungs with air. Miles placed a hand on her shoulder, turning her to him. She looked up at his face, which was a mask of stone, his eyes blazing. Rather than softening, however, he grew only more intense.

"What has he done to you?" he whispered. He turned her head to the side with a gentle hand that was at odds with his demeanor. He briefly rested his hand against her hair and then traced it down her neck where, she realized, she must be marked, the bruises visible even in the dim light. "I will kill him."

"No." She clasped his wrist and held his hand to her cheek. "Please, no. The PSRC will come after you, and even though you're a peer, you'll be executed. I cannot bear it." Overwhelmed, she felt her eyes burn with tears.

"Damn him to an eternal hell." Miles swept Lucy into his arms and made his way around the veranda to the front of the house where he waited for a moment—to be certain there were no witnesses, she assumed—and then up the front stairs with a speed that shocked her.

He passed the bedchamber she shared with Kate and went instead to his own, where he opened the door and kicked it shut behind them. She thought he might lay her down on the bed, which really was more pampering than she needed, but he instead walked to a small settee by the hearth. He set her down and walked to the mantel, resting his elbow on it and plowing his fingers through his hair. He breathed less from exertion, she suspected, and more from anger. He slowly closed his eyes.

"I will kill him," he murmured.

"I love you, Miles," she whispered.

Everything about him seemed to still. His anger seemed to drain away. He finally lifted his head and looked at her. "I love you, Lucy Pickett. I adore you. So much that it hurts."

She was quiet, drinking in the sight of him before acknowledging to herself that circumstances beyond their control must intrude. "I've also come to a conclusion," she said with a sigh. "One of the Charlesworths killed your wife, likely also Marie, and is trying his or her best to kill Kate. The good thing is that we can safely eliminate one suspect. Were Arthur the vampire, I believe he would have attempted to bite one or both of us on the veranda."

He made his way to her side and crouched down. "I think you should kiss me."

She placed her hands on his cheeks and kissed his forehead.

"Not quite what I had in mind." He sat next to her and draped an arm around her waist. "Very well, then," he said, closing his eyes and looking relaxed. If not for the slight bouncing of his knee, she might have believed it was genuine. "Murder and mayhem, death, misery, and cursings. My life in summary." He opened one eye. "I still plan to kill him, you know."

"No, you do not. And be still—you're going to bounce us both onto the floor." She glanced pointedly at his knee.

He frowned, looking at her. "I apologize. I must still be rather . . . agitated."

"I find that I am quite affected, as well. I wonder if I might have a moment to myself to rest while you return to the ball?"

His eyes narrowed. "I'm not returning to the ball without you."

"You must. It is unseemly for you to be absent during a celebration in your brother's honor. And I honestly need some time to rest and think. I am exhausted." She paused, hating to play on his sympathy. "And sore."

His eyes flew to her neck and arm where Arthur had manhandled her. He gently laid one hand against her chest, his forefinger resting softly at the hollow of her throat. "He will pay for each and every bruise," he murmured, his hand slowly circling around to the back of her neck, where he gently nudged her forward to kiss him slowly, deeply.

"He already has paid," she said softly when she pulled back, breathless for at least the hundredth time that evening. "I would wager he's still lying in a heap on the stairs outside."

Miles released a heavy sigh and stood, rising to his full height. He ran a hand through his hair again. "I will be back in thirty minutes. I dare not leave you alone any longer."

She smiled. "If you keep all of the Charlesworths in the same room, I shall be perfectly safe. We will need to devise a plan of attack later on."

"You will leave the planning and attacking to me," he said and leaned in for a quick kiss before making his way to the door. He examined it briefly, frowning. "Looks like I broke it when I kicked it shut, but it will still lock."

She crossed the room and, with a final kiss, closed the door behind him and slid the bolt home.

He had reacted exactly as she had known he would. He would rush in, guns blazing and making his own set of plans, when what was required was a bit of stealth and finesse; he would end up killing someone and find himself investigated by the Committee. She hated the deception but knew it was a necessary one. She had to get into the Charlesworths' bedrooms while they were still empty.

Chapter 32

Lucy checked her pocket watch as she crept down the hallway for the third time. Figuring she should start at the top of the list, she had gone to Eustace's room first, but a cursory check had yielded nothing but some extra-large garters, a hidden stash of laudanum, and some empty gin bottles.

She gave Arthur's room a quick look just to be on the safe side. It was as neat as a pin and utterly boring. That he had a painting of his own likeness hanging over the mantelpiece opposite his bed was especially nauseating but not necessarily incriminating. She hadn't found any evidence to suggest either mother or son was a denizen of the undead.

She had fifteen minutes left before Miles returned to take her back to the ball, and she didn't relish the thought of not being in his bedchamber when the time ran out. He would be angry that she had snuck into the rooms of suspected murderers without his help or knowledge. But one look at how he had handled things with Arthur was all she needed to convince herself she was right to conduct the search alone.

Like the other two doors, Candice's was locked, and Lucy made quick work of it using a trick Daniel had taught her when they'd played hide-and-seek as children. She entered the room and clicked on the small torch she'd grabbed from her bedroom. The light was faint; it needed to be connected to a Tesla charger soon. She hoped it would hold out long enough to make a quick search of the bedroom.

Something Arthur had said about Candice played in her mind as she opened drawers, first in the bureau, and then in Candice's vanity. He had said Candice had showered Miles with attention, which Miles, of course, wouldn't have recognized as *attention*. He would have seen it only as unwelcome adulation from a cousin who had always annoyed him and brushed it off. She doubted he had realized that Candice may have wanted to be the countess.

Lucy made quick work of the vanity. Jewelry, hairpins, perfume bottles, and jars of face paint—all things she expected to find and nothing of any use to Lucy.

With a sigh, she straightened and crossed the room to the tall wardrobe that stood against the wall near the bed. She opened the doors to find dozens of lavish dresses and accessories to match. Pushing aside the masses of fabric, she knelt down and opened one of two drawers at the bottom. She knew that when she found whatever it was she was looking for, she would recognize it, and as she examined the drawer's contents, her heart began to thump painfully in her chest.

She lifted a jar of medicinal herbs and held it to the light of her torch—which flickered and went out.

"*No,*" she whispered. She glanced at the window where the curtains were drawn. She made her way to the drapes, and lifting one aside, read the label by moonlight.

It told her, unfortunately, nothing other than the maker of the bottle. With a glance at the door, she carefully twisted off the lid and brought it to her nose. She recognized the scent. She licked her fingertip and dipped it into the mixture, barely touching it to her tongue to be certain she had correctly identified it. She carefully replaced the lid and clutched the jar tightly in her hand.

When she and her fellow researchers at the Botanical Aid Society had begun the search for the Anti-Vampiric Assimilation Aid, they had been required to learn the smell and taste of the drug itself.

How long had Candice been a vampire? And more importantly, how long had she been taking the Aid? The drug only worked for one year, and if Candice were nearing her time limit, it could explain her desperation to secure a position as the Countess of Blackwell. She would have access to nearly unlimited funds, not to mention a title, which could sustain her while she waited for someone to develop a more permanent assimilation aid that could grant her the ability to walk among society undetected indefinitely.

The doorknob turned, and Lucy dropped the curtain, diving to the side of the bed. She crouched down and held her breath. Someone entered but didn't bother with the light. It made sense—Candice wouldn't need it. To Lucy's immense relief, the room remained blessedly dark as Candice made her way over to the vanity, her back to Lucy.

Lucy could make out little more than the woman's shadow as she tossed aside a few items on the vanity's surface with a curse. Lucy was amazed that the frantic beating of her heart wasn't audible to the creature not ten feet from her.

Candice suddenly clutched her head and let out a frustrated roar. She whirled around and stomped to the other side of the bed where she flung open a drawer on the bedside table, searching for something in a furious rush.

"Arthur," Candice ground out. "What have you done with it?"

Lucy heard her move away from the table. She lifted her head just enough to see Candice pacing back and forth in front of the door leading to the hallway.

Lucy's brow wrinkled. Candice must not have been looking for the Aid or she'd have walked straight to the wardrobe where Lucy had found it.

Candice placed a hand on her forehead, muttering to herself, and while most of it was meaningless to Lucy, she did catch the words, "Blasted diary."

Whose diary?

Lucy realized with a stab of panic that if Candice crossed to the other side of the bed to search in the night table behind Lucy's back, she was done for. She lifted the bedcovering from the floor to see if there was enough clearance for her to hide beneath the bed. She was beginning to cramp from crouching so long, and her ankle throbbed horribly. She wondered if lying on the floor might be more comfortable in the long run when the door opened again and closed quickly.

"Arthur! What on earth happened to you?" Candice's gasp told Lucy a couple of things—first, that Arthur was still alive, and second, that he must look absolutely horrible.

"He is insane." Arthur coughed violently. Lucy heard water being poured and then a pause before the man continued. "He tried to kill me!"

"Keep your voice down!"

"Did you hear me, Candice? He wanted to kill me! I think he *is* a shifter. I think he *did* kill Marie, and I am going to prove it."

"Where is the diary?"

"Why is it so dark in here?"

Candice paused. "I have a headache. I know you have the diary because it's gone. I want it back. I need it."

"I need it more than you do, especially now. I'm going to expose him to the PSRC; he will be executed in a matter of weeks."

"You're a fool. I am going to give you one final opportunity to tell me where you've put the diary. Is it in your room?"

"'One final opportunity'? Are you daft? What is that supposed to mean?"

There was a slight pause, a hiss, and then Lucy heard Arthur's horrified gasp. "Candice! What are you doing? What are you—"

There was a loud thud, and Lucy lifted her head fractionally to see that Candice had thrown Arthur against the wall. With a snarl, she bent to his throat. His scream was cut short, and after several agonizing moments, Lucy heard him hit the floor with a sickening *thunk*. She ducked her head and lay flat, sliding under the bed, using the temporary chaos as cover for the noise she made.

It was silent in the room, and Lucy closed her eyes tightly before turning her head and looking out across the floor. She could see dark shadows but nothing definitive. She heard Candice swear, vicious and low, as she made her way to the vanity with a swish of sound.

According to the letter from the Society that Lucy had read during her original flight to Blackwell, Candice had just given herself a good three hours of energy if she'd consumed enough of Arthur's blood when she killed him. It wouldn't require much, unfortunately, and Lucy realized grimly that it was one of the Vampiric Assimilation Aid's biggest perks to the undead. Walk among the living, enjoy the daylight, eat food normally, maintain a healthy appearance with a natural-looking complexion, and, if desirous of maintaining the vampire assets at full strength—admittedly for a limited time—drink the blood of the living.

Candice had just tipped her hand, however, and she had to have realized it. Unless she could calm herself enough to play innocent once Arthur's body was discovered, she would be forced to take drastic measures. Lucy didn't know her well enough to determine what Candice would do when pushed to extremes. She'd already murdered two women—possibly more—but she had absolutely nothing left to lose. If Candice blamed Kate, or even Miles, for her lot in life, Lucy imagined revenge would be high on her list of priorities.

Lucy heard water droplets hitting the pitcher, and she imagined Candice desperately washing her face and anything else that might have been splattered in the slaughter. The wardrobe door was flung open, and still muttering a litany of curses, Candice changed her clothes. It was several long minutes—it was never easy doing up small buttons without help—before Lucy finally heard Candice take a deep breath and open the door.

The earsplitting scream that followed had Lucy squeezing her eyes closed. Candice was very, very good. It wasn't long before the scream gave way to frantic sobs, and with the light from the hallway spilling into the room, Lucy saw Candice crumple to the floor just outside the doorway.

The running of feet, the added exclamations of horror, and additional screaming soon filled the hallway, turning the scene into absolute chaos.

When Lucy heard the deep rumble of a voice that was all too familiar, she cringed. She feared that to show herself at that point and try to explain what she'd been doing in the room and then point to Candice as the murderer might well send the vampire into an additional frenzy. Kate was likely in the hallway, and it wasn't worth the risk. Lucy would have to wait under the bed, though Miles would soon be frantic with worry over her absence.

Lucy heard Miles firing directions, ordering everyone from the hallway and shouting for Oliver. He told Sam to enter the room and examine Arthur, and Daniel to find Lucy in his bedchamber. What Daniel thought of Lucy's supposed location, she could only imagine. Eustace had only just arrived on the scene, apparently, because Miles told her to go back downstairs.

"What is it?" Eustace shrieked. "What is that? Is that blood? Where is Candice?"

Miles told one of the 'tons to escort Eustace to the parlor and then gave instructions to another to summon the constable, if he was in attendance. Lucy doubted it—a constable would hardly be the sort Eustace would have invited to her elegant ball. Lucy felt drained of all energy and wished the room would clear, if only for a moment.

Sounds of the chaos eventually faded down the hallway, and Lucy listened carefully, identifying only two voices. Slowly, carefully, she slid out from under the bed on the far side and stood, brushing dirt and dust from her dress.

"What the *devil*?" Miles ground out.

Daniel appeared in the doorway, wide-eyed. "She's not in there, Blackwell," he said and then stopped when he saw her.

Sam knelt on the floor next to Arthur and looked up at her as well, his mouth agape. Oliver paused in the act of telescribing a message and whistled low.

"There's no time to explain," she said as she moved toward the four men, faltering on her sore ankle and cramped muscles. "It's Candice. I found this—it's assimilation aid." She showed them the jar and glanced out into the hallway. "She's hell-bent on finding a diary, something that apparently could be detrimental to you," Lucy finished, looking at Miles.

Miles watched her with something akin to fire shooting from his eyes, and she knew she would be forced to endure a blistering lecture on her safety. It would have to wait, and she said as much to all of the men.

"Where is Candice?" she finished. Her stomach dropped at the next thought. "And Kate?"

Chapter 33

"How the blazes did she get her out of the house?" Miles shouted as he pushed his way through the crowd. The crush of people attempting to leave the ball separated him from the butler he was trying to interrogate. When word had reached the partygoers that a vampire was not only in the house but had also just killed someone, they had stampeded for the exit, most without bothering to retrieve their coats or wraps.

"I do not know, sir," the butler yelled at Miles across three heads. "One moment Miss Candice was in the parlor, and the next she was gone."

Miles crushed the paper he held in his hand. It was a note from Candice, hastily scrawled, that she had Kate and if they wanted to see her unharmed, he was to meet her at the hunting lodge in one hour. He spied Lucy in the mass of people, coming from the hallway that led to the kitchen. She was pale, her face drawn in a near panic. He pushed his way to her, dodging elbows and throwing a few of his own.

Grabbing her hand, he pulled her toward the parlor. He shoved her in the room ahead of him and slammed the door, taking a deep breath. Sam, Oliver, and Daniel were there, as he had instructed. A maid hovered over Eustace, who was wringing her hands, clearly at a loss.

"Out," he said to the maid and motioned with his head. Without a backward glance at her mistress, she bolted for the door and left.

"Did you check the third floor?" Lucy asked Daniel. "She's not in the kitchen or den."

Oliver plugged his telescriber into a connector on the wall, checking for news or messages.

Miles gritted his teeth together, hating the news he had to deliver. "Sit down," he murmured to Lucy.

She must have seen something in his face, because she swallowed and nodded, sinking slowly onto a window seat.

"Where is she?" Eustace wailed. "Where is Candice? First Arthur—she will be next!" The woman coughed, choked, and Sam poured her a cup of tea from a tray near her elbow.

Miles had no love for the woman, it was true, but her world was about to be utterly crushed. He found he wasn't entirely without decency as he quietly delivered the news to his aunt that her only daughter was a vile murderer and that she'd kidnapped Kate.

He expected her to deny it, but her face drained of all color and she gaped at him, mute. Miles glanced at Lucy, who stared at him for the space of a few heartbeats before getting to her feet.

"What is she thinking?" Lucy asked. "If she actually wants to meet at the lodge, we'll need more than one hour."

"Once we're airborne, it's only a ten-minute flight," Daniel said. "My personal airship has . . . capabilities."

"I am to go alone," Miles's pronouncement was met with a moment or two of silence.

"Unacceptable," Oliver said. "You're not going alone. And Kate may need Sam for medical attention."

"I am not staying here," Lucy told him. "I'll not attempt any heroics once we are there, but I will not wait here. We must tell Jonathan. He's checking the grounds outside for any sign of her." Lucy glanced at Eustace, who was rocking slowly in her chair, her face a mask of shock. "I'll find some help for her." Lucy made her way to the door. Looking back at Miles, she said, "Do not leave without me."

"I don't like it," Miles said to the room in general after she'd left. The thought of what could happen to Lucy made him sick to his stomach, and he paced, shoving a hand through his hair.

"I don't either," Daniel agreed, his face tense.

"Kate will need her there," Sam said as he placed two fingers on Eustace's wrist. "Lucy's a smart woman. She said she'll stay out of the way. The last thing she will want to do is cause more trouble for Kate."

Miles felt his eyes burn and cursed the vulnerability. His heartclock had nearly stopped when he'd realized that not only had Lucy not rested but she had gone after the vampire herself. She'd said she'd had her reasons, that she would explain later, but he was a combustible mixture of fury and gut-wrenching fear.

"I'll alert the airfield to have my ship ready," Daniel said.

"Use the connector," Oliver told him. "I'm finished. The locals are on their way—should arrive in five minutes." He moved to kneel by Eustace, taking one of her hands. "The police will help you take care of matters here," he told her. "Is there anyone we can send for? Clergy, perhaps, or a lady friend?"

Eustace shook her head as tears slipped from her eyes. "I have no one."

The door opened, and Lucy entered with the head housekeeper on her heels, followed by Jonathan, his face ashen beneath red cheeks that evidenced his time outside. Lucy spoke with the housekeeper while Miles gently grasped his brother's arm.

"I'll explain on the way," he said. "And she will be returned to you whole."

The airship descended quietly in the open area just outside Blackwell's hunting lodge, Daniel at the controls and Oliver assisting him. The building was dark, and Lucy wondered if Candice had intentionally led them in the wrong direction. What could she possibly gain by keeping Kate alive? As much as she wanted to remain hopeful, Lucy fought back waves of despair.

"We fan out." Oliver vaulted up to the railing, preparing to climb down the side ladder and secure the moorings as soon as they touched the ground. "She'll see the airship, undoubtedly, but it doesn't matter." With a quick, apologetic glance at Jonathan, he added, "She wouldn't have bargained with Miles if she had made other plans. Our one chance will be to catch her unaware. We'll have to get Kate away from her because she's not going to willingly hand her over."

"Are you certain she's already in the lodge?" Lucy watched as Oliver lowered himself down the side, followed by Sam, who ran to the other side of the ship to secure the rope that hung to the ground.

"No." Miles checked his ray gun. "But either way, we approach by stealth. If she's not there yet, then we have the advantage of setting up first. I will bring Kate to you, Lucy. You must promise me you will remain here." He wrapped her in his arms. She nodded, and he nudged her face upward for a kiss. She made every effort not to cry, but the tears gathered anyway, and she clutched his lapels, swamped with fear.

"Please, Lucy. Please, no heroics," he whispered. "I will not think clearly if you are in danger."

"I promise." She wiped at a tear with her hand. She wished she could be of use to them, could help in some way or be an important element of their team. As it was, she was exhausted and terrified, still healing and trying to forget the sounds of Arthur Charlesworth having his throat ripped out.

She gave Miles a final squeeze and then turned to Daniel, who was finishing his landing procedure checklist. "I'm not shutting her down completely," he said. "We may need to get away quickly, so she's idling."

Lucy placed a kiss on his cheek. "Be safe."

"Always."

Miles embraced Jonathan, who wasn't happy at staying behind with Lucy but who also seemed to realize he'd be more of a hindrance than a help. He was armed with a ray gun that he claimed he'd shot before, but

Lucy had her doubts. Miles patted Jonathan once on his face and then moved to the railing. He gave Lucy one last, long look before climbing down and disappearing over the side.

Five minutes became ten, and then fifteen. Lucy stared out into the night from the safety of the dark wheelhouse. The wait was agony, as she had known it would be. Jonathan prowled the lower deck. She saw his shadow as he moved back and forth, the ray gun an extension of his hand.

The blurry flash across the bow had Lucy blinking in momentary confusion before she heard a faint thud, rather like someone hitting the deck. Her heart tripping, Lucy ran for the wheelhouse door and wrenched it open, stepping outside and squinting into the dark.

"Jonathan?" she called softly.

Something clamped around her waist from behind, and she felt a cold sensation against her neck as her head was wrenched painfully to the side.

"So predictable," Candice murmured, her teeth scraping against Lucy's skin. "I tell him to come alone, and he brings you and his ridiculous brother. Most likely his trio of cronies are somewhere around, as well."

"Where is Kate?" Lucy managed. "If she's still alive, let her go."

Candice squeezed tighter, her arm like an iron band around Lucy's torso. "She's down there with her beloved," she said and shoved Lucy forward to look down over the deck. In the dim starlight, she saw Kate's crumpled form in her white dress lying against what Lucy could only assume was Jonathan. Neither moved.

"And where is *your* beloved?" Candice murmured in Lucy's ear, nipping it hard enough to draw blood. "Oh, dear," she sighed. "How clumsy of me." She pulled Lucy away from the wheelhouse and dragged her down the stairs to the main deck. "And I doubt you happen to have any anti-vamp with you this time."

Lucy felt the trickle of warm blood trailing down her earlobe and onto her neck. *Keep her talking, keep her talking . . .*

"Why did you poison Clara?" Lucy asked. "And why have Marie killed? You could have just bitten them both, and nobody would have been the wiser." She grunted in pain as Candice lifted her and flew down the last few steps. "They would have blamed it on some 'local rogue vampire.' No one would have even thought to look in your direction."

"Because I didn't have these abilities then!" Candice snarled.

The air whooshed painfully out of Lucy's lungs as Candice ran with her and leaped into the air.

They flew toward the top of the hunting lodge, but Candice faltered, dropping drastically before they surged upward again, barely clearing the roof.

They stumbled to a halt on the center of the roof, skittering and nearly falling, but Candice again hauled up on Lucy's midsection so tightly that she saw black spots dancing before her eyes. There was a small portion of roof that was flat, and Candice dropped Lucy onto it.

"You're nearly spent," Lucy said, trying for a laugh that she couldn't manage. Pain stabbed her ribs. "You used so much energy flying Kate here that you're almost done for."

Candice kicked her, catching the side of Lucy's face with her boot and sending her tumbling down the roof. She came to a halt at the roofline, where a row of tall, wrought-iron spikes were evenly placed. Candice caught her, throwing her back up to the top. Lucy hit the stone chimney with her shoulder and bit her lip to keep from crying out. She refused to give the other woman the satisfaction of hearing her distress. Her face and shoulder throbbed, and she clung to the chimney, her head spinning and her ear on fire where Candice had nipped it. She took shallow breaths to keep the encroaching nausea at bay.

Keep her talking, keep her talking . . .

"I don't understand," Lucy gasped.

Candice crouched down and wrapped her fist in Lucy's hair, pulling her head back. "Of course you don't," she spat. "You can't imagine what it's like to be in love with someone your whole life and then watch him marry another!"

"You killed Clara because you're still in love with Miles!" Lucy exclaimed as the pieces began to fall into place.

"Clara was a stupid, sniveling girl." Candice wrenched Lucy's hair tighter, and Lucy gasped again. "Once I programmed the 'ton to do the work for me, everything else was simple. With Clara gone, I was going to step in and console Miles and take my place as his wife."

Candice abruptly released Lucy's head and stood, forcing Lucy to look up at her. "But then my mother sent me to London to meet potential suitors." She smiled, and Lucy shivered. "And I met Oliver Reed's brother."

Lucy frowned. *Oliver's brother?*

"Lawrence Reed was the one who turned me. Met me at a soiree in London just after Miles's wedding. He established a 'friendship' by saying his brother and my cousin were bosom friends, and that was as good as a proper introduction."

Lucy closed her eyes against Candice's snarling face and wicked teeth, and then she opened them again, willing herself to stay strong, to not give an inch.

"And then," Candice continued, her voice low, "he lured me outside, promised to court me, said he planned to ask for my hand. And by the romantic light of the spring moon, he bit me. Turned me into this." The vampire's eyes took on a red glow, her face all the more haunting because of its beauty.

"But you must have started sending the notes to Miles before leaving for London. How did you know—"

"—that my cousin is a dog? I thought it odd that he kept coming to this lodge so religiously, like clockwork. So I spied on him one weekend when my mother thought I was in Bath with friends. When I was sure of the truth, I devised a plan and sent the notes. He was already making plans to marry his American heiress, and I decided to convince him otherwise."

"By coercion? Blackmail?"

Candice's eyes flashed. "By whatever means necessary! Love requires dedication. But Clara's family was all too eager for a quick courtship and before anyone knew what had happened," Candice threw her arms wide,

"Miles had himself a countess!" She crouched next to Lucy. "And it wasn't me."

"But Marie wasn't the countess. She didn't stand in your way." Where was Daniel? Where was Miles?

"She got in my way once she discovered the programmed 'ton cards in my chamber before I could properly destroy them. She knew I had poisoned Clara. She was going to tell Miles, so I lured her to her garden. Had a stable boy complete the task—and then I sent the note for Miles to find her. And hopefully be caught shifting. He would face charges for murdering his sister and for being a predatory shape-shifter." She clapped her hands and smiled. "Problem solved!"

Lucy scoffed in spite of her fear. "I thought you said you loved him."

"But I do! Don't you see?" Candice's eyes blazed again. "It's better this way. He will be humbled and ready for me to save him. He swore after Clara died that he would never remarry, but I *must* be the countess. It is no longer about love. Now that I am what I am, I need money, resources. Power." Her nostrils flared, and she sucked in a breath. "And *you* will not stand in my way. My mother told me of your engagement earlier this evening. I would congratulate you if the blessed union were to ever be a reality."

Lucy was dizzy, and pain radiated from head to toe. *Keep her talking.* "But what about Oliver?"

Candice's face contorted. "Oliver is a pawn. I am not yet strong enough to confront Lawrence, but when I am—"

Lucy lunged, trying to get away, but Candice backhanded her with enough force to send her flying. She scraped her fingers nearly raw trying to scramble for purchase and keep from falling off the roof.

Candice stopped her from falling to the ground by stomping on her left wrist, and Lucy finally lost her battle with bravery. Crying out in pain, she cast desperately about for what she knew of vampires, of their destruction. Direct sunlight wasn't an option; even if it were daylight, Candice had enough Vampiric Assimilation Aid in her system to withstand it.

301

Lucy had nothing with which to impale her through the heart, and she didn't possess the strength to rip Candice's head from her body.

"Why Kate?" Lucy fought to keep her voice steady, but tears formed unbidden. Her wrist was the only thing supporting her body weight, and the pain caused spots to form before her eyes. "Jonathan isn't the earl. You have no reason to want her dead."

Candice shook her head. "Oh, Miss Pickett, I really did imagine you to be brighter than you are. If Miles refuses to marry me or is killed, Jonathan is my contingency. I *will* be the countess of Blackwell one way or another."

Candice had been delusional before she became a vampire, and the mania now was only amplified. "What do you want from me?" Lucy finally managed through gritted teeth, a welcome surge of anger supplanting her despair. "What are you waiting for?"

"Silly girl." Candice smiled. "We are waiting for Miles. I will explain his options, and he will decide how we shall proceed. Arthur's interference has forced my hand, I'm afraid. I no longer have the luxury of time."

"And what are Miles's options?" Lucy inhaled, trying desperately to catch her breath.

Candice's smile widened. "How fortuitous that I didn't kill you that night at the manor—although you were a dreadful nuisance and very nearly derailed everything. 'I don't want anything to touch Kate's lips that I haven't tested first!' You delayed my plans by weeks! But I need you now as a bargaining chip. Miles will decide whether or not you live. If he agrees to marry me, I will tell him I shall return you to your mother none the worse for the wear. If he does not, you die here before his eyes."

Lucy shoved at the roof with the toes of her boots, trying to relieve the stress her body weight caused on her wrist. "You will not let me go home," she managed.

"You are a smart girl after all. Your death is one more feather in my cap; I will gain high favor indeed for ridding the vampire world of a botanist bent on destroying the Vampiric Assimilation Aid. And once Miles and I are married, he will introduce legislation in Parliament that will reverse the banishment order—if he wants his brother to continue to live."

Lucy laughed, and to her surprise, it was genuine. "You are an absolute fool," she said, sprawled atop the roof, held in place by nothing but a foot on her wrist. "You honestly believe he would do that."

"You think he values you so highly, then?"

"Not me," she said, her arm going blessedly numb. "There is no way in the depths of hell he would introduce that legislation. My friend, you have wasted a large amount of time and energy."

Candice screeched in outrage and picked up Lucy by the wrist. The vampire's energy clearly was fading; Lucy saw her chance. She pushed up on wobbly legs and shoved the heel of her hand into Candice's chin.

Candice staggered and grunted. The vampire's head snapped back, and she released Lucy's arm, giving her momentary reprieve, yet her relief was short-lived as she lost purchase and began sliding down the rooftop.

"Drop, Lucy! Drop straight down!"

Lucy appreciated the advice Miles shouted to her as he grabbed Candice from behind but figured she didn't have much control over the matter. She fell off the roof and braced herself for impact with the ground.

<hr />

Miles had finished searching the lodge when he heard noises coming from the roof. When he climbed to the top, he fully expected to see Candice struggling with Kate, not Lucy. He had told the other men to position themselves on three sides of the house and hope for the best should the hostage fall.

His heart in his throat, he'd been wondering how to distract Candice enough for her to relinquish her hold on Lucy when his sweet little fiancée nearly shoved the vampire's head from her shoulders herself.

Candice's strength surprised him. Even in a weakened state, she twisted free from his grasp and snarled at him, her pretty face eerily evil as she took a swipe at him with nails that could, he knew firsthand, dispense lethal venom. He dodged her movements and moved forward slowly as she began to retreat, her ability to hover diminishing. She slipped but regained her footing at the top of the roof, and he pursued her with a rising sense of rage that was heightened by hours of worry and fear.

"You have made my life quite interesting this year, Candice," he said softly, watching her every move, every twitch, as she pressed herself against the chimney. "I do not much appreciate it."

"You should be thanking me," the woman snarled at him. "If Clara were still alive, you wouldn't be free to propose to your precious botanist!"

"And I was under the impression that you were reserving the role of countess for yourself."

"I will kill her after I finish with you. I will drink every last drop of her blood, and I will do it slowly. She will die knowing that you could not save her." Candice smiled at him. "Or perhaps I shall turn her instead."

He knew she bated him, and still his vision filled with a red haze. He grabbed her shoulders, but she had anticipated his movements—he'd left her just enough of an opening to lunge at his neck. He felt the barest brush of her fangs against his jugular before he picked her up over his head. He allowed himself to slide sideways down the roof until they reached the roofline's wrought-iron spikes.

With a snarl, he impaled her on one of the spikes and then held fast to the metal with one hand as his body swung over the edge. Slinging a foot over the edge of the roof, he climbed back up and looked to be certain the vampire had been staked through the heart.

"You regained your strength," Candice murmured as a trickle of black fluid escaped the side of her mouth and ran down her cheek. "Impossible. Your heartclock . . ." The same black liquid spread from the spear through her heart and stained her dress as she bled out. Any affection he might have felt for his cousin was absent as he looked at the creature who had replaced her.

Her eyes widened slightly and then she was still.

Chapter 34

Lucy climbed from the bed in her guest room at Charlesworth House and looked out the window at the softly falling snow. She was sore from her head to her feet—there wasn't a bit of her that didn't hurt—and yet she hadn't taken a pain reliever for fear it would put her into a deep sleep. It would soon be dawn, and there was one thing still left undone.

After Daniel had caught her when she'd fallen from the roof, he had run to the airship, intending to use it to lift Miles from the rooftop. He had told her he was going to "blow the vamp's head from her shoulders" with some high-powered weaponry Lucy figured he probably was not legally allowed to have aboard a civilian ship. It hadn't been long, however, before Lucy heard Candice's shriek, followed by the sickening *thunk* of her impalement.

Miles, Daniel, and Oliver had disposed of the body—first severing the head for good measure—while Lucy had accompanied Sam back to the airship to tend to Jonathan and Kate. He'd revived both of them, and treated Lucy's wounded ear with a supply of anti-venom he'd procured from London. Her beautiful ball gown, to say the least, was no longer beautiful.

The flight to Blackwell Manor from the hunting lodge was short, but Lucy found a moment to share with everyone what Candice had divulged about Oliver's brother. Oliver had taken the news with the stoicism Lucy had come to recognize in the man as his preferred mode of defense against all things emotional.

"How long has it been since you've seen him?" Miles asked Oliver.

"Not since before the war. We were never close." Oliver moved to stand by the railing, and the others left him in peace.

At Blackwell Manor, Lucy gave Kate a good dose of restorative tea and as much toast as she could manage to shove down her throat. She kissed her cousin good night and left her with Jonathan, gratified to see Kate's features at peace and some color returning to her cheeks.

Miles announced that he had to return to Charlesworth House to help Eustace handle affairs, and Lucy decided to accompany him now that the danger to Kate had passed. Daniel set the course for the airship, leaving Oliver and Sam behind to watch over Blackwell Manor.

Charlesworth House was still ablaze with lights when they arrived. Not only was the local constabulary investigating, but they had also alerted the Scottish authorities who specialized in vampire attacks. Lucy listened in on the proceedings in the library, her head resting on Daniel's shoulder as Miles relayed the events of the evening to the gathered officials.

Lucy felt her eyelids droop, and Daniel squeezed her shoulder.

"You should rest," he murmured. "I'll walk you up to your room." Lucy caught Miles's eye. He looked as exhausted as she felt, and she wished they were far away from everyone and everything.

A maid helped Lucy wash and change into nightclothes. She waited until the maid left before procuring a small torch. She was tired but she knew she couldn't rest until she found the elusive diary the Charlesworth siblings had argued over, and doing so while Miles was occupied elsewhere was her best chance.

She made her way to the family's bedchambers at the other end of the long hallway. The bloody mess inside Candice's room had been only perfunctorily cleaned, as a dark stain extended from under the closed door and out onto the hallway carpet.

With a shudder, she continued past it to Arthur's room, where she twisted the knob, fully expecting to find it locked. It turned in her hand, and her heart sank. Had Candice found the diary before leaving the house with Kate? Surely she hadn't had enough time.

Lucy closed the door behind her and stood at the threshold, her eyes adjusting to the shadows of the room. In her earlier search, she'd not come across anything resembling a diary. She crossed to a small desk near one of the windows and sat in the chair. There were three drawers, each of which held paper and a couple of writing instruments but nothing else.

She turned around in the chair and examined the room, trying to see it with fresh eyes. The room was still neat as a pin, evidence that Candice had not had time to look for the diary. Lucy looked at the portrait of Arthur still hanging over the mantelpiece. Ridiculous and horribly sad. He was gone and had expired in such a horrifying manner. He had been a cad, had assaulted her mere hours before, but she still mourned the loss of a young life wasted.

That portrait . . .

On impulse, she rose and went to the painting, lifting it slightly and shining her torch behind it. With a grim smile of triumph, she reached forward and carefully untied a string that anchored a small, black book to the portrait's hanging wire. She held the book to her chest and quietly made her way out of the room and back to her own.

Lighting her bedside lamp, she climbed up on the mattress with a groan. There wasn't a movement she made that wasn't painful, and she wondered if she'd ever feel normal again. Situating herself against the fluffy pillows, she pulled the blanket over her legs and opened the book.

Seeing Marie's neat, flourished handwriting on the front flyleaf was jarring, as though she were experiencing a visit from beyond the grave. Marie's own pen had touched the pages, and Lucy lost herself in the musings, daydreams, and wishes of a young woman of privilege who was navigating her place in the world. Unable to inherit, she felt displaced from the estate, and a string of suitors proved so unsatisfactory that she eventually decided to be done with the lot of them and set up her own home in one of her mother's former estates.

It was toward the end of the diary that Lucy found the passages that the Charlesworth siblings had valued. Marie suspected Clara was being poisoned, and as much as she faulted the girl for being such a ninny, she didn't want to see her murdered. She had made a list of possible suspects, Candice first among them.

Lucy wondered why Candice hadn't simply burned the diary, but as she continued turning pages, she found reference to what Arthur had said about the book containing evidence against Miles.

Marie had known that Miles was a shape-shifter, and she had written that she wished he would have confided in her, that she knew he carried the heavy burden alone. Lucy's eyes filmed over with tears, the beautiful script blurring as she read the words of tender affection from a sister to her beloved elder brother.

A quiet knock sounded on her bedchamber door, and before she could answer it, Miles cracked it open and peered inside.

"Why aren't you asleep?" He closed the door quietly and stood just inside the room, jacket off, shirt wrinkled and filthy, cravat long gone.

"I had to find something first." She patted the bed and motioned with her head.

He tossed the jacket onto a nearby chair and rolled up his cuffs as he slowly approached. His eye caught on the book she held, and his mouth dropped open. "You went looking for that infernal diary alone? Lucy, for the love! You were supposed to wait for me."

She smiled. "I didn't want to wait. Come here. There are some things you need to read."

He shot her a look of frustration, but he pulled his boots off and settled down next to her. He sighed and swung his legs up onto the du-vet. He placed his arm around her shoulders, gently pulling her close. "I should have dragged you to the vicar on the way back tonight. I don't suppose I shall sleep well again until we are married. Where did you find the diary?"

"In Arthur's bedroom." She handed him the black book. "I'll give you some space to read it. I believe you'll find it of great value."

"Stay here. Don't leave me." He held her close against him and flipped open the book. She knew the moment when he realized the enormity of what he held in his hand with his sharp intake of breath. He closed the cover and set it on his leg. "I cannot read this. Not right now."

"Will you read one small segment?" She reached for the book, and he handed it back to her. She opened it to the end and held it up for him to see.

"Just read it to me."

She looked at him to see he'd closed his eyes. Lucy paused. "Miles, I am sorry. This seemed like the right notion a moment ago, but it can wait."

"No," he said, squeezing her shoulder with his hand. "I want to hear it."

She read aloud what Marie had written about Miles, emotion thick in her throat as she glanced at him and saw a single tear escape his closed eyes and roll down the scar that she never really noticed anymore. When she finished, she closed the book and shifted in the circle of his arm, wiping the tear from his face and placing a kiss on it.

"She was an amazing woman," Lucy said. "And I do believe she adored you."

Miles finally opened his eyes. "She *was* amazing. I miss her terribly. I can never apologize enough for what my family has put you through, Lucy. When I realized you were on the roof with Candice . . ." He shrugged, his eyes glistening. "I would have given my life to keep you safe. You're the best, most amazing thing that has ever happened to me."

He sat up and took Lucy's face in his hands. "You are a miracle. My miracle." He kissed her, and she decided that finding a vicar—and soon—might be a good thing.

Epilogue

The wedding was a lavish affair, lavish but tasteful, and Lucy was satisfied with the results. Their loved ones were in attendance for the intimate ceremony, followed by a grand reception to feed and entertain all of London. Miles had rolled his eyes at the extent to which she'd taken the festivities, but it was her only wedding, she'd told him, and she meant to do it right. Besides, he'd insisted she arrange it in less than a month, so he had no room to complain.

She had to admit her motives weren't entirely pure. She fully intended to launch her husband into polite society and demand that they accept him. She would die before she saw him snubbed ever again, and heaven help the person who did it in her presence. In truth, the enormity of the celebration was for him; she had definitely made her point.

Miles had invited Eustace to the ceremony and told Lucy that perhaps they should extend an invitation for her to visit after their honeymoon. Lucy readily agreed. The poor woman was still reeling from shock, to the point that she'd lost an alarming amount of weight and looked rather gaunt.

Kate and Jonathan had moved into a small estate thirty minutes away, and Kate had been ecstatic to turn over the reins of Blackwell Manor to Lucy. She said she was looking forward to managing a smaller home and grateful they would still live close by.

Hazel Hughes was in attendance and seemed to be healing well from her injuries sustained during the vampire attack. Lucy regretted that they didn't have more time to talk and obtained a promise from the young woman that she would visit Blackwell, hopefully for an extended stay. Lucy took note of what she thought was a fair measure of tension she couldn't quite define between Hazel and Sam and filed it away mentally for later perusal.

Since the attack at the lodge, Daniel had checked in repeatedly with Lucy as if assuring himself she was still alive. He promised a vacation with her and Miles as soon as he could manage the time away from his business. Lucy worried quietly about him but finally accepted the fact that he would come to her in time, if at all. His demons were his own to work through, she supposed, although it bothered her like a rock in her shoe that she wasn't able to fix everything for him.

Sam kept close watch on Miles, insisting on routine maintenance checks for the heartclock.

Oliver busied himself with work—a "secret project" that Lucy suspected involved finding his errant brother. The guilt he felt for the whole of Miles's troubles was tremendous, although Miles told him repeatedly that it wasn't his fault. Oliver had left the wedding reception early, telling Miles it was for business. A "do-gooder" woman, he said, was in the thick of the debate on repealing the Predatory Shifter Extermination Act, and his superiors wanted him to handle it with a measure of "discretion."

For her part, Lucy was glad to hear that *someone* was in the thick of the debate. The sooner the act was repealed, the sooner she would sleep at night knowing Miles was safe from legalized extermination. It didn't sit well with her at all that the vampire who created Candice was at large and likely knew of Miles's condition.

Once dinner had wound down and Lucy had shaken more hands than she could count, Miles whisked her away to the airfield, barely allowing her time to hug family and friends on her way out. They were spending the night at the manor before leaving the following morning, and while she found it odd, he had insisted.

Lucy stood before the mirror in the bedroom that was now officially hers, examining her beautiful wedding ensemble once more before ringing for a maid to help her undress. After returning to Blackwell Manor from Charlesworth House, Lucy had reinstalled the original punch cards for the 'tons, and she intended to reprogram each and every one of them with some pleasant personality traits after her honeymoon.

Miles had made it clear that he didn't care which bed they slept in but that they would spend the night together, each night, for the rest of their lives. She smiled, grateful that the nightmares were lessening. She no longer saw Candice in her sleep, no longer feared for her life, or Kate's.

The night after she had given Miles the diary, she had awoken to see Marie sitting in the chair beside her bed, watching her. The light was on but turned low, and Lucy blinked, gathering her bearings.

Marie smiled gently, and Lucy had returned it, wishing more than anything that she could hear the woman talk, if only once.

"I will take good care of your brother," Lucy whispered, her eyes burning at the loss of what would have been a warm friendship with Miles's sister.

Thank you. For everything.

It wasn't audible, but Lucy heard it clearly. And then Marie Blake was gone.

A quiet knock on the door pulled Lucy from the memory, and Miles entered, still in his wedding finery. She cocked a brow in surprise as he approached to stand behind her.

"I thought you were changing your clothes," she said as he wrapped his arms around her waist. She couldn't help but laugh at the image reflected in the mirror. "I should be taller," she said. "You are enormous, my lord."

He rested his chin atop her head. "You are perfect, my lady. And I have something I want to show you." He led her out of her chambers to the main hallway and down to the double doors that opened into the ballroom.

"Cover your eyes," he said.

She complied, and as she heard him turning the door handle, the soft strains of a waltz spilled gently into the hallway. He led her into the ballroom and then whispered, "Open."

The ballroom sparkled and gleamed, chandeliers polished and wall frescoes restored. She placed her hand on her chest, completely overwhelmed. "Oh, Miles."

"We were interrupted the last time we were in here," he said, and for a moment, he looked the slightest bit uncertain. "Do you like it?"

"It's breathtaking," she said, her eyes stinging. "Absolutely beautiful."

"Lady Lucy Elizabeth Pickett Blake, Countess of Blackwell," he said with a brief bow over her hand, "may I have this dance?"

"It would be my pleasure." She dipped into a curtsey with a smile.

He pulled her close and swept her onto the floor, and she felt as though she were flying.

"Thank you," he said to her quietly.

She looked at him in question.

"For saving me."

Acknowledgments

My heart is full at seeing this book in print. It was a long road to this point, and I am grateful to so many people. To my agent, Pamela Howell, for taking me on and believing in the book. To Pam (again) and Bob DiForio, my everlasting thanks for navigating the publishing waters for me. To Lisa Mangum, Heidi Taylor, Chris Schoebinger, and everyone at Shadow Mountain—the day you told me you loved this book was one of the best days of my life. I am so happy you saw the potential in it, and I'm so grateful for my association with you.

Thanks always to my writing support groups for the brainstorming and retreats—specifically to the Bear Lake Monsters and Goldenpens. My work is better because of my association with you, and I cherish those friendships.

To Josi S. Kilpack (*Forever and Forever*) and Jennifer Moore (*Lady Helen Finds Her Song*), your love, support, and shared tears over the past three years have sustained me and kept me writing. All the thanks in the world will never be enough. I love you both dearly.

To my family and Mark's, for their unflagging love and support. I am so humbly grateful. Words aren't enough, and that probably says something, coming from a person who makes her living by them. I love you, each of you, and hope to always make you proud.

Last but not least, my love, devotion, and profound gratitude to my husband and children. They have been in the trenches with me, have witnessed the joys and frustrations, and have shored me up continually. My life is full and good because they are in it, and nothing I do would mean half as much if I couldn't share it with them. I am richly blessed, and so grateful.

Discussion Questions

1. The original "Beauty and the Beast" fairy tale was published in the mideighteenth century. Why does this particular story have such lasting appeal? What elements of the fairy tale are present in *Beauty and the Clockwork Beast*? Where do the two stories diverge?

2. Steampunk is a specific genre that blends a classic setting with steam-powered or gear-powered technology. What other steampunk novels have you read? In what ways did the steampunk elements in the story help establish the setting, develop the characters, or advance the plot? What was your favorite steampunk invention?

3. Lucy is one of the few female botanists studying the vampire problem and looking for a solution, though she does not seem bothered at being a minority in her profession. How is her situation similar to modern-day experiences? Discuss how society is currently encouraging women to pursue professions in math and science.

4. Lucy and Kate, though cousins, have a family relationship that is more like sisters. How does that relationship sustain the women over the course of the story? Miles and the Charlesworth siblings are also cousins, but they have a much different relationship. Discuss how family relationships—either in a close family or an extended family—can influence you positively or negatively.

5. Miles's bond with Oliver, Sam, and Daniel was forged during war. Is enduring a dangerous experience the only way to strengthen a relationship? What other ways can you develop a lasting friendship? How did you meet your best friend?

6. Marie's ghost cannot rest until Lucy solves the mystery behind her murder and Clara's murder. Do you believe that those who have passed are able to return for important reasons or to seek justice? Do you have any personal experiences with ghosts?

7. Who did you suspect was the murderer? What clues did you see in the book that supported your suspicions?

Marie's
STORY

A Prequel Novelette to

NANCY CAMPBELL ALLEN

Lady Marie Blake stepped into the apothecary shop, shaking her umbrella and then removing the hood of her cloak. The rain in Coleshire had been relentless for two weeks—not altogether odd in the springtime, but irksome nonetheless. Marie's patience ran short regarding things over which she had no control.

She ran a hand over her midsection, straightening the ties on her burgundy corset and adjusting the neckline of the ruffled white shirt that fit snugly beneath it. She shook out the black lace–trimmed burgundy skirts, thinking she ought to have opted for riding breeches, even though she hadn't arrived by horseback.

If she couldn't manage the rain, she could at least see about curing her sister-in-law's mysterious illness. Marie took stock of the shelves at the back of the shop, not quite certain what she was looking for, but feeling the urge to do something. Clara Appleton Blake, Miles's new American bride and the Countess of Blackwell, was afraid of her own shadow and had fallen ill with some indefinable malady.

Marie had not approved of Miles's decision to marry Clara, but it was done now, and Marie certainly hoped the young woman would eventually display the fortitude necessary to bear children. Marie loved her older brother and wanted to see him content. Miles was unhappy, and had been long before his return from deployment to India with Her Majesty's finest.

Marie had been wracking her brain to find a solution to ease her elder brother's disquiet. She had hopes that perhaps the thought of a young heir on the way might bring him a measure of peace.

The apothecary shop was warm and cozy, the walls lined with shelves that hosted a wide assortment of cures for nearly everything under the sun. The containers varied in size and shape, and the glass bottles ranged in color from green and blue to brown and black.

Marie rubbed a hand across her forehead and regarded the medicinal bottles with some frustration. She had no idea what she was looking for. When she spied the apothecary, she made her way across the room to his side.

"My sister-in-law, Lady Blackwell, is suffering from an illness that has left her weak and often nauseated," she began.

The man regarded her for a moment, his face reddening slightly.

Marie refrained from rolling her eyes, but only just. "She is not ex-pecting a child," she told him, wanting to be clear about the symptoms so that Clara wouldn't be treated with wrong kind of medicine. Marie didn't tell the man how she knew her sister-in-law wasn't carrying a blessed bundle of joy; Clara had yet to allow Miles into her bed. The staff gos-siped, even the 'tons, and they were loyal to Marie. There wasn't much that transpired in the house without Marie knowing all the details.

"Very good, my lady," he said and lightly cleared his throat as he tipped his head up to meet her direct gaze. She stood a good two inches taller—but he was slightly short for a man and she was tall for a woman. Had she been wearing her favorite black top hat with the hunting goggles and green feathers, the height difference would have been even more pronounced.

"Perhaps this might ease Lady Blackwell's discomfort," the man said, reaching for a bottle on a high shelf. "And I do have one other herbal mix-ture due to arrive this afternoon. It treats nausea and fatigue quite well—if it pleases you, I can have it delivered to the manor."

Marie scrutinized the bottle he handed her, nodding absently. She would see to it personally that Clara at least tried it. Miles and Clara had been married six weeks, and Marie had little patience with the young American's reservations about taking her place as lady of the estate. Marie had an estate of her own awaiting her, a home thirty minutes to the north that had been part of her mother's holdings. Marie had hoped to move there, renovate the place, and begin her life as a truly independent woman of means when Miles married. Clara had had ample time to familiarize herself with Blackwell Manor, but she still made no move to take on her responsibilities. Perhaps if she were no longer ill, she might be more willing to become a proper wife to Miles.

Miles needed a companion, someone who might provide a supportive shoulder and listen to his troubles at the end of a long day. There had been a time when he had confided in Marie, when they had been the very best of friends. That had changed one night in his eighteenth year. He had come home with a frightening gash across his face that had taken weeks to heal and left behind a jagged scar in its place. He had withdrawn, had laughed less with Marie, and any kind of meaningful conversation ceased altogether.

Marie signed her name to the purchase slip and thanked the apothecary with a nod. The paper bag crinkled as she folded it closed and made her way to the door. She didn't bother with the umbrella, but simply pulled her hood back up over her head. She braved the deluge of rain and quickly crossed the street to her waiting Traveler. She climbed inside, slamming the door and gritting her teeth against the cold before settling behind the steering wheel. She fired up the vehicle by twisting a crank and pushing a series of buttons on the dash.

It wasn't entirely unusual for a woman to operate a Traveler herself, but Marie was well aware of the image she presented to society. Mid-twenties, unmarried—she did as she pleased without a man by her side. She was fairly certain most of her friends, if not her family, were baffled by her. She had had her choice of suitors but found them all lacking. Marie had decided at a young age that she would marry for love or not at all.

Sitting for a moment to allow the coils in the seat to warm, she flipped on the window-washer blades and sighed, feeling weary. Miles's "accident" had been years earlier, and he had never once spoken of it. She had pestered him about it once, and, at his angry, abrupt response, had resolved to leave it be. She had felt his withdrawal keenly at the time, but she still occasionally saw a spark of his old self in him. Miles had his secrets, things he didn't want her or their younger brother, Jonathan, to know.

Their mother had died giving birth to Jonathan, and their father had passed several years ago; the former they missed greatly, the latter engendered no tender emotions whatsoever. Although not the eldest sibling, Marie often felt the urge to fill the gaping hole left by their mother's death, and her self-imposed responsibility likely contributed to her unmarried state. She adored her brothers and had decided she would be the favorite aunt to their future children, the one person who would serve dessert before dinner and take them to the carnival.

She thought of her own aunt who was in residence at the Blackwell estate, along with her two cousins, and grimaced. They were visiting despite the lack of an invitation and showed no signs of departing any time soon. She pulled the Traveler onto the road and headed for home. One bright spot, she supposed, was the fact that Miles's three best friends from his military deployment were also visiting. They helped diffuse some of the familial irritation that made Marie want to disown the lot of them.

As she passed Coleshire Airship Field, Marie glanced out at the rows of airships in the process of either landing or preparing to lift off. Standing head and shoulders above the rest in both structure and quality was the Pickett Airship line, owned and operated by none other than Miles's military friend Daniel Pickett. His quick engineering and entrepreneurial talents had created a small empire, built on transporting England's citizens all over the globe. He was handsome as sin, and Marie might have expressed an interest in forming an association with him had he not been rather remote and unapproachable.

She continued along the heavily wooded paths that stood between Coleshire proper and the Blackwell estate. The thick vegetation sheltered the Traveler from the rain, but the darkened interior of the tunnel-like paths made for a poor trade. She always felt slightly uneasy making the journey, and she experienced a sense of relief when Blackwell Manor's tall turrets came into view.

Marie drove the Traveler to the stables and garage, leaving the Traveler with the garage master. As she made her way up the sloping lawn to the manor, she clutched her purchase from the apothecary shop tighter in her hand. Miles was away from home for a few more days—Parliament, he'd said—and Marie hoped Clara's health might begin to show some improvement before his return.

Something wasn't right. Marie sat by Clara in the library after dinner and examined her sister-in-law. Clara was paler than before, and while the doctor who visited that afternoon had praised Marie's herbal purchases, he had expressed privately to Marie that he doubted they would do much besides ease some of Clara's symptoms. He was still baffled by the nature of the illness and could offer no new insight despite examining her for the third time in as many weeks.

Marie frowned at the burst of harsh laughter sounding from a small gaming table where Aunt Eustace Charlesworth sat with her two adult children, Arthur and Candice, and two of Miles's friends, Oliver Reed, a Bow Street consultant, and Dr. Samuel MacInnes. Eustace was in hostess mode, attempting to charm the gentlemen without realizing, apparently, how dearly she lacked social graces. His friends didn't seem to mind Miles's absence. They had even said that, given Miles's expected return in a couple of days, they would be happy to wait, if it wouldn't be a bother for Marie, Clara, and Jonathan.

Eustace laughed again and snorted as well, and Marie briefly closed her eyes. A bother? Were it not for Oliver, Sam, and Daniel, Marie would be obliged to entertain the relatives herself. The presence of Miles's friends was anything but a bother. She never would have believed it possible that she would prefer Clara's company to anyone, but the thought of joining her aunt and cousins at the gaming table set her teeth on edge.

The fire was warm and crackling, casting a cozy glow and warding off the springtime chill. Clara didn't seem to be benefitting much, however; she shivered despite the blanket Marie had draped around her shoulders. Marie glanced at Daniel Pickett, who sat near them at the hearth. He met her gaze, and his eyes flicked to Clara and back. Marie lifted her shoulder in a small shrug, and Daniel's brows knit in a frown.

"Is there something I can do for you, Lady Blackwell?" he asked Clara softly. "Perhaps some tea?"

Clara shook her head but managed a smile. "Thank you, Mr. Pickett, but I find I haven't an appetite for much of anything." She looked at Marie, and added, "And thank you ever so much for the herbal concoction. It settled my stomach quite nicely."

Marie nodded and felt a tug on her heart when Clara managed to hold her gaze for longer than her customary two seconds of eye contact. There was something almost pleading in her expression, but Marie was at an utter loss to help her.

"When Miles returns," Marie said, "I will see to it that he takes you to London for a thorough examination."

Clara smiled, but it lacked any genuine sense of joy. "Dr. MacInnes mentioned the same thing to me earlier," she murmured. "He said he has access to laboratories with the latest equipment and associates with many years of experience."

She coughed, and Marie winced at the sound. Sam looked up from the gaming table along with Eustace and the others, his expression tightening as he glanced at Clara. He excused himself, rose, and joined them at the hearth. He placed the back of his hand to Clara's forehead and pressed his fingertips to the pulse point at her wrist.

Sam said something to Clara, but Marie missed it. She made her way across the room to the massive bank of windows that opened out onto a large patio at the back of the house. Sam's instincts as a personable doctor would probably never fail him, but he couldn't hide the anxiety in his eyes when examining the sick young woman. Marie looked out into the night but saw only her reflection in the glass. Her face was stoic enough, but the emotions roiling beneath the surface had her heart increasing its rhythm uncomfortably.

Miles needed to come home. He could fix things, she was sure of it. But he would be gone for at least one more day if her suspicions were correct. For years now, his pattern of activity had taken him away from home on a monthly basis like clockwork. He often used business and Parliament as excuses—which were valid enough—but she knew that, more often than not, he'd spend at least three days at the family hunting lodge on the coast.

Marie glanced at Clara's reflection in the dark window and felt a familiar surge of frustration. If only the girl were stronger! Clara was perfectly kind and lovely, and Marie knew her disdain of the girl might be misplaced, but Miles needed someone strong. Life wasn't kind to those who lacked the strength to fight.

Two of the household's 'tons entered the room and noiselessly cleared the teacups and small dessert plates. They were perfect replicas of humans, programmed to have personalities, traits, and physical abilities that were often deceivingly human from a distance. They would finish their duties in the kitchen and then retire to their chambers where they would plug in to the Tesla connectors in order to be fully charged by morning.

Marie turned when she saw Jonathan's reflection in the window. He crossed the room to her with a smile, and she felt her heavy mood lift. He was dashing with his dark hair and his poet's soul, and he smiled as he placed a kiss on her cheek. He was nearing twenty-two and had plenty of prospects for marriage, but he had yet to settle on a significant pastime. He had written volumes of poetry, but she couldn't convince him to submit any of it for publication in London. Their father would have thought it a vulgar display, and Marie was afraid his memory loomed large over Jonathan.

"Out courting?" Marie asked him.

"Regrettably. Another money-grubber."

"You're finding those in plentiful supply of late."

Jonathan nodded. "And I tire of it. Would it be so much to ask that I find a woman interested in me rather than Miles's deep pockets?"

"Take comfort in the fact that you do not suffer alone. Nor will you be the last."

Jonathan offered her a half smile and turned his attention to the room. "Are they ever going to leave?" he muttered and gestured toward their relations, who sat at the gaming table with Oliver Reed and now Daniel Pickett, who must have filled Sam's vacant seat. Sam was still conversing with Clara by the hearth.

"I suspect they are waiting to see Miles," Marie told him. "Eustace likes to be able to tell her friends she spent ever so much time with her darling nephew, Earl Blackwell."

Jonathan nodded toward Clara. "And how does she fare this evening? She wasn't looking well this morning at breakfast."

"She's not looking well now," Marie said with a frown. "Jonathan, I am concerned about how this will affect Miles."

"How what will affect Miles?"

"Her death."

Jonathan's eyes widened. "What are you saying?"

Marie pulled him by the elbow to the far side of the library. She felt the absence of warmth from the fire but she wanted the privacy the dimmer corner of the room offered. "I do not believe she possesses the fortitude to conquer this illness. I suspect something nefarious may be afoot, and society is suspicious enough of Miles as it is. The scar on his face, his dismissive demeanor, his unwillingness to participate socially in circles that befit his station." There was more, of course, but Marie was not about to share the true nature of her concerns with her younger brother. Not yet.

Marie spent the next morning in the Tesla control room, reading through the transcriptions of telescribed messages that had been sent and received by all of the manor's guests. She then perused the programmable tin punch cards that served as the brain functioning for the 'tons. There were a few missing, and Marie's suspicions grew.

The lunch hour was at hand, and Marie had only just left the Tesla control room when a high-pitched cry sounded from the second floor. Her heart filled with dread, Marie rushed to the front hall and up the stairs. Mrs. Farrell, the human housekeeper, rushed from the west wing, eyes wide and fists clenched. Marie grabbed the frantic woman by her shoulders and ground her to a halt.

"Is it Lady Blackwell?"

"Yes, my lady," the older woman choked out. "She is dead!"

Marie's head spun, and she tried to pull her thoughts together. "Summon the doctor and the constable," she said. "And gather all the guests in the library. I must speak with them."

Mrs. Farrell shook her head, her eyes still wide with terror. "The Charlesworths left for London after breakfast and will not return until late evening. And Mr. Pickett has also departed. Something about trouble with one of the airships at the landing field."

Marie felt her nostrils flare. She ought to have looked earlier, ought to have investigated the Records Room when she first suspected something was awry. She clenched her teeth and briefly closed her eyes. "Find Mr. Reed, then, and send Dr. MacInnes to me in the countess's chambers. And instruct the maids to stay out of the guest rooms until further notice. I do not want anything touched."

Mrs. Farrell nodded, her pulse throbbing noticeably at her throat, and hurried off.

Marie clutched at the banister as she stumbled her way up the stairs. She ran the length of the hallway to the massive doors that led to the earl's and countess's suite. Mrs. Farrell had left one of the doors open, and Marie entered, weaving through the sitting room and into a small hallway on the left that housed the countess's chambers along with dressing rooms and maid's quarters.

The room was dark. The curtains had yet to be opened, and Marie impatiently flung the fabric to the side, wondering if she were merely postponing the inevitable. She needed to look at Clara, and she didn't want to.

The figure on the bed lay horribly still. As Marie approached her, she held her breath and hoped that Mrs. Farrell had been mistaken, that Clara was still alive and hadn't died mysteriously under the same roof that had sheltered Marie her entire life. Her throat thickened as she looked upon Clara's face, no paler in death than it had been the night before. Thoughts of the missing 'ton programming cards swam through Marie's head. She reluctantly placed two fingers against Clara's neck.

"She is gone, then?"

Marie jumped at the intruding voice. Sam MacInnes stood in the doorway and regarded the young countess. He shook his head and approached the bed, checking for a pulse as Marie had done and opening one of Clara's eyes with his thumb.

"Who discovered her?" he asked.

Marie shrugged. "Probably one of the 'tons. They would have checked on her when she never rang for a tray or to dress for the day." She looped an arm around the footpost and leaned against it, surprised to feel faint. She had seen death before—her parents had both passed—but they had died of natural causes. Marie harbored strong suspicions that someone in the house had murdered Clara. And the most difficult part of all was that Marie now had no idea who to trust. Guests had been in residence for weeks, people had come and gone, and her suspect list was long.

Mrs. Farrell returned to the room with Jonathan and Mr. Arnold, the butler. Jonathan looked at Marie with huge eyes and made his way to the bedside.

"What . . . what has happened?" he managed.

Marie shook her head.

"I must call Miles home," Jonathan said. "Is he in London today?"

"I believe he is at the hunting lodge." Marie left the room and crossed the sitting room, her emotions in turmoil. Perhaps the only silver lining in the tragedy was that Miles probably wouldn't be implicated in Clara's death should Marie be able to prove foul play. He hadn't been in residence for more than one or two weeks since marrying the young woman, and he clearly wasn't present when the poor soul passed.

Marie heard someone knocking at the front door as she passed the second floor landing but she was on a mission. The visitor could wait. She approached the guest rooms in the east wing, looking for signs of the spent tin punch cards or anything that might give her a clue to the killer's identity.

She heard voices in the hallway as she moved from one room to the next and spied Oliver speaking with the local constable. She considered sharing her suspicions with Miles's friend, but he might be the guilty party, Bow Street consultant or no.

Marie made a quick examination of each guest room, using a hairpin to unlock those that were locked. When she found the spent punch cards and slipped them into her telescriber to read the programming instructions, her heart pounded in her chest.

And near the punch cards was an equally damning piece of evidence in the form of an illegal medicinal aid.

"Well, well," she murmured, stunned, "we have a vampire among us."

Miles returned to the manor that night and, after briefly acknowledging Marie and Jonathan, went straight to his study. His eyes were bleary and his expression more drawn than Marie had ever seen. She'd determined to tell him what she'd discovered, but she wanted to wait until they had a moment alone.

The house was swarming with people, and Miles had his hands full speaking with the constable and Oliver and handling preparations for Clara's burial and notifying the family. Marie had been on pins and needles the entire day but had stayed busy helping the frantic Mrs. Farrell.

The night wore on, and as the home finally began to clear of people, Miles disappeared. Marie searched for him but to no avail. He was home a day early, after all. She supposed he needed to get away from the house.

Her nerves were strung tight, and her heart ached as she thought of her brother facing his demons somewhere alone. Things had to change. She would talk to him, tell him that she knew of his condition and convince him to allow her to help shoulder the burden.

As the hours crept onward, she returned to her room, exhausted but pacing the floor. She heard a commotion at the front of the house; her relatives had returned. She placed her fingers to her temples. Taking a seat at her vanity, she opened a drawer and pulled out her diary and pen. Scribbling furiously, she tried to make sense on paper of what she had discovered. Her diary was her release, her one safe place to write everything down and see it all before her in black and white. She flipped through some of her earlier entries—observations of the household, the guests, Clara's worsening illness—and realized the clues had been there all along. The evidence was definitive, and she felt a grim sense of satisfaction that the guilty party would suffer.

A knock on her door sent the pen flying from her fingers, and she cursed under her breath. Opening the door with a little more force than was strictly necessary, she eyed the 'ton on the other side. He held out a paper to her and bowed. Marie grabbed it with a mumble of thanks and closed the door.

It was a note from Miles, telling her that he needed to speak to her privately and to meet him at her garden gazebo around midnight.

She looked up from the missive and stared out the window into the dark night. Perhaps Miles had decided to take her into his confidence after all. The timing made sense—if rumors were accurate, midnight was the magic hour. Marie glanced at her pocket watch that was attached to her hip pocket with a copper chain. She had less than fifteen minutes.

Quickly selecting a cloak from her wardrobe and grabbing a Tesla torch from a table near the door, she made her way through the house and into the night. Her cloak did little to protect her from the damp cold that accompanied the thick pockets of fog hovering over the ground. The path behind the gardens wound through a dense, darkly wooded area, and the beam from her torch scattered in the heavy mist, offering little guidance.

Her breathing sounded loud to her own ears as she picked up her pace. She ran along the twisted path until she saw the familiar tall stone walls of her own sanctuary, her garden. Enclosed on four sides, the garden had been unofficially hers since childhood, and she had spent hours there, tending it with Mr. Clancy, the gardener. Her mother had loved it, had spent hours in it herself, which was probably why Marie adored it so much.

There was a lock on the gate, but it was never employed. She swung the gate open wide and frowned. The fog had a light, eerie quality to it that lifted some of the darkness, but she was unable to see more than a few feet. The gazebo situated at the back wall was lost in the mist, but she felt fairly certain she would have seen the glow of a lantern or a Tesla torch if Miles were already there.

She made her way to the gazebo, the familiarity of the garden offering scant comfort as her torchlight bounced in the fog but offered no real help. It was so incredibly, awfully quiet. She hoped desperately that Miles would hurry; the sense of urgency she felt at having discovered that Clara had been murdered weighed heavily on her. She needed to speak with him.

She climbed the steps into the gazebo and turned. A faint light appeared in the fog as she rubbed her arms, and she wished she'd have taken the time to find a better wrap. She felt her heartbeat in her throat, and chided herself for allowing the eerie night to try her nerves.

"Miles?" she called softly and heard a twig snap as the light grew ever closer. She stood at the edge of the steps but drew back into the gazebo when the torch shined directly in her face so she was unable to see who held it.

"Miles!" she repeated, her tone sharp as she continued her retreat, feeling a surge of anger that finally had her standing her ground in the center of the structure. "Take the light from my eyes, I cannot see you!"

Her corset felt tight as she breathed harder, and she moved to smack the torch away when the one who wielded it clutched her by the throat. Her head spun as she gasped, trying to draw a breath through her crushed airway. She grasped at the wrist that first lifted her from her feet and then released her, hurling her down onto the stone floor.

Marie rolled to the side and tried to crawl away when she felt a slash come down across her face, raking from her forehead down to her neck. She reached up desperately as she fell back to the ground, blood obscuring her vision as she clawed wildly at her attacker. She ripped a button free, but when her head made contact again with the unforgiving floor, her arm flung outward and the button slipped free.

Her gaze followed along the length her arm to her extended fingers where the button rolled to a stop. Her thoughts were scattered, frantic. She tried to move her limbs but found them unresponsive. Conscious, coherent thought dimmed as the world slowly enclosed her in blackness and searing pain sliced across her midsection and chest.

Miles . . .

Her lips formed the name but no sound issued forth as she finally registered a blissful deadening of the pain, a measure of peace. Feeling as though a hand had reached down and pulled her into the air, she looked around wildly to see who had rescued her even as the choking, blinding pain ceased altogether.

She hovered in the gazebo, her vision suddenly sharp and clear. She saw through the dark, through the fog, noting her attacker leaning over a prostrate and bloodied form. Fury bubbled in her chest as she lashed out, only to realize that her hand passed ineffectively through her assailant's head.

Marie looked down again, her senses reeling, as she regarded her own earthly end. Stunned, she watched as her attacker rose, straightened clothing, and turned and left the gazebo. The Tesla torch, dropped and forgotten, rolled slightly and then was still, the light casting a ghostly glow over Marie's mortal remains.

Sorrow replaced the fury in her chest, and she screamed, hearing it echo only inside her head. She sank down next to her battered body, noting the direction her eyes had taken in those last, frantic moments before her corporeal form had succumbed to the assault. Her mortal, sightless eyes gazed down the length of her arm, the line of her bare hand pointing to the one piece of evidence she had managed to take from her murderer.

Alone . . . She was utterly, devastatingly alone. She heaved breaths that weren't breaths at all, felt the frantic, ghostly heartbeat of an organ that lay still and lifeless on the floor before her. She welcomed the surge of anger that swelled around her until the air fairly pulsated with it. She would not leave. She would remain at her home until she and her sister-in-law were avenged.

As she felt her eyes burn with tears that weren't really there, she thought of her brothers and sobbed.

About the Author

NANCY CAMPBELL ALLEN is the author of twelve published novels, which span genres from contemporary romantic suspense to historical fiction. In 2005, her work won the Utah Best of State award. She has presented at numerous writing conferences and events since her first book was released in 1999. Nancy received a BS in Elementary Education from Weber State University. She loves to read, write, travel, and research, and enjoys spending time laughing with family and friends. She is married and the mother of three children.

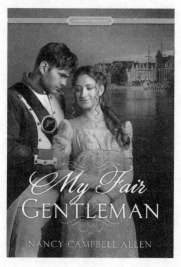